# CHARADES WITH A LUNATIC

# CHARADES WITH A LUNATIC

To Phoebe,
Just enjoy!
Love you!
Your cuz,
Thea

Thea Phipps

Thea Phipps
11-20-09 Little Rock

| Library of Congress Control Number: | | 2009900225 |
|---|---|---|
| ISBN: | Hardcover | 978-1-4415-0192-9 |
| | Softcover | 978-1-4415-0191-2 |



This is a work of fiction. Names, characters, places and incidents either are the product of the author's imagination or are used fictitiously, and any resemblance to any actual persons, living or dead, events, or locales is entirely coincidental.

This book was printed in the United States of America.

**To order additional copies of this book, contact:**
Xlibris Corporation
1-888-795-4274
www.Xlibris.com
Orders@Xlibris.com
56048

For you, Randy, the one who still writes me love notes,
The one who still calls me "beautiful"
after twenty-six years of marriage . . .
I love you.
And to all the Friends, you know who you are . . .

# 1

The part I played in my insane uncle's "great treasure hunt" began when my friend, Tamsin, and I picked my great-aunts up from the airport in London. My great-aunts, two elderly missionaries from Gilead who had spent the last forty-five years in Peru, were coming home to Cornwall to live with us, and by the word "us," I am referring to my own sizeable family.

"Treasure hunt"—a romantic concept to some, and to others juvenile. For me, the word "treasure" always brought to mind Errol Flynn with a dagger between his teeth, moonlight on the high seas, and daring maidens with curvaceous hairdos; but then that was before I experienced the underwear-clad parade of mannequins, Confucius in boxer shorts, or being chased by Chihuahua-sized rats. Now when I hear the word "treasure," I have the urge to giggle maniacally. That, or hide in a wardrobe with the dust bunnies. Not only at the word "treasure," but also when I recall the poetically challenged clues thought up by the lunatic we played "charades" with, the lunatic being my great-uncle Desmond, now deceased, not the two utterly fascinating and discombobulating elderly ladies I was bringing home.

We were seated at the Dog and Crown, a pub we had stopped at on our long drive from Heathrow to Cornwall.

"Scary genes, Bella." Tamsin grinned at me and skewed her brown eyes sideways to watch as my great-aunt stirred her hot tea with her finger. Great-Aunt Astrid pulled her digit from the cup, sucked it clean with a noise like a wet kiss, and pointed it accusingly at the barmaid.

*"Donde esta Cuzco?"* my great-aunt asked the startled woman, reverting to her Peruvian Spanish even though we were just outside of London. Poor Aunt Astrid seemed to have trouble remembering that she was now in the United Kingdom, not South America.

"Cuzco?" Tamsin raised an eyebrow. "Isn't that the Incan capital?"

"Ah, Cuzco." My other great-aunt, Aurora, smiled wisely and leaned into her face, her earnest eyes resembling blue Ping-Pong balls behind her glasses. "It means 'navel of the world' in Incan, dear. I don't believe we've passed it yet, unless we've just missed the road signs."

This wasn't good. Great-aunt Astrid may have temporarily forgotten what continent she was on, but Great-aunt Aurora had apparently been on the lookout for road signs directing us to the globe's belly button. Wondering fleetingly if that was where the world's largest ball of string was nestled, I grinned into my cup of tea.

From what I can see from my fly-on-the-wall perspective, it's a terrible thing to lose one's mind. At least I know that it's pretty unnerving to take care of the one losing their mind, and I didn't have just one to look after. I had two. We had no clue as to how far my two great-aunts had mentally scattered. We all knew that they were gently forgetful at times, we just didn't know that they had been getting a bit past that. Maybe it was the plane journey from Peru to England that had finally nudged them over the edge. Countless grueling hours of pressurized air, confined children, and toilets smaller than their own bladders.

And to make matters slightly worse, my nineteen years of age compared to their collective one hundred and thirty-one years made me feel as green and as raw as an embryonic pea still growing in the pod. It had certainly strained my herding skills to the limit to get them and their luggage out of the airport and into the Range Rover, but we did it without getting arrested or losing someone, which, speaking candidly, should have earned us a round of applause.

However, in the interests of excruciating honesty, I guess they weren't exactly losing their minds. They just kept misplacing them like car keys.

Pete Lord, the head cook at the Iron Rose, an inn owned by my parents, claims that their forgetfulness is caused by "all that llama meat they eat out there. That and those roasted monkeys." Pete is a fifty-year-old American built like a seedy prizefighter. He is comprised of bulging muscle, rock-hard slabs of fat, and ears that look like they'd been chewed by cats. He says things like, "The pope ain't no Englishman," which, incidentally, no one knows what he means by that.

Rayvyn, our thirty-five-year-old self-proclaimed "Child of the Cosmos" who works at the inn full-time doing everything from cleaning rooms to waiting on tables, claims that mental glitches were caused by eating flesh. Never mind that as a vegan she eats lard-laden snack cakes so fast she's been known to pick bits of the wrapper from her teeth.

"Senility, Isabella," she told me one day as we were cleaning out a vacated room at the inn, "is the temple's reaction to myriads of flukes traversing the pathways, causing disharmony and stagnation in the central meridian." I think that she meant that my great-aunts are mentally clogged up because they've eaten meat. A sort of geriatric "cork of pork."

Rayvyn's answer to all the wars, violence, broken homes, and diarrheic children in the third world is for the globe to quit eating meat and submit to a collective enema of warm water and unsulphured, unprocessed, organic, blackstrap molasses. And being a bit of a vigilante obsessed with humanity's collective colon, Rayvyn constantly tries to reform my eclectic eating habits.

Never mind. I'm getting ahead of myself. At least Pete and Rayvyn agree on the "you are what you eat" angle when it comes to my two great-aunts, Astrid and Aurora. But to do justice to the phrase "begin at the beginning," let me back up to the bit when Tamsin and I had to fetch them from the airport.

I had never seen my great-aunts in the flesh before I had to pick them up at the airport. All I had ever seen of them was the blurry photograph that they had sent to their sister, my grandmother. It showed two blurry women with blurry book bags standing next to some blurry Amazonian tribal chief. He was all dressed up for the photograph in a ceremonial loincloth, mud paint, and bone ornaments piercing his body in bloodcurdling places. At the time that I had first seen the photograph, I was glad that it was blurred since I didn't want to see any of the painful bits any clearer. But I later regretted it. I had to retrieve my great-aunts from the airport, and I had absolutely no idea what they looked like.

My parents knew, having seen more than one photograph of them, but for some inexplicable reason, my great-aunts had decided to bump their flight up a day and were scheduled to arrive in England that Sunday afternoon, not on Monday when they had originally planned, and only a handful of hours after their phone call to alert us of their untimely arrival. That last-minute schedule change completely blew apart my parents' carefully laid plans to welcome them.

That Sunday morning, everyone in my family was engaged in something that couldn't be rescheduled. The only one, not counting myself, without anything pressing to do was Gabriel. But since my baby brother was only six years old, no one was allowing him behind the wheel of the Range Rover for another decade. Since my great-aunts weren't going to wait that long for a ride, I had been hastily elected to take my parents' place as welcoming committee. That caused my parents some consternation since I had never driven the distance from Cornwall to London by myself before. They didn't say anything, but I knew they envisioned me getting kidnapped for the white slave trade as soon as I stopped for petrol, or getting lost at the first turning and ending up in Wales by nightfall.

So, assuaging their fears, they had my oldest brother, Dante, loan me his fully charged mobile phone, and they asked Tamsin Hugo to go with me. Tamsin, my best friend, is Welsh in spite of her French surname, and is a relatively new addition to the Cornish village of Halfmoon. She is only six months older than I am, and we do almost everything together. My parents no doubt envisioned me as being vulnerable alone. To my thinking, however, lanky, leggy Tamsin with her exaggerated startle response didn't seem to be much more of a challenge to wandering criminals. I guess my parents had thought that while one of us was being assaulted, the other one could go for help like Lassie.

This was how on that overcast Sunday Tamsin and I, barely equipped for the task ahead of us, had found ourselves at the airport holding up a huge cardboard sign that said the following, ATTENTION ASTRID AND AURORA WILDEVE. As we were scanning the faces of the arriving horde limping toward us, I heard a breathless voice coming up beside me from the wrong direction.

"Imagine, Astrid, those two young things have the same name as we."

Tamsin and I had turned in unison at the words.

Great-aunt Astrid was tall, topping my five feet three inches by another good set of five more inches. She was so thin and tan she resembled those bog men that archaeologists dig out of the peat. She was clad in a heavily embroidered poncho, a long magenta skirt, huarache sandals, and her head was crowned with one of those tall rounded hats peculiar to Bolivian Indians. To my unaccustomed eye, it looked like she had gotten the point of her head stuck in a black pipe, and a rescue team had to saw her loose. I didn't know it at the time, but the hat was merely a souvenir and not her sartorial preference. When I looked at her, her face cracked into a friendly smile that made the air between us glow.

By contrast, Great-aunt Aurora was plump, short, and smelled inexplicably like fruity marmalade. Her apricot-colored skin was soft, downy, and powdered; and she was dressed in a periwinkle dress of weathered cotton. Her eyes were very wide and very blue behind the lens of her glasses, giving her the look of perpetual surprise. Her smile, however, was quick, tremulous, and warm like watery sunshine breaking through clouds.

I fell in love with them at first sight.

"Great-aunt Astrid? Aurora?" I smiled back. At the sudden look of recognition on Great-aunt Astrid's face, I dropped my half-of-the-cardboard sign and enveloped them each in a hug.

"Sister, it's Isabella, Luc's daughter," Aunt Astrid had informed her sister, patting my cheek with a heavily be-ringed hand. "Goodness, child, you certainly do have your mother's hair."

"Yes, doesn't she?" Aunt Aurora beamed and had tried to pat my other cheek.

"Who's this?" With her hand still on my face, Aunt Astrid had turned to look at Tamsin. "Surely this isn't little Gabriel all grown up?"

Tamsin's eyes glazed over.

"She's a good friend of mine." I grinned and slid the cardboard out of her slack hands. "Tamsin Hugo. She regular pioneers with me."

The words "regular pioneer" brought up visions of six-guns and bonnets, cowboys and Indians, and plows and mules to most minds; or perhaps a calico vision of Laura Ingalls running through a wheat field, flapping her arms in agitation, yelling, "Pa! Pa!" like an earthbound crow. But in that instance, "regular pioneer" was merely a term used for one who volunteers to spend at least seventy hours a month teaching others about the Bible.

The Bible, not the world's religions. It's amazing how much the two had absolutely nothing to do with each other.

"Forgive me." Aunt Astrid's mouth had twitched. "All I saw was that mop of dark hair, and I thought it was little Gabriel in the middle of a growth spurt."

Tamsin smiled feebly, not sure what to say. I didn't know what to say either. My baby brother Gabriel, being six years old, barely came up to my hip. Tamsin is nearly six feet tall with breasts.

"Let's go get your luggage," I suggested brightly.

My great-aunts had packed all their belongings in old-fashioned trunks, which meant that Tamsin and I had to drag the heavy crates free from the rapidly spinning carousel by small ragged, petrified straps. It also took longer than I had expected since Great-aunt Aurora had complicated things a bit by toddling off into the men's lavatory. I had to drop everything when I noticed what she was doing, dart in with averted eyes, and snatch her before she could wash her travel-stained hands in a urinal next to a startled priest.

But after three tries, two brawny helpers, and one bruise on my shinbone later, we finally had their luggage on trolleys and could escape through the lobby and into the drizzle outside. Between the three of us—a porter, Tamsin, and I—we managed to load the four trunks into the back of the Range Rover. As I called my parents on Dante's mobile phone to give them a brief progress report, Aunt Astrid tipped the bewildered porter a Peruvian peso and tried to get into the wrong car, setting off an alarm. I intercepted her, steered her to the Range Rover's backseat to place her beside her sister, climbed in the front seat, hung up the phone, made sure everyone was buckled in, and started the engine. I put the vehicle in gear, engaged the automatic door locks for obvious reasons, and backed out of the narrow slot.

We were off.

Well, at least two of us were, bless their hearts.

I kept glancing at them in the rearview as I drove, thinking about what brought them from the mountains of Titicaca to England. I had to back up quite a bit, sixty years or so, and mentally search my fund of ancestral knowledge. Our family's history, or more accurately our family lunacy, seemed to be the seed that started it all.

Their father, my great-grandfather Sir James Wildeve, had a total of four living children, three stillborn offspring, and five miscarriages before impregnating Great-grandmother Destiny into an early grave. Then two years after her death, he had accidentally impaled himself on a rusty farm implement, ironically poetic I thought, and died, leaving the Wildeve estate in Cornwall to his only surviving son, my great-uncle Desmond, who had been thirty-five years old at the time.

Tanglewood Manor, or Wildeve Manor as the locals still call it, is an imposing three-storied house, counting the attics, and is built out of pale gray stone. The manor contains no central heating, one huge bathroom fitted out like a Roman public bath, and an erratic rat-gnawed electrical system. The whole gloomy rambling structure peers out over the ocean from atop a high cliff outside of the Cornish village of Halfmoon. The Tanglewood Estate, or what is left of it, is nothing but a huge frog in the little mud puddle of village.

Halfmoon, home to my father's maternal family line for hundreds of years, is a quaint, picturesque, ancient, crooked, inbred little village that had managed to escape being commercialized even if it hadn't escaped tourism. Tourism and fishing are its main industries. Pretty much its only industries. You can't count rat breeding, sheep droppings, and ageing as moneymakers. In fact, if the southern Cornish light wasn't so clear and Halfmoon's buildings so quaint, the rats, the sheep, and the locals gutting their fish by the pub would put a giant damper on most visitors' desire to visit.

So when my great-grandfather, Sir James, had died, Great-uncle Desmond had sold off what land he could of the family estate, keeping the acreage that ran in front of the cliff and that bordered the shoreline below, and, instead of sinking the money into remodeling, left to explore the world and buy its souvenirs. When Great-uncle Desmond had inherited the estate, my grandmother Bryn, my father's mother, was only ten years old, Great-aunt Astrid was eight, and Great-aunt Aurora was seven.

The governess that Great-uncle Desmond had hired to take his little sisters off his incapable and disinterested hands was a young unmarried International Bible Student named Rosella Tregarth. Rosella raised my grandmother and my great-aunts with no interference from Great-uncle Desmond, and by the time all three girls had entered their late teens, they had chosen to involve themselves in the same volunteer Bible courses their governess had.

But Great-uncle Desmond, having survived a car crash when he was fifteen, had random glitches in his mental machinery and did not grasp the meaning of their decision. Great-uncle Desmond had mistakenly thought that his sisters were becoming "Bible Student nuns" and he panicked. He came home from Bora-Bora to find an "antidote."

One of his solutions was to throw financially suitable bachelors at them with the same fervor he launched clay pigeons, hoping that marriage would "nullify their vows." In an effort to get away from her strange older brother, my grandmother had selected the handsome Irish horse *handler* of someone in the suitor parade, married him instead of the selected suitor, moved to the Aran Islands, and proceeded to have seven children, my father being the first. My great-aunts Astrid and Aurora left home afterward, taking up full-time missionary service, ending up in Peru via Gilead missionary school in the United States.

My great-uncle Desmond was so angry at their choices he never spoke to Astrid, Aurora, and my grandmother again.

Then two years ago, when I was seventeen, my father inherited Halfmoon's Iron Rose Inn from an extremely distant cousin, whose direct family line had died out with her. Instead of trying to find a buyer for the inheritance, all eight members of my family moved from London back to the ancestral village, including my three oldest brothers, Dante, Brandt, and Jude, who were already outside of the house and living on their own. Full circle, back to the family seat my grandmother had successfully escaped from, perhaps, but apparently she had fled with a bungee cord strapped to her ankles. Two generations later and the Wildeves were back through no intent of our own. It just happened.

My grandmother, however, never came back to Halfmoon, even to visit. My great-aunts never came back, either. They stayed in their service assignment in Peru.

No one really knew where Great-uncle Desmond was at any given time of his life. He ran amok. Expeditions down rivers, up mountains, and behind frontiers. He explored, collected, aged, and became even more moldy and peculiar. Most of his life was spent abroad, coming home only long enough to deposit his treasures and thrash his servants. As time passed, his staff became smaller and scantier until he was left with a manservant as old as he was. Both were legally blind, profoundly deaf, and proudly incontinent. And for the last fifty years of Uncle Desmond's strange life, he allowed absolutely no visitors into Tanglewood Manor, his home. By then Great-uncle Desmond was so old his spine had collapsed like a deflated accordion and his age-shrunk head would peer out tortoisewise from between his collarbones. He was a village legend.

But so was Tanglewood Manor. It was an eerie structure by the time I had first seen it when I was seventeen. The stone archways that had bordered the original entry to the property are still standing even though they are in someone else's sheep pasture. The house is sturdily built, covered in swathes of ivy, cobwebs, and grime, and squatting in a nest of overgrown weeds, twisted bushes, and vermin. It's a bit eerie, but not unpleasantly creepy. When I had first laid eyes on it, it reminded me a bit of a dusty old man that had fallen asleep and had been forgotten in the corner chair while everyone else went to dinner.

No, the house definitely wasn't a woman, but male, in spite of the walled flower gardens in the back. The mansion is too large and ungainly to be anything else, a haphazardly stacked chunk with huge rippled windows thick with decades of bug crust. Towers and pointless turrets abound, along with miles of metal gutters, carved stones, and odd niches, not to mention the sudden abutments that confuse the symmetry. Definitely a man—crabby, neglected, imposing and snoring—but with sweets and treasures stuffed in his pockets. Someone who could tell you faerie stories if you could just wake him up.

I was fascinated by what was left of Tanglewood Estate, but not fascinated by Great-uncle Desmond. Great-uncle Desmond unnerved me. Age had apparently enhanced the effects of the automobile accident he had survived at fifteen. He would stare at me, his horn rims magnifying his faded eyes to three times their normal size. He looked like a fly. A plotting, scheming fly, and I half-expected to see him preen the back of his dusty suit with his legs.

And then Great-uncle Desmond died from natural causes. Natural . . . you can't get more back to nature than lightning. He was struck by a bolt, apparently, while he was swimming during a storm, and turned instantly into glass, or something very like it. I know what you're thinking, and you would be right. I told you he was crazy.

His stiff body was discovered one horrible morning on the beach below his house by hysterical trespassers. They thought at first that he was a rare piece of driftwood until one of the girls got close enough to see the splash of scarlet Speedo and the bright blue snorkel bolt upright in his stiff hand like a property marker.

My father arranged Great-uncle Desmond's funeral, and even though we were the only relatives there, the whole village turned out, more out of curiosity than out of any kind of respect. He seemed to have been the Yeti of Halfmoon, Cornwall. Never spotted by reliable sources yet talked about by everyone when stale spore turned up, usually in the form of his one surviving servant, Rawlings, running errands.

The undertaker made the most of the occasion even though the snorkel was still fused to Great-uncle's hand. He covered the melted bit of blue plastic with a strategically placed bouquet of lilies, painted Desmond's lipless mouth with rouge, and fluffed his matted fringe of wispy hair into a pompadour. He was more unnerving dead than he was alive, looking like a rather warty blue Phyllis Diller nestled in a cloud of white casket pillows.

His lawyer, Mr. Ambrose Hobhouse, pensioned off Uncle Desmond's manservant, Rawlings, who promptly scooted off to America, leaving Great-aunts Astrid and Aurora, the sole beneficiaries of everything, to fend for themselves. The problem was that no one knew exactly what was meant by "everything." The house was to remain securely bolted until my great-aunts could arrive and take possession of the keys.

So there I was, leaving the airport in my parents' Range Rover amidst four steamer trunks, bringing them home to live with us.

The drive back to Cornwall was highly educational, if uneventful. No near accidents on the rain-slicked roads, no emergency stops, and no delays. I did learn a lot, however, about the breeding habits of the Peruvian boobies even though half of Great-aunt Astrid's fascinating discourse was delivered in Spanish.

By the time we had stopped for dinner at a small roadside pub, deep clouds were stuck overhead, and it was raining big splashing drops. Aunts Astrid and Aurora refused my offer of umbrellas and sloshed purposefully to the pub's entrance like they were fording the Amazon, something they may have done regularly in the past forty years for all I knew. At least there were no piranhas darting about the floating gum wrappers.

It wasn't very crowded in the Dog and Crown, and we found a cozy table by a window. Sheets of water drummed on the small leaded panes and obscured any view we might have had, but the pub was warm and dry.

"English food," Aunt Aurora enthused as we looked at the menu board propped up by the fireplace. "What a treat."

"I haven't had a Scotch egg since I was seventeen," Aunt Astrid stated loudly. And for some reason, Tamsin blushed.

I took everyone's order, gave it to the barmaid, and then carried a tray of tea things back to the table. While Aunt Astrid tried to tip me with a crinkled peso, Aunt Aurora added a healthy slug of whiskey from a miniature airline bottle to one of the four cups, claiming it as hers. The rest of us stirred cream and sugar into the other three cups and cradled the heat in our hands. Another wet gust hit the windowpanes next to our table, and the sheets of water coming down grew more intense.

That was when Aunt Astrid asked the confused barmaid where Cuzco was. I decided not to intervene, explain, or apologize. Any scanty social graces I possessed weren't deft enough. Besides, their leaps from reality beat small talk hands down, and I was tentatively beginning to enjoy myself.

As I took my first mouthful of tea, Dante's phone rang in my purse. I hurried to swallow the scalding liquid, which was a bit painful, but more civilized than spitting it back in my cup, and fished for the mobile. It had somehow worked its way to the bottom of my bag and was buried under weeks of purse debris, trilling away merrily like a tiny car alarm.

"Dearest," Great-aunt Aurora's breathless voice wobbled beside me, but I didn't look up. I knew she was talking to her sister. "I believe I have that ringing in my ears again."

"It's in mine as well, dear," Great-aunt Astrid said dryly. "I believe that sound is coming from Isabella's purse."

"Got it!" I chortled and yanked the mobile out, checking the screen to see if it was for me. It was my parents. I answered it as I got up from our table and made my way to the niche where the lavatories were hidden away.

"Hello, *bambina*," my mother's Italian-accented voice said through the static. "How is everything?"

My Italian mother had met my Irish father in Rome when, at fifteen, she had agreed to model for one of his paintings. At only four inches over five feet, she was as delicate looking as an angelic child. Her waist-long hair was a silvery blond mass of Botticelli curls, her slanted Sophia Loren eyes were a deep, dark violet, and her Italian skin was the milky brown of hot cappuccinos. My teenaged father had been instantly smitten.

Even at that young age, my father was as big and as dark as my black-browed grandfather, but without his violent dissipated nature even though he had the same explosive energies. His passion was "Art" with a capital *A,* and he channeled all his vitality and frustration into painting enormous canvases of savage scenery. Or enormous canvases of beautiful women. Or beautiful women doing unlikely things in savage scenery. In the first picture he had painted of my fifteen-year-old mother, she was walking over storm-lashed waves, modestly carrying an enormous sheaf of wine-colored roses placed strategically over her unclothed body. Ruby petals whipped away in the wind behind her like drops of blood.

The propinquity of romantic Ireland versus hot-blooded Italy in the sweltering rooftop studio had engendered a marathon of passionate painting interspersed with passionate fighting. They were throwing constant sparks, not to mention paintbrushes, canvases, pretty much anything that can be lobbed to express emotions, but it wasn't until my mother torched my father's sofa bed in a fit of theatrical Italian rage that they knew it was true love. He proposed to her, and the chemistry between them came out in his work. The art commissions began piling up. He was fought over by galleries. They got married. And all this happened when she was only sixteen, and he wasn't yet nineteen.

At that time, my father was an exotic product of the bohemian art world. At four and a half inches taller than six feet, he had a huge presence to match. His brogue was musical and pronounced, and his voice resonant and deep enough to intimidate the shy. His black hair was long and wild; and his eyebrows were thick, pointed, blue-black slashes, overscoring his intense emerald green eyes. He stayed barefoot, wore paint-streaked jeans, ripped tee shirts, a wickedly pointed goatee and moustache, and accessorized with a tiny gold earring that came from a long-dead pirate. Unfortunately, it was genuine, not artistic packaging to attract buyers and galleries.

By the time my parents were married and had two children, they developed a healthy curiosity about the Bible, finding out quite by accident that the artistic depictions of hell portrayed in the Vatican could be traced to the Etruscans, not to Christianity, and belatedly decided to follow the course of my grandmother, finding an older couple to teach them what they knew. My father terrified them, of course, as he would any sane humans. It wasn't until he cut his hair, shaved off his goatee and moustache, and threw away the earring that the elderly couple was brave enough to look him in the eye. Not long after that, my grandmother's baton of volunteer teaching was picked up by my parents and turned into a family career. That made six of us doing it for seventy hours each month. All of us, bar Michael, who was volunteering fifty hours each month as an auxiliary pioneer, and little Gabriel, who was scheduled to start school in another year.

My mother still describes my father as the most charming man on earth, with hair the color of midnight, a lilt in his voice that can woo cold statues off their pedestals, and a passionate way of throwing himself at life that sweeps you along like a leaf in a torrent. I guess that's one way to explain why they had six kids. I'm number five.

As I talked with my parents on the phone, hiding beside the lavatories in the Dog and Crown, I watched Tamsin's expression of polite interest evolve into one of consternation at Aunt Astrid's words. Tamsin looked as if she had just trodden barefoot on a dead squid, and I wondered what was being said. I found out once I hung up and returned to the table. Aunt Astrid had apparently been imparting creepy little factoids about Great-uncle Desmond.

"Bonkers," Aunt Astrid was saying calmly. "Not dangerous. Just off a little. Even before the car accident."

"Even before," Aunt Aurora added breathlessly.

"Strange," Aunt Astrid continued. "When he was a child, he had habits that distressed Papa greatly. He began collecting his toenail clippings in a jar."

I saw Tamsin glaze over. I knew she was picturing what I was. A massive glass jar with eighty years of toenail, the last layers near the top resembling doggie treats. I looked down at the table, feeling a bit queasy.

"We knew he was bad," Aunt Astrid continued, "even before his phone call to us. But when I talked to him, it was obvious he had long since gone over the edge."

"He called you?" I looked up from contemplating the bowl of nuts in the center of the table. I had found myself fixated on the cashews, thinking of my great-uncle's toenails. "When did he call you? I thought he hadn't talked to you since you left home."

"Oh, he called us only days before he died."

I looked from Aunt Astrid's weathered face to Aunt Aurora's. Aunt Aurora smiled at me, her expression tremulous, and poked my arm with her pudgy forefinger.

"Once I knew it was Desmond, I cried."

"Poor dear couldn't speak," Aunt Astrid said briskly and took another sip of her tea. "I had to take the phone from her."

"Why did he call?" I asked.

"He ranted on about something. I couldn't really understand him." Aunt Astrid put her cup back on to its saucer and frowned at the table top in front of us. She suddenly looked like a haunted Shar-pei. "Something about mother. And then he recited some awful poetry."

"I like poetry," Aunt Aurora interrupted wistfully.

"What kind of poetry did he recite?" I persisted. Aunt Astrid looked up at me, perplexed.

"I can't remember," She said simply and sighed. "At least not all of it. I can only remember part of it because it was so ghastly."

"What did he say?" Tamsin breathed, her eyes wide, and leaned forward in spite of herself.

"Roses are red, violets are blue. It's not quite dead, just like you."

Tamsin and I drew back involuntarily at Aunt Astrid's words. Aunt Aurora, however, beamed mistily and clutched her bosom with clasped hands.

"Oh, Desmond," she breathed. "He was always so clever with rhyme."

"Order!" the barmaid shouted and thumped down four plates.

"I'll get it," I said hastily and got up to bring our food to the table.

As we sorted our meals, I could see that Aunts Astrid and Aurora were exhausted and disjointed. I decided to steer the conversation away from the distressful subject of Great-uncle Desmond, filing away the phone call to tell my parents about later.

We finished our meal without incident. Without incident only if one isn't counting Aunt Astrid's first bite of Scotch egg. Her partial plate of incisors embedded itself into the chewy crust of sausage and got as tightly wedged as a thong on a sumo. It took Aunt Aurora, myself, and a fork to free the teeth; but other than that, we finished the rest of the quick meal in relative peace.

Once we finished dining, we left the pub, I secured them in the Range Rover, and we began the last leg of our journey to Halfmoon. By the time we reached the winding lanes close to home, Aunts Astrid and Aurora were asleep. It was after dusk, and I could see the monstrous silhouette of Aunt Astrid's hat in the rearview mirror as I drove through the sporadic traffic. The rain had slackened, but I knew it was only a lull in the storm since lightning continued to fork the horizon out to sea.

"I don't see it." Tamsin sighed quietly in the front seat, keeping her voice low. I could barely hear her over the intermittent swipe of the wipers.

"Don't see what?" I asked.

"I don't see how they're going to manage their legacy of the manor house. I've seen the outside of it. The place is a ruin. It has to be just as bad on the inside."

"Probably. Mom has already fixed up the two guest rooms downstairs so they can stay with us until they decide what to do with the house."

"When will you see what the inside of the manor is like?"

"Great-uncle Desmond's solicitor is supposed to turn the keys over to them tomorrow after they sign some papers." I paused. "I'll have to admit I'm very curious about Great-uncle Desmond's treasures. The ones he was supposed to have collected from all over the world."

"If they're real and not a figment of the village's imagination." She gave the dash a thoughtful frown. "Who's going to inventory the estate?"

"My parents and great-aunts have already discussed that. We need to see the inside to see what has to be done. For all we know, it's as bare as a monastery. If it isn't, then all of us, I suppose. We're all going to have to muck in, but I will probably be over there the most since I'm the only one in the family with free time right now."

"How fun," Tamsin said faintly. I glanced at her to see if she was being funny. She wasn't.

"Want to help?"

"Are you serious?"

"Why not? I can tell you're dying to find out what's in Tanglewood Manor just as much as I am. You're just as curious."

"Actually, I've wanted to see the inside since I'd moved here." She suddenly grinned, capitulating. "I thought you'd never ask."

We had already driven past the outlying farms that bordered the village, and I could see Halfmoon nestled in the cleft below us like a handful of fireflies that had been flung at the sea. We had to climb down from the cliff road to the waterfront to enter the village and then climb the winding streets to the inn sitting on its own promontory above the water. Blinding daggers shot overhead as I tried to negotiate the slick labyrinth, and thunder broke free to roll down the streets.

I reached into my purse and handed Tamsin the mobile phone. "Can you call my parents and tell them we're here?"

She took the phone from me and did as I asked, keeping her eyes on the twisty street in front of us. After a few moments, we passed the Iron Anchor pub and turned into the inn's long sweeping drive.

The Iron Rose Inn started its life as a stately home. It became an inn when it housed sailors during the nineteenth century; after which, it became the home away from home for tourists and artists migrating south to the Cornish coast. It was large, rambling, and ancient, with a rose-filled courtyard and roughly hewn steps leading from the adjoining cliff to the bathing beach below. I pulled around to the west wing and into the family's private drive, where an outside light had been left on in welcome.

Another streak of lightning fragmented the blackness overhead, thunder boomed, and I turned off the engine, feeling suddenly very tired. I rubbed my eyes, yawned, and turned to peer over the back of the seat at my slumbering great-aunts. A gusty growl rattled the backseat, and I couldn't tell which aunt had snorted in her sleep.

"I almost hate to wake them," I murmured. Ahead of us the front doors opened, and my parents stepped out, carrying umbrellas. The night was too dark and full of damp to see anything more than their welcoming silhouettes as they approached the Range Rover.

Aunt Astrid suddenly sat up, abruptly pressed her be-ringed fingers to her hat, and snorted, instantly wide-awake.

"Why did we stop, dear?" she snorted again and lowered her hand. "May I, perhaps, use the facilities somewhere? Of course, if there's no toilet, I can manage quite well in the bush."

"But once she squats, someone will have to help her back up," Aunt Aurora said placidly, obviously awake at her sister's voice. "I can't with my stiff knees. The last time I had tried to help, we both got stuck, and Carmen had to come looking for us. We had been squatting together for nearly an hour before we were assisted. By then we had to be carried back to the bus."

"Oh my goodness!" Tamsin blurted out involuntarily.

My father reached us just then, pulled open Aunt Astrid's door, and flashed all of us a welcoming smile.

"Aunt Astrid? Aunt Aurora?" my father's brogue filled the car. "How are you?"

"Welcome." My mother opened Aunt Aurora's door and smiled warmly at my two aunts. "Come in before the storm breaks."

"Luc?" Aunt Astrid accepted my father's helping hand as she slid to the ground. "Oh, my goodness! How tall you are! You look just like your father, but you do have Bryn's smile."

"And Raphaela!" Aunt Aurora's plump face broke into a tremulous glow. She clasped my mother's hand as she slid from the car. "How very nice to finally meet you, my dear!" She released her grip and bent to straighten her travel-rumpled dress.

"Aunt Aurora! Aunt Astrid! Aunt Aurora! Aunt Astrid!" My pajama-clad little brother squirted from the open doorway of our apartments at the inn, chanting ecstatically, and ran toward us. Before I could open my car door and intervene, he cannoned straight into Aunt Aurora's ample buttocks and nearly jackknifed her back into the car. His face disappeared as he wrapped skinny arms around as much of her as he could. My mother grabbed at Aunt Aurora, who, in turn, turned to see what kind of missile had been launched at her buttocks. She seemed to be delighted to find that a small boy had been embedded.

"Gabriel!" My oldest brother, Dante, materialized suddenly out of the darkness and bent to extract my baby brother from Aunt Aurora's derriere.

"Well, now that we got that over with," my father said, his voice amused, "why don't we get inside before it starts raining. Isabella, child, go ahead and take Gabriel so your brothers can bring the luggage in."

Lightning shot over us, and a drop of rain plopped warningly on my forehead.

"Tamsin, *bambina*, stay the night," my mother said, leaning over to give me a kiss on the cheek before escorting Aunt Aurora toward the front door. "I don't want you out in this storm. It's about to break."

I looked at my friend and could see that she was torn between getting home to her own bed and staying to see the family reunion.

"Come on," I said and motioned to her over the hood of the Range Rover, taking my little brother's arm with my free hand. He turned to me in welcoming delight and swarmed up my body like a Tahitian child swarming up a palm tree to harvest a coconut. I got an exuberant kiss on my chin as another huge drop of rain hit my eyeball.

"Thanks," she surrendered suddenly and grinned at me as another stab of lightning illuminated us.

As we toddled inside, my four older brothers hauled the trunks into the house and deposited them in my great-aunts' rooms. By the time they joined us around one of my mother's lavish snack trays in the front room, the full fury of the storm had broken loose and was attacking the windowpanes in a fusillade of grapeshot.

"Bella, *bambina,*" my mother said, preparing to carry a protesting Gabriel back to bed, "fix your aunts a plate. There are pastries, fruit, smoked cheeses, crackers, olives, and quiche."

While I did as I was bid, my father settled my great-aunts on to one of the sofas and poured them cups of tea.

"Oh, my," Aunt Aurora breathed, eyeing the massive painting over the fireplace. "One of yours, Aodhagan?"

Tamsin gave me a strange look, selected a quiche from the tray, but didn't ask me what Aunt Aurora meant when she called my father "Aodhagan." I didn't volunteer to explain, either.

After my parents began their volunteer teaching work all those years ago, my mother became extremely embarrassed at the paintings that had catapulted my father into artistic fame. My mother never tells anyone that the exuberantly nude blonde in his early works is her at fifteen and sixteen. To guarantee discretion, my father legally changed his name from Aodhagan (the Gaelic form of "Egan," said the same except with a healthy sprinkle of spit) Quinn to Lucien Wildeve, using his first name instead of his middle name and using his mother's maiden name instead of his father's surname. But no one would recognize a Luc Wildeve signature, so he still signs his work "A. Quinn" in an illegible, but recognizable, scrawl.

My father grinned as Aunt Aurora took the cup of tea from his hand.

"To be sure, Aunt," he said mildly, handing the other cup to Aunt Astrid. "It's one of mine."

"Lovely," Aunt Astrid barked, following her sister's gaze to the painting. I handed her a plate of food and watched as her eyes roved over the massive family portrait.

It wasn't a family portrait in a conventional sense since my father had never been a conventional artist. Not only was the canvas large enough to double as a dyke, my father had put us all in a setting worthy of Edgar Allan Poe. All six of us—my mother, my older brothers, and myself as a toddler—were poised atop a windswept cliff. The ocean and a luminous electrical storm formed our backdrop. Even though we resembled a family of lemmings about to take the plunge, the whole effect was one of poignancy and exhilaration. When viewing it, one half-expected to hear thunder clapping or an aria soaring in the background right before we turned and leapt.

I looked around the rest of the front room, trying to see my home as Aunt Astrid or Aunt Aurora might, and made the amusing observation that everything, from the dancing harlequin end tables to the crystal wall sconces, was either as nonchalantly irreverent as my father's grin or as elegant as my mother's profile.

"How did it go, *poca*?" Michael, my fourth-oldest brother, spoke into my ear as he reached over me to snag a pastry. "Took you long enough."

"Peruvian warts," Aunt Aurora said complacently, apropos of nothing, forestalling any comment I might have made. Michael turned to watch as she poured a tot of cognac from another airline bottle into her tea. "Hector had them in 1963. They hung from his chest in big purple balls. I'll never eat another fig off a tree again."

"Enough said." Michael grinned at me. At the mention of swollen boils, Tamsin put the cheesy quiche back onto the tray and gingerly retired her plate.

"So who's who?" Aunt Astrid barked out, turning her gaze from the family portrait to roam about the room. "Bryn sent me some photographs over the years, but I've gotten hopelessly muddled."

My oldest brother, Dante, gave my great-aunts an amused bow, his loaded plate balanced precariously in his hand.

"Allow me to help you keep us in order, Aunt Astrid," he laughed and introduced himself, Brandt, Jude, and Michael, giving my great-aunts an expurgated version of our family history.

Dante, named after Rossetti, the pre-Raphaelite poet and artist, was born first, only eleven months before Brandt, who was named after the Dutch painter Rembrandt van Rijn. Four years later, Jude came into the world.

Big families and rounded hips run in my mother's Italian blood, along with a fiery temperament and garlic in everything, so she kept having children. Undaunted, still trying for a girl to balance out the accruing testosterone, my mother became pregnant again three years later and gave birth to Michael. Finally, when Dante was eleven, Brandt ten, Jude six, and Michael was three, I was born. My mother was only twenty-eight. Relieved to finally have the girl she wanted, she decided to leave well enough alone and quit having babies since postpartum bellies have a tendency to sag into kilts. She had almost succeeded. When I was twelve, my baby brother Gabriel was born, astonishing everyone, especially my mother when he was first discovered growing inside of her.

Growing up as the only girl at the tail end of so many brothers had its drawbacks; one of which was the unfortunate tendency I had developed when I was three years old of burping my name when introduced, something that my parents thankfully rubbed out with the ruthless efficiency of a mafia hit. But being the only girl at the tail end of so many older brothers also had its good side. I can hit a moving target with just about anything, I'm cruelly proficient at laundry, and I had no shortage of affectionate attention while growing up.

As Dante finished his introduction to our rather unwieldy family, my mother flowed back into the room, her presence serene in contrast to my father's electric energy. Aunt Aurora gave her a misty smile.

"Such beautiful children, my dear. A striking family."

The rest of us, save my father, Aunt Astrid, and Tamsin dubiously looked at one another.

I don't look like my mother. It's sad and rather disappointing for me, but true. I have her blond hair and nearly the violet color of her eyes, but not her exotic, charming, wild, lovely looks. I look enough like her to make it obvious I'm her daughter, but my mouth is my father's. Somehow that sucked the wild grace from my face and made me look as though I thought life was nothing but a private joke. My mouth smiles by itself, even when I'm not amused. I suppose it's the Irish in me. And my curls don't swoop and swirl in neat glittering masses like my mother's does. My curls are longer and more exuberant than her own shoulder-length hair and have a tendency to misbehave with a mind of their own, waving at passersby even when I'm merely sitting on a park bench reading my magazines. I would shear some of it off, except I was mildly afraid that I would look like I was licking a light socket if I did.

My brothers, however, are striking enough merely because of the larger-than-life vitality they inherited from my father.

Once a young woman on the street told Dante that his emerald eyes and black hair were "imprisoned angels in a dark, dark forest," which embarrassed him acutely. She was carrying a booklet of poetry at the time, and I told him later that she probably knew so many quotations, she fired them off at random. Jude suggested Tourette's syndrome.

Brandt is the family changeling, with dark brown hair, eyes that are somewhere between blue and green, and a lone dimple in his right cheek when he smiles. As far as anyone knows, it is the first dimple in our family history. He claims he is trying to evolve out of the family gene pool.

Jude, my third-oldest brother, had inherited our mother's blond hair and her Italian skin; but my father's stature and his far more masculine features, which, to be candid, makes Jude look like Dante's negative. When Jude was a fat little baby, he looked like Cupid in an evil mood, having feathery duplicates of my father's winged eyebrows over his green eyes.

Michael is the only sibling with the specific combination of my father's black hair and my mother's violet eyes. Rayvyn, the inn's Child of the Cosmos factotum, swears that he resembles Michelangelo's statue of *David,* something I can't see no matter how hard I squint. Whatever her private hallucinations, Rayvyn thinks she's in love with Michael, who, in turn, hasn't a shred of vanity and has absolutely no clue as to her interest.

Dante, Brandt, and Jude—the only ones not precisely living at home—share one of the inn's three guest cottages tucked away on the edge of the property. Their two-story cottage is separated from the others by a century-old yew hedge intertwined with wild apple trees and white-veined ivy. Ancient, quaint, and modernized, with just enough room to house three large men without cramping, it frees them from paying a much higher rent in the village. It is also conveniently close to our mother's cooking, which they eagerly trade in for a substantial contribution to the household expenses.

At Aunt Aurora's compliment, my mother smiled serenely, happily, looking naturally exotic and gilt-edged in spite of Gabriel's fingerprints of tomato sauce on the shoulder of her blouse. "Thank you."

I settled myself beside Tamsin on the crimson sofa across from my great-aunts and took a bite of garlic quiche, trying unsuccessfully to keep the crumbs from cascading beyond my plate.

"Aunt Astrid said that Great-uncle Desmond called them just before he died." A spectacular clap of thunder accompanied my bald statement, and I turned to share an amused grin with Tamsin at my celestial timing.

"Really?" My father looked up from the cup cradled in his large palm like a boiled egg. "I didn't know."

"We didn't tell Bryn," Aunt Astrid confessed. "It was all rather grisly."

"What did he say?" My father's right eyebrow lifted.

"He kept reciting a little rhyme," I answered. "Roses are red, violets are blue. It's almost dead, just like you."

My mother and father frowned at each other in silent communication, and there was another clap of thunder, this time preceded by a wicked strobe of lightning. The resultant echo nearly drowned out Aunt Astrid's next words.

"I couldn't really understand him, you know. It had been so long since I spoke English, and my ear wasn't tuned in. He seemed to be, well . . . 'giddy' is the word that keeps coming up in my mind. Giddy, dearest?" She turned to her sister, who nodded, her expression oddly nostalgic.

"I didn't want to say anything," my father said slowly, putting his cup down on the coffee table, "but he called here as well, right before he died, and left a message on the machine."

Tamsin skewed her eyes at me, and I shrugged. I hadn't known anything about it, or I would have mentioned it in the pub when the subject came up. Michael, who was standing in front of the fireplace, ran fingers through his shock of black hair.

"I was the one who listened to it," he said. "It was a bit hard to make out at first. Twice he recited a few lines, laughed, and then hung up."

"Recited what?" Brandt asked from his seat on one of the peacock-embroidered wingbacks.

"More awful poetry." Michael looked at him and grinned. "If I remember it correctly, he said that 'Wildeve is lost, the land is sold, and for Astrid and Aurora heads had rolled.'"

Thunder and lightning cracked across the windows, hitting the inn's roof, and the electricity went out. Tamsin jumped, her elbow upsetting the plate of food balanced on my outspread hand; and for a few wild seconds, we scrabbled around in the dark retrieving bits of pastry, quiche, and rolling olives. I thought of the rolling heads in Michael's words and wondered if Great-uncle Desmond had finally slipped off the edge he had spent his life teetering on.

The generator kicked in, as I knew it would, and the lights flickered back on.

"Well, that's that," Aunt Astrid said briskly and put her empty plate down on the eviscerated food tray, making as if to rise from the cushions. "If someone will help me straighten my cranky legs, I believe I'll toddle off to bed." She looked at my mother who, being the nearest, rushed to help her stand. "Thank you, dearest, the food was lovely, especially those ham sandwiches."

My mother smiled, nonplused, and Tamsin stared involuntarily at the food tray with perplexed eyes.

"Sandwiches?" she whispered to herself, her eyes vainly searching the remnants of food for bread crumbs. "But we didn't have any."

# 2

It rained all night. Large hard drops hit the panes of my bedroom windows, keeping me awake for most of the night but somehow lulling Tamsin. She slept like a corpse in the big four-poster next to me while I lay on my back, my hands behind my head as I stared at the ceiling. It was a pretty ceiling. My father had painted apricot clouds, a silvery moon, and luminous stars on the yellowed plasterwork when we had moved to the inn two years ago, but I was too tired to appreciate it that night. I didn't drop off until the wee hours of the morning, my mind snagged on my great-aunts and the intriguing prospect of getting to see the inside of Tanglewood Manor.

The next morning, Tamsin and I were in the front room with my parents, Great-aunts Astrid and Aurora, and Great-uncle Desmond's solicitor, Ambrose Hobhouse. Tamsin seemed to be well rested, whereas I was far from fresh. I was balled up next to my friend on the huge crimson sofa with my face buried in a silk pillow.

Dante, Brandt, and Jude were out, doing their volunteer work; and Brandt had taken Gabriel with him to one of his Bible students, an elderly man who ran the bait shop by the docks. Gabriel was fascinated with Mr. Peevey's wooden leg and black silk eye patch, the result of a car accident and not from a shark encounter as Gabriel firmly believed. To a little boy of six, the arrival of two great-aunts paled next to the chance to play with a glass eyeball in a jeweler's box.

Michael, however, was taking inventory of the inn's restaurant and making sure that Pete, the inn's cook, and Rayvyn, the inn's all-around help, didn't maim each other in their habitual bickering. Pete and Rayvyn fight like two divas forced to share a mirror.

My brothers were due back for lunch and afterward were scheduled to go to the manor house with my father and my great-aunts to check the cobwebbed structure from the cellars to the roof for safety. I wasn't exactly sure what that entailed, but after hearing the discussion the night before, I knew it involved grimy dirt and the use of dangerous tools. My brothers have a love of all things powered by big extension cords, and they were looking forward to the task like children looking forward to a carnival.

Mr. Hobhouse completed the necessary paperwork with my great-aunts and my father while my mother cleared away what was left of the refreshments. Aunts Astrid and Aurora asked questions about what they were signing, surprisingly lucid after a good-night's sleep. After the legal forms were filed away, Mr. Hobhouse produced an enormous key ring from his satchel and held it out to my great-aunts.

"Oh, dear." Aunt Aurora blinked distressed blue eyes at the laden iron, making no move to touch it. "So many of them. And not labeled. I'll never remember what they all unlock."

"Ah yes," Mr. Hobhouse said noncommittally and cleared his throat. He was a tall middle-aged man, but so thin and reedy that Aunt Aurora could have easily pinned him to the mat in a wrestling match.

"Which keys open which doors?" Aunt Astrid took the plate-sized ring from the solicitor's hand and shook it, setting the keys crashing like discordant wind chimes. "Do you know?"

"Ah no," Mr. Hobhouse said, managing to sound vaguely regretful. Aunt Astrid frowned and tried to hand them back, but Mr. Hobhouse, obviously determined to keep the keys out of his possession, ignored her, reached into his satchel, and freed a heavy yellow envelope crisscrossed with thick slabs of packing tape. It looked faintly ominous and waterproof enough to use as a raft.

"At your brother's instructions, should he predecease him, Mr. Rawlings sealed up this missive from Mr. Wildeve and left the envelope with me. I was assured that this envelope contains the keys to all of the manor's outside doors."

"So that's why no one could see if the house was livable," my mother interjected as she reentered the room, having finished whatever she had been doing in the kitchen. "Why didn't he want a proper inventory done by an executor? That seems like a very complicated and inefficient way to handle everything."

"Exactly." Mr. Hobhouse inclined his head at my mother. "Mr. Wildeve had insisted that the manor remain secure until his sisters took possession. It seems that he became even more . . . ah—"

"Crazy," Aunt Aurora supplied innocently and without pretense.

"Ah no," Mr. Hobhouse's mouth twitched involuntarily. "I was about to say 'cautious.'"

"You mean paranoid," Aunt Astrid snorted.

"Whatever his reasons," Mr. Hobhouse continued tactfully, "when he made his last will, he gave explicit instructions that no one was to enter the house except for his two younger sisters living in Peru."

"No one? Ever?" Aunt Astrid frowned in disbelief. "So how are we to move in? We'll need help. I assure you that even though my sister and I have lived in a somewhat primitive corner of the world for most of our life, we have absolutely no idea how to remodel. My nephew tells me that the house is dilapidated."

"Pardon me?" Mr. Hobhouse looked confused.

"No, indeed," Aunt Aurora breathed. "Sister is right."

"There are, however, many things we can do," Aunt Astrid went on, "but I doubt that any of our skills will be useful in this situation. I have defended myself from wild boars, using nothing but Aurora's old book bag. I had left mine in the canoe, you see. And I have swung on a rope—"

"You can't count that, dear," Aunt Aurora interrupted worriedly. "You didn't do that as a daily exercise. The bridge broke, and it was pure providence that you hung on and hit that ledge."

"That's true." Aunt Astrid swiveled her gaze to her sister. "But we have many other skills, dear. However, you are a better aim than I am with a dart and a blowgun."

"How kind of you to say so." Aunt Aurora smiled sweetly and waved her sister's compliment away with a deprecating hand. "But that was just a lark. And it was so many years ago, I doubt very much if I could handle a blowgun now."

Aunt Astrid turned and smiled at Mr. Hobhouse.

"So you see, dear, we don't know the first thing about fixing electricity or unclogging pipes. I don't see how we can honor Desmond's strange instructions about letting no one in if we are to make it a home."

"Pardon me?" Mr. Hobhouse was still staring at her.

"We'll need repairmen in. At the very, least we would like to have our nephew and his family over for supper one evening. Aurora makes an absolutely delightful llama roast."

"Ah!" Mr. Hobhouse blinked a few times in rapid succession. He seemed at a loss. Either he was trying not to think about llama rumps swimming in gravy, or he was picturing Aunt Aurora launching a poisoned dart at a howler monkey with a six-foot blowgun. As we all were. "Ah . . . I see. Of course. Of course. I didn't make myself very clear, I'm afraid. No one was to enter until you had gained legal possession, which you had done once you finished signing the papers I had brought today. Mr. Wildeve had merely wished for you to read the missive in the envelope before you open up the house. I believe that is why he had Rawlings seal the keys to the main doors inside the envelope with the letter."

"That's easily done," Aunt Astrid said briskly and held out her hand. "We'll just have a peek at it now."

"Perhaps you would like to read it in privacy," the solicitor suggested delicately. "It is, after all, your brother's last words to you."

"If you prefer," Aunt Astrid said, taking the proffered envelope. "But it would be silly to expect sentiment from him. Our brother had stubbornly refused to acknowledge us for over forty years."

"Perhaps he wished to make amends. He did leave you all his property."

"Amends." Aunt Astrid's mouth creased in a fleeting smile, and she looked pointedly at the enormous mass of unlabelled keys lying on the table between them. "Amends? Perhaps it's more of a revenge."

Mr. Hobhouse permitted his mouth another small twitch. "Perhaps. I would like to stress again that if you have any questions or need assistance, please feel free to call on me. You have my card." He closed his satchel. "I'll leave you to it, then, and see myself out. It's time I return to the office. Good day." He bowed formally to my great-aunts and left, quietly shutting the foyer door behind him.

"Well," Aunt Astrid sighed, "is there a letter opener somewhere?"

"He has such nice blue eyes." Aunt Aurora beamed, obviously more taken with Ambrose than with her inheritance.

Michael entered the room just then, running an exasperated hand through his black hair.

"Has he left? I tried to get finished earlier, but Rayvyn wouldn't let me go." Michael dropped on the sofa next to me, punched up a pillow, put it behind his head, leaned back, and shut his eyes. I brought him up to date on the session with Mr. Hobhouse while my father used his penknife to slit the envelope, handing it back to Aunt Astrid. She frowned and pulled out a sheet of paper wrapped around a second envelope, this one smaller and also sealed.

"Read the letter out loud, dearest," Aunt Aurora encouraged as her sister unfolded the creased missive.

"Certainly." Aunt Astrid cleared her throat and began, "Remember the day you left for America to go to your missionary school and I told you as you left that I wouldn't give you a penny of Father's money? If I remember correctly, I had said, 'Over my dead body.' Well, apparently that has come to pass. My little joke. Well, my dear sisters, I have another joke for you. Maybe you will find it. Maybe you won't. But it is there, all right. You have two months. If you don't, the National Trust is willing to pay the death duties in exchange for the house and all that is in it. Perhaps it is more desirable to you to just let it go. You never did have any sense of family heritage. You were too eager to leave. However, since I couldn't take it with me, as the saying goes, the wealth is all there. More, perhaps, than you can guess. No one knows where it is. Not even Rawlings was let into my secret. I trust no one. I never have. I give you one clue. Desmond."

We all sat in stupefied silence as the grandfather clock ticked loudly in the corner. After a moment of forehead-puckering contemplation, Aunt Aurora spoke, sounding more tremulous than usual, "Well, dear, I do have to say that it's such a relief not to worry about paying the death duties. And the missionary work can always use the contributions."

"It is a load off my mind as well, sister," Aunt Astrid agreed and began to tear open the second envelope. "Desmond had always been a few bobs short of a stew."

"Soup," My mother gasped and jumped up from her seat to hurry out of the room, obviously in pursuit of turning down a flame she had forgotten in the kitchen. My father's gaze followed her as she rushed by; then he turned his attention back to my great-aunts, one eyebrow raised as he studied them.

"You do know that you are welcome to stay and make your home with us. If you have no desire to bother with it, you can just let Tanglewood Manor go to the National Trust."

"Thank you, dear." Aunt Aurora beamed at him, her downy cheeks quivering gently. "But in the short time that you had known him, perhaps you had noticed that your poor uncle really wasn't as cunning as he liked to assume."

"Sister is speaking the truth. Desmond was never very good at mind games. He was much better at shooting bunnies with father's old rifle," Aunt Astrid said matter-of-factly and pulled a sheet of paper from the second envelope. As she unfolded it, a key ring with five large keys fell out and hit the table with a metallic clatter. Taking a deep breath, she read the short note in a puzzled voice.

"Roses are red, violets are blue. It belongs to Destiny, and so do you." She paused. "Another one of those silly rhymes."

I saw Michael's mouth curve up in a smile.

"No," Aunt Aurora stated sadly, "he wasn't very cunning."

"That's it?" Tamsin asked, sounding disappointed.

"There seems to be something penciled on the back." My father pointed out gently. "It's a little faint."

Aunt Astrid turned the paper over, squinted at the scribbling, and then frowned as she read aloud, "Perhaps you know what this verse means, but you don't know me well enough." She paused. "I wonder what Desmond meant by that? We knew him better than anyone."

My mother reentered the room just then, and the enigmatic clues were reread for her benefit.

"It belongs to Destiny, and so do you?" my mother echoed the last snatch of Uncle Desmond's rhyme. Aunt Astrid smiled, tapping the paper in her hand.

"That part is easy enough, dear. Our mother. Destiny Olivia Wildeve. He must have been referring to something that belonged to Mother."

"Didn't Mother have some nice pieces of jewelry?" Aunt Aurora's blue eyes blinked ingeniously at her sister. "I recall a choker of garnets and seed pearls though that doesn't seem to be very valuable."

"I believe she did, sister, I believe she did. Though my memory is far too hazy to rely upon. Perhaps Bryn can recall," Aunt Astrid said, referring to her older sister, my grandmother, and gave a hard sigh.

"So what does he mean by the second part of the clue written on the back?" I asked. But before anyone could hazard a guess, the foyer door opened to admit Dante, Brandt, and Jude. Brandt smiled at my mother's questioning look as Dante shut the door behind them.

"Gabriel is at Violet's. I told him it was all right to spend the night."

Violet Pengarth—the elderly wife of Albert, the only elder the Halfmoon congregation had before my father, Dante, and Brandt moved in—reminded me of a happy sparrow. Dressed in perpetual tweeds, she is forever hopping about on spindly legs the size of towel rods.

Albert Pengarth, her husband, reminded me of an ancient spy. Tall, lean, handsome, wrinkled, white haired, and clever, he had a habit of studying everything through a perpetual squint. Nothing daunted him. I had once seen him fend off a rabid dog with a series of bizarre kicks, looking like a suit-clad ninja master until he lost his loafer through the pub window. Violet's comment, once the crash and tinkle of breaking glass had subsided, had been, "Oh, pooh Albert!" Albert, typically distracted by the proximity of the pub, had replied, "Hey! Anyone fancy a ploughman's before we head back?"

Violet and Albert were presently raising their seven-year-old great-grandson, Eli, who had been orphaned by a plane crash. Gabriel and Eli were inseparable.

My brothers were dressed in working uniforms of jeans and tee shirts, obviously ready to investigate Tanglewood's dirtier nooks. I knew that it was going to take them and my father all day to complete the task, perhaps longer if they ran into problems. I also knew that I wasn't going to be allowed to accompany them into the manor on their first trek in. That had been made painfully clear the night before. My brothers were convinced that I was going to explore unstable masonry, end up brain damaged, and be forced to dribble my liquid veggies into an adult nappy.

Since Tamsin and I were barred from accompanying them inside, we planned on spending the afternoon wandering about the tangled outside, looking for the gardens that I'd heard about from my grandmother but had never yet glimpsed.

"How was service?" Aunt Aurora asked, referring to their volunteer work, and smiled at her great-nephews as they settled themselves in the room to wait for lunch. My mother left once more to check on it.

"More eventful than usual," Dante sighed as he lowered himself into one of the wingbacks that flanked the fireplace.

"Zephyr proposed marriage to him this morning." Jude grinned and settled himself into the facing armchair.

Originally from Arizona, Zephyr Callahan is a two-time divorcee with a frantic need to find a third husband. She wears long gauzy dresses, sprinkles blossoms in her hair, glitter on her collarbones, and decals on her fingernails. She also has an aggressive seven-year-old daughter named Aura. Aura is big for her age and spends her time after the meetings leading Gabriel around by his head.

Zephyr had moved to Cornwall to take care of her aging great-grandfather, who is suffering from Alzheimer's. Charlie Radcliffe is not interested in anything outside of his own tea cakes, being a staunch philosopher who spouts garbled quotes from Nietzsche while pottering aimlessly about the cottage in his slippers and apron. Or naked, as I once discovered much to my horror. On that profoundly disturbing experience he had intoned Nietzsche's motto "Long live the Superman!" before darting outside into the street to stop traffic in its tracks.

"Did you accept Zephyr's proposal?" Michael grinned, his eyes still closed and his arms still crossed lazily over his chest.

"No." Dante leaned back in his chair and gave the toes of his work boots an amused look. "But I imagine I'm merely a booby prize on her list."

"Well"—I kicked Michael's leg with my unshod foot—"she's not going alphabetically, or Brandt would have had first refusal. You might be next."

He opened one eye to swivel it in my direction. I could see a suspicious glint between the black lashes.

"Why?" he asked bluntly.

"She told me that she's into 'raven locks.'"

"Don't say Rayvyn," Michael groaned and closed his eye again.

"Did everything go well with Mr. Hobhouse?" Brandt asked, quirking an eyebrow at our great-aunts.

"Read the letter," I urged. "Tell them about it."

"Tell us what?" Brandt's eyebrow rose even higher.

Aunt Astrid read her brother's bizarre letter, following it up with the silly verse and the sneering words penciled on the back. She explained their deductions about Destiny, their mother, and suggested that the hidden wealth could possibly be jewels even though neither of them could remember any.

"Would he be crazy enough to make it all up?" Dante asked when the recital was over.

"No, dear," Aunt Aurora breathed. "He was most earnest about money."

"Almost a savant," Aunt Astrid agreed with her sister. "As a child, he ate the chalk when the tutor had his back turned, but he was most advanced in accounting. He could glance at a jar of pennies and tell you how many there were."

"Well, we really won't know what could possibly be hidden in the house until we've been inside," my father broke in, openly amused. "And no one is going to be free to take inventory until we know it's safe enough to wander about in."

"Safe is good, dear." Astrid smiled at my father. "But no one needs to concern themselves if it's sanitary or not. Aurora and I have learned how to be clean in the most unsanitary places. All we'll need is a stick to dig a hole with and some coca or cinchona leaves. Not banana leaves. Banana leaves are too slick and unwieldy. I made that common mistake soon after arriving at the foot of Nevado Coropuna."

"Leaves are biodegradable," Aunt Aurora said, took a deep breath to add another innocently graphic tidbit, but was mercifully silenced when my mother came in to announce lunch, ignoring our involuntary grins as she waved the long wooden spoon in her hand like a wand.

Later, after eating fresh rosemary bread and bowls of my mother's minestrone, we divided ourselves into two groups, piled into the Range Rover and Brandt's truck, and drove to Tanglewood Manor. The remains of the estate was only three miles from the inn as the crow flies, but as the lane rambles, it is closer to five, two of which travel the cliff's edge right up to the house.

As we drove the two-mile cliff drive, the oceanfront cliffs with its dangerous hewn-rock steps going down to the beach below was on our left, and a long shrubby, overgrown strip of lawn was on our right. That long overgrown strip of lawn on our right fronted a medieval forest that now belonged to someone else, and in front of us as we drew near was the manor house itself. The cliff-side access brought us to the front of the house and the original graveled sweep that circled an ancient fountain. The gravel had long since been scattered by the elements, leaving ruts and a packed mix of soil and cliff stone, and the fountain had long been dormant, the stone mermaids frozen in mid-cavort by lichen crust. The house itself, all weathered gray angles and overhangs swathed in ivy and vines, was nestled in a cushiony backdrop of more medieval forest. As far as I could tell, the forest behind the house still belonged to Wildeves.

We circled the fountain, pulled up to the wide steps leading to an enormous stoop, and turned off the engines. A relative silence descended, and I was abruptly aware of waves crashing, sea birds calling, and thick loneliness. Aunt Aurora was the first to break the curious spell.

"Oh, my," she said breathlessly, opened the Range Rover's door, and slid out. Aunt Astrid climbed out after her and disapprovingly surveyed the property.

"What a mess. Well, sister, we might as well get this part over with. Ready for ghosts, Aurora?" she sighed. "Let's see what Desmond's been doing with his life these last forty years." They toddled away, arm in arm, making for the steps and the enormous front doors. My brothers exchanged amused glances and respectfully trailed behind them, their heavy tool bags clanking in their gloved hands.

My father saw the wistful look on my face and laughed.

"I'll tell you what," he stopped and cupped a consoling hand around the back of my head, drawing me to him in a quick squeeze, "if we're reasonably sure that it's safe enough to tour, you and Tamsin can look it over this evening after dinner."

"Are you coming back tonight to work on it?"

"No, child, we've got shepherding visits tonight," he said, referring to their calls on various members of the Halfmoon congregation. "But Jude and Michael should be free to take you out here for a quick run-through." He patted my shoulder and released me. "Stay away from the outbuildings in the courtyard. We won't have time to check any of them until later."

"We'll be careful," I assured him and then thought about my farcical expedition the day before in the crowded airport. "But please keep an eye on Aunt Astrid and Aunt Aurora."

"We will, child." He smiled and handed me his mobile phone. "Here, keep this with you. Dante and Jude have theirs, but Gabriel accidentally knocked Brandt's into Mr. Peevey's toilet." He turned and began his ascent up the long sweep. "We'll call you when we're ready to leave."

We watched him cross the deep stoop and disappear inside, closing the doors behind him. Fat lavender clouds began scudding overhead, rolling blue shadows across the neglected feral lawn. I took a deep breath to inhale the salty ozone wafting past us.

"Rain tonight," I predicted and gazed around at the unkempt vista. A slow-growing breeze rose up the cliff's side, and the shrubbery began to stir and rustle.

"Is it just me, or does the lawn seem to be beckoning to us?" Tamsin grinned. I stuffed the wafer of phone into the front pocket of my jeans.

"Ready to go around back?" I asked and began wading carefully toward the wooded side of the house. Tamsin bounded over a low shrub and sidled up to me.

"Have you been all around the outside yet?" Tamsin asked as we walked. I shook my head.

"No. Great-uncle Desmond would have potted me from a tower. The closest any of us had gotten was to knock politely on the front door to make sure he was still alive."

As we neared the side of the house, brambles began to snag at us, and vines tried to wrap tendrils around our feet. I told Tamsin to be wary of broken glass and nails.

"Do you think it's booby-trapped?" she asked and circumvented a random bush that had apparently sprung up years ago from a bird-recycled seed.

"Mr. Hobhouse had already sent someone out here to check what he could. I think that he was half-afraid that Uncle Desmond or Rawlings had put out mantraps."

Tamsin halted in midstride, her foot still in the air, and skewed her wide brown eyes to me.

"You look like Bambi," I remarked.

"Mr. Hobhouse's man." She lowered her foot gingerly and wrapped long fingers around my arm. "Did he check carefully?"

"Of course," I laughed and pulled her along behind me. We reached the grassy verge that bounded the north side of the manor and found ourselves staring up at the imposing expanse of hewn stone, windows, and gryphons guarding the gutters. It seemed an inordinately long way up to the roofline.

"It looks so big and neglected." Tamsin shuddered in faint distaste and stepped over a baby yew.

"I'm especially curious after that letter he wrote to Aunts Astrid and Aurora," I said as we waded around the short clots of shrubbery, most of it unidentifiable.

Ahead of us we could see a long verandah encircled with a stone balustrade and empty pots the size of bathtubs. We wandered to it and climbed its mossy steps. Paved in large smooth flagstones, the narrow verandah stretched down the rest of the manor's north side, ending at the corner that led to the back of the house and the gated courtyard. Strategically placed benches ringed a fountain of flying sea horses, the benches' granite seats nothing but chipped slabs resting on the backs of stone swans, their arched necks the benches' armrests.

Even neglected it was utterly enchanting. Tamsin and I turned slowly and stared. Tiny trees, their sapling trunks the size of licorice whips, along with wild vinca, pushed up through cracks in the stones where soil had pooled.

I went to the dead fountain and looked in. I could see tiny waves of sapphire tiles under the puddle of last night's storm. Just then, an unidentifiable bug, indigo and iridescent, floated down, hovered over a matching tile, probably hoping to mate with it, and then flew off highly disappointed, breaking the spell. I smiled and raised my eyes, having caught a flash of movement in the French doors.

"There's Aunt Aurora," I said and pointed at the wavering of flowered print behind the glass. "Let's go see how the inspection is coming along. Maybe we'll get a glimpse inside."

We trotted over to the glass and made a tent of our hands to peer in. Aunt Aurora seemed to be sifting through the papers stuffed in the pigeonholes of an enormous rolltop desk. I knocked on the glass panes. Aunt Aurora jumped at the sound of my knuckles and stared at the ceiling above as if angels were summoning her.

"Juanito?" Aunt Aurora called upward, her voice tremulous and hopeful. I rapped again.

"Aunt Aurora!" I called loudly through the glass. "It's us. We're out here."

I kept rapping until she eventually found us standing outside and hastened to open the doors. She gave us a sweet, vague smile, eyes peering myopically at us like cloudy sapphires.

"Hello, dears," she greeted us before I could speak. "I'm afraid Astrid isn't here right now. She's with the Machu Picchu Indians today, teaching them hygiene. It's not at all nice where they pierce themselves. And did you know that they worship corn? Or is that the Aztecs? Anyway, if you come back next week, she should be home."

We stood there with our mouths open, words dying on our tongues before they could be formed. Patting my cheek, Aunt Aurora shut the doors, latched them, and trotted back to the massive desk. I could see Michael's amused figure in the far doorway, his teeth flashing white in the dimness.

"Well," Tamsin said after a moment, "aren't they extinct? The Machu Picchu, I mean."

"At least someone is with her," I said and tried to dismiss my unease. I knew from experience that my brothers were diligent babysitters and was certain that my great-aunts would come to no harm. Shrugging to myself helplessly, I turned and made my way toward the back of the property. Tamsin tagged along behind, gathering sprigs of wildflowers as she went.

We eventually ambled to the back corner of the north wing. Ahead of us spread the previously hidden back lawn in its entire unruly, neglected splendor. It was an undulating mass of overgrown greenery, ghostly outlines of long-ago gardens running wild, and shaggy rolling knolls, terraces, and steps, along with a couple of withered trees. Plop a glossy raven on one of the dead trees and a few storm clouds behind it, and the atmosphere would be complete.

In the distance, one of the lawn's scrolled stone arches opened onto a winding flagstone path bordered by riotous rosebushes. The rosebushes meandered down to the medieval forest and disappeared into its green-lit depths, scattering dark pink petals in its wake like windblown confetti.

"Look." I pointed to what the roses had led my eyes to. Nestled in the forest of age-gnarled trees, barely discernible, was a long meandering yew hedge that had to be nearly twenty feet high. It looked forgotten, scruffy with wild vines and ivy, but you could still see the phantom ghosts of old topiary. And it boxed something in, disappearing into the dimness and blending in with the surrounding foliage until it was lost. I knew it had to be the walled gardens that my grandmother had told me about.

"Come on. I think we've found them." I clambered over the balustrade of the verandah and leapt past a clump of shrubbery. "Let's see if we can get in."

Dodging bushes and wading through knee-high weeds, we cut across the lawns to the block steps under the arch and started down the path, our attention carefully fixed on the uneven stones so we wouldn't trip. The flower-strewn flagstones bumped over the ground as if they had been laid years ago, years before my grandmother was born, years before the distant trees could stretch out their roots to shift the underlying soil.

"Grandmother said that there are two ways inside. One is through an enormous iron gate in the back that was always kept locked. The other way in is a bit harder to find." I paused to circumvent a long thorny arm of fat rosebuds. "She never told me the key to getting in the garden. She said that I would have more fun if I found it myself." I glanced back at Tamsin. "A secret garden. A bit Frances Hodgson Burnett, don't you think?"

She grinned at me and ducked under the arms of an untamed bush bursting with pink petals. None of the bushes that we had passed were hybrids. There were no willowy wands with delicately layered buds. These were old, wild, and hardy, with masses of shedding flowers. I finger-combed my hair, dislodging a shower of petals that had gotten tangled in my curls.

We reached the dappled shade of the forest's rim. The rosebushes had already begun to thin out and be replaced with shaggy tufts of grass, woodsy ferns, and bare stones pushing through the soil. Up ahead I could see the flagstones suddenly turn and meander down the hedge line behind a massive beech tree. As we neared the path's abrupt change of course, we found ourselves having to clamber over twisted roots and broken pieces of statuary. Tamsin tripped over a nymph's head and would have gone sprawling if she hadn't reached out and caught herself by my jeans. A belt loop came away in her hand, and I staggered into the massive bole of some tree. The foliage overhead was alive with birds, and all about us the light was a deep golden green, glowing like old gilt on a Renaissance masterpiece.

We followed the flagstones around the wavy perimeter of the yew hedge, and the more we adhered to the path, the more I got the feeling that the flagstones were merely leading us to the locked gate. Tamsin slowed, stopped, and lowered herself onto a thick slab of engraved marble. A butterfly flickered past us, bobbing and weaving, looking like a dancing rose petal in moving coins of light.

"Is that a grave marker?" I said thoughtfully, pointing at the slab she was sitting on. Her eyes widened comically, and she bobbed up from the marble, jumping to one side as if she had been shoved.

"I didn't say it was," I laughed. "I just thought it looked like one."

"Very funny." She gave me a suitably unimpressed look and then bent to study the faint weathered markings her thighs had been resting on. "You're right, though. It does. The engravings look like letters, but it's hard to make them out."

I squatted beside her legs and ran my fingers over the chiseled grooves.

"It's old," I said. "There are hardly any edges left."

"Let's scoot it into a patch of light and see if we can read it," she suggested. "Maybe it's a pedestal to some of those broken bits."

I thought back to the bits of statuary we had seen scattered about and half-buried under fern fronds—mostly hands, limbs, and heads, with nary a torso to connect them to. Some pieces were tiny and delicate, others large and roughly hewn. I wondered, not for the first time, where the statue bits came from. Either there had been some ancient statues that hadn't survived the elements, or they were planted as bits and bobs during the same Gothic revival craze a few hundred years ago that had wealthy landowners constructing fake ruins in their gardens. Or maybe some lazy Wildeve had remodeled and thrown the unwanted parts out into the forest the same way some people tossed discarded tires into an alley.

I experimentally rocked the heavy slab and was surprised to find that it wasn't so embedded into the soil that it couldn't be shifted. Perhaps the same things that had slowly displaced the flagstones had eventually displaced the slab.

"How about over there," Tamsin suggested and pointed to a large shifting patch of sunshine that had managed to weave its way past the canopy of leaves.

I agreed, and, kneeling on the springy ground, we managed to push the slab toward the sunshine, killing ferns and grass in a solid, muddy path of evisceration. We stopped at the wavering edge of light and collapsed across the sunbeam.

"Are you sure we aren't displacing an ancestral gravestone?" Tamsin moaned and slowly unfurled her lanky body until she was flat on the ground like a flounder. "I've herniated something I know I'm going to use later."

"If it is an ancestral grave marker, we'll just turn around scoot it back," I laughed and swiped a bead of sweat from my eye so I could get a better look at the etched notches. "Oh," I said, disappointed, "I know why we couldn't make it out. It's in Latin."

"It *is* old," Tamsin gasped and scrambled around until she could see the marks in the shifting light.

"Do we know anyone who knows Latin?" I asked. Tamsin sat back on her heels, looking into the woods as if trying to find inspiration in the deeper shadows.

The only readily available Latin in my father's mind was for translating inscriptions on old paintings. My brothers might remember their Latin, having been taught some of it in school, but I knew that if I asked them for a translation, there would be a good chance that their response would be something ridiculous and completely made up. I'd rather try to coerce a Latin translation from a heaving cat than to try to wring one from my brothers when they're in one of their hilarious moods.

"What about Basil Brett?" Tamsin suggested after a few moments of contemplation. "He used to sell old manuscripts. He might know enough Latin. At least he'd have something readily available to look it up in."

"That's a good idea."

Basil Brett is a prim tiny elderly ministerial servant in the congregation, who looks like he'd been polished by wads of old money. There is no showy display, so no one knows if he actually has any. He just looks incredibly groomed, tasteful, and plush from his buffed leather shoes to his coifed silver hair. Looking beautiful and courteous must have been one of his job requirements when he worked in his London auction house selling rare antiques. Even his voice is beautiful, polite, and discreet, making him sound like the hybrid offspring of a BBC announcer and an undertaker.

I found Basil's number in my father's directory, punched it in, and was a bit surprised when my summons was answered on the second ring.

I gave Basil my request, which he readily assented to; then, once he had a pencil in his hand, I read out the letters and the spaces. He promised me he would look it up to make sure his memory wasn't playing him false and call me back in a few moments with a translation. I shut the mobile and sat down on the stone slab to wait. He didn't take long.

"Most curious, my angel," he said fulsomely when I answered the phone on its first ring. "Loosely translated, your Latin inscription says, 'I wait beyond the flames where I dance above light. Silver are my feet, and black is my crown.' Does that help you?"

"In a way," I said guardedly and then repeated the quotation for Tamsin's benefit. I needed her to help me remember the exact wording until I could have it written down. "Thank you very much."

"You are most welcome," he said and hung up. I hastily punched in Dante's number on the speed dial and waited until he answered.

"Dante, can you write something down for me, please, and keep it in your pocket to give to me later?"

"Sure. Just give me a few minutes to get to the library. I saw some parchment on a table in there."

"Library," I echoed, thinking of enormous fireplaces and miles of leather-bound books. "Is the house really in good-enough shape for Tamsin and me to see it this evening? What's it like inside?"

He grunted. It was an ominous and guarded sound. "You'll have to see it for yourself. It's unbelievable. And, yes, at the rate everything is going in here, you and Tamsin can probably see it this evening." He paused, and I could hear the dry rustle of what I pictured to be large scrolls of paper. "Okay. I'm ready. Dictate."

I repeated Basil's words, and, as odd as they were, Dante, obviously preoccupied, asked no questions.

Tamsin and I spent the rest of the afternoon exploring the hedge line for the key to the secret entrance. We weren't successful. All we had managed to stumble across were flagstones, more nymph heads, and tree roots. We never wandered to what we had decided was the back of the garden for fear of coming across the locked gate. According to my grandmother, the huge gate was of wrought iron, and I didn't want to accidentally find myself cheating by peeking in at the garden the wrong way around. Besides wanting to see the garden as my grandmother had seen it, we were having too much fun searching for the secret way in.

The sun was hovering over the trees when my father called it a day and finally came out of the manor house, his clothes covered in cobwebs and beaded with the transparent bits of long-dead insects. He found Tamsin and I stretched out on the Range Rover's hood like lizards trying to suck the last vestige of warmth from a rock. The cloud-dotted sky had long since turned soft and hazy, and the earlier warmth was fleeing steadily with the lowering sun. We were feeling lazy, hungry for dinner, and pleasantly cool. I rolled over and smiled at him as he descended the wide sweep of front steps.

"Hi," I greeted him cheerfully and propped my hand under my head. "Will Tamsin and I get to see the house after dinner?"

"Hi, yourself, rosebud," he said amiably and touched a knuckle to my face. "It seems safe enough. Not very livable, but if you're careful, nothing should happen."

Dante came out just then, escorting Aunt Astrid and Aunt Aurora. Glassy-eyed and dusty, Aunts Astrid and Aurora toddled slowly down the steps as if their bones ached. My father saw my face.

"I know, child, but short of tying them to chairs, there was no way to get them to take it easier," he said gently. "As much as I would have liked for them to rest, there was no way to bar them from coming to see their home today. Your aunt Aurora escaped Michael for a few minutes and tobogganed down the great stairs on a tea tray. I'm going to get your grandmother to talk to them."

Aunts Astrid and Aurora saw us reclining on the Range Rover's hood and waved.

"Oh, my dears," Aunt Aurora gasped as she eased herself down the front steps, "what marvelous fun."

"How we wished that you both could have been with us." Aunt Astrid's smile was grim. I thought the grimness was due to the obvious effort expended on bending her arthritic knees, but her next words clued me in. "It was unbelievable. I used to feel it was such a shame that my brother never got himself a nice wife and settled down. Now I'm rather relieved that he pulled the plug on his gene pool."

"Aunt Astrid!" Jude came out of the door behind them, carrying a stack of paper-filled boxes that he had to peer around, pretending shock over her statement, and Aunt Aurora giggled, sounding like a teenager.

"Tell us." I sat up on the hood and slid to the ground, fishing my father's mobile phone from my pocket to hand it to him. "What was it like? Are all the stories about Great-uncle Desmond true?"

"Yes and no," Jude laughed and stepped past the slow progress of Dante and Aunts Astrid and Aurora to throw the boxed papers, his tool bag, and tool belt into the back of Brandt's truck. "And, no, I won't tell you what it's like. You'll have to see it for yourself. I'll bring you and Tamsin tonight after dinner."

Just then Brandt and Michael came out of the front doors. Michael, looking as if he had spent the day rolling in soot, took the tools from Brandt, who shut and locked the great doors behind them, then turned, and saw us staring at him. He flashed a tired smile as he came down the steps.

"So far, Jude and I reamed thirty-two chimneys," he laughed and tossed the long chain that had been used to knock the soot from the chimneys, along with the tool belts, into the back of the truck.

"I told him we just need to buy a goose and drop it down the stacks," Jude laughed and opened the Range Rover's doors to help my father and Dante install my great-aunts onto the cushioned seats. I ran to my oldest brother and took the piece of paper he slid from his pocket, knowing it was Basil's translation.

"We found a slab of marble with some words in Latin inscribed on it, so we called Basil Brett and asked him to translate it for us," I told my father and then read from the scrap of paper in my hand.

"I wait beyond the flames where I dance above the light," Brandt repeated slowly and tiredly fished the truck's keys from his pocket. "Why does that make me think of something?"

"Do you know what it means?" I asked eagerly. "Is it a quotation?" He shook his head slowly and shrugged.

"I don't know, *poca*. I'll have to think about it. Maybe it will come to me."

*Poca* is a feminine corruption of *poco,* the Italian word for "little bit." The family story behind that stems from Michael, who was three years old when I was born and just learning the more advanced intricacies of Italian. At least it beats what they call Gabriel, which is *uvetta. Uvetta* means "raisin," and it delights my baby brother to no end. My brothers tell him it's because he was tiny, blue, and wrinkled right after he was born.

"That's an idea," Dante said and looked at my father. "Basil Brett can help with evaluations. And he can recommend someone if Aunts Astrid and Aurora want to unload some of it."

"I'll call him tonight," my father answered and got into the Range Rover.

"Please try to remember what the Latin inscription makes you think of." I flung at Brandt and climbed into the Range Rover after Tamsin, putting me in the backseat with her and Aunt Aurora. Aunt Astrid was in front with my father. As we pulled away from the house with Brandt's truck following the Range Rover, my father and Aunt Astrid began to talk about their afternoon.

The house seemed to be in far better repair than anyone had anticipated. The only problems were cosmetic.

Handymen had installed the electricity in the nineteen thirties. Cleverly hidden cloth-covered conduits snaked all over the walls, providing an adequate but fairly primitive and limited electrical resource, all of it leading back to ancient fuse boxes in the cellars, all of which seemed to be haphazardly and precariously attached to a set of crusty generators. It was anyone's guess as to why there were generators when England's Electricity Board had added the manor to the electrical supplier in the village. No one could even hazard a guess as to where my great-grandfather had the cables buried. It must have cost dearly and been quite a project in its day.

Also, luxurious when it was first installed, the plumbing boasted a thronelike toilet, a hot and cold tap at the sink, and a massive bathtub with gold-plated fixtures. Even the gold-plated towel rods were connected to the boiler and heated with hot water. It was just that the boiler seldom boiled anything. Its fuel source used to be felled trees shoved into the cellar's furnace, but Great-uncle Desmond had converted the boiler to electricity as well, which for some reason was temperamental. So the advent of hot water was about as rare and as exciting as a lunar eclipse. The most one could hope for was that the toilet wouldn't back up when flushed and that cold water would be there for washing. The water supply was potable, running clear and bacteria free but smelling of old horseshoes.

The floors were a bit creaky in places, but solid, the stairs and railings firm, the roof hardly leaking, and the chimneys so far sound and freshly reamed by Michael, who had to ride all the way home in the back of Brandt's truck.

There was one telephone line out of the study with one black rotary dial telephone at the end of it. There were no computers, no televisions, and no radios, just plenty of candles, matches, and one old Victrola record player according to Aunt Astrid.

"Even fifty years ago, it was a wee bit old-fashioned," Aunt Aurora commented as we drove the cliff-edged road away from the manor toward home. We had to go slowly since the drive was potholed and rutted with decades of neglect.

"But it used to be so beautiful inside," Aunt Astrid lamented. "Now it is just a mess."

"Tamsin and I talked about it, and we can work on it tomorrow, cleaning it up a bit," I said, and I saw my father's green eyes glitter at me through the rearview mirror.

"I'm going to hire a cleaning firm to tackle the house once the contents are evaluated and sorted," he said and navigated around a pothole the size of a child's wading pool. "It's too large, too far gone, and too inaccessible. If you would like to help tomorrow, you can find out where all the keys on the key ring go, *leanbh*."

"Should I try to find out which keys belong to the outbuildings as well?" I asked. My father shook his head.

"We'll get to those later. The buildings are all locked, and we didn't have the time to try to find the right keys. Brandt looked in the windows, and he said that as far as he could tell, the outbuildings were empty—"

"Desmond should have used them for storage," Aunt Astrid snorted.

"So don't worry about them yet. If you end up with a handful of keys that you can't find locks for, then just hang on to them, and we'll try them on the outbuildings later. Right now just concentrate on the inside of the manor. There are some locked wardrobes, drawers, cabinets, and closets. And one of the tower rooms is locked as well. That bothers me. Try to get that open tomorrow."

"How will I label the keys?" I asked, painfully aware that I wouldn't know which room I was in unless it had an oven or a toilet.

"You don't have to label them, child." My father smiled at me, reading my mind. "Just leave the keys in the locks that they fit, and I'll take care of it later."

"You might as well have these now," Aunt Astrid said and fished through her enormous tote for the outside door keys and the saucer-sized key ring. "And whatever you see tonight when you go in, just don't be frightened. And wash your hands if you touch anything. Especially that revolting wildebeest."

I glanced meaningfully at Tamsin as Aunt Astrid reached over the seat and put the keys in my hands.

# 3

After dinner, as promised, Jude drove Michael, Tamsin, and me to Tanglewood Manor in his van, a great white shell of fiberglass bouncing on demented shocks. Besides the driver's seat and the front passenger seat, which had been surrendered to Tamsin as the guest, there are no places to sit unless it's on the floor next to tools, car parts, diving equipment, fishing tackle, or other male accoutrements. I always feel like the last marble in the box when I have to ride in the back of Jude's van. For safety's sake, I wedged myself somewhere between Michael's solid form and an immovable box with something heavy inside. I wasn't sure what was in the box, but it beat sitting next to the empty scuba tanks that had a tendency to roll across the floor like loose torpedoes.

Brandt had already taken his truck and Albert Pengarth on shepherding visits, and my father and Dante had long since left in the Range Rover on theirs. Even though Jude usually accompanied them, he was free for the night and available to take us on our tour of Tanglewood Manor.

It was more than could be said for Michael's old midnight blue Saab, which was stuck at home with a flat tire and an alarmingly soft spare, something that we were all beginning to regret. It was dark and blowy when we left the house with nothing more than a faint scent of rain hovering in the blackness, but now the wind was beginning to grow with alarming rapidity, and when Jude's flat-sided van caught the storm winds, it bobbled more violently than a fat lady running for her life.

"Maybe we should turn back and try again tomorrow," Jude suggested and turned on the dash's blower to clear the growing condensation from the windshield. "If we're turning back to go home, we need to do so now. The storm's building quickly, and it looks like it's going to break any second."

"You mean we'll have to wait until the weather is calm?" Tamsin asked, sounding as disappointed as I felt at the thought of aborting the long-awaited excursion. A sudden gust of wind sprung up, buffeted the van, and sent two of the scuba tanks spinning in opposite directions.

"Look, I don't really want to go back," I said. "Tamsin and I have waited too long to see the inside of the manor house. Do you think we'll make it? Can we keep going?"

"I know we can make it to the manor. Depending on the violence of the storm that's blowing in, we might not be able to make it back though. But if you are that set on seeing it now, we can go on to the manor and just take our chances. If we have to, we can always hitch a ride back with Dad after he and Dante finish tonight," Jude said and turned onto the rutted lane that led along the cliff's edge to the house. "Then tomorrow Brandt can drop me off to pick the van up."

Driving through wind gusts charging up a cliff face is like riding your bicycle with Toto in Kansas. I kept expecting the tin man to crash through the windscreen and kill us.

"It's getting worse," Jude remarked a moment later, expertly dodging a pothole. I guessed that he was used to his van and knew how far to push it. The rest of us were so buffeted and jarred that we couldn't speak without biting our tongues off. I could hear the loose change clanking violently in Jude's ashtray. "The wind is starting to hit the cliff pretty hard, but it may not be this bad down in the village."

"Hopefully, later, it will die down a bit," Tamsin grunted timidly between potholes, then screeched when a fork of lightning hit the water somewhere beside us.

Heaven was beginning to crack, and by the time we had pulled up to the front steps, lightning was avidly attacking the ocean in a breathtaking celestial display. The violent riptide of wind swirling maniacally around us shot a wriggling fish up and over the cliffs and plopped it across the windscreen like a splat of jelly. It was a toss-up as to who was more startled, the fish or us. We all jerked back, watching in surprised horror as the windscreen wipers ricocheted back and flung it into oblivion. Jude turned off his engine, and large pelting raindrops began to thunder and roll over the van's roof like hurled marbles.

The grime-encrusted manor had never looked more welcoming.

"Sorry!" Jude shouted. "The storm seems to have beaten us! And to top it off, I gave the umbrellas to Aunts Astrid and Aurora! Can you believe they didn't have any?"

"Yes!" Michael yelled over the racket the storm was making in the echo chamber we were sitting in and scrambled to his feet, yanking me up behind him. "Come on! Run!" he commanded and shoved open the heavy sliding door. I barely had time to snag my rucksack with the keys in it before he propelled me out of the van and into the rain. Doors opened behind me, slammed shut, and we all ran for the deep front stoop. A brilliant stab of lightning hit the water nearby with a loud crack, sucking the air from our lungs.

Jude snatched the outside door keys from my hand as I fumbled, unlocking the door for me and shoving all of us into the house like he was ramming a plunger through a clogged drain. We exploded into the blackness in a stumbling damp mass of warm bodies and eight feet. I got mine tangled up with Tamsin's and cannoned into another body. This one was stiff and meaty and didn't move when I landed, both of us flat on the floor with a body-jarring thud. Either I was embracing a horizontal corpse with advanced rigor or I had just killed one of my brothers. I froze in horror. Overhead a light clicked on, and I found myself staring at Margaret Rutherford. Her hat had been knocked off, and I found my left knee up her skirt, exposing her cotton bloomers and rolled stockings.

"Are you all right, Bella?" Jude asked and pulled me off the mannequin's immense bosom. I could see Michael against the wall, his hand on the light switch, and Tamsin staring openmouthed at something behind me. I whirled around and swallowed a gasp. We were in a soaring cavern built of hewn blocks. Flagstones the size of mattresses paved the floor, medieval weaponry and tapestries the size of sails hung from the walls, and a wrought-iron chandelier the size of an upended sapling hung above us. But that wasn't what had wrung an involuntary gasp from my throat.

Bizarre curios filled every chunk of floor space. There were antique Bavarian dirndls on dressmakers' dummies, a worm-eaten Viking funerary ship floating on the flagstones like a bulbous, petrified canoe, grimy marble cherubs frolicking on chipped feet, and several suits of armor, only to mention a few of the objects crowding out the Great Hall. There was even a row of cancan dancers, arm in arm in a perpetually frozen pose, their raised feet exposing brittle yellow bloomers. One more kick and the ancient knickers would fall off in leprous dust.

The vast room was as crowded as a fevered dream closet. The light was dim and smoky, surreal shadows hunkered and flitted through the clutter, and the objects regarded us with comic malevolence. The air was still, cool, and musty inside while the lightning, thunder, and tempest raged beyond the walls.

I experimentally sniffed the stale air, recognizing the scent of Great-uncle Desmond. It was a sort of soil, dust, mold, and age mix, with an underlying scent of exotic spice and decay. In the past, I had always thought that the tang clinging to my great-uncle's person erupted from his haphazardly aligned ninety-year-old teeth. I didn't know then that I had been inhaling the odor of his house.

"Are these tombstones?" Tamsin gasped and pointed to a row of lichen-covered slabs leaning drunkenly against the wall beside her. Michael leaned past her and gently pried a slab from its nest, looking at the other side where the writing appeared to be incised.

"Yes," he said briefly and returned the slab to its place. Tamsin took a small step away from it.

"It's unbelievable!" I said and took a tentative step into the morass of clutter. I never knew one could experience the macabre and hilarity at the same time. I finally understood Aunt Astrid's cryptic comment about the wildebeest when I spotted the taxidermist's nightmare peering at us from behind a four-beast carousel.

"Ready for the tour?" Michael asked.

A hedgehog-sized dust ball rolled to my foot and stopped like tumbleweed against a saloon wall. I lifted my foot to shake it off and was surprised to see a fluffy goose feather stuck to the bottom of my shoe.

"We're as ready as we'll get," I said and scraped my foot across the age-buffed flagstones.

We began our tour of the manor to the atmospheric accompaniment of thunder, lightning, shadows, drafts, and an olfactory overload that clung to the back of the throat like molasses. I couldn't take it all in. There was just too much eclectic horror in cobweb icing. By the time we were headed for the massive dining hall, I had seen a dead cobra varnished to a plaque, a Ping-Pong table next to a signed-Picasso lithograph, a moth-eaten stuffed zebra leaking stuffing from improbable cracked udders, a baby human Cyclops in a pickle jar, a happy-face bowling ball, lab equipment in the kitchens, and a stunning collection of Venetian masquerade masks. And we had gone through only a fourth of the rooms on the ground floor and hadn't actually peered into the darker shadows.

Plastic dummies with wax heads were everywhere, positioned for startling effect. A bikini-clad Marilyn Monroe crouching behind a sofa, Elvis admiring a soot-blackened painting over a fireplace, Willie Wonka with a martini glass that was empty save for the petrified olive stuck to the rim like a shriveled wart, a nude Churchill in a tête-à-tête with an equally nude Captain Kirk, along with unidentified plastic mannequin guests lounging in dark niches.

When we reached the formal dining hall, Tamsin and I jerked to a standstill in the doorway to stare at the mannequins seated around the long dining table. At that moment, lightning lit up the French doors, quivered, stabbing our retinas with its brilliance, blinding everyone, then abruptly quit. Thunder crashed and echoed, rain continued to slam against the panes, and the lights flickered once, twice, and then died.

"Oh, my goodness," Tamsin's disembodied exclamation was disorienting in the vaulted dark room. The lights had gone out before we could take in details of the dining room itself, but not before we had a good look at the mannequins.

Every chair at the elegantly laid long dining table was filled, all except for the one at the head, and every mannequin was dressed to the hilt in formal eveningwear from the flapper era. The top half of the unexpected tableau looked like a scene straight out of P. G. Wodehouse. The bottom half didn't quite give the same impression since the mannequins were naked from the waist down, their bare plastic cheeks having been plopped with cavalier abandon on the faded elegance of the chairs. One could only hope that Great-uncle Desmond didn't dine with them in the same state. I made a mental note not to sit on the empty chair heading the table.

"I don't think the lights are coming back on," Michael's voice floated from somewhere in the dark. He sounded like he was laughing.

"Probably not tonight," Jude agreed with him, his smile also audible. Lightning shot overhead again, accompanied by an immediate explosion of thunder, and once more the startling tableau was illuminated as if we were under missile fire.

"The storm is right over us," Tamsin observed. I felt her fingers touch my arm in a faint brush. "I don't think it's going to move on anytime soon."

"I guess it's here to stay," Jude sighed, sounding cheerfully resigned. "Nothing is letting up tonight, I'm afraid. We have a choice. We can stay, or we can make a dash back to the van and try to make it home. Personally, I'm not too sure of my van in this wind."

I thought of the two-mile stretch of drive that ran not ten uneven feet from the cliff's eroded edge and shivered. A good gust, a flash of lightning, a dash of disorienting thunder thrown in, and a slick spot of road all at the same moment and four cubes of people in a crushed van would wash up a week later in France. Michael must have pictured the same thing.

"I wish we could have brought my car," he murmured. I heard him rooting around in a drawer, and a second later I heard the scratch of a match. "We can use these," he said and began to light the candles in the three ornate silver candelabras. As each wick flamed one by one, I could see the pinpoints of light in the mannequins' glassy eyes. Jewels sparkled, cufflinks glowed, and the whole bizarre apparition wavered and warmed in the candlelight, suddenly becoming lifelike. I felt a chill flush down my spine as Michael handed me a heavily tarnished candelabra. Lightning flashed, windows rattled, and I expected the five flames that I held in my hand to flicker.

I saw Jude pull his mobile phone from his belt and punch in a number.

"Are you calling Dad?" I asked and raised my light to peer closer at the faceted crystal stemware on the table. It had the silver blue sheen of old Waterford.

"I hope the lines aren't down all through the village," he said absently and leaned against a massive sideboard that could have garaged a Fiat. "If I can't find a safe ride, we'll have to stay until the storm blows over."

"Are these real?" Tamsin gasped and pointed to a ruby-colored choker on a mannequin's throat.

"They're probably just those garnets Aunt Aurora was talking about. Or paste," I said thoughtfully and turned to Jude, who was punching another number into his mobile phone. "Basil would be able to tell us when he comes."

"Come on." Michael grinned and picked up a second candelabra lit with wavering flames, leaving the third one for Jude, who stayed behind to find someone who could answer their landline. "Follow me, and we can finish looking this place over."

The rest of the tour was about as festive as a weenie roast in a crematorium. Shadows shifted and flitted, lightning blinded and disoriented us, and thunder kept startling us with a regularity that shredded my sleep-deprived nerves. The bizarre clutter of Great-uncle Desmond's fantastic collections added an unspeakably weird twist to an already-dreamlike exploration. There's nothing quite as atmospheric as stumbling across a gritty sarcophagus in a ballroom by flickering candlelight. The mannequin of Cleopatra draped over its lid in an attitude of deep mourning didn't make it any more palatable, especially since she was scabby from age and the color of a little boy's earwax. She should have joined the shriveled pharaoh inside decades ago.

"Is this thing real?" I gasped and crouched to peer at the sarcophagus's hieroglyphs etched in its stone side.

"Very," Michael answered and touched the rough lid. "But knowing Great-uncle Desmond, only the sarcophagus is genuine, and the mummy inside is probably made of the same raddled wax as Cleo."

"There's something in it?" Tamsin asked, her brown eyes wide and shiny in the candlelight. Michael shrugged.

"We haven't opened it yet."

At his words, Jude materialized into our pool of light, coming up behind us.

"Did you find a ride to get home tonight?" Michael asked as Jude rested a light hand on the nape of my neck.

"That's what took me so long. No, I didn't. The lines are already down in most of the village. I did manage to get Patrick on his mobile, but he slurred his words, and there was too much background noise."

"The Anchor," Michael murmured. Patrick McCauley was the owner and driver of the village's only taxicab, and the Anchor was his favorite pub. "What about Dad?"

"Glynnis's mother has had a minor stroke and is being stabilized in a London hospital. Dad and Brandt are taking Glynnis there now, and they won't be back until the morning."

Glynnis Polwen is an ancient little spinster in our congregation. She's short, unendingly cheerful, and always smells of gingersnaps and milk. She's also so plump that her dress rides up her hips in tiny crepelike wrinkles when she walks, making her look like an ambling baby rhino from behind.

"So how are we going to get home? What can we do?" I asked.

"Spend the night here if we can't get Brandt at Albert's before he goes home. The storm is supposed to last all night. I could get through to Violet, but our phone is down at the house," Jude answered. I knew that he was referring to the phone in the cottage he shared with Brandt and Dante, and not the phone at the inn. "Violet is going to keep an eye out for Brandt, and she'll try to stop him before he drops Albert off and leaves. I'd already called Mom, told her not to expect Bella and Tamsin any time soon, and that we'll probably end up spending the night here."

"Spend the night here?" Tamsin repeated, dismayed. "Are any of the beds in good shape?"

"Good enough, I suppose." Jude shrugged. "If you stay dressed."

"Does the bathroom work?" I asked, having more pressing matters.

"Most of the time, according to Aunt Astrid," Michael laughed.

"Good," I said. "Where is it?"

"Upstairs on the courtyard side of the house," Jude answered. "Come on, I'll take you."

I stared at the flames of my candelabra; my tired brain kept flitting back to the wax Gandhi we had found plopped unceremoniously on the lid of Uncle Desmond's ancient Victrola. Great-uncle Desmond had filled Gandhi's palm-upward hands with dust-furred clots of sticky cough drops and a lone button that looked like it had been severed from a suit jacket.

"The upper rooms are all pretty harmless," Michael laughed, reading my mind. "Just bedroom suites with mannequins on some of the beds."

"Are you serious?"

"Queen Elizabeth is in Uncle Desmond's room, along with a stuffed squid and a chunk of the Berlin wall."

I assumed that the last two items mentioned weren't actually sharing Great-uncle Desmond's mattress. I wasn't too sure about the royal mannequin.

We trooped en masse through the maze of junk, following Jude, and up the grand staircase to the upper floor, navigating the dark hallway until we came to the lavatory. Ushered in, I shut the door behind me and held up my candelabra to look around. A second later, I wrenched the door open.

"What's this?" I demanded and gestured toward the ancient claw-footed tub.

Napoleon, dressed in scarlet Speedos and his famous admiral's hat, reclined stiffly at the bottom of the deep basin of porcelain and cast iron. The surreal tableau included diver's flippers on his feet, an empty brandy snifter, a chocolate box full of bonbons so petrified they resembled goat droppings, and an open book facedown on the mahogany surround.

"And this?" I gestured toward the thronelike toilet on a raised dais at the back of the room. Sitting bolt upright, his embroidered robe hitched to his knees, his boxers lowered to his ankles, and his hand raised in serene blessing was Confucius.

"Could somebody move him?" I leaned out into the hallway and plucked Jude from the laughing group. "It's urgent."

"We found it like that." Michael grinned. "We figured it had to be the work of Rawlings before he left. Great-uncle Desmond may not have been too keen on bathing regularly, but he would have needed the rest of the facilities free while he was alive."

Following me back in, Jude plucked the mannequin from the toilet and strode across the bathroom to plop him on the tub's mahogany surround next to Napoleon's raised hand.

"That's so grotesque." I wrinkled my nose in disgust but couldn't help laughing. "It looks like they're chatting."

"There's nowhere else to put him," Jude protested, stepping back to admire the effect. "I can't straighten his legs. If I put him on the floor, his legs will be in the air and his skirt up."

"You're right. Leave him," I agreed and then waited with crossed legs for Jude to exit the cavernous bathroom. Right before I shut the door for the second time, I heard Tamsin's succinct psychoanalysis.

"Scary genes, Isabella."

Once I finished, I had to search for the toilet's flushing mechanism. It turned out to be a gilded flaking chain with an ivory pull that I had to stand on the toilet seat to reach. When I flushed, I heard a loud clanking echoing from the plumber's grate at the base of the dais. After I washed my hands, I stepped out into the hallway and found the others discussing the sarcophagus in the ballroom.

"Why not look in it tonight?" Jude switched the candelabra to his other hand and leaned a shoulder against the wall. "The seal is already broken."

"Why would you want to do that?" Tamsin's eyes were huge. "What if there is a real mummy inside?"

"If there is, we won't touch it," Michael laughed. "But I think we ought to at least look to see what's in there. Jude's right. I noticed it earlier today. The seal has already been broken, and the sarcophagus has already been tampered with. It looks like someone had already opened it."

"Are you thinking that the treasure might be in the sarcophagus?" I asked as thunder crashed outside, sounding like the echo of a distant cannon. The light from the thirteen candles wrapped us in a cozy golden glow. Suddenly, I didn't care that we were stranded by the storm, that all we had were candles, and that we were utterly cut off from rescue. I was having fun. Tamsin caught something of what I was feeling, and she gave me a small tentative grin.

"It could be," Michael said lightly and shrugged. "I'll have to admit that it was the first thing to occur to me when I saw it."

"Won't you need pulleys and things to get the lid off?" Tamsin asked practically. Jude shook his head.

"Michael and I can manage it easily enough. It's only the secondary lid, not the heavier outside slab. All we will need to do is just shift it to see inside."

It took us nearly five minutes to creep through the ballroom's maze to the sarcophagus. Only Basil Brett would know what was valuable enough to scavenge and what was to be discarded. The room was crowded with suits of armor, a Venetian gondola, more statues and mannequins, more everything. The sarcophagus was in the center like a hidden prize.

While Jude removed Cleopatra from the stone coffin, I tried to look at what I could see of the ballroom itself. Instead of the medieval barrenness of the Great Hall, the ballroom had been painstakingly finished. It was beautiful, but was as filthy as the rest of the manor. There were web-shrouded chandeliers above us, a marbled floor of cream and blue harlequin diamonds, and pale walls covered in French molding. Searching the high walls around us, I barely made out the plastered fretwork of the minstrel's gallery. I was to find out later that the gallery also looked out onto the dining hall nearby.

I tried to imagine the strains of music floating down and the opulently dressed dancers swirling by. My fantasy was abruptly shattered by a crash of thunder and a pulsating, quivering fork of lightning so brilliant the inside of my wince turned bloodred.

"Ready?" I heard Jude's voice. I opened my eyes.

He and Michael faced each other over the covering slab of the coffin, all three candelabras resting on the top of a nearby upended trunk. Shadows flickered and danced, my brothers' muscles tensed and bulged, and the slab began to move, inch by careful grating inch. It sounded exactly like what it was, a door to antiquity opening and widening. I felt an anticipatory chill rush up my spine, and I saw Tamsin raise her fingers to her mouth. Dropping his hands from the shifted slab, Jude leaned over, lifted one of the candelabras, and held it over the black opening. He and Michael peered inside and stared.

"What's in there?" I asked and tentatively crept forward when they didn't move. Tamsin's scrabbling fingers found my hand, and we inched closer. I could feel her heart hammering in her fingertips. We peered in.

A withered, unwrapped, decaying twig of humanity peered up at us through eyeless sockets that caved inward. The nose was gone. The lips were gone. Patches of skull showed through the human jerky. Hands with fingernails like flattened raisins modestly covered the body's pelvis, and gold coins rested on the shriveled nipples.

Jude pried a coin from the pharaoh's chest and curiously held it up. My stomach lurched. Tamsin made a low moan like the mating call of a dove and fell over backward, taking me with her. We crashed onto a stack of books, and for one horrified second, I thought that I was going to lose my dinner on Tamsin's baby blue tee shirt.

"This whole thing is wax!" Michael said incredulously and then turned at the crash we made, falling on the pile of tomes. "Are you all right?"

"What happened?" Jude's anxious voice floated through my nausea. I felt Tamsin stir under me. Lights were brought closer, and hands helped us sit up. Michael's exclamation finally penetrated my disorientation, and I started laughing. It took Tamsin a second longer to understand what was so funny. Laughing, we hauled ourselves to our feet with our arms wrapped around each other. Michael and Jude stared at us in concern when tears began streaming down my cheeks.

"You're tired," Jude said kindly, which sent us off into another fresh peal of giggles. Tamsin began to snort.

"Did you see the note?" Michael interrupted our convulsive hilarity and held up a slip of yellowed paper.

"In the sarcophagus?" Jude raised the candelabra in his hand and read the writing sprawling across the parchment. "You've got to be kidding."

"What?" I asked, finally letting go of Tamsin to swipe the back of my hand across my cheeks. "Let me see."

Michael obediently lowered the paper to my gaze, and I read out loud what was undoubtedly another missive from Great-uncle Desmond. The disjointed note looked as if someone had freed a spider from a bottle of ink and had shooed it across an old sheet of paper.

"Roses are red, violets are blue. Men aren't the dead. This is a clue."

Tamsin and I went off again on another peal of laughter.

"So does anybody know what 'men aren't the dead' means?" Michael's mouth twitched into an involuntary grin, and another of the many streaks of lightning flickered brightly, temporarily blinding us.

"I can't figure out what the focus of that idiotic statement is." Jude took the paper from him and stared at it. "I guess he had to find something to rhyme with 'red.'"

"Is he trying to tell us that it's women who are dead, or is he trying to tell us that the men are alive?" Michael picked up his candelabra and bent low to look at the underside of the note Jude continued to stare at. "Is this clue like the first one? Is there something on the back?"

Jude flipped the note over and raised his eyebrows. "It says to try again."

"When is Brandt due to get back tonight?" Michael asked, looking at his watch.

Jude shrugged and pocketed the crackly bit of parchment.

"I told Violet not to stay up to intercept him. If they come in too late, we'll have to wait until morning when Dad and Dante get back from London. They'll call when they get in."

Michael and Jude looked at each other a moment, each reading the other's expression. Michael sighed.

"Why don't we put Bella and Tamsin in the nursery?" he suggested. "It looks the cleanest."

"Bed already?" I leaned past them and grabbed the remaining candelabra from the trunk. "We haven't seen the rest of the house. We haven't even made it up the stairs except to go to the bathroom."

"It's late. We have a lot to do tomorrow before the meeting," Jude said, referring to the Tuesday-night Bible study.

"At least check to make sure that the piece of paper in your pocket was the whole clue," I protested and pointed at the open sarcophagus. "Look thoroughly. Please? I'm not touching that thing inside."

They faced me with identical expressions of amused indecision. I waited for a couple of beats and tried to look hopeful and worthy. I felt like Beatrix Plimpton's Pomeranian when she holds up a livery chunk of her homemade doggie cookies.

"Might as well," Michael sighed good-naturedly. And they put their candelabras back down on the upended trunk. They were in the middle of hoisting the stone slab to the floor when Jude's mobile rang.

"Get it," he grunted and braced himself under the weight of the shifting lid, taking most of the burden until Michael could reposition himself at its end. I leaned forward and hurriedly unclipped the phone from his belt. I flipped it open and answered it, assuming that it was Brandt as I watched my brothers wedge something under the slab before setting it on the floor. Rayvyn's breathless voice broke through the atmospheric static in my ear, surprising me, "Listen, Isabella, is Michael there?"

It took me a minute to identify the background noise as chewing. I pictured the self-proclaimed "Child of the Cosmos" vegan eating one of those lardy snack cakes she was fond of and playing with her long braid. Unbraided, her hair reaches to the tops of her thighs. A true redhead, she dyes her hair coal black to match her chosen name. Grooming, however, is not her strong point, and I had never seen her with anything less than three inches of red roots showing above the black. It always looks like her part is bleeding.

A valiant survivor of breast cancer, she scorns undergarment support, white bread, deodorant, and petrochemicals as tools of the devil designed to bring brain damage the human race. She has only one gravitationally challenged breast left, and it swings freely under her muumuu like a tetherball that has been whacked into orbit. It's very disconcerting, especially when she tucks it under her armpit so she can scrub the toilet bowls with vigor.

"Yes, why? Do you need to talk with him?" I asked, watching as Jude hoisted the wax mummy from its bed. He propped it against the trunk with the candelabras and began to root with Michael through the leavings in the sarcophagus. The mummy's remaining nipple coin came unstuck and rolled across the floor to Tamsin's foot. She gave it a horrified kick, and it pinged madly across the gloomy ballroom. I started laughing.

"I'm being serious, Isabella," Rayvyn said reproachfully in my ear. "I need to ask you something, and I'm glad I got you and not Jude. He might tell Michael and spoil the surprise."

"Ask away."

"What is Michael's favorite color? I despair of ever synchronizing him with nature." The buzz and crackle of the static played itself out on the phone, reminding me of the sound stiff cellophane makes when you unwrap old candy.

"What?" I said after a moment.

"Isabella, try to think." Rayvyn's voice was impatient. "It's lightning outside. Do you know how dangerous that is? If I'm on the phone longer than two minutes, all my vortexes begin to run in a counterclockwise direction. Listen carefully. I need to know because I have a friend who makes personalized health aids . . . you know, like art. And I thought I'd get something for Michael as a gift. I thought he would also appreciate one of those bottles of mint-flavored chlorophyll to use with it."

Art? Health? What on earth was she buying him?

"Mint chlorophyll?" I echoed stupidly and watched the waxen head of the mummy begin to soften from the heat of the nearby candelabras. A shiny patch on its cheek began to blossom like leprosy, and a drip formed into a tear.

"Some people put it in their herbal teas as well." I could hear her long-suffering sigh through all the chewing and static. "It comes with instructions so you don't need a friend to help you. There's even a cute little illustrated guide. You still haven't told me his favorite color."

I thoughtfully looked at Michael, examining a wad of brown mummy wrapping in his hand. "Fuchsia," I said, not having the faintest idea. "I have one favor I want to ask in return."

"Name it."

"I want to be there when you give it to him."

I hung up before her vortexes could reverse direction and handed the phone back to Jude, who clipped it back to his belt.

"Who was it?" Michael asked and leaned into the sarcophagus to run a hand around the inside corners.

"Rayvyn."

"What did she want?" he asked absently and dusted his hands across the thighs of his jeans.

"You'll find out later." I grinned evilly, but Michael wasn't looking. Jude saw my expression and raised an eyebrow.

"Look at this," Tamsin interjected abruptly. I turned to see her crouched behind the melting mummy with one of the candelabras in her hand. "There's something etched on pharaoh's bottom."

"Another clue?" I asked excitedly and crouched next to her. Jude leaned the mummy away from the trunk and peered at the shiny patch Tamsin was pointing at.

"Madame Tussaud's," he read, amused, and hoisted the pitiful object to replace it in its nest. "There's nothing here. Come on, it's time we all went to bed."

Ignoring my half-hearted protests, Jude and Michael escorted us up another staircase and through the attic maze to leave us in the nursery suite with one of the candelabras, tired wishes for us to have a good night, and advice to keep our clothes on when we climbed between the sheets. The advice was well stated since it was obvious to us that the sheets hadn't been changed since my grandmother and great-aunts had slept in the nursery as the last children of the house.

Once Michael and Jude were gone, I walked over to one of the three beds and looked down on the nearly smooth counterpane. A childish handprint still marred its surface. Surprised, I put my own spread hand over it.

"Too bad the wind is blowing the rain so violently," Tamsin said over the lash of the storm behind the drawn curtains. "It would be nice to open the windows and let in a little fresh air."

I put the candelabra on the night table next to a music box and a glass-shaded lamp. There were no mannequins, no stuffed wildlife, and no traces of Great-uncle Desmond even though he must have spent his time in the nursery as a child.

"You want to sleep in this bed?" I asked, nodding at the bed I was standing beside. She smiled. Without much hesitation or ritual, we tiredly slipped off our shoes, blew out the burning candles, and burrowed under the clammy covers toward the center of the lumpy mattress. It was a bit like nestling together in a sack of gravel. We wrapped up snugly, turned our backs to each other, and listened to the raging storm. It seemed to have gotten snagged on the cliffs and was dropping all it had to break free.

After a moment, I felt Tamsin stir and roll over to face the ceiling. "Are you asleep?" she whispered quietly. I barely heard her over the drum of the rain. I rolled over and tucked my hands behind my head.

"No."

"Your mom told me that your grandparents will be here in a few days to see your great-aunts. What is your grandmother like? I've never met her."

I stared up at the blackness and thought about how best to describe her.

I knew from old photographs that she used to be small, delicate, and beautiful; but years of living with my grandfather had brought out her steel. She was still small, but wiry instead of delicate, her face careworn and stretched over beautiful bones. Her hair was long and white; and her eyes were brilliant, defiant, and the color of polished green glass. She always wore faded colorful dresses, sturdy leather working shoes, and a long thick braid like a silver rope down her back.

She seemed to be serenely oblivious to my grandfather's frequent tirades, but she had a phobia about flying in an airplane. Traveling by boat wasn't any better, which was unfortunate since my grandparents lived on the Aran Islands off the coast of Ireland. If she needed to go somewhere far away, flying was not an option. She would rather walk on cobras than fly or sail, which is why she never visited her sisters in Peru even though my father had offered more than once to pay for a trip.

I told Tamsin.

"My grandmother hasn't seen Aunt Astrid and Aunt Aurora since she got married and moved to Ireland. They've kept in touch, but her sisters haven't been back to England since they left, and England is as far as Grandmother's phobia lets her go."

I could see Tamsin blink at me in the darkness, the whites of her eyes glinting as she tried to make out my expression. "So what is your grandfather like?"

He was even harder to describe than my grandmother was. I sighed at the ceiling and gathered my thoughts.

He was once as large and as lean as my father, but age had restructured his powerful body into whipcord muscles over long knotty bones. His wild black hair had turned silver, and he wore it long because he never had the patience to groom it. His outrageous hair was always gathered out of his way at the nape of his sinewy neck with a scrap of something he could tie.

Dealing with him was a bit like standing on an iceberg next to a roaring, blasting furnace. You would shove in a bit of yourself by way of conversation, and you would get either burned or frozen. It was always easier for me to take him with a lot of air between us. All our cousins call my grandparents by the more affectionate and intimate terms of *daideo* and *mamó*, Gaelic for "granddad" and "grandma." I call them Grandfather and Grandmother. "Grandmother" because we speak English when we converse, and she's English. "Grandfather" because he unnerves me too much to attempt coziness.

When I was three months old, my family went to visit them on the Aran Islands. My grandfather wasn't particularly interested in meeting me, the latest in a straggly line of grandchildren. Enraged by his attitude, my grandmother took me, forced me on him much to my mother's horror, and snapped a quick picture. Somewhere in an album is a snapshot of my grandfather holding me out in front of his face with an expression of bafflement as if he was trying to figure out what he had just put his hand in.

"He used to drink," I sighed. "He was the kind of drinker that got thrown out of pubs. But he stopped a few years ago."

"Is he still studying?" Tamsin asked, referring to my religion-hating grandfather abruptly agreeing to study the Bible, an event that seemed to disorient the rest of us, rather in the way of pigs flying, and I sighed again. "Didn't he just start a couple of months ago?"

"Yes, he's still studying, but he won't talk about it. No one knows what he thinks yet."

The rain continued to lash outside, and my eyelids began to feel heavy. I yawned and thought about what I was going to do in the morning.

"Are you going to stay around tomorrow, or are you planning on doing something else?" I asked after a moment. She shifted to tuck her hands behind her head.

"I'm staying and helping, if that's all right, but in the afternoon, I have to go in to work."

Tamsin worked part-time at the village's lending library. She did everything that the aged librarian couldn't do on her own such as reading fine print, bending low to shelve books, swabbing out the rusty loo, or killing the insects that perpetually shot out of the floor vents. She was paid well and spent much of her time at work with nothing to do but read and brew endless cups of tea. She enjoyed everything about her job except for the delegated chore of waking the older patrons at closing time, having been attacked once with a cane when she woke Colonel Arbuthnot during one of his frequent World War II dreams. For a few prewaking sputtering moments, he was back in a *bierstubbe* in Berlin being "put through an experience" by a German barmaid with thighs the size of logs.

I yawned again and rolled over to look at the curtained windows, feeling Tamsin's warmth at my back. An occasional flicker lit up the slit between the heavy velvet panels.

"Oh, bother," I heard Tamsin murmur a moment later. A fitful gust of wind shook the windows. I turned to look at her. "Oh, bother, bother, bother," she repeated and struggled to a sitting position in the clammy feather bed, sighing loudly as she swung her legs free of the covers.

"What is it?" I asked even though I knew the answer.

"Can you light the candelabra for me? I've got to go."

"No."

"Why 'no'?"

"I don't have any matches."

The sound of rain suddenly intensified as a fresh fury hit the house, and I saw the whites of her eyeballs glow like hard-boiled eggs in the gloom.

"Can't you use a chamber pot or something?" I asked a second later. "This room hasn't been touched in over fifty years. There's bound to be one under the bed." She continued to stare at me. I could read her thoughts as easily as if she had spoken them out loud. "Quite," I said after a rain drummed moment. "I wouldn't either."

"Isabella, I'm not using anything that's housed spiders for the last fifty years."

"So what do you want to do?" I blinked at her, trying to make out her expression in the muffling darkness. "Hope the lighting has passed and hang yourself out of the window?"

"Help me find something, will you?" she asked and slipped from the high bed to the floor. "Preferably something considerably larger than one of those test tubes from the kitchen."

"What?" I struggled to a sitting position and surveyed the dark room around us with eyes as good as blind. "You've got to be kidding."

I could see her moving across the floor in a shuffling squat, her arms stretched out in front like minesweepers.

"Tamsin." I frowned at her. "What are you doing?"

Her sudden giggle pierced the sound of the rain around us.

"I wonder what your aunt Astrid would do."

"Would you get up?" I said and swung my legs free of the ancient blankets so I could stand on the clammy floor. "Look, let's see if we can find the bathroom."

It was going to take the homing instinct of a spawning salmon and plenty of blind groping to locate the toilet in the vast cluttered manor. Uncle Desmond's décor had been frightful enough by candlelight. I didn't want to feel any of it in the dark.

I knew better than to suggest going to the foot of the attic stairs and shouting for a more knowledgeable and a more fearless escort for two reasons. I wasn't at all optimistic about our chances of being heard over the rain and the battlement-thick walls. Besides, I had no idea where anyone else was sleeping. And, secondly, Tamsin was raised by gracious Welsh parents in a tiny prudish Welsh village. She would rather relieve herself discreetly in the sarcophagus and repent later than to ask any of my brothers to escort her to the nearest plumbing.

Tamsin stood up and groped for my hand as I shuffled hesitantly toward her.

"I hope you remember your way better than I do." She giggled nervously as we began shuffling in the general direction of the door.

Tamsin always giggles when she's nervous. She had laughed hysterically through her older sister's wedding. It was also impossible for me to be her assistant in a "talk," or demonstration, at one of the meetings. The last time we tried, she burst out laughing while we were on the stage together. It was a little incongruous since I was playing the role of a New Age Traveler protesting the destruction of our planet. When I got to the part about homeless Amazonian Capavari Indians, she had to leave to stem a nosebleed that resulted from holding her breath too long and too ferociously. We could hear her laughing hysterically from the bathroom while I stayed in place, wondering if I should get off the stage and follow her.

We found the stairs to the lower floor without too much mishap, but safely descending the uneven treads was another matter. In the end we sat down and thumped our way to the lower story one hard tread at a time. At any rate, it was better than free falling. By the time we reached the last step, I could feel twinges in the depths of my own bladder. The incessant sound of rain certainly wasn't helping, either.

We got to the bottom landing and stood up, still holding hands. I set off to the right, dragging my free hand on the age-warped wall beside us, using my fingertips as a tactile guide. I don't know what I would have done if my groping fingers brushed up against the stuffed wildebeest haunting the hallways in the dark. I knew one thing. If I did, the resulting scream would be loud enough to resurrect the wax mummy in the sarcophagus, let alone my brothers, wherever they were. I laughed nervously at my thoughts, and Tamsin giggled back.

"What?" she asked and was nearly drowned out by an enormous clap of thunder.

"I keep thinking about that sarcophagus in the ballroom," I answered her question, groping inch by inch along the wall.

"About the note?"

I didn't answer, pausing when my fingers found a crack in the paneling. I cautiously traced the outline of what seemed to be a slightly recessed doorjamb.

"What do you think the clue means?" Tamsin murmured. I could feel her listening presence behind me as I groped unsuccessfully for a door latch. I knew it wasn't the bathroom, but after all the tension, thunder, and Tamsin's nervous starts, I was hoping for at least a basin or a bucket in a forgotten linen closet. I would have even welcomed the scorned test tube.

"I have no idea what any of the clues mean," I admitted and ran the flat of my palm along the wood, giving it a shove, hoping that the door was not locked.

"What are you doing?" she hissed.

"I'm trying to figure out if—" I broke off, choked by surprise when three things happened at once.

A wild arc of lightning finally hit the house, skimming the slate roof in a series of ricocheting cracks, Tamsin and I let loose full-throated bloodcurdling screams so pure and piercing our teeth rang like tuning forks, and the wall gave way into nothingness, pitching me headlong into it. I jerked Tamsin behind me, failing to let go of her hand as I fell. I landed on my face, Tamsin landed on me, and the wall simply shut back up. Shocked and stunned, I was barely aware of her scrambling off my inert body.

"Isabella, what happened?" She began to pluck at me frantically. "Are you all right? Isabella?"

I groaned, peeled my face off the gritty floor, and managed to prop the upper half of my body on my elbows. I wriggled experimentally and felt my face with a shaking hand.

"I think so," I gasped, touching my nose to make sure it hadn't been shoved up somewhere behind my eyeballs. "What about you?"

"I'm fine. What happened?" The edge of adrenaline was still rattling her voice. "Where are we?"

"I'm not sure." I cautiously raised myself to an awkward squat and sat on my heels. "Let's not move around much. For all I know, we are somewhere unsafe."

"Unsafe?" Tamsin echoed me. I heard her abrupt cessation of movement. For the next few seconds, the only sounds were our ragged breathing and the faintest far-off hum of the storm. "You mean," she said quietly after the relative silence stretched around us, "this isn't a room?"

"I don't know," I answered frankly. "That really wasn't a door we just popped through." I remembered with the clearer interpretation of hindsight that what I had mistakenly thought was a barely recessed doorjamb to a work closet or a servants' passage was actually an irregularity in the paneling. We hadn't stumbled through a servant's door. There hadn't been a latch. I frowned in the total blackness and then dropped from my squat to land on my knees, barely noting the bone-jarring impact as my bones connected with stone.

"Tamsin." I tried to sense her nearness in the dark. "The treasure, Tamsin. We have just stumbled into a secret room." I raised my voice excitedly. "We are in a secret room!" I repeated and groped toward the sound of her breathing, brushing against some kind of hard object that tumbled over and rolled away. I found her jeans and then her hand. She pulled me carefully to my feet.

"I think," she said faintly, attempting to bring me down to earth with her next words, "that I need to find the bathroom in the next thirty seconds, treasure or no treasure."

"Oh, great." I let go of her hand, dropped back to my knees, and began cautiously sweeping the floor in front of me with spread fingers. "Start looking."

"For what?" she hissed back.

"For anything you can aim into." I heard the rustle of her body as she dropped to her knees to comply. "Just be careful," I admonished and then froze as my fingers brushed the cold curve of a stone object. It teetered into my palm. It was heavy and had a loosely fitted lid. I picked it up, and the lid fell off, rolling away like a giant coin. I heard it settle in some dank corner away from me. "Wait a minute. I found something you can use." I caressed it cautiously, trying to gauge what it was. I heard the zip of her jeans. "Wait a moment. It has something in it. Let me dump it somewhere first."

I inched along, feeling the floor once again, and discovered something oblong and soft. It felt like a soft sack to my hurried fingers. I dumped the container's contents into it, put it down, and then inched backward to put the stone bowl into Tamsin's fumbling hands.

"Thanks," Tamsin's murmur echoed in the blackness. I sat back to give her room to maneuver and felt a feather-light brush of something trail across the back of my hand. Then I heard a squeak and a stealthy rustle a few feet away.

"Tamsin," I said after a moment, goose bumps rising up all over my body. I hugged myself, and the skin on my arms felt like the skin of a plucked chicken. "Tamsin, was that you?"

"Was that me what?" she asked breathlessly. A second later I heard the sound of water filling a container.

"Did you just touch me?" I asked and willed myself to hold still.

"No. Why?"

"Are you sure?"

"Yes. What is it?"

My mind suddenly conjured up unbidden images of rats. Feral rats the size of dingoes. Rats scurrying across the floor in the blackness. Rats with hairless, pink, scaly tails like trailing whips. I felt my whole body contract, my bladder distend, and a scream rise up to my neck. Clap. I read somewhere that clapping low to the ground chases them away. Or was that snakes? Did it make any difference? I started clapping with a runaway urgency that made a sound like machine-gun fire bouncing off the walls around us.

"What?" I heard Tamsin's startled shriek, the violent clink of stone on stone, and the heavy thud of someone falling down.

And lights. Wonderful, blessed, amazing lights, all going on and off like strobes at a nightclub.

"A Clapper?" Tamsin said a breathless moment later, her eyes screwed shut against the sudden flickering brilliance, her jeans half-mast, her body prone on the stones, and the stone jar cradled to her bosom like a dying child. I halted as her one-word explanation filtered through my panicked disorientation. At my last clap, the lights went out.

"Your great-uncle Desmond installed a Clapper?" Her disbelieving voice echoed in the darkness. Abrupt silence settled as the last echo died. I thought of the generator in the cellars that didn't seem to be attached to most of the fuses, and then I thought about Uncle Desmond's obvious love of gimmickry. The Clapper, an American-born contraption that allowed one to turn lights on and off without touching the switch.

"Isabella," she said a moment later. "Could you clap one more time? My hands are a bit full."

Dazed, I complied, and the room sprang into eye-watering brightness. Shading my eyes, I gazed around me as Tamsin put the vase down and adjusted her clothes.

My mouth fell open as if my jaws were unhinged.

# 4

Directly in front of me was a hallway receding into gloom. A hallway filled with a long line of mannequins dressed in women's underwear. A chorus line of coyly posed, partially clad plastic bodies. Faded satin chemises, lacy camisoles, yellowed petticoats, garters, feathers, straps, whale-boned corsets, jewel-hued garments running like watercolors in the tunnel's mildew and damp. Female instruments of torture, ancient and rusted, shut like forgotten mantraps, half-gnawed away by the resident rodent population.

Boxes and crates stacked around and in between the mannequins spilled silks, brocades, robes, dresses, stockings, gloves, shoes, and mangy furs that had been nearly picked clean to line rats' nests. Plastic heads were skewered on to the disused wall sconces with every conceivable size and shape of wig adorning their baldpates. One fantastic headpiece of hair looked like a miniature ship made out of unwashed lamb's wool. One wig was braided, teased, and knotted into an elaborate birdcage complete with a tiny wooden canary on a perch.

I looked down by my knees at the object I had emptied the vase in.

A shoe. A blue suede shoe. Filled with ashes. An unmistakable bone splinter gleamed dustily in the naked overhead lights. Numb, I lifted the suede shoe over my head, careful not to spill the ashes into my face, and read the brass plaque that had been hammered into the hard heel.

"What?" Tamsin asked, her question a very faint monosyllable.

"Elvis. December 1967."

Wordlessly Tamsin held out what I now knew to be a funeral urn. She had filled it half-full, and as I took it from her, I noted the tarnished plaque on one side of the square base. Not bothering to read the name of the person I had emptied into Elvis's old shoe, I set it down on the stone floor, unzipped my jeans, and carefully perched myself on its cold edge.

Tamsin's belated giggles filled the room. While I carefully concentrated on the task at hand, Tamsin's eyes roved incredulously about the hallway and its portal.

"This stuff looks really, really old. Why am I not surprised that your great-uncle collected women's underwear?"

Finished, I looked up from fastening my jeans and noticed that a nearby box of feathered headpieces had a swirled hole gnawed into the center of its lid. The rim of the hole had the packed look of a nest, and I wondered if little rodent babies were curled up inside like squirming little wads of pink bubble gum.

"Do you think any of this is valuable?" Tamsin asked as I carefully set the urn behind me so it wouldn't get kicked over.

"Not anymore." I looked around at the open crates and boxes. "Unfortunately, I took care of Elvis's shoe myself."

"By the way," Tamsin began, her voice casual and faintly curious, "who was in the urn?" Ignoring my snort of laughter, she stooped and carefully hoisted the brimming container to squint at its etched base. "Clarisse De Mornay," she intoned, slowly sounding out the name as she deciphered the tarnished engraving. "Born 1756, died 1792."

"Seventeen ninety-two," I repeated, impressed with its age. Clarisse had certainly been around a lot longer than Elvis's shoe had. "Over two hundred years ago. She died young. I wonder who she was." I looked at her frowning profile. "Tamsin?"

"The terrier." Her voice was thoughtful. I stared at her for a moment and then shifted to peer at the base, careful not to jog her elbow. She indicated the last two words of the engraving. "Or, maybe it says 'terror.' Whoever engraved this did an appalling job."

"Why would Great-uncle Desmond have the cremated remains of someone's terrier?" I squinted. "Where's that engraved?"

"Right there. Maybe it's an epitaph?" Carefully putting the alabaster urn on the floor, she straightened, turned to the blank expanse of wall, and nodded at the portal we had just burst through. "So how do we get back out?"

"That's a good question. I don't even know how we got in here in the first place." I looked at the wall we had somehow tumbled through. There wasn't a latch, a knob, an indentation, a protrusion, not anything. I ran a hand over the tightly fitted planks. It was as smooth as the proverbial baby's bottom. And just as sticky. It needed a good scrape and polish as much as the rest of the house.

Tamsin startled me by abruptly rearing back, running, and flinging herself at the would-be door, hitting it with her shoulder and hip in a full-body slam. It sounded like someone dropping a watermelon from a balcony, and the impact shot her backward with so much force she stumbled past me and into the first mannequin before I could do anything. They went down, and the mannequin's plastic Barbie head popped off like a champagne cork, hit a crate, and then lolled around slowly until it was looking at us. Tamsin, still recumbent on the decapitated mannequin, stared at the head. Both of them looked a little stunned.

"Are you all right?" I gasped and darted over to my friend. She groaned and shifted to rub her shoulder.

"My hip's fine, but remind me next time to use something a little less brittle and bony than my shoulder."

"Did you break it?"

"No." She gave a weak giggle as she struggled to disengage herself from Barbie's embrace. I helped her up and then frowned, doing a doubletake at the mannequin. An old pot holder was peeking out of the chemisette's satin cup. Barbie was a Ken. Ken in a French lace chemise stuffed with souvenir pot holders. I could read "Present from Brighton" from where I stood. I looked back at the stubborn wall.

"I don't think we're going to get out this way. Not unless we can find the secret."

"We can't wait here to be discovered," Tamsin sighed, struggled to her feet, and surveyed me with her long arms crossed over her abdomen. She looked disapproving of the whole secret passage concept. "It will take forever."

"I know." I spun around and peered past the receding line of mannequins. "Maybe it will lead us to an exit. Let's keep going and see where it takes us."

We set off with trepidation. As exciting as it was to find a secret passageway in a five-hundred-year-old manor house, it was a bit of an ordeal to pick our way past Great-uncle Desmond's unsettling treasures. Especially when I was proved right in my earlier guess, and a rat's nose poked out of the hole in the box of feathers like a quivering whiskered finger. Little red eyes like phosphorescent beads glared out at us, and a menacing squeak echoed from beside our feet. Tamsin shrieked and took off, running blindly down the passageway, dodging giant Barbies like she was on a slalom. Gurgling incoherently, I darted off after her. Together we managed to demolish a good part of the orderly march of mannequins, leaving strewn bodies in our wake like so many fallen soldiers on a battlefield. We didn't stop and gather our wits until we hit the edge of more gloom.

Pausing and panting, Tamsin gave a tentative clap, and another set of lights sprang on ahead of us. The sudden illumination was fortunate because we were panting at the threshold of a sharp turn. If we weren't more scared of the dark than of rabid rats, we wouldn't have stopped to clap. We would have continued to run straight-ahead and hit the stones in front of us.

We forced ourselves to continue on at a more decorous pace.

"There's a starving ginger tomcat hanging around the boardinghouse," Tamsin panted as we circumvented a stack of empty crates. I wondered briefly if Great-uncle Desmond would hide treasure in the middle of a storage room of junk. I brought my mind back to what Tamsin was saying. "Maybe we ought to bring him here and see what he can do to control the rats. And the mice. I'll bet he's an excellent mouser."

"Good idea," I panted. The passageway climbed and descended short stairs, rounded right-angle turns, straightened back, and in general meandered crazily like a maze designed to throw off pursuers, which, for all I knew, could have been its original purpose. Five hundred years ago when the manor house had been first built, Saxons were still sporting ebullient skin diseases and eating their meat raw. For a wealthy person, hidden passageways with hard-to-detect random niches was probably the medieval equivalent of a good insurance plan. And there were Uncle Desmond's Clappers at every turn, ready to lighten our way when the gloom threatened.

We had gone perhaps fifty yards when the passageway abruptly ended in a blank wall of paneling. We stopped and stared at it in despair. Tamsin blanched and reminiscently rubbed her sore shoulder. I put a hand on her arm.

"My turn," I said and tried to figure out if we were facing another one-way entry or the passage's exit.

I wasn't about to trust my brute strength and bounce off the dead end like a demented tiddly wink, so I leaned forward and gave the wall a tentative push. Nothing. Tamsin stepped back and gave me more room. Taking a deep breath, I lunged forward, putting as much power as I dared behind the shove, and smacked both forearms against the panel. Taken utterly by surprise, the wall caved as if it had never been there, and I pitched headfirst into nothingness. The panel swung shut as soon as I cleared the threshold, and I suddenly found myself in a disorienting wad of bent legs and arms with my backside in the air and my right knee pressed to my ear like a phone receiver. The second wall I had crashed into abruptly sprang open behind my back, and I tumbled out onto a stone floor, finishing the somersault to the accompaniment of thunder and lightning. Finally freed from the secret passageway, I found myself plopped into a room of the house, my assaulted tailbone shoved up somewhere exotic and inappropriate to humans.

I didn't think that any of what happened this evening was what my father had in mind when he gave me permission to explore Tanglewood Manor.

I had just stood up, barely clearing the space I had been in, when Tamsin burst in on the scene much like I had. She tumbled onto the floor by my feet and caught herself on my legs.

"Look!" I pointed to the familiar outlines of blackness against the storm-lit gloom. The admiral's hat poking out over the edge of the massive tub was just as hard to miss as the philosopher's raised hand. Confucius looked like he was waving at us, blessing our crash landing into the bathroom. "If I had known where the tunnel was leading, we could have been spared the urn."

I looked at our portal back into the manor's dimension. We had tumbled out of the bathroom armoire. Well over ten feet tall, the armoire looked far more appropriate for a bedroom than for a bathroom, which is probably what the room had been before the advent of indoor plumbing. Lightning flickered fitfully and illuminated the crusty gray bathrobe hanging from a peg on the inside of its open door.

"Regency?" Tamsin guessed my thoughts as she eyed the simple scrolls carved on the armoire's edge.

"Maybe. If it is, then it would had to have been added over two hundred years after the tunnel itself," I said and climbed back into its stygian depths to feel along its back wall. I began to run my hands over the panels. I decided I'd better touch the rough wood lightly, wondering what the shelf life of bubonic plague was and if I was likely to contract it by a splinter.

"What are you doing?"

"I'm looking for some kind of a latch. I'm not even sure where the door is." I lightened my touch and swept my fingers in an arc, spanning the inside wall from edge to edge. On the third pass, my fingertips brushed over a finely etched irregularity on level with my waist and close to the left side of the armoire. Frowning in the dark in a vain attempt to see, I squatted and traced my fingers over and over the scratches, trying to decipher what I felt.

"What is it?" Tamsin's voice was breathless in my ear as she leaned in behind me. I reached back, found her arm, and brought her hand forward to touch her fingertips to the etched lines. I could see her pale hand moving gently in the blackness.

"A word?" she hazarded. "It feels like three squiggles that aren't connected. Letters?"

"It feels like a 3, a zero, and an *A* to me," I said, stood up, and slipped past her, jumping back down onto the bathroom floor.

"Thirty, *A*?" Tamsin murmured. "Or 3, *O*, *A*? The builder's mark, do you think?" Lightning flashed a split second before thunder boomed and rolled down the cliffs. She pushed halfheartedly on the back of the armoire, and it pivoted open, surprising both of us.

"What are you doing?" I asked when she grinned and stepped back inside the exposed passage we had just traversed.

"I'll be out in a minute. I'm going to go back and turn off the lights."

"What about the rats?" I asked, and she paused, her hands still in place against the wood. "Do you want me to go with you?"

"So we can both get rabies? No. Don't worry, I'm not getting that close to them." She grinned and was gone, leaving me in the dark to wait for her. Restless and not wanting to even think about the groping wandering trip back to the nursery, I went to the window and looked out into the rain. The tempest outside showed no signs of letting up. The drops hit the warped panes with enough force it sounded like flung pebbles. It was a bit like being in the middle of one huge automated car wash. Waves of water lashed, drops sprayed, and any moment I half-expected to see a giant brush loom up out of the darkness and start scrubbing the house down. I sighed. It would be nice and convenient if only one would. Lightning forked above the windows, spread, and I heard the crack of electricity hitting the water.

Moving away from the window, I rubbed the burns from my eyes and wandered over to the bathroom's door, pushing it open. I was about to step out to get my bearings when Jude's anxious voice arrested me.

"I can't find them anywhere. Are you sure they aren't upstairs in the nursery?"

"I'm sure." Michael sounded as anxious as Jude, and I stepped out to peer at their faint, candlelit figures at the far end of the hallway. Apparently, bloodcurdling shrieks do carry beyond battlement-thick walls.

"We're fine!" I called out. They started convulsively at the unexpected shout, turning to stare blindly into the deep gloom of the enclosed hallway.

"Where are you?" Jude raised his candelabra. "Are you at the bathroom?"

"So what happened?" Michael asked, sounding worried. They strode down the hallway toward me. "Are you and Tamsin all right?"

As they stepped into the bathroom, wild streaks of lightning arced past the windowpanes behind them and imprinted my retinas with a scene straight from a horror film. Looming over me were two silhouettes brandishing menacing candelabras.

"Watch this." I said, hearing the scrabble of Tamsin forcing her way back into the armoire. As if on cue, she pushed open the armoire doors, looked startled to see my brothers, and froze, holding the passage door open behind her with her arm. I clapped, and the lights that she had just turned off behind her sprang back into life.

"The insane old sot," Michael murmured disbelievingly. Jude gave a low laugh of surprise as he stepped forward and leaned into the armoire. He peered into the exposed passageway as Tamsin stepped down into the bathroom, giving him room to maneuver his bulk in the enclosed space.

Feeling that an account was called for, I sat down next to Confucius and began to recount our nocturnal adventures. Without considering the mirth it would invoke, I didn't leave anything out. Maybe I should have. It was going to take a long time to live down the urn. When I finished my recital, with much amplification from Tamsin, she was sitting on the other side of Confucius, obviously just as tired as I was.

Jude's phone abruptly rang, echoing over the rain in the cavernous bathroom, and I jumped, inadvertently elbowing Confucius in his midsection. He teetered, but kept his perch above Napoleon.

"Brandt?" Jude answered the summons, knowing who it was without looking at his screen. "Are you at Albert's? Can you come to Tanglewood and get us?"

While Jude dealt with explanations of our predicament, Michael handed me his candelabra and climbed into the armoire.

"What are you doing? I asked, looking up at him.

"Look through the secret passageway." He gave me a tired smile. "What else would I do in a raging storm?"

The next morning dawned soft, wet, and blowy, with low clouds overhead like blue pearls rolling out to sea. Tamsin spent the night with me again, but left before breakfast to go back to her lodgings for a bath and a fresh change of clothes.

She lived inexpensively in an attic room of a boardinghouse that was run by two ancient women. Fleshly sisters Arabel Bunt and Zinnia Bunt-Joliet were harmlessly eccentric. Arabel had never married, but had never said why. Zinnia, in contrast, had run away at the age of seventeen to marry an older French émigré named Jean Baptiste Joliet, an artist painting his way through Cornwall. Both Arabel and Zinnia had a gossipy interest in Tamsin and looked after her with the same interfering zeal they bestowed on the three other boarders.

Rising fairly early to study for the meeting that night, I decided to eat a heartier-than-usual breakfast in the dining room of the inn instead of fending for myself in the kitchen at home. My mother had left before we had stirred, taking Great-aunts Astrid and Aurora and leaving a note at the kitchen table:

> Clive came by this morning and took your great-aunts in for a checkup. I went with them, but afterward Clive is bringing us back for the Range Rover. Your father should be home by then. There is leftover pasta in case anyone wants to eat here for lunch. Otherwise, I'm taking Astrid and Aurora out to the Moonstone to eat early if anyone wants to join us around noon. I'm stopping by the manor beforehand, Bella, if you and Tamsin would like to join us.

She ended the cheerful note with the usual admonitions and reminders along with her maternal blessing on the project.

Clive Chaucer, a ministerial servant in our congregation, also happens to be the village doctor. A widower only a few years younger than my parents, he is tall, thin, with light gray eyes, slightly graying black hair, and a wickedly dry sense of humor behind a good-natured personality. He loves quoting poetry and ballads, most of them obscure.

It's always disconcerting to me when I have to go to him professionally. I never know where to look, what to say, or what expression to allow on my face when he is examining me for whatever ailment I was sent to him for. Even when he's just looking into my ears, I feel horribly self-conscious. Call me hypersensitive, but it's hard to look poised while the congregation's "territory servant" checks your armpits for swollen lymph nodes, all the while quoting a ballad such as Ireland's "Carrighfergus." He'd poke flesh while saying things like,

> I'm drunk today, but I'm seldom sober,
> A handsome rover from town to town.
> Ah, but I'm sick now, my days are over,
> Come all you young lads and lay me down

As a general rule, I would rather suck razors than admit I'm sick.

I was sitting at a corner table in the inn's dining room, halfway through my breakfast, when I saw my father and Dante enter. Spotting me at the doorway, they signaled to Rayvyn, who was waiting on tables in her usual eccentric fashion, gave her their orders, and then made their way through the other sparse late-breakfast diners to join me. My father planted a weary kiss on my damp hair before he sat down.

"Good morning, rosebud. I heard about last night," he began and shifted his chair closer to the table. Dante lifted a rasher of bacon from my plate before he sat down on across from me. "Jude called when Brandt was taking you and Tamsin home."

My father and Dante looked like pirates with dark stubble on their jaws, finger-raked black hair, and crumpled white shirts. There was even an irregular splash of something dried on Dante's breast pocket, and I pointed at it.

"Rum? Or parrot droppings?"

"Coffee." Dante grinned and took a bite of bacon. I looked back at my father.

"What did Jude tell you?" I asked as I watched Rayvyn approach with two cups and a fresh pot of coffee. I waited until she had poured and left before continuing. "Did he tell you about the secret passageway that we found?"

"He did." My father smiled, his green eyes narrowing in amusement as he lifted his coffee cup and studied me over its rim. "I'm surprised that you had found one of them so quickly."

"One of them?" I echoed, startled. "You mean that there is more than one? You knew about it?"

"There's definitely more than one," my father admitted and took a sip as he settled back in his chair. Dante reached for a piece of toast, so I pushed my plate toward him. He gave me a tired perfunctory wink, picked up a clean fork, and began to finish what was left while it was still warm. My father warmed his fingertips against his cup. "Your grandmother told me a little about the house when I was growing up. I don't remember much about it except that there is more than one passage or secret room."

"I heard that you and Tamsin disinterred a Clarisse De Mornay," Dante laughed, his fork pausing halfway to his mouth. "Is she still in Elvis's shoe?"

I made a face.

"Remind me to restore the urn today. I'll do it before Mom comes with Aunt Astrid and Aunt Aurora."

"Basil should be there as well. He said he'd do inventory for us, and he's coming by this morning," my father said, taking another sip of coffee. "Show him the passageway. He's actually an expert on old houses, not just on antiques. Maybe he can show you how you and Tamsin got in the passageway in the first place."

"Basil's there?" I belatedly wondered what I had done with the front door keys last night. "How did he get in?"

"Jude is there with him. He made copies of the outside door keys this morning for all of us and a set for Basil," Dante said. I suddenly remembered Jude opening the front door the night before and pocketing the keys. I still had the giant key ring in my rucksack.

"I'll try to open the locked tower room today and find out where some of the keys go."

"After Basil is done with him, Jude is going to clean the worst of the garbage out of the house," my father said and then suddenly turned to look across the dining room, an inscrutable expression on his face. I turned to see what he was looking at and spotted Rayvyn doing something strange to the back of a dining chair. When she coughed, I knew it was a do-it-yourself Heimlich maneuver to dislodge one of those Fisherman's Friend cough drops she was forever swallowing by accident. She wiped her hands down her long braid and then cheerfully trotted off to the kitchens. My father sighed and turned his attention back to me. "There's only one trash bin in the whole house, so Jude said he's bringing a supply of liners. He'll take what we clear out to the tip later."

"I know Michael has to work today, but where is Brandt?" I asked. "Is he going out, or is he working at the house this morning?"

"Neither," Dante reminded me and drained his cup. "He has to dig his phone out of Peevey's pipes. Which reminds me, he said that he's going to try to clean some of the manor's windows sometime this week."

Rayvyn suddenly materialized behind us, balancing two plates of food and a pot of coffee, plunking them down without ceremony. She poured my father and brother a second cup of coffee and managed to look queasy, disapproving, and self-righteous all at the same time.

"Here are your breakfasts," she said mildly and then turned on her heel and left. I looked at what they had ordered and knew what Rayvyn had been dying to say but wouldn't dare with my father present. Breakfast would have been announced as, "Here are your poached fowl ovum and dead swine." Dante caught my eye and grinned.

I checked my watch and realized that I only had a few minutes before Tamsin was due to pick me up. I stood up and dropped my napkin on the table.

"Are you starting now?" my father asked. And I nodded. I leaned over behind him and wrapped my arms around his neck, planting a kiss on his whisker-rough jaw. He smelled very faintly of aftershave and hospital.

"How's Glynnis?" I asked, my cheek still pressed to his and my eye only an inch away from whisker burn. "Tell her I love her when you talk to her next."

"She's fine, child, and I will." My father reached back and patted my hair affectionately.

"Be careful," Dante said, his mouth close to a triangle of toast. He looked too tired to eat it. He gave me another grin. "And try not to damage anything. Especially yourself or Tamsin."

"I won't," I said cheerfully, snagged my rucksack from beside my vacated chair, smiled in farewell, and left, passing Rayvyn on the way to Reception. She struck a pose as I walked by, putting both palms over her eyes and lifting one sandal-clad foot in the air like a circus elephant. She hissed at me, and I stopped.

"Isabella. Guess."

"Guess what?" I asked, genuinely curious. An elderly couple dressed in travel-wrinkled clothes came in just then and stood behind me waiting to be seated.

"Guess. What am I?"

I knew that "disconnected" wasn't the answer she was looking for, so I shrugged, painfully aware of the watching couple behind me.

"I don't know. What are you?"

Without warning, she arched her back and flung her hands in the air over her head. It was a cross between a diva hearing applause and a convulsion. Her maverick breast almost met her chin, and I was absurdly glad for the elderly couple behind me that it hadn't finished its arcing flight by plopping out of the loose neck of her peasant blouse. The poor old couple didn't look heart-strong. But then again, they did look faintly blind, so maybe they would have just thought it was an exotic pendant flying about and survived the shock.

"Anonymity," she trumpeted. "I'm anonymity, silly."

In spite of myself, I smiled, wanting to laugh, but was hindered by the dampening realization that it would either encourage her or enrage her. Neither was good in a crowded dining room of paying customers. She saw the utterly startled older couple still standing behind me and calmly plucked two menus from the basket beside the door.

"Will you please come this way?"

I stayed a few seconds longer to watch her seat them and for my father to signal her over to his table. My parents had never hired her. She came with the inn as a proviso when my father had inherited it two years ago. Once, when Dante had asked my father if she does drugs, my father merely sighed.

"No," he had said, "her personality precludes hallucinogenics. She breaks through to the other side all by herself."

I left the inn by way of Reception and reached the bottom of the front steps a moment before Tamsin pulled up in her red Mini, looking as if she was driving a maraschino cherry on steroids. Slipping my rucksack from my shoulder, I opened the passenger door and slid in next to her, only to have the pungent scent of ammonia pierce my brain.

"What's that?" I peered into the back of the car.

"I brought whatever cleaning supplies I could find at the Bunts's. In case we need them," she answered as she let off the clutch with a tiny jerk. "Arabel found out what I'm doing today, and she wanted to contribute to the cause."

"That was nice of her," I murmured and visualized the rotund little woman in her ubiquitous flower print dresses. Tamsin seemed determined to keep Arabel and me from meeting, even though she had pointed her out to me from a distance. I had, however, been in Tamsin's room many times and had used the top floor lavatory on occasion. The only thing that I remembered about those times was the hand-crocheted toilet roll cozy in the shape of a bloated kitten.

"Poor thing," Tamsin suddenly laughed. "She's angling to trade favors. She'll contribute the gear if I contribute the gossip. She's dying to know what the inside of Tanglewood Manor is like. When I didn't volunteer anything, she asked me to invite you to tea tomorrow."

"Why not? She's harmless."

Tamsin stopped laughing, gave me a skewed look from brown eyes, but didn't say anything.

Moments later, we pulled up in front of the manor. Jude's van was no longer in front of the stoop, and I realized that Brandt must have dropped him off on his way to Mr. Peevey's plumbing. I wondered if the van was parked in the back of the house by the courtyard where the soon-to-be-full bin liners would be easier to cart outside. Tamsin pointed to a sleek gunmetal gray Mercedes sedan parked under a tree.

"Basil Brett is here."

Neither one of us was getting out of the car. In the blowy morning, the mansion looked every bit as intriguing as it had the day before, but instead of the gritty walls and sunlit ivy of yesterday, it was silver under the wet blue sky. A gust of wind stirred the creepers over the windows, and they made one of those beckoning gestures I was starting to associate with Tanglewood. After a few more seconds of staring, we finally opened the Mini's doors and stepped out.

"What's first?" Tamsin asked as I hoisted the rucksack to my shoulder and shut the car door.

"We're supposed to find out where all the keys go," I answered as we started toward the front doors. "Don't forget, one of the tower rooms is still locked."

We crossed the scattered potholes and let ourselves in the unlocked double doors.

The Great Hall was even larger than I had remembered it to be. More spacious and even dirtier, if that was possible. Watery sunlight slanted in through the crusty windows, highlighting every swirling dust mote and making the vast vault overhead appear smoky. We looked around with renewed interest.

The tapestries on the walls were so moth eaten and moldy it was hard to decipher their subjects. After a minute of judicious squinting at one tapestry, I realized that I was looking at a scene of Adam and Eve selling us into sin. At least I hoped that's what it was. The scene involved two nude people, masses of strategically placed foliage, a snake, and what looked like an Australian kiwi in someone's hand. I pictured the first couple greeting each other every morning with a hearty, "G'day, mate!"

I dropped my rucksack by the door, fished out the plate-sized key ring, and surveyed the mass of clinking metal with a frown. Tamsin stared blankly at the mismatched assortment.

"They seem a bit rusty," she said dubiously. "Do you think the locks will still open?"

We heard the faint murmur of men's voices overhead and looked up at the heavy balustrade of the gallery ringing the Great Hall above us.

"If Jude's here, he might have an oil can with him to use in the more stubborn locks." At the mention of his name, my older brother's blond head shifted into view, and he peered down at us.

"What do you need an oil can for?"

"We're supposed to match the keys to the locks, and we're afraid that the keys are too rusted to work or that the locks are too dry."

"Just a minute." His head withdrew from sight, and I heard Basil Brett's unmistakable voice speaking to him. We waited. The carpets in the overhead gallery and on the stairs were thick enough to mute a jackhammer, let alone the footfalls of two men, and they just suddenly materialized on the stair landing above us.

"Good morning, ladies!" Basil Brett's voice rolled down the staircase, making us start. "Two of our most lovely treasures! A Sandro Botticelli angel and one of El Greco's dark maidens!"

For a moment, I thought that Great-uncle Desmond had actually collected something valuable. A Botticelli and an El Greco would buy a fleet of new missionary homes. Then Tamsin's amused whisper brought me back to earth.

"You're the Botticelli."

I smiled uncertainly at Basil. His erudite compliments always make me feel like I should just giggle and pull my dress up over my head. At Jude's grin, I collected my wits.

"Thank you for saying so, but at the moment, I don't feel very angelic."

"What is the problem, Miss Bella?" Basil flashed a perfectly polished smile. His teeth were so white they looked like glazed porcelain, which was odd since most seventy-year-old teeth look like they're chipped walrus tusks or like a mouthful of peanuts trying to fall out. "Can we help?"

"We have to find where all these go," I sighed and held up the rusty key ring. "There are ninety-eight of them. I counted."

"You might need more than an oil can." Jude circumnavigated the hopping cherub stationed at the foot of the stairs and took the keys from my hand. At least I think it was a cherub. It was intensely grimy and had buttocks and wings. "My van is out back. I have some mechanic's acid that should eat the rust off your keys." He grinned at me. "Come along, my little *cattiva panciuta far scomparire.*"

Come along, my little evil potbellied dwarf?

*"Cretino."* (Twit.) I smiled back.

*"Parla Italiano."* (He speaks Italian.) Jude smiled even wider.

"What?"

"That I do, young lady." Brother Brett's face creased in a delighted smile. "*Si, invece si.*"

I managed to restrain myself from pulling my shirt up over my head and running off the cliffs outside. Instead, I tried to ignore the blush invading my face and was unexpectedly saved by the welcome voices of Great-aunts Astrid and Aurora. But if I was hoping their arrival would salvage some of the dignity that I had just lost, I was doomed to disappointment.

"I'm telling you, sister," Aunt Astrid was chiding Aurora as they opened the front doors and filed in, "you smelled absolutely fetid. Going on the Amazon with you was rather like standing downwind from wet donkeys."

"With festering saddle sores," Aunt Aurora supplemented breathlessly. "Yes, you've already told me many times. Would you rather I had the malaria?"

"Of course not, dearest, but that homemade mosquito repellent was most foul."

"What you say is true. It used to make me quite light-headed when we ascended above the tree line. But you can't deny it was effective. I never had even the tiniest fever—"

"That may be true as well," Aunt Astrid interrupted her, "but that lovely Clive was not too impressed with those leech scars all over that hump on your . . . ," her voice trailed off when she came around the carousel and spotted all four of us standing there and staring, which was just as well, since the next words of her sentence were better left unuttered.

My mother entered in behind them looking faintly amused and fiercely determined to stay out of the conversation. There was only the tiniest of pauses before Aunt Astrid resumed speaking.

"Good heavens, Aurora," she barked, "what a lovely man!"

We all looked at Basil. Completely unflustered, he bowed to all three newcomers in a precise movement. My mother began to make introductions. Tamsin sidled up to me.

"I was just thinking," she whispered, "while you're getting what you need out of Jude's van, I'm going to clean up Clarisse's urn and Elvis's shoe."

I nodded in approval and watched as she sidled discreetly past my mother to disappear out of the front door. My mother smiled at Tamsin as she passed, then looked at me.

"Good morning, *bocciolo*," she said warmly. "Where is she going?"

"She's going to the car to get some cleaning materials."

Jude plucked the key ring from my hand and walked off. I took one step, intending to follow, then stopped, hearing the last of Great-aunt Astrid's words as she conversed with Basil.

"More than one secret room." She grasped his arm. Her long weathered fingers completely encircled his bicep. In her magenta dress, she looked a bit like a macaw landing on a twig. "Aurora and I have been trying to remember where they all were, but of course, we aren't sure. It's been so long since we played in them. Our father used them for storage before he put new slates on the roof. The attics used to be so damp."

"In fact"—Great-aunt Aurora peered at him earnestly—"Luc's daughter explored one of them last night."

"How did Aunt Aurora know?" I glanced at my mother. She patted my shoulder.

"I called your father from Clive's this morning."

"Has Jude taken you through the passageway yet?" Great-aunt Astrid asked. "Aurora and I can't seem to remember one in that particular hallway."

"Not yet. And please call me Basil. And I would very much like to see the passageway."

"Oh, my goodness, call me Astrid. And my sister is Aurora. Perhaps Isabella can take us to it."

Just then Tamsin came back into the Great Hall with a loaded bucket. I could see a pair of yellow latex gloves hanging over the edge. She saw my look, read my mind, and nodded.

"Excuse me." She smiled, ducked her head, and scurried up the stairs to the first landing. She paused and looked back. "Clive Chaucer is here," she said and then continued her rapid trot up the staircase, the yellow gloves waving cheerfully at us as she went. I tried to figure out how to stall until she could pour out the urn still entombed in the passageway with the ash-filled shoe. Pour out or hide.

"Clive wants to see the house?" I looked at my mother.

"We invited him to lunch with us, so I asked him if he wanted to see the manor first. He doesn't have surgery today."

Just then Clive Chaucer came in through the open double doors and wandered thoughtfully around the clutter until he came to us.

"Well, well," he laughed, his eyes roving quickly over the massive walls, the massive chandelier, the massive junk, and the massive dust balls rolling over the massive flagstones. He crossed his arms over his chest and let his eyes come to rest on the grime-encrusted cherub at the foot of the stairs. His smile faded as he squinted at the statue. "Now in Kilkenny, it is reported, they've marble stones there as black as ink. With gold and silver I would transport her but I'll sing no more now, till I get a drink."

Great-aunt Astrid beamed at him.

"'Carrighfergus,'" she trumpeted the name of the traditional Irish song the doctor was quoting from and then turned triumphantly toward her sister. "I am one up on you, dear."

"'Carrighfergus.'" Aunt Aurora pouted. "I should have remembered that ballad. Dear Bryn used to sing that one when that dreadful Finghin was wooing her."

Finghin is my grandfather in Ireland. It's pronounced "Fin-jin." "Fin-jin" Quinn. I often wonder what my grandmother was thinking of when she picked someone with that name. Especially since her first name is Bryn. "Fin-jin" and Bryn Quinn. Maybe that's why my grandfather always used to get into pub fights.

"'Carrighfergus,'" Clive confirmed with a grin, and after greeting Basil he turned a friendly smile on me. "What is this I hear? You found a secret passageway in the middle of the night?"

"She was just going to show it to us," Aunt Aurora breathed.

"These old house secrets are a passion of mine," Basil said fulsomely. My mother and I smiled. The word "passion" isn't one you'd associate with precise wee Basil. "Houses tell you a lot about the family that built them."

I wondered what Tanglewood Manor told Basil about our DNA, and my smile became a wince.

"Usually," he continued, "these passageways or secret entrances were put in for easy access to a particular room. It was either installed for a philandering husband or to keep an eye on a guest, perhaps to steal from him. Rarely was a first-story room used for imprisoning. Cellars and dungeons were used for that. The Saxon's culture was psychologically unsound during the time this dwelling was constructed. Comprised mainly of warring landholders, the rich classes' only defense was paranoia, thievery, and sexual conquest."

Egads. Forget the manor house itself. What would Uncle Desmond's rusted underwear collection tell him?

"Are you ready, dear?" Great-aunt Astrid smiled at me. "Lead the way."

I wondered how fast Tamsin would be able to travel through the obstacle course of fallen mannequins to get to the brimming urn. This brought up the much more imponderable worry of how fast she would be able to trot back to the bathroom with it and keep her tee shirt dry.

"The only way to get to the passageway is through the bathroom armoire," I said and began leading the way up the wide staircase to the next floor, curious to see what Basil and Clive were going to make of it. I was glad that at least Confucius had been moved off the toilet though I didn't recall anyone pulling up his boxers.

"I know which secret passage it is now, dearest," Aunt Aurora said briefly, obviously saving her breath to climb the stairs. "Our dear papa installed plumbing in it."

"What did Clive say? How are they?" I whispered to my mother, being far enough ahead to be unheard by the others. I was given a reassuring smile as we rounded the first landing.

"They're fine. Basically, their hearts are tired. It's just a combination of having battled tropical disease and of being oxygen deprived from swift altitude changes. It's all coming together now in their old age. They're easily exhausted, and when that happens, they don't get enough blood and oxygen to their brain. Nothing that a more sedentary life and a lower altitude can't improve. Coming to England was the best thing for them physically."

Cornwall was definitely closer to the earth's core than the Peruvian mountains, but convincing my great-aunts to lead a less physically active life was going to be the tricky bit. If anyone could do it, it would be my grandmother.

"Clive thinks he can regulate it with medication, though they want to try herbal remedies first," my mother continued. "Either way, it's apparently going to take quite a while to get it under control."

As we drew closer to the open bathroom door, we could hear a whoosh of water and the sound of old pipes clanking. Tamsin must have just tipped the urn. When we trooped in, Tamsin was at the sink holding the urn under a trickle of water coming from the gilded taps. She looked over her shoulder at us and gave me a grin. On the window sill, nestled in a clean dust rag, was a pyramidal pile of ashes with Elvis's shoe upended beside it.

I noticed a charcoal smear on Tamsin's cheek and went over to her to thumb it off. We both made a face at the grittiness of it. We were losing bits of Clarisse all over the manor, and I wondered how much of her was scattered down the secret hallway or lodged in our sinuses.

Basil went straight to the armoire and began exploring the back panel.

"Give it a good shove," Tamsin instructed, shutting off the water and shaking the wet urn over the sink.

"Ah. A spring-loaded pivot," he said, climbed nimbly into the massive wardrobe, and was swallowed whole. Aunts Astrid and Aurora and my mother stood behind him trying to peer at what he was doing. We heard the faint slap of flesh on wood as Basil thumped the armoire's back panel in an effort to gauge the size of the hidden door.

Clive seemed to be more distracted by the mannequins than by the soon-to-be-revealed secret passageway. He was standing in front of them with his hands on his hips in some sort of silent commune with the figures. He glanced at Tamsin and me watching him.

"O who can stand? O who hath caused this? O who can answer at the throne of God? The Kings and Nobles of the Land have done it! Hear it not, Heaven, thy Ministers have done it!" His stage-deepened voice rolled around the bathroom like thunder, and then he toed the elastic of Confucius's boxers until they twanged like a loose guitar string. He looked at us, his face openly amused. "The harlot and the wild beast, eh?"

"A poem by William Blake!" Aunt Aurora's triumphant voice echoed hollowly from the depths of the armoire. She was bent over, peering in the immense wardrobe with Aunt Astrid's magenta-skirted derriere beside hers. I couldn't see their heads. There was a prim little grunt from the armoire's depths and a faint scrape of wood on wood.

"Good show, Basil. Good show," Aunt Astrid applauded. "Come along, Aurora. Let's step in."

"Clap," my mother instructed Basil, laughed, and helped Aunt Astrid hoist Aunt Aurora over the high edge. It was a bit like pushing a water bed up the stairs. Clive jumped forward, putting a shoulder into it, and Aunt Aurora giggled as she suddenly shot forward into the armoire.

"It's hard to believe I used to load myself with literature and hike above Lake Titicaca in the summertime," she said and crept into the passageway behind Basil.

"Are you coming with us?" my mother asked Clive, pausing before stepping delicately into the cavernous wardrobe. He smiled and waved them on.

"Probably. I'll be there shortly."

She flashed me a white smile, brushed her hands over the sides of her linen capris, and disappeared from view. Clive turned to rest his speculative gaze on the pile of ashes next to Elvis's shoe.

"What have we here?" He came closer and prodded the ashes with a clinical forefinger. It looked like he was sculpting a Zen garden out of Clarisse's remains.

"Clarisse De Mornay," Tamsin answered, her gaze a fascinated stare as she watched Clive sculpt a decorative swirl.

"I beg your pardon?"

"She was in here," Tamsin said and held up the freshly rinsed urn, turning it so he could see the name etched in its square base. "Clarisse's remains. Someone or something who died in the eighteenth century." She frowned. "I think she might have been someone's terrier. Bella thinks it was some woman. We don't know exactly."

"Hmmm." Clive drew a happy face in the ashes. "Clarisse, you say?" He picked up a large bone splinter and held it up to the light streaming in through the crusty windows. He frowned, sniffed it, touched it to his tongue in a tentative lick, and then rolled his eyes up in pretend ecstasy. "Mmm-mmm . . . all we need now is a dry white wine."

My breakfast tried to jump out, and I clapped a hand to my mouth. I darted forward, fighting Tamsin for sink space.

"I'm sorry." Clive's hands were steady and apologetic on our backs. He was laughing. "I'm sorry. It was too good to pass up. It's animal bones. Not human. My guess is chicken, actually. Come on. Take some deep breaths."

Tamsin, the first to slowly straighten up from the sink, turned to stare at him.

"Are you sure?"

"Of course, he's sure," I gurgled and turned to rest my forehead on Tamsin's shoulder. "He's a doctor."

"Chicken bones? Do you think Great-uncle Desmond knew?" Jude laughed. I looked over at my brother as he came into the bathroom. He walked over to me and picked a dust ball from my hair, where it must have migrated like a dandelion spore. "The keys are sitting in a bowl of solvent in the kitchen. Give them a few hours, and you should be able to scrub them clean under running water. I've left you a pair of gloves and a wire brush." He looked back at Clive and pointed at the ashes. "So you think he might have put the chicken bones in the urn himself?"

Clive shrugged, still smiling, and rinsed the ash dust from his fingertips. Tamsin began to dry the damp urn with a clean rag, a thoughtful expression on her face, and I wondered what had just popped into her mind.

"The bones certainly aren't that old. Three? Four chickens perhaps? I assume that he must have filled the urn himself since the urn certainly isn't two hundred years old like the inscription implies. You should ask Basil."

"Isabella, come here." Tamsin's thoughtful look gave way to a frown. Slipping past me, she walked to one of the windows and tilted the urn into the light of a weak sunbeam. I did as she instructed and peered inside the urn's cored depths. It was difficult to decipher, but once seen, there were no mistaking the three tiny figures. I glanced reflexively at the still-open armoire. The back panel had swiveled shut behind Basil and the others, exposing it to the faint daylight.

"What's in the urn?" Jude broke into my speculations.

"The same thing that's over there," I said and went to the armoire to point at the figures carved into the back panel. I passed the urn back to a curious Clive as Jude joined me.

"It's a 3, and then a zero, and then the letter *A* all stacked on top of each other," Jude said slowly, peering at the etching I indicated.

"Or the letter *O* and not a zero," Tamsin supplied.

"We found it last night, but I thought it was a builder's mark," I continued, watching as Jude ran his fingers over the rough carving. "But it can't be, can it, if the same mark is in the bottom of the urn?"

"Under chicken bones," Tamsin's voice reminded me dryly. I turned to look at her, knowing what she was thinking. One of Great-uncle Desmond's weird clues? We wouldn't know until we asked Great-aunts Astrid and Aurora. Or perhaps my grandmother. Jude straightened up and looked back at Clive, who had moved on from examining the urn in his hand to staring suspiciously at Elvis's shoe. The doctor felt my brother's look and glanced up.

"It's a long story," my brother said, grinning. "Unfortunately, it isn't ours to tell, or we would let you in on it. But, then, perhaps Aunts Astrid and Aurora have already told you?"

"About the great treasure hunt?" Clive suddenly grinned and carefully set the urn on the windowsill next to the pile of ashes. "They did, indeed. I take it that the etched figures have something to do with that?"

"Possibly," Jude laughed. "Had you met Desmond Wildeve?"

"I had dealings with him a few times," Clive said thoughtfully. "But not as a patient. The first time I had met him he had brought Colin Rawlings in my surgery."

"What was their great-uncle like?" Tamsin asked, wanting a more professionally objective opinion than mine. I had already told her what I thought of him, but words like "shriveled," "peevish," and "liver spotted" weren't cleverly insightful and didn't tell her any more than she already knew.

"That's hard to say." Clive crossed his arms over his chest and stared thoughtfully at the scabby bathroom floor. "A bit odd, certainly, and unbalancing more than unbalanced. A natural-born lateral thinker."

"A natural-born lateral thinker?" Tamsin echoed. Clive looked up and smiled at her.

"Unbalancing?" I added my echo. He nodded.

"His effect on other people. You could have a conversation with him, and it wasn't until you had walked away that you realized that he was on another subject entirely and that neither of you knew it."

As I was digesting this view of Great-uncle Desmond, Clive's mobile phone went off. He answered it, had a brief conversation, and then rang off, smiling at us as he hastily exited the bathroom.

"Emergency," he said succinctly. "Tell your mother I'll meet everyone at lunch." And then he was gone, leaving us behind with the chicken bones. I looked thoughtfully at the unappetizing mound and carefully lifted the ash-laden rag by its four corners, tucking it into a ball.

"I'm throwing the ashes away," I began and then looked at Jude. "Where are the bin liners? In the kitchen?"

He nodded, plucked Uncle Desmond's stiff gray-yellow bathrobe from inside the armoire, disturbing its odiferous crust, and draped it over my arm. The unexpected aroma of pickled eggs swelled into my face.

"Throw that away while you're at it."

"I know something I can do while the keys are derusting," Tamsin said, veering away from the malodorous cloud enveloping me as if she had bounced off a wall. "I'll go with you and get the bin liners. Then I'll distribute a couple to each room. We're going to need them."

"And I know another thing," I said and glanced down at the balled up rag in my hand as we walked to the doorway. "I'm not ordering chicken for lunch."

# 5

The Moonstone began its life hundreds of years ago as Halfmoon's only inn and public house. Rambling, whitewashed, thatched, and twisty like the rest of the village, its leaded windows have peered at the water beyond the sea wall on the Low Street for over three centuries. The building is a dark maze of snugs and niches where the myriad fireplaces are huge and faintly lopsided with heavy mantels.

Pete Lord's younger brother, Frank, had bought the Moonstone a year ago and had transformed it into Halfmoon's version of the Savoy, and now added to the antiquated look of rustic pub was a bizarre touch of faux French.

We had been placed at a secluded table tucked into one of the large bay windows overlooking the beached fishing boats. Aunt Aurora sat on one side of me and Tamsin on the other. Jasmine seated us. Jasmine was to Jude what Rayvyn was to Michael.

Twice divorced in her twenty-two years, Jasmine Burke had moved to Halfmoon when she was eighteen. At about five feet tall and a hundred and seventy pounds, she resembled a tattooed and pierced fireplug. Being a barmaid was obviously a career choice and not merely a way to pay her rent. Regularly attiring herself in black thick-soled boots and minidresses, she gels her inch-long orange hair into lethal spikes, smokes like a flaming brush pile, and has blue fingernails with ochre tips. She doesn't paint them that color. They are that color. And she has a thing for Jude.

Jude doesn't seem too disconcerted by her persistent pursuit. He responds to her attempts to flirt with a cheerful amusement, letting everything she says bounce off, and it's obvious when I watch her that she can't decide whether to force her attentions on my brother or harpoon him to the wall. A smarter woman would have given up after their first encounter two years ago, but Jasmine wasn't smart. That was obvious in her tattoo choice of a third eye on her sternum. The choice and location were silly enough, but to top it off, as she steadily gained weight her growing cleavage had long since crept up, captured it, and squashed it between her breasts like a forgotten raisin fallen from a teacake.

As she handed out our menus, Jude placidly ignored her fluttering eyelashes. She snorted in disgust, sounding a bit like a chain saw snagged on a cedar knot, and stomped off in her Doc Martens.

Basil Brett watched Jasmine go with speculation in his bright blue eyes.

"I would be willing to wager that the charm hanging off her nose is an authentic Egyptian scarab. One from antiquity and not forged."

"That was a charm?" Tamsin's confused voice was only loud enough for me to hear.

"Isn't a scarab just a dung beetle by another name?" Aunt Astrid snorted calmly, obviously unimpressed with Jasmine's sartorial choices. "Didn't I see some of those in one of the tower rooms?"

"Scarabs? In one of Desmond's collections?" Clive raised a black eyebrow and regarded Aunt Astrid over his menu.

"No. Scurrying about on the floor." She slapped her menu shut and folded her hands over it. "I think I'll have a pizza. I've never had one of those."

"Oh, that does sound properly exotic, sister," Aunt Aurora breathed. "Perhaps we could share one. I don't believe I can eat much today. I feel a bit fatigued."

"So, Basil, can you tell us what the marks in the armoire mean?" Jude leaned forward to look at the older man, resting his forearms on the table's edge. "Bella did show you the urn, didn't she?"

"She did," Basil said primly and slid his napkin-wrapped art nouveau silverware across the scarred table until it was directly in front of his neat figure. "First of all, I have no idea what those etched marks in the armoire and urn mean. And I certainly don't believe the urn to be two hundred years old. It looks much like the urns mass produced after the Second World War."

"That's what I thought," Clive added. "Did she tell you that the bones inside were chicken bones and not human?"

"She did," Basil answered and then stopped as Jasmine tromped up to take our varied lunch orders. As she jotted everything down on her pad, Jasmine tried to bat her kohl-ringed eyes at Jude a second time, but he had turned to stare out of the window at the gently ebbing waves. Twice frustrated in her attempts to force a smile from him, she stomped away to bring our order of tea, thumping an irritable hand against a vacant table in passing as if the tabletop were Jude's head.

"She did tell me about the bones," Basil began where he had left off. "But the only thing I can tell you about the armoire is that it predates Prince George's reign by about twenty years. It isn't Regency."

"If the remains in the urn aren't authentic," my mother chimed in, "then who is Clarisse De Mornay?" She looked at my great-aunts. "Have either of you heard of her?"

They shook their heads in unison, and Aunt Astrid shrugged.

"Perhaps the name is one of Desmond's rather silly clues."

"That's what we think," Tamsin blurted out and then waited as Jasmine returned with the tray of tea things. We were silent as she slapped the cups and saucers down in front of us. She followed up the cups with three teapots plopped down in quick succession. Then after she dropped the sugar, cream, and lemon slices on to the center of the table, she clutched the now-empty tray to her third eye, glared at Jude's profile, and stomped off.

"The name has to be some sort of clue since it isn't a real funeral urn," Tamsin finished, watching as I snagged the pot closest to me and poured Indian tea into Aunt Aurora's cup.

"Thank you, dear." Aunt Aurora smiled, fished in her enormous purse, and pulled out a miniature airline bottle of cognac. She poured the equivalent of three drops into her cup, stirred in a lump of sugar, and then dropped in a lemon slice.

"So how can we find out what the name means?" my mother asked, pouring out a cup of tea for Aunt Astrid. "Any ideas?"

Aunt Astrid snagged the cognac from her sister's plump fingers before she could drop the bottle back into her purse, unscrewed the tiny cap, and upended the rest of the contents into her teacup. A burst of fumes wafted over the table and dried our eyes up.

"If the armoire predates the Regency period by about twenty years, that would make it the late eighteenth century, wouldn't it?" I looked across the table at Basil's twinkling blue eyes. They looked like happy agate marbles embedded in pink folds. "What do those numbers make me think of?"

"That armoire was put over the passageway's entrance a little over two hundred years after it had already been built." My mother looked at Basil thoughtfully. "I wonder what it had replaced."

"Possibly just a paneled door leading to a servants' passage," Basil answered, smiling gallantly at both of us. I could tell that he was respectfully enamored of my mother. I suspected that he would greatly enjoy rescuing her from something. If we were living in medieval times, he would trot up on his snowy white steed and defend her honor. Unfortunately for Basil, my mother's feelings for him would have never exceeded anything more precious than the desire to pinch his rosy cheek, take him home in her purse, and feed him cheesy lasagna until his skin filled back out and he was shiny once again. Then she would free him back to his natural habitat. Or put him on the mantel with her grandmother's rococo clock.

"Don't forget the clue in the sarcophagus," Jude reminded everyone at the table. I assumed by everyone's thoughtful, nonstartled response that they had already been told about our tomb raiding of the night before. I looked at my brother, remembering how he had pocketed the clue before lifting the mummy out of his box.

"Do you still have that paper we found in with the mummy?"

He nodded and extracted it from his wallet, handing it to me. I read it out loud.

"Roses are red, violets are blue. Men aren't the dead. This is a clue." I flipped the paper over to look at the message penciled on the back. "Try again."

"May I see it, dear?" Basil asked. I leaned over the table to give him the slip of parchment. He held the thin skin up to the light and frowned at it. It wasn't the clue he wanted to see; it was the paper it had been written on. I remembered that he was an expert in antique documents.

"Hmm," he exhaled thoughtfully. "This parchment is actually fairly old and was made by splitting vellum into layers. They used to pickle it in salt, stretch it thin, dry it, and bleach it in the sun. It was a kind of legal paper that was commonly used. I wonder how he had gotten a hold of a blank piece."

"Old?" My mother leaned her forearms on the table beside her teacup. "How old?"

"Looking at the coloring, I would guess that this piece is perhaps a couple of hundred years old." He paused. "Unless Desmond forged its obvious antiquity. Not impossible if you know what you're doing."

"I do appreciate a good education," Aunt Aurora breathed respectfully, looking properly awed by Basil's superior knowledge.

"A couple hundred years?" I blurted out. "Shouldn't we be more careful with it?"

Basil twinkled at me and folded it back into the square it was in when Jude had extracted it from his leather wallet.

"No, my dear. It's quite indestructible from mere handling. The professions used it just for that reason. Now the older parchments were a bit more fragile. This is really a form of tanned sheepskin."

I took the parchment from Basil, gingerly slipping it into my rucksack as it sat under my chair. I knew it was my imagination, but at the words "tanned sheepskin," I could suddenly detect a faint odor of goat.

"Men aren't the dead," Clive repeated thoughtfully. "Try again. I'll have to think about that one."

Just then the familiar stomp of Jasmine's boots began approaching, and we fell protectively silent, knowing that if Jasmine heard one word about the great treasure hunt, so would the rest of the village in less than an hour. For half a century, Halfmoon had speculated about Great-uncle Desmond's travels and treasures, but no one had actually believed the tales enough to get up and look for themselves. However, if one word of what we were doing escaped, the tiny part of the village that wasn't embedded behind Zimmer frames would be scrabbling about the mansion like Elvis fans at Graceland.

Jasmine entered our niche, carrying a tray, and plopped four of the lunches down in front of us, presenting Jude's plate with a flourish, which was amiably ignored by him while the rest of us thanked her with varying degrees of enthusiasm. She narrowed her eyes into angry slits and stomped away to pick up the last four orders. No one spoke until she had stoically completed her service and the last echo of her combat boots had faded into silence. Somewhere in the pub's bowels, a jukebox started playing "Love Me Tender."

"So what have we come up with?" Aunt Astrid stared at the pizza wheel that had been placed between her and her sister. I knew she was talking about clues and not about her lunch. Picking up a knife and fork, she hovered over the platter indecisively. "How do I eat this?"

"Goodness," Aunt Aurora breathed. "I do believe, sister, that it is much larger than the hubcaps on Papa's Bentley."

My mother leaned over to work the pizza slices loose from their moorings of melted mozzarella.

"Here you go," she said, slipped the freed wedges onto the provided plates, and set them before my great-aunts.

"Thank you, dear." Aunt Astrid beamed and tentatively cut a chunk off with her knife, putting it in her mouth as carefully as she must have slid in her first bite of roasted monkey over forty years ago. She chewed, and everyone watched, including her anxious sister.

"Oh my," she barked, swallowed, and sawed off another piece. "Eat up, Aurora. It's even better than your monkey stew with sun-dried corn and wild yams." Tamsin shuddered next to me as if someone had grabbed her stomach and yanked it. Aunt Astrid swallowed her second bite and began to saw loose her third.

"So, as we were saying, what have we come up with?"

Jude put his fork down and rested his fingers around his indigo cup of tea.

"We have the clue that whatever it is belongs to Destiny, which is an odd way to phrase it when you think about it. Not 'belonged,' but 'belongs.' Present tense. I have a feeling that Great-uncle Desmond may not have been much of a poet, but his words were carefully chosen."

"I hadn't thought of that, but you're right." My mother nodded thoughtfully, picking through her shrimp salad to spear a black olive. It rolled around her plate, resisting her tines, and it looked like she was attempting to impale a fleeing cockroach. "What else do we have?"

"There's the second part of that clue. That we would never find it unless we knew Great-uncle Desmond better." Jude paused thoughtfully, waiting until Aunts Astrid and Aurora looked up from their wedges of pizza. "What would he mean? Do you know if he kept some kind of journal?"

"Possibly," Aunt Aurora breathed. "I know Mother did."

"Your mother kept diaries?" my mother asked, and at the unified nods from my great-aunts, she looked at Jude and arched a delicate eyebrow. "That somehow seems a good place to start. A mother certainly knows her children."

"Where were her journals kept?" Clive asked. Aunt Aurora smiled tremulously at him.

"Father kept her room intact after she died. I used to sneak in there and read them, you know."

"So we look for her journals," I said while my mother worked another slice of pizza loose from its wheel, setting it on Aunt Aurora's proffered plate. "Tamsin and I can do that."

"What do they look like?" Tamsin asked. "Can you remember?"

"No, dear," Aunt Aurora sighed. "It's been too long."

"I guess we'll know them when we see them," I said dubiously.

"What other clues?" my mother continued to prod. "What about the one found with the wax mummy?"

"I've been thinking about that one," Clive interjected. "The part that intrigues me is that the men aren't the dead and to try again. Think about it. Where did you find the clue?"

"In the sarcophagus," I said obediently.

"That's right." Jude gave Clive a speculative look. "In a coffin."

"With a fake body," Clive hinted.

"A fake grave?" Jude raised his eyebrows, and I could see the glint in his eyes mirror Clive's. "The insane old sot."

"Tell us," I begged and put my fork down by my plate. "What did you just think of?"

"A fake grave." Jude turned his amused green glint to me and began to tick the items off on his fingers. "A note that says that it isn't the men who are dead and the directions to try again. Put them together, *poca*."

"Try to think laterally, luv. What did you see a lot of in the Great Hall?" Clive prodded gently. I cast my mind back over our candlelit trek through the maze of junk. What was there that had to do with graves? The Viking funerary ship? Then I had it.

"The tombstones," I said wonderingly. "There were tombstones along the wall."

"Put that with the rest," Jude said, watching my face. I wondered if the chaotic thoughts flooding my head were apparent in my expression.

"The sarcophagus didn't have anything real in it. It was nothing but a fake grave. We need to look at the tombstones propped up in the Great Hall since they obviously aren't real graves, either." I paused, another thought striking me. "Wait a minute. The note said to try again. Put that with the first part of the clue. What did we do to find the clue to begin with? We opened the sarcophagus. We opened a grave."

"Ohhh." Tamsin read my mind, shuddered, and put her fork down on what was left of her pommes frites. "So you're saying that we need to try again by opening another grave."

"Somewhere is a fake grave that needs to be opened," I said excitedly. "'Try again,' Uncle Desmond said. There is a clue in the tombstones in the Great Hall which will lead us to a grave that we need to open."

"I hope not," Basil said thoughtfully, staring at the pile of pepperoni that Great-aunt Aurora had been meticulously pulling off the pizza and stacking on the table while no one was watching.

"Oh, goodness," my mother suddenly sighed. "I feel rather like I'm part of a sane group of people trying to play charades with a lunatic. We are all calling out answers, but we don't know if we have anything right because there really isn't any logic to any of this."

"Charades from beyond the grave," Aunt Astrid said dryly.

"So what do we have so far?" Jude interlaced his fingers, put his elbows on the table on either side of his plate, and rested his forehead on the backs of his hands. He looked as if he was praying over his coq au vin. "We need to look for Destiny's diaries. We need to look through the tombstones." He looked up and grinned. "And Bella needs to dig up somebody's grave. Now if we could just figure out whose."

"And we need to find out who Clarisse De Mornay is," Tamsin reminded us. "That's something I can do at the library."

"At the library?" My mother frowned thoughtfully and then cleared her face with a smile. "Ahh, I remember. Doesn't the lending library have computer files that you can check?"

"We have access to an extensive registry on the Internet. It goes as far back as England's records. Well," she paused, "maybe not that far, but we can hook up with other databases. Births, deaths, marriages, even inheritances. Property deeds. Everything. It just takes a bit of digging if you know where to look."

"Do you know where to look, dear?" Aunt Astrid asked placidly. Tamsin grinned at her.

"If I can't find it, then Ms. Dilly can." Ms. Dilly, the head librarian, was old enough to remember Queen Elizabeth's father as king. Her trifocal spectacles were as thick as pancakes, and they hung from a cord of Bakelite beads that she had strung herself when Bakelite was new. She always wore hand-knitted twin-sets and a dab of vanilla extract behind each ear. "I should have time to look today when I go to work after lunch. Is there anything else I should be looking up as well?"

"How about Desmond Wildeve?" Jude suggested, surprising me. I hadn't thought of my great-uncle as a cipher that needed defining. "He seems to be the center of all this. He did tell us in a clue that we needed to know him better."

"Good idea," Tamsin said thoughtfully. "Why not?"

"Is that too much, *bambina*?" my mother laughed. "We seem to have loaded you up."

"It's not too much," Tamsin reassured her. "The computer does all the work. It shouldn't take too long."

"Well, that takes care of the urn," I said. "But what about the 3-0-A in the urn and in the armoire? Any ideas on that?"

Just then Jasmine's boots started up their heavy tromp in the back reaches of the pub, and we fell silent. It was obvious that she was coming our way. She suddenly materialized at Jude's side, parked a hand on her hip, cocked her body his direction, and pasted a flirtatious smile on her face. Her nicotine-colored teeth looked like some of that sun-dried corn in Aunt Aurora's monkey stew.

"Look 'ere, Jude," she began ominously and picked at the scarab in her nose like she was dislodging an inconvenient scab. "Okay. I remembered what you had said last time about Hebrew and all that. I, like, really, really want to study the Bible."

All eyes swiveled to Jude.

"Ms. Burke, if that is what you want, my sister or my mother would be glad to come by—"

"I want you," Jasmine interrupted, her eyes smoky. "And call me Jazz."

"Certainly, Jazz," my mother broke in smoothly. "If you would like to name a time for us to talk, then I could—"

"Forget it," Jasmine snorted in disgust and stomped off.

"That was an experience for the yearbook," Clive said cheerfully and peered sadly into his empty teacup. "And here I was hoping that she was bringing us a fresh pot."

"The 3-0-A," Basil spoke thoughtfully as if we hadn't just witnessed the worst return visit in Christian history. "That's what intrigues me. I had seen it on the back panel of the armoire, and I'm convinced it is some kind of indication from Mr. Wildeve. Otherwise, it wouldn't have been etched in the bottom of the urn."

"Perhaps it's only one-half of a clue, and we just haven't found the other half yet," Aunt Astrid said thoughtfully and then put her half-eaten slice of pizza back on her plate, freeing her hands to rub her forehead. "Goodness. I'm so tired, my dears. I can't seem to think anymore."

Everyone but my two great-aunts and Basil looked at one another with varying degrees of consternation. Basil was still staring thoughtfully into space, his blue eyes glassy and sharp. Aunt Astrid continued to rub her temples distractedly, but Aunt Aurora, however, was busily holding a pepperoni slice up to the light.

"Astrid, dear, look," she said excitedly, her eyes as round and as unfocussed as a newborn's. "Does that, or does that not, look like dear Papa?"

"Time to go," my mother said serenely and shoved her chair back from the table.

My mother took Aunts Astrid and Aurora home for their naps while Clive and Tamsin left for work, leaving Basil, Jude, and me free to go back and spend what was left of the afternoon sorting through more of Great-uncle Desmond's appalling souvenirs.

It had taken me well over three hours of scrubbing to bring the derusted keys back to their nearly original splendor. Now, newly dried and oiled, they rested in a tangled mass in the bottom of a chamber pot.

Carrying the clinking mass of metal and porcelain, I went in search of my brother to ask him where the locked tower room was. I found Jude with Basil in the bowels of the manor house, hearing their voices floating eerily up a staircase placed in one of the huge larders. I called down and was told to descend.

The cellars of Tanglewood are huge, rambling, mazelike, cold, and chiseled out of the cliffs, resembling dungeons more than storage. Or more like the secret dwellings of some forgotten sect of religious lunatics than a wine cellar. It was too rough, too cavelike, and too full of surprise niches. I kept expecting a robed and tonsured monk to step out of the shadows and bid me welcome.

I found Basil and Jude near the steps by a row of shelves. They were brandishing a tiny penlight and squinting together at a cobwebbed bottle in Basil's hand. They turned as I came down the last stone step.

"What do you need, *poca*?" Jude asked absently and turned back to deciphering the handwritten label.

"What's that?" I asked curiously and ventured closer. I could sense Basil's suppressed excitement.

"Come here," Jude said and shifted to draw me to his side. "It's a bottle of wine that looks to be over two hundred years old. See here?" He indicated the lip of the scoured looking glass. It bulged out in a bulbous rim of dense green. "This is hand-blown and very old. Now look at the label." He turned the bottle slightly in Basil's hand. Inked letters and numbers on rough, yellowed paper dissolved downward into tobacco-colored tears.

"What does it say?" I asked. Basil gave me a distracted smile.

"We aren't able to make it out, angel." He swiped his thumb over the label in a futile effort to make something clearer. "Perhaps we should just bring it up into a brighter light." Basil turned the beam of the tiny torch to the ascending staircase, and we climbed the steps up and out into the faint sunshine penetrating the kitchen-attached workrooms. Basil held the bottle up in a beam, and we crowded around him.

"It's French," I said, pointing to a barely discernible "aux" written in drippy brown ink.

"Very probably," Basil said and squinted blue eyes at the smeared letters. His feathery lashes were nearly transparent in the slant of sunshine. "Can anyone make out a date anywhere?"

"That's what I've been looking for," Jude said and touched the edge of the label. "That looks a bit like an 8 and a 3. Or perhaps another 8."

"Is the exact date important?" I asked and shifted the heavy key-filled chamber pot to the crook of my other elbow. "What about where it was made?"

"Both are important, my angel." Basil fingered the cork and turned the bottle in his hands. "Perhaps I can find another in the cellars. One without a ruined label."

"Are they valuable?" I asked, thinking about some of the aged crates of wine that had been sold in estate auctions.

"Perhaps." Basil handed the bottle to Jude and started back to the cellars. "But this is more about supporting a little idea I have." He held his hand up before either one of us could ask what he meant. "Patience, my dears. I will tell you about it when I find enough evidence to support my little theory."

I watched him leave and then snagged Jude with my free hand when he began to follow Basil back into the bowels of the manor house.

"Wait. Can you show me where the locked tower room is? I want to see if any of these keys fit."

"You don't have much time, *poca*," Jude said and stepped past me to deposit the wine bottle on a dirt-encrusted work surface. He looked at his watch. "I have less than an hour before I have to get back for the meeting. Can we make it quick?"

The locked room was placed midway up a tower overlooking the ocean cliffs. The architect of Tanglewood must have loved mazes since nothing about the manor was orderly or symmetrical. I was hopelessly lost by the time we reached our destination, and every time I rounded a turn, I expected to face the red eyes of a Minotaur.

Jude walked me to the closed door of the locked tower room, but didn't leave, waiting to check the room for safe entry once the door was opened. It took almost ten minutes to find the key that turned the tumblers in the lock, mainly because the lock needed to be oiled, and Jude had to go back downstairs to find the oilcan. When I finally did turn the key, my fingers were reddened from wrestling with the rough bits of iron.

The door creaked open like the gate to a crypt.

It was a bedroom. I don't know what I expected, but it wasn't the ragged dissolving splendor that greeted me. I felt shivers run up my body, one after the other, fluffing up my hair like a spooked dog. The decades of neglect were obvious. Swags of cobwebs hung from the chandelier and from the canopy of the immense bed that took up the center of the octagonal room. Late-afternoon sunlight streamed in the crusty windows, riding on slabs of fairy dust refusing to land. Thick smears and pale dirt coated everything, and the air smelled like the prehistoric basket of Uncle Desmond's unwashed socks that I had tripped over earlier that morning. The shivers of apprehension turned into shivers of revulsion as Jude stepped past me to kick away the carcass of a spider. It spun away from the toe of his shoe like a dirty prune.

"Stay here, *poca*," he said unnecessarily and took a slow tour of the room, looking at the walls, checking the insulation wrapped electrical conduits, the immense fireplace, the furniture, and testing the floorboards that creaked as he stepped on them. After a few moments, he gave me the okay to step in. I wasn't sure, anymore, that my curiosity was bigger than my desire to avoid the decay.

Dead spiders were everywhere in crusty lumps along with the shriveled specks of dead flies and vermin pellets. The dust crunched underfoot, and I felt like I was walking on mildewed talcum powder. As I stepped into the room, I couldn't help but feel a pang of regret at seeing such a splendid room left to disintegrate.

The bed was a canopied four-poster that looked big enough to cradle a sleeping soccer team without crowding. The bedspread and drapes hanging about the four posts were of rotting blue damask and matched the drapes bracketing the windows. The room was crammed with furniture, all of it beautifully carved with rococo handles and scrolls while the immense armoire was still tight and straight. Various built-in shelves and paintings covered the walls below and in between the mahogany molding.

The room looked forgotten, airless, and very, very still as if no one had entered for decades, but it was more than abandoned space. It looked as if the last person to leave, the last one to lock the door, had left in haste. It was in the forgotten ashes still left in the hearth. It was in the displaced hairbrush left on the mantel. It was in the chamber pot peeking coyly out from under the disarranged folds of the bed skirt. It was in the hastily discarded riding habit. I peered closer at the habit, unwilling to touch it.

Stained and crumpled, it was wadded up on the lid of a huge carved chest as if it had been stripped from a warm body and flung onto the nearest surface. Riding boots, spotted and cracked from neglect, were propped up at the foot of the chest as well, enhancing the impression of hasty flight.

I frowned at the chamber pot and then looked down at the one I held encircled in my arm, the obvious twin to the one peeking out from under the bed.

Then without any preceding thought, the fuzz on my arms stood up again, and a chill ran through me in a wave. I looked back at the riding habit and consciously identified what my subconscious had noted a few seconds earlier. Pinned to the lapel of the crumpled riding jacket was a brooch in the shape of a starburst. Half-hidden in the folds of cloth, its exact contour and color was obscured, but I recognized it. Clean and polished, the grimy starburst would be silver and robin's egg blue with the multifaceted stones shooting sparks in the light. I knew because my grandmother had one just like it. Hers was the twin to the one her mother had owned.

A long-forgotten story filtered back to my mind. My grandmother had told me that my great-grandmother was six months pregnant when she was thrown from her horse and hemorrhaged to death. When I had heard the story, I was not yet ten years old, and, not knowing much about the details of childbirth and pregnancy, all I could wonder at was my great-grandmother's folly to ride a horse with a child in her belly. Now, as the story came back, I stared at the discarded riding habit.

I was standing in my great-grandmother's bedroom. The one she had died in. I suddenly noticed something I had missed earlier because I hadn't been looking closely enough. Dark rust stains spattered the riding habit's divided skirt and seemed welded to the jacket on top of it.

Jude's hand touched my shoulder, and I shrieked, nearly dropping the chamber pot.

"What's wrong with you?" he asked, amused, but didn't wait for an answer. "It's time to go."

"Jude, I think this is Great-grandmother's room. I think this is the room she died in."

"How do you know?"

I gestured toward the riding habit encrusted with blood long since dried into glue and dust.

"You mean this?" he asked and leaned down to snatch the disgusting garment from the chest. He held it up before I could stop him and pried the stains apart. It crackled under his tugging hands, and little powdery flecks of brown floated away. Horrified, I took a step backward as he held the stains up to his nose and sniffed.

"The insane old sot," he murmured. Dropping the jacket back to the chest, he leaned toward the bed and swiped a finger across the thick dust. He contemplated his gritty fingertip for a moment and then touched it to his tongue.

"What are you doing?" I burbled crossly and pressed the chamber pot into my stomach. Ignoring me, he reached up, freed a string of cobweb hanging from the bed's drapes, and dragged it over his tongue, grimacing at the taste. He wiped his mouth with his forearm and surveyed the room.

"The insane old sot. I wonder what he's up to now."

"What?" I demanded and hiccupped deep into the chamber pot. Jude suddenly noticed me and laughed.

"Bella, it's not real. Not any of it. The blood is gravy, the dust is flour, and the cobwebs are spun sugar. Old, stale, and sprayed heavily with hair lacquer to hold its shape, but still spun sugar."

"This isn't Great-grandmother's bedroom?"

"I'm sure it's her bedroom, all right, even though it's not the customary suite of rooms like Uncle Desmond's," he said and looked around with slow appraisal, taking the chamber pot from me to drop it on the bed with a musical clink. "But this whole room, all of it, is a setup from Great-uncle Desmond."

"How do you know?"

"I smelled gravy when I first disturbed the jacket. Then when I looked around, it became obvious." He grinned and toed a wooden leg of the immense bed. "Think about it. Why would they leave a blood-spattered riding habit on the chest, but make the bed with clean sheets?"

"So this is another clue," I said, feeling stupid for succumbing so easily to atmosphere and missing the obvious.

"Probably," he admitted, turning a slow circle at the foot of the bed, his eyes slowly raking the walls. "But I don't know how yet."

"Nothing makes sense," I sighed and touched a fingertip to the floury bedspread. "Why would Great-uncle Desmond taunt his sisters that they wouldn't be able to find what he had hidden and then make the clues obvious?"

"They aren't, *poca*. Would you have normally looked into that urn under the ashes? Would you have climbed into the armoire and felt the etchings on the back panel?"

"No." I found myself staring at a framed watercolor hung up between a set of tall windows overlooking the ocean. The picture was a blue wash of fog rolling over a sea.

"It's the same for the sarcophagus. For it to be valuable, the sarcophagus has to remain sealed. Normally a person wouldn't have taken the chance to open it." He paused and then came over to look at the watercolor I had been examining with interest. "And this room. Aunts Astrid and Aurora wouldn't have had the strength or the interest to clean it themselves. If it was to be done at all, professional cleaners who wouldn't have had a clue would have been hired."

"What I don't understand is why did he go through all that trouble? Why bother to even leave them anything? Why not give it to the National Trust to begin with?"

"Who knows?" Jude gently lifted the framed watercolor from its hook and held it toward a dusty slant of light. "Maybe he wanted to play one last joke. He probably thought he was going to be somewhere watching it all."

"'A natural-born lateral thinker,'" I quoted Clive Chaucer's assessment of Great-uncle Desmond's personality. "This makes me think that the first thing to check in this room is the gravy-covered riding habit."

"That's what I think as well." He replaced the oddly compelling watercolor back to its place on the wall. "But we don't have time right now. We have only forty minutes to get back, change, and make it to the meeting. You'll have to come back tomorrow."

"I don't want to wait until tomorrow to find out what's in Destiny's bedroom." I frowned and followed my brother out of the room. "Want to come back tonight after the meeting?"

"No."

"Why not?"

"Ask Brandt. As far as I know, he's free after his meeting. I've got to get up early tomorrow and go to the Frazer's."

Lottie and Rory Frazer own a farm just outside of the village's boundaries. Well into their seventies and as tough as stale jerky, they claimed that the best time to talk about the Bible with them is before their breakfast of eggs, bacon, kippers, toast, and homemade preserves. On a Cornish farm, that's about one hour before the sun sets in China.

"What are you doing tomorrow?"

"I have to finish putting together a talk for the Service Meeting this Thursday. I might have to substitute for Albert."

"So you aren't coming back here tomorrow?" I asked as we entered the kitchen, and I grabbed my rucksack from beside the cookers. Jude spotted the ink-smeared bottle of wine on the counter with a note under it from Basil. He paused to snag the note and read it, shaking his head absently at me as his eyes passed over the beautifully scrolled handwriting.

"I don't know, *poca*," he said, put Basil's note back on the counter, and urged me toward one of the crooked doors leading to the courtyard where he had parked his van. "We're going to be late if we don't hurry. Go get in."

Within seconds we were in the van and speeding down the manor's drive. Even though we missed most of the potholes, the van's worn chassis danced from rut to rut like a drunk tied to a pogo stick. We bounced with wild abandon, and if it weren't for my brother's skill at maneuvering his cantankerous vehicle, we would have bounced sideways to the cliff and into the sea.

The van doesn't hurry well on cobblestones, either. When Jude stopped in front of the inn to let me out, I stumbled from the passenger door to fall on my face on the wide steps and kiss the smooth stones.

"Cute," Jude said dryly and waited for me to get up and reclaim my rucksack from the seat. "At least I got you back in time to get cleaned up."

"So are you going to ask Brandt to meet me at the manor tonight?" I frowned and picked a vermin pellet that seemed to have gotten hung in my hair like a misplaced earring.

"I'll tell him to call Dad's mobile and leave a message if he can't." Jude was Brandt's assistant. "He'll call in time to let you know."

"Thanks. I'll probably see you tomorrow then," I said and squinted at my brother's watch dial before slamming the door. He drove off with a quick wave.

I had just enough time for a hurried shower. I probably had enough unwanted pellets and flour on my body to make raisin cookies for the whole group tonight. I slung my rucksack over my shoulder and decided to take the shortcut through the reception area instead of wending my way past the landscaping to the private wing where we lived.

As I neared the front doors, Rayvyn passed me, going in the opposite direction and leading a small clot of Japanese men arrayed in polyester and cameras. I paused, torn between the need to be on time to the meeting and the desire to know what she was up to. If I hurried, I could do both. I paused long enough to see her reach the ancient mossy fountain in the forecourt.

I let go of the front door and ran back down the steps and on to the circle of lawn to stand with her grinning audience. I edged around them until I found an opening where I could stand in front of everyone.

Kicking off her sandals, Rayvyn clambered up onto the pitted edge of the fountain and balanced herself on its rim. As a rule, I never know what Rayvyn is going to do until she has already done it. I stared with as much interest as her entourage did except I wasn't smiling, bobbing my head, and aiming a camera.

She raised her arms over her head and clasped her hands, looking like an organic virgin about to offer herself to the volcano. Surely she wasn't going to dive headfirst into the shallow water?

"I call this," she said, stretching out a hairy leg and hooking her bare foot around the head of the stone maiden pouring water from her urn into the basin, "Cosmic Gambols of Innocence."

Oh, great. Interpretive posing on a slick edge with sharp stony protrusions. I felt faint. Short of using a bazooka to pick her off the edge, I had no chance of stopping her. I tossed my rucksack behind her admirers and held up my hands like I was trying to safety spot a gymnast. Or stop a train, which I had a better chance of doing.

"Rayvyn," I heard the familiar voice of my brother and saw Michael in his suit and tie pushing his way through the crowd at the opposite edge of the fountain. Either she didn't hear him over the appreciative noises of the smiling men, or she was lost in creative concentration. Or perhaps this wasn't her first interpretive pose of the day, and she had already bounced headfirst off a stone scroll.

Michael looked faint as she suddenly arched her back in a spine-defying curl backward. It didn't look much like a cosmic gambol, whatever that was in Rayvyn's brain. It looked more like she had just taken a snort of strychnine and was convulsing in an astounding death agony. Everyone held their breath.

Then with a double-jointed flutter that would have impressed even a carnival freak, she tightened her spinal curl, touched the crown of her head to her ankle, and let her arms fall gracefully into the water. You could have heard a pin drop if it wasn't for the noisy tinkle of the fountain. No one moved.

We froze in astounded awe, our mouths agape, our eyes dilated, our cameras poised, but still.

It was a tribute to the utter grotesqueness of the moment. I had never seen a human so not-human-shaped before. She should have called the pose "Cosmic Pretzels." The only movement in our tableau of shock was her long braid bobbing about in the water.

And then her bosom gave way to gravity. It slid free of its blousy confines and plopped noisily into the water like a bobber at the end of a fishing line. Or an apple in the toe of a very long sock.

The spell was broken. Cameras clicked around me in a frenzy, Michael blanched and turned away, and the little knot of entranced Japanese men surged forward like the police line in a riot.

Oh, why not. I started clapping. That degree of selfless exhibitionism for the sake of art deserved acknowledgment. It was the least I could do before she got dismissed. I added a whistle to my shout of "bravo!"

"Isabella!" A firm hand spun me around in midclap, and I found myself face to necktie with my father. Rayvyn must have registered his presence as well because she fell off the slippery edge of the fountain into the water with a Japanese spraying splash behind me. I felt the cold water flick across the back of my shirt. The frenzy of clicks around me intensified.

"Get in the house, child," my father's brogue was pronounced, and his tone grim. "Get cleaned up and get ready."

"Yes, sir." I ducked and hastily retrieved my trampled rucksack, sneaking a quick peek behind me at Rayvyn climbing out of the fountain. She was covered in helping hands, and one elderly gentleman was draping his jacket over her shoulders. Wasting no more time, I ran home to wash and get dressed for the meeting.

The meeting that night was made up of the congregation broken up into smaller groups. The one I was assigned was held in an extra room at the inn and was almost ready to start when I darted in the door and found a seat next to Tamsin. We always perched together in the corner on a set of hard stools, risking early hemorrhoids to spare those who already suffered from them.

The room is furnished with our elderly congregation in mind. The chairs are plush and upright, the lamps are high wattage, and the toilet has guardrails and handgrips. There's even an economy-sized tube of denture fixative next to the caddy of laxative tea that somebody had brought for snack nights.

My baby brother Gabriel was newly returned from Violet's and sat by my mother. He chose that moment to notice me seated next to Tamsin.

"Bella!" he called out excitedly as if we had lost sight of each other during a dangerous expedition and had just now regained contact. "Look! I have a loose tooth!"

Before my mother could restrain him, he jumped from his seat and ran to me, dodging bunions, arthritic knees, canes, Zimmer frames, and bulging purses with a hand fixed firmly to his mouth. Grinning, he clambered up the stool to my lap, removed his hand from his mouth only long enough to give me an enthusiastic kiss that echoed over the overlapping voices, then opened wide, showing me the wiggling tooth pinched between his thumb and forefinger. It suddenly came out, and blood welled up in a huge crimson bubble.

I grabbed his clip-on necktie as if it were a disposable tissue and staunched the trickle of blood running rapidly down his chin before it could spot his pristine white shirt. Or more importantly, the cashmere blouse I had borrowed from my mother. I rolled my eyes at my mother and then stood up with my little brother tucked sideways under my arm like a parcel. He seemed oblivious to the necktie I held wadded to his face as he studied the newly ejected molar with disbelieving green eyes. I made my way to the loo as discreetly as I could.

When I returned with my freshly laundered little brother, the meeting was in full swing. My father asked a question as I settled on my stool with Gabriel. He waited for me to open my book before he called on Great-aunt Aurora, who was sitting on one of the sofas with her sister beside her.

"Babylon's reputation for pleasure seeking is well documented," Aunt Aurora began coherently, cluing me in as to what paragraph we were on. "And as Historian Herodotus claimed . . . ," and that was the last of the English words to be uttered in her comment. She suddenly switched into rapid Spanish without even a pause. It was like the smooth switch of a railway train onto a different track with the waiting crowd watching it veer away from them into the horizon. Jasper Penhallow popped out his deaf aid and began tinkering over it with a yellowed fingernail.

When Aunt Aurora was done, her sister gave her an incredulous look and then began a loud argument in stage whispers that echoed sibilantly around the room.

"It is not, Aurora."

"It is too, dear."

"That simply isn't true."

"It certainly is."

"I believe you must be tired, dearest."

"Am not," she hissed.

My father gave Aunt Astrid an amused smile and asked her if she would like to translate her sister's comment for the rest of the group. Looking suddenly aware of the fixed gazes around her, Aunt Astrid smoothed an already-smooth page of her open Bible, coughed primly, and delivered the English translation of Aunt Aurora's Spanish words.

"She . . . er, basically said with so many words that the . . . uh . . . mark of the beast was that . . . er . . . mole on Hitler's neck."

The silence that greeted Aunt Astrid's translation was profound. You could have heard a rat burp. Jasper Penhallow was the first to break it.

"Is that a new thought?" he barked loudly and vigorously scratched the inside of his nostril with a gnarly forefinger, his one good eye swinging over to pin my father to his chair. "Eh, young man? It's not in my book. I must have studied an old one. Anyone care to trade?"

Michael wasn't faring too well. While my mother radiated compassion, my brother was resting his chin on his hand and pressing a finger to his lips so hard they were becoming bloodless. I quickly vacated my stool, plopped Gabriel on my seat as a marker, and darted to the lavatory before I could even glance at Tamsin's studiously averted profile, regrettably missing my father's response.

After the meeting was over, Tamsin and I retired to a quiet corner to have our first words together since we had parted after lunch at the Moonstone.

"You won't believe what I found out at the library today," Tamsin murmured, her eyes on elderly Chloe O'Rourke as she tottered over to my father to sit down beside him. Chloe made me think of a tiny parrot that had been caught in a blender. She's small, veiny, frail, and colorful, with oversized shaggy tropical-print dresses and wigs that hang askew on her cantaloupe-sized head. Her lips are always glossed in crimson that bleeds outward like a sunset, and her dark eyes are always streaked with brilliant indigo. That evening her shaggy wig was the color of overripe tomatoes.

"Did you find out anything about Clarisse De Mornay?"

"No." She managed to tear her eyes away from Chloe to look at me, and the look she gave me was mildly perplexed. "I couldn't find out anything about her. But I did find out something about your great-uncle Desmond."

Before I could reply, Gabriel came skipping up to us. He opened his mouth at Tamsin, showed her the gap in his teeth, and then solemnly fished the grisly tooth from his pants pocket to offer it to her as a love token. Gabriel had somehow gotten it into his head that once he receives a biweekly allowance, he and Tamsin will wed.

"I thought I told you to put it in the trash," I said and closed his fingers around the tiny clotted object, hiding it from Tamsin's stoic gaze.

"Now?" He looked at me with wide green eyes, his lashes longer than any girl's and twice as thick. He looked like an underfed cherub in an Italian fresco. "I thought you meant later."

"Put it back in your pocket. Tamsin's seen it," I said and squeezed one of his plump cheeks. "Can you do us a favor, *uvetta*? Can you go get Dad's phone and bring it to me?"

"Okay," he said happily and bounded away to Chloe and my father who were sitting side by side engaged in earnest conversation. I spotted my mother sitting in a group clustered around Aunts Astrid and Aurora. I looked back at Tamsin.

"Can you go somewhere tonight?"

She nodded, not asking what I had in mind.

"I found something in the manor I want to show you, and while we go there, we can talk—," I began and then paused as Gabriel came back with my father's mobile phone held out in both hands as if he were transporting a gem-encrusted chalice. I took it from him. "Thank you, *bambino*."

I turned the mobile on and checked for messages. There were none, which meant that Brandt had agreed to meet us at Tanglewood. I smiled and turned off the mobile, slipping it into my skirt pocket.

"Do you want to come to the manor with me?" I asked Tamsin. Gabriel suddenly lunged, wrapped skinny arms around my thighs, and pressed his face into my hip like he was trying to smother himself.

"Oh mistress, by the gods, do nothing rash!" Gabriel said indistinctly into my left buttock, quoting a snatch from Matthew Arnold.

"What?" I jerked sideways, startled, then looked up at Tamsin's amused stare. "Did he just say what I thought he said?"

"Yes," Gabriel answered, his voice muffled.

I pried his anaconda-like grip from my middle and hoisted him up by his shoulders until we were nose to nose. His green orbs were magnified in my vision like a bug's. "Where on earth did you learn that?"

"Clive Chaucer." He grinned, his feet dangling. "Bella, can I go with you? If you love me, you would take me with you."

"No, you can't go with me and Tamsin."

Gabriel's eyes slowly rolled to the back of his head like green marbles. Tamsin looked faintly alarmed when Gabriel's head lolled backward.

"Oh no." I gently shook Gabriel's floppy body, grinning. "Oh, what have I done?"

I walked over to my father and Chloe and solemnly draped Gabriel's limp figure over my father's knees as if I were ceremoniously gifting him with a dead baby.

"What's this?" my father asked.

"I broke his heart," I sighed. One of Gabriel's eyelids flickered open.

"Bella, you're supposed to kiss me awake."

"You're shameless, you little dwarf," I told my baby brother. Chloe peered up at me out of startled eyes. They looked like licorice jelly beans hidden in tissue paper.

"I know, I know," she warbled at me and patted her sharp little rib cage with age-palsied hands. "But I'm lonely, and he's got all his hair."

"Pardon me?" I blinked at her, realizing that her statement was directed to me, and for one disorienting second, I thought she was referring to my father.

"Jasper Penhallow has asked her to marry him, and Chloe was just asking me if I would do the wedding." My father grinned.

"We want a white wedding, and I would like Gabriel to be the ring bearer," she warbled. Both of Gabriel's eyes shot open at her words, and he tried to sit up. My father put a large hand across my little brother's stomach, anchoring him. Gabriel exhaled noisily, gave up trying to interrupt, and dropped his head back to peer upside down at Chloe.

"Congratulations!" I said and impulsively leaned down to plant a kiss on Chloe's pleated cheek.

"Thank you, dear," she chirruped and smiled coyly at me, accepting my kiss. I fished in my skirt pocket for the mobile phone and held it out to my father.

"Tamsin and I want to go with Brandt to the manor tonight. Is that all right? We won't be too long," I said. My father shot his cuff to look at his wristwatch. Chloe wobbled in her seat at the sudden movement.

"Have you had dinner yet?" he asked. I shook my head. Chloe smiled tremulously at my father, interrupting us.

"I appreciate the offer, young man, but Jasper would be jealous. We aren't seeing other people."

My father grinned at both of us but otherwise ignored Chloe's bemused misunderstanding.

"Pete and Rayvyn should still be in the kitchen, rosebud. Take Tamsin with you and get something to eat."

"So it's good?"

"After you eat, child. Don't stay out too late and go ahead and keep the phone with you." He smiled and gave me a paternal pat on my rear. I had been dismissed with his blessing.

"Thanks." I blew a kiss at my baby brother, left them to discuss the wedding, informed my mother where I was going, and gathered up my books, my purse, and Tamsin to go change our clothes into something more practical.

It took less than five minutes to finish changing. Tamsin always left a change of clothes in my closet, and I always kept a pair of jeans at her room in the boardinghouse. I found two hefty torches in the pantry and loaded them into my rucksack before taking Tamsin to the inn's kitchen for a quick bite to take with us.

Rayvyn and Pete were in one of their habitual confrontations when we pushed our way through the swinging doors.

Pete was bellowing and snorting like a frightened bull caught in quicksand. Rayvyn, however, with eyes clamped shut, was serenely embracing herself in the center of the room and exhaling so loudly through her sinuses she sounded as if her head had sprung a leak. Whatever she was doing, it was pretty much the New Age version of "la, la, la, la, la, I can't hear youuuuu . . ."

I tuned Pete out when I caught the gist of the argument we had walked in on. It somehow concerned Pete's dinner of chops and the resultant likelihood that Pete's offspring will be born with pork for pea brains. Tamsin stood frozen in the doorway while I walked in and found a fresh loaf of bread.

"Is roast beef all right with you?" I asked. She nodded wordlessly. I found a large serrated knife and began sawing off the required slices of rye while Pete threw his hands up in disgust and disappeared into the walk-in cooler. Even though Rayvyn's eyes were shut, she seemed to sense his bodily withdrawal. Her pose relaxed, and she opened one hazel eye to look at me.

"I have Michael's gift."

It took me a minute to recall her plans to order some kind of health aid for my brother. I glanced up at Tamsin, stifling my smile, and then focused on cutting the last slice of bread. Rayvyn opened both eyes and bent forward across the table to lean toward me. Any closer to me and she would have to splay herself out like roadkill over its wooden surface.

"When do you think I should give it to him?"

I laid out the four slices of bread and pondered what to tell her, rolling the remainder of the loaf back in its paper.

"Do it at lunch after the crowd have been in." I walked into the cooler for the pan of roast. Pete was sulking behind the mutton, his arms crossed over his massive chest as he leaned back against the cooler's wall. It was obvious that even the cooler wasn't cooling his temper yet. He gave me a frustrated glance and shifted to stare balefully at the bacon.

"I'll be in for a late lunch, so come get me for the presentation," I called out to Rayvyn and walked back out carrying the homemade horseradish sauce and the pan of beef. I began spreading the sauce on the rye.

"What gift?" Tamsin murmured from the doorway, breaking her silence in a hesitant voice.

"I'll tell you later," I said quickly. Tamsin was appalled by Rayvyn's eccentricities, and she already looked primed to bolt from the kitchen.

I laid the slabs of roast on the prepared bread and salted them. Rayvyn looked down at the half-made sandwiches of roast beef as if I were seasoning blobs of poison-laced lard and took a deep breath. Pete, having seen me carry out the pan of beef, knew what was about to erupt from Rayvyn's mouth.

"Don't even start." Pete's big bullet-shaped head appeared from around the edge of the cooler door, and he surveyed Rayvyn with irritation. She whirled to glare at him. Her gypsy skirt flared out like flames at her abrupt movement, and she looked down, distracted by the swirl of drama. The horror on her face was replaced with a small smile. Then she swirled again.

"Why don't you go hug a tree?" he growled at her as I wrapped the finished sandwiches in waxed paper and handed the pan of beef to him. He took it from me and put it down in the cooler with exaggerated self-control. "Not everyone wants to be a cud chewer, you dingy hippie."

Their nightly ritual was threatening to erupt again. Entertaining as it was, it was time to leave and get Tamsin to a socially safe place. I snatched the sandwiches from the table, barely having time to grab two cans of soda before Rayvyn swooped down on the serrated bread knife with its nonexistent point.

"I heard that!" she yelled and spun around again, watching the wild arc of her cherry-colored skirt with approval. Then she turned and brandished the knife like she was leading a cavalry charge, stabbing its dull point toward the ceiling. "I will now do the dance of anger!"

There was a swirl of air, and Tamsin's body was gone.

"Don't kill him," I murmured to Rayvyn, ducked away from her, and made my way toward the door. Caught up in the dramatic flare of her skirts, Rayvyn barely flicked a glance in my direction as she began whirling around the kitchen like a cog that shot its moorings. I wondered fleetingly if she would even notice if I exchanged the somewhat dangerous knife in her hand for the innocuous melon baller sitting by the sink, but then I remembered her rather protuberant eyeballs and thought better of it.

I found Tamsin waiting nervously at the inn's front doors. I snagged my rucksack from the reception desk and handed her a sandwich and a can of soda.

"Don't worry," I told her cheerfully and led the way outside to the front car park and its sweep around the fountain. "They always carry on like that. If they didn't hate each other so much, they'd get married."

She looked doubtful and followed me to her red Mini, unlocked her door, and then unlocked mine so I could get in. She started the car, put it in gear, and began to circle around the front sweep toward the lane out.

"Tell me what you found out at the library today," I prodded once we had cleared the inn's massive wrought-iron gates. The night was cool and clear with stars flung overhead like a spray of frost, and I could see the starlight reflected on the waves below us as we drove toward the village. Tamsin rolled her window down, and salted air eddied into the car around us.

"It's pretty strange," she said and ran her free hand over her forehead to untangle her flying bangs. "I don't know how to tell you."

"Start at the beginning," I suggested and studied her perplexed profile in the green light thrown by the dash.

"First of all, I couldn't find any kind of mention of a Clarisse De Mornay. There were three De Mornays registered in the computer records, but they were all males. Unmarried as far as I could make out. And there were only two Clarisses born in 1756, and they both died young. One died in her teens. She was Constance Clarisse Shelwood. And the other, Clarisse Hart, died as an infant."

"What's odd?"

"If Clarisse De Mornay existed, she should have been in the computers. We have more than one program to research the name." She paused to navigate the sharp turn into the village, carefully descending the hillside of smooth cobblestones in front of us. "I can't think, though, why she isn't mentioned in any of the records unless, of course, I was right, and she really was a dog. Someone's terrier. Or she never existed and was a figment of your great-uncle's imagination."

"Maybe that's it," I said. "Maybe the only clues on the urn are the figures etched inside and not the name on it."

"This brings me to the really odd thing I found out this afternoon," she said and waited until we reached the outskirts of the village and was forced to a crawl. Ancient buildings leaned over us, nearly blocking the moonlight. I rolled my window down and leaned out to peer up at the sliver of stars directly overhead.

"What?" I asked quietly and savored the cool air lifting the hair from my neck.

"I don't know for certain. Most of this is a guess, but I think I'm right. I never saw him. Ms. Dilly would let him in about an hour before the library was officially open."

"Who?" I pulled my head back in to look at her.

"Your great-uncle."

"Uncle Desmond?" I echoed her, startled. "What was he doing in the library? Uncle Desmond avoided coming into the village whenever he could. That's the only reason he kept on Rawlings. To run errands for him and to shoot trespassers." I paused, thinking of the homemade laboratory in the manor's kitchens. "That, and to play Igor. What was he doing?"

"According to Ms. Dilly, he came in for a few weeks for about four or five months before he died. She said he sat in the local section."

"The local section?" I repeated and tried to picture the layout of the library. "Isn't that where books on local history and all the maps are kept?"

"And books and charts on local genealogy," Tamsin said and glanced at me.

"You think that he was looking up something in local genealogy?" I asked. Tamsin shrugged. Finally clearing the heart of the village, we began the long climb to the hills and crags behind Halfmoon. She shifted down, and the car began to chug.

"There's more. I'll tell you why I think he was looking over genealogy." She paused. "Of course, all I can find are the records. Do you remember that you asked me to check him out as well as Clarisse?"

I nodded.

"Well, I found your great-grandparents' marriage certificate." She waited until we crested the hill overlooking the back of the village and then pulled over to the side of the lane, stopping the car and sliding the gearshift into park. She fished her bulging purse from the back of the Mini and pulled out a sheaf of papers, handing them to me. "Your great-uncle Desmond was born almost three years before they were married."

"What?" I said incredulously and took the scroll from her to unroll it as she turned on the car's overhead light. "He wasn't legal then?"

"He was legal. It's just that Destiny wasn't his mother. Your great-grandmother was Sir James Wildeve's second wife. His first wife was Sarah Entwhistle from London. She bore him Desmond."

She waited as I scanned the sheaf of papers. The topmost sheet was a copy of my great-grandparents' wedding lines. Later, I was to find out that there was something in their wedding lines that I should have seen if I had been alert enough, but I was too gobsmacked by the news that my great-grandfather had married twice. As it was, I merely saw the date of their wedding. The second sheet was Great-uncle Desmond's birth certificate. The third paper was of Sarah's wedding lines, and the fourth sheet was a death certificate. I held it up.

"Sarah's."

She nodded.

"Where's Tyne Hospital?" I asked and then noted Sarah's cause of death. "Pneumonia."

"I can't find it yet." Tamsin shrugged. "It isn't in operation anymore, and it wasn't local, so I'm going to check other places next. Perhaps it was in London."

"So Desmond's mother died when he was two years old," I said and dropped the handful of papers to my lap to look out over the rooftops of the village. The sea beyond us stretched away in silvered ripples. "Did you tell Mom or Dad?"

"No." She smiled, turned off the dome light on the car's ceiling, and put the car in gear. We eased back onto the road. "I thought I'd leave that bombshell to you. I almost couldn't stand myself at the meeting. I wanted to tell you so badly."

"I guess we must be on the right course," I sighed and thought about Desmond's sneering clue that Great-aunts Astrid and Aurora would never find the hidden treasure unless they knew him better. I repeated the parts of his clue that now made sense. "You never did have any sense of family heritage. Since I couldn't take it with me, the wealth is all there. It belongs to Destiny, and so do you," I sighed. "This must be the part of Desmond that Aunts Astrid and Aurora didn't know about their brother. Do you think he just found out who his real mother was, and that was why he was poring over the genealogy?"

"Maybe. But if he was, it really doesn't make much sense either. It's local genealogy, remember? Sarah Entwhistle was the daughter of a London solicitor. It's on the marriage lines. She wasn't originally from Cornwall."

"So Great-uncle Desmond must have been looking up Destiny. I wonder how long he had known that Destiny wasn't his biological mother." I turned to stare at Tamsin. "Do you think a three-year-old child would remember?"

"It's hard to tell," she laughed. "I can't even remember last week with any clarity. He was probably raised by a nanny anyway."

"I wonder what Aunts Astrid and Aurora are going to make of this," I said and rolled the sheaf of paper back up and inserted the tight little tube into a side pocket of my rucksack.

"So what are you going to show me?" Tamsin asked and slowed down to turn onto the manor's long pockmarked drive. We began creeping around the potholes like a giant red turtle on a slalom course.

"We unlocked the tower room." I looked out of my window at the cliffs tumbling away from the side of the car. The horizon of sea looked endless. Smiling at the memory of our trek into the room, I began to describe it all and to tell her of Jude's discoveries.

"So you want to go back and look it all over," Tamsin guessed and paused to concentrate on navigating the tiny Mini over a deep rut. "Do you think that there is a clue in there?"

"Probably."

We eventually pulled up in front of the manor, and Tamsin turned off the engine. The strange silence from the day before engulfed us, broken only by the distant sound of the sea. We ate our dinner and stared up through the windshield at the imposing facade in front of us as if we were watching television. The ivy beckoned to us, and I ducked down to peer up at the attic. The windows looked like silver eyes, and the roofline was sharp and clear, cutting off the expanse of stars with a hard edge.

"Are we waiting for Brandt, or are we going in?" Tamsin eventually asked as she crumpled up her empty sandwich wrapper and stuffed it into the overflowing sack she used as a trash receptacle.

"I guess we can go in," I said. "He probably won't be here for another thirty minutes."

Brandt's study group is the farthest out from Halfmoon. He conducts it in a square little farmhouse owned by the oldest sister in the congregation. Chlotilde Tregaren had already overtaken a hundred years of age, and, partaking every year, she is deeply frustrated that she isn't dead yet. To add insult to injury, she is still vigorous enough to get up an hour before the sun does to milk her three cows. She invites Brandt and Jude, his group assistant, to supper once a month before the meeting so she can complain bitterly to them about the splendid state of her bowels, being afraid that she'll be on the earth during Armageddon as a mere spectator and not in heaven as a warrior.

"I've got some good torches." I rummaged through my rucksack and pulled them out, handing one to Tamsin before I shoved my father's mobile into my jean pocket. "Let's go in. I want to show you something in the kitchens first."

"What's in the kitchens?" Tamsin asked as we got out of the car. I dug the front door keys from my other pocket.

"A bottle of wine that Jude and Basil found in the cellars. I want to see if you can make out the label. The ink is all smeared, and Basil was trying to decipher the date."

We let ourselves in the front doors, and, with the aid of the torches, I managed to guide us to the kitchens. The lone bottle with Basil's note sat on the only clear patch of counter below the windows where Jude had left it. I handed the bottle to Tamsin and let her examine it while I read Basil's note.

"Wait," I halted her in middecipher, wondering why Jude didn't tell me what Basil had written. He must have had his mind on the meeting and not on the manor, or he would have readily seen the significance of Basil's words. "Basil says that he found other bottles like this one, but without the labels too far gone. The wine is French like we had thought and had been fermented in 1788 and bottled about five years later." I looked back down at the note. "Why does that keep meaning something to me?"

"What?"

"I don't know. I can't quite catch it. It has something to do with the bathroom armoire, but I can't put my finger on it." I looked up at her again and waved the note under our noses. "But that isn't the exciting part. Basil said that the others he found led him to a wall where there's an inscription chiseled in the stones."

"What's the inscription?" Tamsin asked quietly and set the forgotten bottle back down on the counter where Basil had left it.

"It's in Latin. Translated, it reads, 'I wait beyond the grave.'"

Tamsin rubbed her hands slowly over the bare flesh of her arms and stared at me with her huge eyes.

"So now we have two similar inscriptions," I said, grinning at her. "The one we had found outside on that slab by the garden that said, 'I wait beyond the flames where I dance above light. Silver are my feet, and black is my crown.' Now Basil's note says that there is another inscription on a wall in the cellars. His says, 'I wait beyond the grave.'"

"Wasn't Brandt the one who was checking the manor's wiring yesterday?" Tamsin continued to stare at me. "He was the one who found the generators in the cellars. I'll bet he had seen the inscription that Basil had found. When we read our inscription, he said that it reminded him of something, but he couldn't recall what."

"Let's go," I said excitedly and put my rucksack and Basil's note on the counter by the bottle. I grabbed Tamsin's free hand and towed her behind me to the larder's stairs that led to the wine cellars.

"Where are we going?"

"To see the inscription."

The stairs down into the core foundation of the manor house were far worse than I had remembered, made even spookier by the intensity of night. The smooth stones were gritty underfoot with dirt and decay, and I still expected a robed monk to waft into view from the deep shadows.

We made it to the bottom of the steps and stood uncertainly in the center aisle bisecting the rows of wine racks. A random half of the bottle-shaped niches were filled with wine, and the other half stood eerily empty with nothing but cobwebs to string them together. A solid wall of casks lined one of the walls and stretched away into gloomy infinity, rounding a distant corner to disappear from sight. I played the beam of my torch over the banded casks with their bunged-up holes and age-blackened spigots. They were taller on their sides than Gabriel was standing up.

"Where did Basil say the inscription was?" Tamsin's voice echoed eerily in the cellars' closeness.

"Over the boiler that doesn't work half the time since Great-uncle Desmond had it converted to electric." I stepped around a rack and peered into what seemed to be an arched doorway that led into deeper gloom. I could make out more racks. "I just don't know where that is. Let's try in here."

After ten minutes of wandering, we found the massive boiler.

Once upon a time there had been two tanks, one above the other and fused together. The lowest one would have held flaming logs the size of felled trees while the topmost tank would have held the heated water. Now, Great-uncle Desmond, in a do-it-yourself home project, had managed to encase the lower water tank in electric coils that never worked properly, leaving the top tank full of tepid water. Everything was a tangled mass of wires and rusty pipes. An accidental electrocution waiting to happen.

I frowned at it and shined the beam of my torch over the surrounding walls while Tamsin let hers wander musingly over the boiler as if she couldn't take it all in. After a few seconds, I found the Latin inscription on one of the wall's hewn blocks. It was almost ten feet from the flagstone floor and was surrounded by embellishments carved by long-dead stonemasons.

"Here it is," I said excitedly and held my beam at an angle.

"I wait beyond the grave," Tamsin whispered after a second of staring at it in silence. "Is that thc whole inscription? We had more to the one we found outside."

"I wait beyond the flames where I dance above light. Silver are my feet, and black is my crown." I paused. "Wait a minute. What if we have it wrong? Think about the outside slab's inscription."

"Wrong how? In the actual translation?" Tamsin asked, her low voice echoing weirdly around us.

"No. The punctuation. Listen to it this way." I took care to emphasize the full stop of my intended pause. "I wait beyond the flames. Where I dance above light, silver are my feet, and black is my crown."

"I wait beyond the flames," Tamsin grunted thoughtfully and then added the inscription on the wall above us. "I wait beyond the grave. If the two inscriptions go together, that makes more sense. So what is the second part of the outside inscription? Where I dance above light, silver are my feet, and black is my crown—what does that mean?"

"I have no idea," my hushed voice echoed into silence, and then, without any warning, I became acutely aware that I was standing in a dank cellar with only Tamsin and two torches for company. I shivered and let my beam play over the wall around the mutilated boiler.

"Isabella," Tamsin's voice came out oddly. I turned to look at her. She was staring at a section of the wall behind the worst of the snarled wires. "Look at this." She played her beam over an ornate patch of stonework that was nearly hidden in the tangled shadows. "Does that remind you of anything?"

I frowned, knelt, and trained my torch alongside hers, recognizing what had gotten her attention. I touched the cut scrollwork.

"It's the same carving that's on one of the fireplaces upstairs." I got down on my stomach and shined the torch's beam under the boiler. Its yellow glow hit a wall of soot-blackened stone. "This is also a fireplace. The boiler was installed in an old fireplace niche. What's a fireplace doing in the cellars?"

"A fireplace? The slab outside said, 'I wait beyond the flames,'" Tamsin said softly. I scrambled back to my feet, sopping up a couple of centuries of grit with the front of my shirt.

"I wait beyond the flames means that something is beyond a fireplace?" I suggested and thought about the fireplace upstairs that apparently was born from the same stonemason that fashioned the fireplace in front of us. "So what do you think 'I wait beyond the grave' means?"

"I wait beyond the grave." Tamsin's profile turned suddenly thoughtful, and she turned to stare at me, her eyebrows a straight line over the bridge of her nose. "What was that we said about the sarcophagus clue?"

"Something is in a grave that isn't real?" I said and tried to clear my sudden influx of chaotic thoughts. "Let's go up and check out the other hearth."

At that moment, a rat chose to make its appearance from under the boiler. I saw the red eyes glowing upward a split second before I registered the rodent. I'm not particularly rat phobic, but this one was large enough to drag dead lapdogs up into trees. I gurgled incoherently and levitated.

"Rat!" the scream that burst out from my throat was loud and somewhere on the frequency that only bats can hear. I was surprised that wine bottles didn't shatter somewhere. Then I turned and ran.

"Where?" Tamsin screamed back as we rounded a line of racks. I didn't answer her, not wanting to waste breath on stating the obvious when my oxygen was better used for bounding up the stairs three treads at a time. I certainly wasn't going to be running toward the glaring rodent; ergo, it must be behind us.

I burst out of the stairs, into the pantry, and shot into the kitchen with my torch beam strafing the darkness like the searchlights of World War II London. I careened around a long table with test tubes, stumbled over one of its chairs, and ran full tilt into the solid figure that suddenly loomed in front of me. A hard arm snagged me.

"Bella!" Brandt's startled voice cut across my panic. "What is it?"

I sucked in a loud gasp, my knees buckled in sudden relief, my face fell somewhere into Brandt's stomach, and Tamsin plowed right into my back. We would have all three gone down if it weren't for Brandt absorbing the momentum.

"What happened? Bella, are you all right?" Brandt demanded and shook me. I think he had assumed that I'd fainted, which would be reasonable since my chin was hung on his belt buckle. Tamsin stumbled backward and landed on a chair.

"Rat," I gasped as he hauled me to my feet. "There was a rat in the cellars."

"Are you all right?"

I nodded, still gasping for air, and he jerked me to his chest in a relieved hug, squeezing my lungs in midpant. I grunted like a Russian weight lifter.

"Of course, there are rats in the cellars, you little idiot," he said, released me, and shoved me unceremoniously onto a nearby chair. He ran his hand through his hair and regarded me with exasperation. "Don't ever do that again."

"Go in the cellars?" I gasped.

"No. Take ten years off my life by running at me and screaming like that. I thought . . . I don't know what I thought."

"Sorry," I said and began to laugh. Tamsin had long since left the chair to clamber on an edge of the table, her long legs tucked under her. She started giggling and snorting into the back of her hand. I considered getting on the table with her, but I wasn't so sure that swarms of rodents weren't huddled among the test tubes.

"What made you go into the cellars?"

I pointed with my torch beam to the lone wine bottle on the counter with its accompanying slip of paper.

"Basil's note."

"Wait until you hear what we found out." Tamsin grinned, peering up at him. "It starts with your great-uncle."

It didn't take us long to tell Brandt our story. We began with Tamsin's discovery that Destiny wasn't Great-uncle Desmond's mother and ended with my discovery of the hapless rodent under the boiler. And somewhere in between it all, Tamsin forgot herself long enough to get off the table and get on a chair with her feet once again on the crusty floor.

Our recital over, we dwindled into silence and watched as Brandt surveyed us thoughtfully, his chin tucked in and his arms crossed over his chest. A shock of his chestnut hair had fallen over his forehead, and the fingers of one hand were drumming lightly over his elbow. I recognized the sign. He was processing the pieces we had laid out, and the busy tic of his fingers was very much like the flickering and humming of a computer while it's loading. After a few seconds, he shifted and uncrossed his arms, putting his hands on his hips.

"First things first," he said. "I didn't see an inscription over the boiler. I saw it on a fireplace up here, not the cellars. Show me the one over the boiler."

I debated about whether or not I was ready to brave the rat again, and then decided that the poor rodent was probably more traumatized by the encounter than I was. Besides, I had my brother to save me from killer rats. I could always climb him like a pole. But then, so could the rat. Brandt saw me looking at him.

"The rat wouldn't dare. Not with the noise you two were making." He grinned, reading my mind.

We followed my brother down into the cellars and to the boiler where we picked out the inscription with our torch beams. He studied it for a moment in silence and then shifted his attention to the niche of the boiler-filled fireplace.

"See this pattern you were talking about?" His beam followed the scrollwork cut into the stones. "It's called a Greek key."

I heard a stealthy rustle behind me, and I whirled to shine my light at the racks. The only things winking back at me were the dust-covered bottles. I bent over, trained the beam under the edges of the rack, and searched the cobwebs for beady eyes.

"Is the Greek key cut into the fireplace upstairs with the inscription?" Tamsin frowned. He nodded.

"We're probably talking about the same fireplace."

"So the inscription 'I wait beyond the flames' could still mean the flames of a fireplace," Tamsin murmured. Brandt clamped his hand firmly on my shoulder.

"Come one, *poca,* leave the wildlife alone," he said and pulled me upright. "Let's go on up and look at the fireplace upstairs."

The fireplace that sported the other inscription was the one that Tamsin and I had remembered, though we would have taken a long time to find it if Brandt hadn't been there to direct us to its exact location. It was in one of the manor's larger rooms. It was hard to tell what the room's original purpose had been since it was full of the usual curio clutter. Brandt led us to the fireplace, circumnavigating the mess, and knelt down on one knee to shine his beam up into the flue.

"It's up there?" I asked and got on my knees beside him. I was aware of Tamsin bending down behind us, and I shifted to make room for her. "How did you see it up there?"

Brandt grunted noncommittally and stood up to shift some of the litter from around the fireplace. Part of what he shifted was a mannequin of Elvis in the early years, wearing his skinny dark pants and a white shirt instead of the spangles and sideburns. I glanced at Elvis's feet as Brandt lifted him bodily from beside us. He only had one blue suede shoe on, and I smiled, remembering our discovery of the secret passageway.

"I didn't find the inscription." Brandt deposited the mannequin by a knobby piece of Victorian furniture. "Michael did, and I happened to be in here checking the conduits when he found it. He didn't have time to decipher it, so I did when he and Jude moved on to clear another flue."

Brandt knelt again, this time setting his light down on its end so that the beam was cast upward, and his hands were free. He began running his fingers over the incised letters high up on the back wall of the hearth.

"There's a Greek key here as well. I imagine that the same stonemason laid this fireplace as well as the other one. Maybe it was his signature mark."

"Why didn't he put it anywhere else?" I asked and shifted closer to the hearth.

"He might have," Brandt answered and continued to prod the hearth's walls. "But a house this size had several stonemasons working on it. He may have only done a few."

"What are you doing?" I asked.

"I wait beyond the flames," Brandt answered my question with the words of the hearth's hidden inscription. "I agree with you and Tamsin. I'm wondering if it's a hint to look beyond the hearth wall."

We watched with interest as Brandt thoroughly searched the sooty fireplace. After a few minutes, he sat back on his heels, wiped his grimy hands on the thighs of his jeans, and picked his torch back up to train its beam on the high mantel above us.

"If it has a trigger, it's not in the hearth," he said. "Perhaps it's somewhere in the mantel."

"Maybe Basil would know," I suggested and stood up.

"Perhaps." Brandt stood up beside me and ran a slow hand over the molding of the fireplace. Above it was an ugly painting of a woman with powdered hair. I recognized the French court of Louis XIV by the figure of Marie Antoinette in the foreground.

"I wonder why the other fireplace says 'grave' and not 'flames.' I have a feeling we will know the answer to that once we understand what this reference to the flames means," I said and looked at Brandt. "So what do we do now?"

Brandt checked his watch.

"We still have time to go upstairs and look through the tower room."

# 6

Brandt led the way to Destiny's tower bedroom. It was even more sinister and eerie by torchlight, and I could feel Tamsin shrug off a convulsive shiver when we stepped past the threshold. Brandt laid a light hand on the back of my neck and looked about appraisingly.

"Where do you want to start?"

"What are we looking for?" Tamsin turned and cast a quick glance at me.

"I don't know what we're looking for," I said and walked over to peer down at the crumpled riding habit. "All I know is that Great-uncle Desmond was trying to put us off this room, so there is probably something hidden here. I guess we just look through everything until we find it. We'll probably know it when we see it."

"If this is your great-grandmother's room, may I look through the wardrobe?" Tamsin asked. I nodded.

Tamsin's mother owns a vintage clothing boutique in the tiny Welsh village that they live in. Tamsin had inherited her mother's fascination with the more spectacular vintage fashions, and I knew that she was eager to sift through my great-grandmother's dresses.

While I stood about indecisively, Tamsin opened the armoire's doors and gasped. I joined my torch beam with hers and gasped myself when she reached into the untidy press of clothes to free a waterfall of ruby chips.

"Look at this. This whole gown is hand-beaded." She held it up reverently and jiggled the hanger, turning the crystal beads into shooting sparks.

Brandt, who is completely uninterested in female fashion unless a female is in it, uncrumpled the jacket of the riding habit and held it up. Tamsin saw what he was doing and frowned.

"Is that the riding habit you said was your great-grandmother's?" She lowered her eyebrows when I nodded. "It can't be," she stated baldly. "Fleur MacPherson had it in her shop."

Fleur MacPherson is the aged offspring of a French ballet dancer and a seventy-year-old Scotsman who had died right after she was born. She owns a used-clothing store on the High Street that was once called "Second Chances." It is now known as the Recycling Center, having been renamed by Fleur's environmentally conscious granddaughter after she came back from Argentina wearing hand-dyed caftans and twine jewelry.

"Are you sure?" I asked Tamsin. She jerked her torch to point at the jacket's lapels with the beam.

"I'm sure. I wouldn't forget that black lace. It's handmade. I was sure that Fleur didn't know how valuable it was."

"When did you see it?" Brandt asked. Tamsin shrugged, going back to her inspection of her gown's beadwork.

"About six months ago."

Brandt laughed and dropped the jacket back onto the floury bed.

"Something definitely must be here in this room," he said. "It's all too much of a stage set."

"But where?" I sighed and thought about my great-aunts stating that Great-grandmother had kept her journals in her room. I wondered if that was what we were supposed to be looking for.

I studied the wall shelves around me with renewed interest and then went to the high shelf closest to the head of the enormous bed. It held the most books. Holding the torch eye level, I could barely make out a set of Shakespeare's plays, each bound separately in gummy-looking leather. I tugged tentatively on a ragged spine, but it didn't budge. After a few more tugs on different volumes, I gave up, tasting mildew spores in the back of my throat.

Time and neglect had apparently glued the leather covers together.

I continued to move my beam over the shelf, pausing every now and again to decipher the faded gilt letters. I saw Chaucer side by side with Virgil. Works of history beside huge atlases. I wondered if anything in the shelf was a first edition.

I looked around for the rolling ladder that was usually attached to the higher shelves in stately homes and found only empty rails and tracks. I snagged the vanity's low stool and dragged it over to the shelf, clambering up on its seat to squint up at the books on the topmost shelf.

A row of identically slim leather books, obviously a set of something, was packed in the shelf as tightly as sardines in a tin, laid neatly and regimentally in a perfectly even row. All except for a set of three huge volumes of something that was packed at the left side like a lone brick that had been crammed in. I looked at the spines of the "brick" first.

"Sir Augustus Wildeve?"

"What?" Brandt asked idly, opening a vanity drawer.

"Sir Augustus Wildeve," I repeated. "There are three volumes here that seemed to have been written by him. I didn't know we had an author in the family tree."

"What are they about?" Tamsin asked. I glanced over my shoulder at her as she freed a crush of peacock satin from the armoire.

"It doesn't say. It just has his name on the spine." I turned back to the books and tried to pull one free, but it stuck in a clump to the shelf as firmly as Shakespeare had done. "It won't come out."

"It's the salt air," Brandt said as he closed the drawer he was looking through and pulled open another one. "We may have to sell them in a giant book clod if we can't restore them."

"What are you finding?" I asked. He shook his head dismissively.

"Nothing but gloves and scarves. Everything smells of mice."

"Speaking of mice, Tamsin, when are we going to catch that wild tomcat hanging out at the boardinghouse and bring him here?"

"Tomorrow. After tea at the Bunts. Don't forget you promised to have midmorning tea with them."

"I haven't forgotten," I assured her, running my torchlight over the slender spines of the regimented set next to Sir Augustus. The gilt figures embossed on their backs were numbers and not letters. Years and not titles. Exhilaration welled up, and I swung my torch to pin Brandt and Tamsin in its beam.

"I think I just found Great-grandmother's journals," I said excitedly and pulled the first book free. It came out with relative ease, surprising me.

"Here's a journal for 1916," I said, opening it as Brandt and Tamsin came over to stand beside me. The pages were blank and untouched. I frowned and flipped through all the pages, finding nothing. "It's empty. Nothing has been written in it."

I handed the blank journal to Brandt and pulled another one free. It was blank as well.

"What's going on?" I said, mildly frustrated, and pulled a handful down for Tamsin, handing it to her to go through.

"I think you just found the clue, *poca*," Brandt said, amused.

"Blank journals," I said incredulously. "How does that tell us anything?" He shrugged, still amused, and reached past me to pull down a handful for himself.

"Perhaps the clue comes in more than one part," he said.

"Anything in those?" I asked looking down at Tamsin's bent head as I gathered the last of the journals and tucked them into the cradle I made from my shirt. With the torch under my arm, I jumped from the stool and walked over to the floured bed to deposit the load of diaries. A dusty cloud puffed up into my face.

"No. I haven't found anything, yet," Tamsin answered and tossed a book on the bed beside my pile.

"Keep looking," I sighed. "For all we know, Great-uncle Desmond had hidden a clue between the pages. Or on a page. Maybe he wrote something down."

"Nothing in these, *poca*." Brandt carried the books he had in his hand to the foot of the bed and deposited them on top of my pile of discarded journals.

It took us only a few minutes to complete our search through the virginal pages. There was nothing in any of them. Tamsin had even tried to pick apart the flaps glued down in the covers of each.

"So now what do we do?" I asked. Brandt strode over to the nearly denuded top shelf to searchingly run a hand over the plank. Dusty flour cascaded down with each swipe. After about three passes, Brandt's eyebrows twitched with surprise, and he stepped up onto the seat of the stool to peer down at the plank of shelf.

"What?" I asked when he finally stepped down, looking thoughtful. Tamsin clambered onto the vacated stool and trained her torch beam on the spot he had been staring at.

"Take a look for yourself, *poca*," he said and bent behind me, pinning my knees with a hard forearm and hoisting me up. I peered with Tamsin at the lightly etched '3-0-A' that showed up under our combined torch beams.

"That again!" I wriggled free from my brother's grip to slide to the floor. "It's just like the one in the armoire and in the urn."

"I thought so," Brandt said slowly as Tamsin stepped down from the stool. "But I wasn't sure. I hadn't seen the others. Why don't you show me?"

As quickly as we could, we found our way to the bathroom; and once inside, I pulled open the armoire, climbed in, and found the etching on its back panel with my torch beam.

"What do you think it means?" I asked and watched as he leaned in to run a hand over the rough lettering. He ran his fingers lightly over the stacked figures from the bottom to the top and back again. And then I knew.

"Oh my goodness!" I blurted out and stared at the etching, finally identifying what we had been looking at and speculating about for the last two days without success. I wanted to make sure I was right. "Just a minute. I'll be right back."

I jumped from the armoire, darted out of the bathroom, and sprinted down the hallway in pursuit of my brainstorm without waiting for the others to catch up. I heard Brandt call out to me, but I didn't stop to hear what he said.

I found my way to the tower room without mishap and ran over to clamber on the stool by the shelf. It wasn't until I tried to peer at the surface of the top plank that I belatedly realized that I was too short to see over its edge to the etchings. In lieu of waiting for my brother's obliging boost, I stepped carefully onto the ledges that held the books below me, carefully climbed the shelf face like I was scaling a ladder, and peered at the shallow etchings.

I was right in my guess as to its meaning. And in my excitement, I forgot my precarious position and slipped.

It's funny what the mind decides and discards in the flash of a split second.

I was falling, and, instead of dropping my father's obviously expensive torch and clinging to the shelf to catch myself, I grabbed a handful of books with my free hand. The same chunk of books by Sir Augustus Wildeve. I recognized the sticky roughness under my scrabbling fingers and what had refused to budge earlier was tilting forward en masse. And shifting with the books was the wall shelf.

Spinning a quarter turn on an invisible axis, I had the utterly disorienting impression that the room spun, not me, and then I was flung off. One moment I was splayed on the shelf; the next I was splayed on the floor. And then the shelf inconveniently closed back up again, leaving me in utter blackness.

How wonderfully gothic. How obvious and ridiculous. How highly painful and utterly annoying. In that disorienting split second before I was flung off, I had dropped the torch. It wasn't destroyed, however, by its fall. It was destroyed when I fell on it and smashed it.

It was a good thing the torch was under my stomach. Any higher and I would be changing batteries out of my sternum for the rest of my life. Any lower and I would be able to go to the bathroom in the dark. I rolled off the torch, fighting for air, and stared into the bursting stars above me until I could pull in my first ragged breath.

After a few minutes I sat up, my hand to the pit of my stomach, and tried to orient myself. A belly flop on stones from such a relatively small height is harder on the body than one would think. Breathing slowly, I waited until the stars cleared before I got gingerly to my knees, feeling cautiously around me for the torch. I found it right by my body, a shard-coated cylinder with its head popped loose like an eye hanging from a socket.

I'd never seen air so black before. It was impenetrable, and I felt swaddled past the forehead in utter darkness. It was like a dense fog around me, and I realized that the air I was breathing was not only without light, it was as close and as still as a sealed tomb. Tentatively and cautiously, I clapped my hands, hoping that Great-uncle Desmond had installed Clappers in this passageway as well. He had. A light blinked on, puckering my pupils into pinpoints and bringing instant tears to my eyes.

I was in an empty space that curved to the left around a corner, and I wondered if I was in another secret hallway circumventing the tower room or merely in a hidden niche like a priest's hole. It wasn't very wide. The dust furring the stones looked real enough and not like a stage set from Great-uncle Desmond, but I wasn't about to lick the floor to find out.

The first rational thing I did was to check the walled expanse before me for an exit. The wall was utterly smooth without an indication as to how to trigger the pivot. I pushed against the wall. It was as solid as any other part of the house. At least to me, anyway. I wondered if I was in yet another hidden place with two ways in and only one way out. Maybe it was just like the other passageway Tamsin and I had stumbled into the night before.

Then I suddenly remembered my father's mobile phone in the front pocket of my jeans. Abject relief was mingled with abject fear as I dug it out and opened it, hoping against hope that I hadn't crushed it as well. It seemed intact, and I could tell by the tiny green light when I turned it on that it was still working. I wondered if I would be able to get a signal in the bowels of the wall, then thought it was at least worth a try.

Not only was I elevated in a tower on top of a cliff, I was inside a wall, making the outside barrier thinner than the inside walls of the manor. Then I debated about whom I should call. I couldn't call Brandt who was currently phoneless, thanks to my baby brother's fascination with Mr. Peevey's plumbing.

In the end, I chose to call my brothers' cottage and see who was still up and able to drive out to free me. I didn't choose to phone my parents even though I knew my father would still be up. I wasn't keen on explaining to him how I had inadvertently eluded Brandt and ended up in between the walls covered in crushed rat droppings. As I flicked a black blob from my shirt, I realized that the room couldn't have been sealed, or there would be little rat carcasses as well. I looked around the walls as I waited for someone to pick up on the other end.

Dante answered on the fourth ring.

"You're breaking up, *poca*, I can barely understand you. You're where?" he said after my short explanation of why I was calling.

"I fell into another secret passageway," I yelled slowly and distinctly into the phone. "I can't get out. Brandt and Tamsin do not know where I've gone, and they're still in the house looking for me. I need someone to come over here and open the wall for me."

I could hear Dante's long chuckle over the static while I was talking.

"Are you all right?" he asked. I raised my shirt to peer down at my stomach. It looked like someone had nailed me with a cannonball.

"Yes. I'm fine. Can you come out?"

"Of course. Tell me how to open the wall, and I'll be there in a few minutes."

After giving him the necessary instructions and thanking him profusely, I hung up, pocketed the phone, and decided to pass the time exploring my prison. Perhaps I'd find another way out.

It turned out that it wasn't a maze like the last one. It also didn't have underwear-clad mannequins parading down its length. In fact, there was hardly any length to it at all. It was a small arc-shaped room that had only two objects stashed in its far end.

Not seeing very clearly since Great-uncle Desmond had installed only one low-wattage lightbulb, I crept toward the dimly illuminated objects in the gloom, trying to make out exactly what I was peering at. Something long and brown was shoved against the far wall like a rug rolled up inside out, and beside it was something like a small crate.

I was only five feet away from it when I noticed the note stuck to the center of the long brown roll with an ordinary pushpin. I knew that it was another clue from Great-uncle Desmond. I snatched it free and held it close, reading aloud the familiar spiky writing: "I had told you to try again. Congratulations."

I frowned and looked up at the fat cylinder that the note had been tacked to. When did he tell us to try again? And what exactly had I found? I wrapped my arms around the oblong package and tried to hoist it up, finding it surprisingly heavy. My heartbeat speeded up when I suddenly wondered if I had actually found the treasure. Ignoring the crate for the moment, I gave up on attempting to lift the heavy package from the floor and concentrated on tucking one end of it under my arm and dragging it around the corner toward the light. It was hard going. I finally dropped it under the light of the bulb, and it landed on the stones with the solid thump of a felled tree, bouncing only once. Whatever it was, I hoped that I hadn't broken it.

Then I went back for the crate. It was full of books. I had found Destiny's real journals.

I was hard-pressed what to examine first, and in the end Destiny's journals won out over Great-uncle Desmond's wrapped package. I could easily open the diaries, but it looked as if I was going to need a knife to hack open the mystery parcel. Dante or Brandt could do that once they freed me.

I selected what looked like the first of the journals and opened it to the first page:

*The journal of Destiny Olivia Wildeve for the year of 1915.*

My heart sped up even more, and I dropped down to perch on the package like a frog on a log, oblivious to my surroundings, and read on.

> *I am not sure that I like Cornwall. But, then, I did not exactly favor France, either. Both places seem to be filled with secretive people. The weather in both France and here is pleasant enough if one doesn't mind the storms hanging onto the cliffs. It is only the people. Aunt Jeanine says that I merely need to get used to being in this village. She claims that it is only the move that has indisposed me to this place. Perhaps she is correct, and I have decided to open my mind a little wider to these strange people. But since I am*

*the foreigner here, then perhaps I am the strange one. Tomorrow Aunt Jeanine is inviting a few guests for supper. It is to be a sort of introduction to my stay here and to my roots. I wish that I knew how long that stay is to be. At least until the war is over. Then I may return.*

The next entry was dated two days later.

*The small dinner party last night was a success according to Aunt Jeanine. I wish that I had thought so. I was placed between Colonel Trevelyan and Sir James Wildeve. Perhaps I would have enjoyed it more had I not been monopolized by the colonel, a man who is at least fifty years my senior. He smells of stale tobacco and of the horses he kept talking about. Sir James Wildeve, however, seemed to be much more of a gentleman. He did not talk about his livestock the way the colonel did, and Sir James was most attentive the few times I had managed to speak to him. But he was so quiet, refusing to be drawn into anything more enlightening about himself in spite of my discreet questions. He is not unprepossessing, and his table manners were impeccable. Perhaps I will see more of him. Aunt Jeanine was most discouraging, claiming that a special friendship with him would not suit me.*

I shifted to straddle my loglike perch, settling into a more comfortable position. I was eager to read all about the budding romance between my great-grandparents. It seemed to have been fuelled by pique on my great-grandmother's part and perversity on my great-grandfather's. Enjoying my voyeurism, I read on, skimming past the shorter passages, stopping only to read when I caught the name Wildeve. The next pertinent entry was dated mid-February.

*I saw Sir James again today just outside the milliners. Sir Wildeve looked very handsome on his gray mount, but Aunt Jeanine continued on when I made as if to stop. I know that Sir Wildeve had observed her desire to spirit me away into the millinery, but he tipped his hat to me as if we had already exchanged civil greetings. Tonight after dinner I asked Aunt Jeanine why Sir James was good enough to place next to me at a dinner party yet not good enough for me to greet in the street. She would not tell me. She said that she would not stoop to gossip and that as her niece I was to be guided by her without questioning her judgment. Poor Aunt Jeanine. I do mean to find out.*

The next mention of Great-grandfather was dated four days later.

*Today I managed to create a little time alone with the vicar during tea. Aunt Jeanine was occupied with Rose Tregarth and her daughter and did not see me. I managed to bring the conversation around to Tanglewood Manor, and, of course, the conversation eventually led to Sir Wildeve. I am sure that the vicar had no unnecessary prodding from me to speak in confidence. I gather that Sir Wildeve has had some great tragedy in his life, and because of his duties and obligations to his estate and the village, he has been unable to leave. Talk dies once there is nothing present to remind people. Other than that, he would say no more. I will have to present myself somehow to Ms. Esterhazey at the teashop. Aunt Jeanine has claimed more than once that Jane Esterhazey is too quick to indulge in gossip.*

A week later, she had managed to initiate a chat with the proprietress of the village teashop.

*This afternoon I had excused myself from Aunt Jeanine, timing my errand at the butcher's with tea, and it was a most opportune time to engage Ms. Esterhazey in conversation. She invited me back into her little room for tea while Esther saw to those in the front. Since the remark about Tanglewood Manor had worked so well on loosening the vicar's tongue, I tried it again on Jane. It seems that Sir James nurses a fear about the stability of his offspring. Jane assured me that it is not without foundation. Tomorrow I am going to bring a recipe to Mrs. Polwen. Perhaps she will let me in Tanglewood, and I will contrive to meet the little boy.*

I started the next entry, wondering if the recipe recipient, Mrs. Polwen, was my great-grandfather's cook at the manor.

*I went to Tanglewood this afternoon. I had gone to the back doors and had been admitted into the house by Mrs. Leyeland.*

Who was Mrs. Leyeland? The housekeeper?

*She escorted me to the kitchens where Mrs. Polwen was overseeing the dinner preparations. When I entered the kitchens, I saw a boy who looked to be no more than two years of age. I could see right away who he was by the set of his dark eyes and by the way his hairline peaked over his forehead. He was sitting on the little scullery's lap while she was peeling potatoes. Every once in a while, the infant would steal a potato peeling and pop the whole curl into his mouth. Twice he choked, and the maid had to put the knife down to clear his mouth out. I wondered where the nursemaid was, but I didn't feel comfortable enough to ask. The little one's name is Desmond James. I left the recipe with Mrs. Polwen and left without visiting her or Mrs. Leyeland. They were rushing about getting everything prepared for Sir James's dinner guests from London, and they would not have welcomed a diversion.*

I paused in my reading to look at the small crate of journals by my knee. I wondered which journal actually had a clue in it. I knew that there had to be something important in at least one, or Great-uncle Desmond would have never hidden them.

Splaying the journal facedown on my knee to hold my place, I reached into the crate and counted out the rest of them. There were twenty-five in all. Deciding to put them back in proper chronological order, I made an oddly frustrating discovery. There was one missing. According to the gilt years embossed on the spines, it was the one that should have come after the one I was reading. I decided to skip ahead in the one I held and look through its last entries. Perhaps it would give me an idea of why the next journal was missing. Perhaps Destiny had herself skipped a year.

I found the first entry to speak openly about Sarah, Desmond's mother.

*I found Sarah's choker of pearls. The ones she hid. They were not where we had thought, but were embedded in the urn by the fountain, shoved in under the roots. They were nearly unrecognizable as the black necklace that she had worn in her portrait. I can see there was no choice. It had to be done, if only for the sake of the child.*

The next entry was far more suggestive, provocative, and even alarming.

> *Today I had tea with Mrs. Leyeland. As housekeeper, she could easily put her hand to the letter opener. It is of Oriental design, gilded, sharp, and the handle is covered in faux cabochon gems. It certainly looked wickedly lethal. Mrs. Leyeland swore that the blood was so copious that it had soaked the underskirts. She held it out to me, but I made no move to touch it.*

It was the last entry in the journal for that year, and I knew that Great-grandmother Destiny hadn't skipped a year. Great-uncle Desmond had hidden it. Frustrated, I smacked the log under me and closed the skinny little volume, inserted the journal back into the crate at its proper place, and pulled the next one free.

Just as I opened the journal's front cover, the wall in front of me began to move. I looked up, relieved, and three blindingly bright torch beams met my smile. The beams stopped short, and I could feel Dante, Brandt, and Tamsin staring at me from behind the beams.

"Guess what I had found," I said gleefully and held up the journal in my hand, waving it like a semaphore flag. "Destiny's journals. And I know what the etchings in the armoire and in the urn mean."

"Bella, *bambina*," Dante's deep voice rolled hesitantly and gently into the cramped room, "why are you sitting on that mummy like it's a bench at a bus stop?"

When I came to, I was splayed out on the gritty floor like a bug on a windscreen. I wasn't out long. It had actually been less than a second. I had fallen backward off the gift-wrapped cadaver, and the thud of my body against the stones had snapped me out of my faint as effectively as pouring ammonia up my nose. It didn't orient me, though. I felt as if my brain was floating in slow motion like a picturesquely scudding cloud and someone else's knees were draped over the mummy. It wasn't until Brandt and Dante touched me that I realized suddenly that it was *my* knees, and my brain suddenly stopped floating.

"Ack!" I said, or some other such unidentifiable noise, and began kicking the mummy maniacally, my legs churning like pistons.

"Easy, easy, easy," Dante said. But I paid no heed. The first thing I was going to do was kick the tattered corpse away from me; the second thing was to wash my hands. The third thing was to . . . What was the third thing?

"Bella, Bella, Bella . . ." Four hands grabbed the seat of my jeans and my armpits, and I was gently airlifted away from my target as smoothly as a helicopter completing a rescue mission. I continued to kick convulsively as I was carried outside the hidden room and deposited carefully on Great-grandmother's bed. Flour rose around me in a choking cloud; and I screamed a long, deep wail of revulsion, kicked one more time, and then stiffened across the counterpane like another corpse. There was silence.

"Bella?" Dante's tentative hand brushed the wads of hair from my face, and I opened my eyes to stare straight-ahead.

"I'm fine," I said grimly and then paused. "Where's Tamsin?"

"Here," came a timid voice from beside me. She paused suggestively for a moment and then said, "I've got hand sanitizer in my pocket."

"Thank you, but I think I'd rather burn my skin off with matches," I said and felt my rigid muscles slowly cave back into place. I struggled to sit up. Feeling a fleeting touch on the top of my head, I turned in time to see Dante leave the bedside. He stepped out of the collective glow of the torches and disappeared into the surrounding gloom.

"Are you all right, *poca*?" Brandt was laughing as he crouched beside the high bed to peer up at my face. He reached out and carefully tucked a chunk of my hair behind my ear before the entangled rat pellets could touch my mouth. "If the mummy wasn't dead before, he sure is now."

I shuddered and pressed fingers to my eyes, remembering how I had dragged the mummy along the floor in a headlock. And then I remembered how it had bounced when I had dropped it to the floor. I shuddered again, and goose bumps flushed down my body.

"Great-uncle Desmond had actually hammered a note to his chest with a tack." I grimaced. "It said, 'I told you to try again. Congratulations.'"

"What did he mean by that?" Tamsin asked and pulled my hand from my face to squirt a huge dollop of sanitizer into my palm. It was cold and pungent. I resisted the urge to rub it all over my body and concentrated for the next few seconds on smoothing it over my hands instead. The skin instantly puckered and shriveled, becoming germ free and smelling like a hospital corridor.

"I remember now," I said. "It was the clue in the sarcophagus. He said to try again." I looked up. "Where's Dante?"

"In here, *bambina,*" he answered and came out of the secret room, the crate of journals in one hand and his torch in the other. "I'm assuming you want to bring these home."

"There's a journal missing." I frowned at the crate as he set it gently on the bed beside me. "Uncle Desmond had hidden it."

"It's probably still in this room," Brandt said thoughtfully and stood up from his crouch beside the bed.

"But we've looked everywhere," Tamsin murmured and surveyed the room with her torch. "I can't imagine where it would be."

"I had thought that the riding habit had held a clue," I said and looked at it still splayed out on the foot of the bed beside me. "But apparently it was just a stage prop from Great-uncle Desmond."

Dante played his torch beam over the habit, lingered gruesomely on the gravy stains, and then grunted.

"What?" I asked as he stepped past me to peer down at the cracked riding boots at the foot of the bed. He shined his light into their depths and then kicked one of them. The boot fell over sideways, and a slim journal slid out. So did a hairy spider, riding the journal like a surfboard. The journal slid to a stop beside Dante's boot, and the startled spider fled into the darkness. I jumped from the bed to lift the journal from the gritty floor and check the spine.

"This is it!" I exclaimed and clutched it to my bosom like an injured pet. "How did you know?"

"One boot seemed stiffer than the other. It looked like something was propping it up inside."

"One of the clues has to be in this one," I said and smoothed fingers over the journal, cleaning the flour dust from its cover.

"Why did he hide the others then?" Tamsin asked reasonably. I shrugged.

"I don't know. I thought of that too, but maybe he separated the journals to separate two different clues. In those"—I pointed at the crate—"Great-grandmother talks about Desmond before she was married to Great-grandfather." I looked up. "Speaking of clues, I finally figured out what the etching means."

"The '3-0-A'?" Dante asked and eased the journal from my fingers to flip through it, his beam trained on the flowing writing inside. "Tell us."

"I'll show you," I said and leaned over the bed where I could see an undisturbed dusting of flour. They trained their torches on the spot as I used my fingertip to write the figures down exactly as they had appeared in the armoire and the urn. I glanced at Brandt, who stood behind me.

"When we showed you the armoire, you ran your hand over it like this." I demonstrated, gliding my fingers an inch above the vertically stacked letters, going from the bottom toward the top. "I was standing in the armoire to the side watching you, and it gave me a completely different perspective. Literally. We were looking at it from the wrong direction."

I grinned, and grasping a patch of the bedspread, I shifted it a quarter turn clockwise.

"Look at it this way."

Dante, Brandt, and Tamsin crowded behind me, and I heard Tamsin gasp.

"I feel so stupid. If I had just turned the urn a bit, we would have seen it."

"It's not a stacked '3-0-A.' It's a monogram. D-O-W," I laughed. "Destiny Olivia Wildeve. I think Great-uncle Desmond scratched the monogram in everything that he intended for us to find as clues."

"If you're right, *poca*, then that means that the etchings themselves mean nothing," Dante rumbled thoughtfully behind me, and touched my shoulder. "It's the urn itself that's the clue."

"But I looked up the name on the urn," Tamsin sighed. "I can't find a Clarisse De Mornay."

"Perhaps it's the date, then," I suggested. And again a connection squiggled away from my grasp. If only I could just see it. There was something that I needed to remember, but I had no idea what. Mildly frustrated, I swiped the flat of my hand over the flour and obliterated my great-grandmother's monogram.

"There is something I would like to do before we go," Brandt said and glanced at the luminous dial of his watch. "I would like to see those tombstones stacked against the wall in the Great Hall downstairs. I keep thinking about the inscription over the boiler in the cellars. 'I wait beyond the grave.'"

"What inscription?" Dante asked. Brandt told him as we trooped down to the Great Hall together, the three torches that were still in working order bobbing erratically as we took the long flight of stairs. Dante was carrying my father's ruined torch and the crate of books.

The Great Hall was as macabre as before, with Margaret Rutherford still prone on the floor with her skirt hiked to her waist. Brandt jerked her to her feet in passing and led us unerringly to the cache of tombstones against the wall.

We found five roughly carved headstones leaning side by side. Crusts of dried soil clung to their bottoms like they had been freshly yanked from the earth, and lichen had long since settled around the edges of the incised letters.

After just having intimately handled the wrappings of a three-thousand-year-old mummy, I suffered from cadaver overload and wasn't too keen to touch the tombstones. Tamsin and I let my brothers handle the heavy slabs of granite. They flipped them from the wall and leaned them back so that we could see the inscriptions.

We fell silent as we studied the dark row of names. Even though the tombstones didn't seem to be in any kind of order, it was obvious that they were to be taken together.

"They're all Wildeves," Tamsin whispered.

"They're all men's names," I added. "So what does it mean in the clue?"

"What part?" Dante asked absently and played his torch over the slabs.

"The men aren't the dead," I quoted. "I thought it meant that we would find a woman somewhere in all this."

"Look at the dates." Dante played his torch beam over the one in the middle. It was small and so scoured by the weather the name was difficult to decipher. "James George Wildeve, born 1760, died 1793. This grave seems to be the oldest."

"He was only thirty-three years old when he died," Tamsin murmured, joining her torch beam to Dante's. "He didn't live long."

"Neither did this one," Brandt said and trained his light on the first tombstone in the row. "Henry Bertrand. He was only twenty-eight when he died in 1886."

"That one seems to be the newest tombstone," I said, stepped closer, and toed the large flake of lichen hanging from the edge of the *B* in "Bertrand." It stuck to my shoe, and I brushed it off on the flagstone floor. Dante suddenly bent down to stare closely at Henry Bertrand's tombstone, training the concentrated center of his beam on the spot where the lichen had flaked off.

"That's odd," he said and ran the tip of his finger over another patch of lichen, pulling free another large flake to hold it close to his eyes. He rubbed it between his fingertips, and it disintegrated into brittle flecks.

"What is it?" Brandt asked quietly. Dante reached out and picked a flake free from the tombstone leaning next to Henry Bertrand's. It did the same thing. Brushing his hand across his jeans, he stood up and surveyed the line of grave markers with a frown.

"It's a fake. That lichen is green paint."

"A clue." Tamsin grinned. "Clive and Jude were right. The tombstones are another clue."

"It's paint?" I leaned down and stared hard at the lichen. "How did you know? It looks real."

"If lichen had actually grown on the stone, *poca*, you would see a discoloration on the granite if you pulled a piece free. These tombstones had never been out in the elements."

"Are all of them fakes?" I asked and Dante grunted.

"Good question. Let's check."

Tamsin and I watched Brandt and Dante as they rubbed the flats of their hands over the face of every tombstone. Brittle green paint flecked off like leprous dust.

"They're all fake. Every one of them," Brandt said, answering my question, and stood up to survey their handiwork. "So we have another clue planted by Great-uncle Desmond. I wonder who they are, then, besides being Wildeves."

"I can look them up at the library," Tamsin offered timidly. "I have to go in to work tomorrow after tea. I'll have time."

"Is Pansy still on for the morning?" I asked. Tamsin nodded her answer.

"Are you going with me?" she countered. I hesitated.

Pansy is one of Tamsin's newer Bible students. Cheerful, tolerant, redheaded with over a million freckles on her arms alone, she is under thirty, husbandless, and has eight children. Eight busy, imaginative, and undisciplined children less than ten years of age.

The last time I had gone with Tamsin on Pansy's lesson, her oldest daughter, Fiesta, an intense redhead child of eight, had managed to cram a fistful of her unwanted lunch down my blouse while Tamsin was helping Pansy locate Lamentations in Pansy's ancient Bible. The resultant struggle that ensued was brief, silent, fierce; and the only signs that anything untoward had happened were the grease stains on my blouse, the fried fish pulp on the coffee table, and the long red hairs snagged in my ring.

That was also the same morning that Prince Charles and Bravo Caesar, Pansy's seven-year-old twin boys, came home with a panicked diarrheic goat that they had kidnapped from the farm down the lane. They freed it in the house while I was reading a paragraph, and it was a bit like trying to dodge the spray from a fireman's hose. I had to wrap up in one of Pansy's bathrobes and ride home in the luggage space of Tamsin's Mini after that, my blouse and skirt in a bin liner along with one of my shoes.

"Prudence and Deirdre are the only ones going out tomorrow," Tamsin said pleadingly.

Prudence is in her early nineties, and Deirdre, only thirty-five but painfully shy, had once collapsed in tears when Jude had unthinkingly removed an aphid from the shoulder of her cardigan while she was still in it. Picturing Pansy's horde carting Deirdre away on their bony little shoulders, I capitulated.

"I'll go," I sighed. "And then we can go to the Bunts for tea before lunch. When are you going in to work?"

"After tea. We can catch the ginger tomcat then and bring it over here, but after we drop him off, I'll have to work at the library until closing."

"You don't mind looking the names up?" I asked and nodded at the grisly line of phony tombstones. "It would be wonderful if you can figure out what Great-uncle Desmond's clue might mean."

"I'm only manning the front desk," Tamsin said. "It's my easiest day of the week. Ms. Dilly will be there as well, doing what ever she does in her office. If I hit a snag, she can help me." She paused, and then laughed. "I'll consider it repayment for dealing with Pansy's children."

"Do either of you have paper or pen to take the names and dates down from the tombstones?" Dante asked. I frowned, going through a mental checklist of the contents in my rucksack. The only contents I was sure of was my nearly empty money purse, my medical directive, and a half-eaten bar of dark chocolate.

"I don't," Tamsin answered apologetically. Dante grinned impartially at both of us.

"Never mind. I'll go find something in the library. I know where there are markers and scraps of old parchment." He left, and I remembered the old sheepskin parchment that Basil had handled when we had all lunched together at the Moonstone. After a few minutes, he returned, handed the torn sheet of paper and heavy black marker to Tamsin, and took the torch from her as she meticulously copied down the names and dates of the tombstones lined up against the wall, listing them in order of appearance in case it was significant.

"Let's hope that at least one of the names is real and not a complete mystery like Clarisse," I said and then jumped as my pocket rang. I hurriedly dug out my father's mobile phone and answered it. It was my father.

"Bella, *leanbh*, it's getting late. I'd rather you come home now and get to bed."

"Okay," I told my father. "I'll be home in a few minutes."

"I'll take you back," Brandt said and bent to pick up the crate of journals that Dante had set down on the floor. "Then Tamsin can go on home."

"I just need to collect my rucksack from Tamsin's car and then Brandt will drive me back," I told my father as we began picking our way through the maze of curios. "I've got a lot to tell you."

"We'll be waiting, child," my father said good-naturedly and hung up.

I wanted to tell them about the inscriptions and the fireplaces. I wanted to tell them about the mummy and about the journals. But that meant that I was going to have to tell them about running thoughtlessly away from Brandt to be trapped in the walls. And about falling because I wouldn't let go of the torch. I knew I would have to downplay the welt on my stomach. That would just earn me a house call from Clive Chaucer who would knead my body for ruptures, and I'd been through enough already.

# 7

The next morning, an unexpected nugget of information about Great-uncle Desmond came from the unlikely source of Pansy Bliss, Tamsin's Bible student.

Tamsin and Pansy were in their usual places on the sofa while Pansy nursed her latest spawn, a hefty ginger two-year-old she had christened Lotus. I was glad she had chosen the name Lotus even though Lotus was a boy. Her other choice, she had confided to us one day, had been "Yummy."

Lotus was attached to her breast like a barnacle to a hull while her three-year-old daughter, Zorro Delighte, was sitting contentedly between her mother and Tamsin, painting her little brother's toenails with glue.

I was kept busy trying to prevent Pansy's five-year-old son, Buzzer, from urinating in my book bag, or I would have caught the first of the exchange between his mother and Tamsin. I had wrestled Buzzer's shorts back up and had shoved him into a tatty beanbag when I caught Great-uncle Desmond's name in the middle of one of Pansy's sentences. Buzzer continued to squat on top of the beanbag like a malevolent toad, the finger of one hand up a nostril and the other hand protectively cupping his sprout while he glared at me.

"Used to know Gran," Pansy was saying as I divided my attention between her and Buzzer's calculating glare. "Gran said he was handsome if a bit on the scrawny side for one who could ride and hunt like he did. Gran had a bit of a soft spot for him, but he never paid her any mind. Gran reckons he was a bit scared of girls. But when I told her that you"—with that, she turned her searching gaze to me, presumably to direct her words to my ears, but was just in time to see Buzzer short out the lamp beside me with a well-directed stream. I jumped back, nearly overturning my chair, the lamp popped, shooting an arc of electricity to the metal casement of the window, cracking the glass; and Buzzer was shot free of the beanbag like a spring loaded arrow, landing bare bottom first into the tower of blocks that nine-year-old Lark was stacking. The tower exploded, Buzzer howled, and Lark scrambled backward onto the table behind him.

"Cor!" he burst out admiringly and jumped to his feet on the tabletop to survey his little brother laid out on the rubble below him.

Pansy rallied quickly, detached Lotus with a pop that rivaled the exploding lamp, laid him out on the floor, and walked over to Buzzer to lift him in her arms and check for damage. There was barely a pause in her stream of words even though she had changed her topic from Great-uncle Desmond to her children's lack of a father's firm hand.

"Ran off like he did after my Lotus was conceived. The boys need a father especially, even more than my Zorro, Orchid, and Fiesta."

Zorro had looked up at the mention of her older sisters and smiled, posing with her raised bottle of glue like an artist with a loaded paintbrush.

"I know something about Fiesta that I promised not to tell."

"But it's really hard on my Lark, him being the oldest and all. Say"—she set Buzzer back on his feet and eyed me as if she had been struck by a sudden brainstorm. Buzzer began methodically kicking Lark's building blocks down the hall. "Them handsome brothers of yours. That dark one with those amazing green eyes . . . Does he like children?"

I stared at her for a moment so I wouldn't be tempted to glance at Tamsin.

"Umm, I'll ask him," I said.

"Do that. I could certainly do with a gorgeous set of biceps like his." she sighed, wedged her breast back into her brassiere, buttoned her blouse back up, and walked to a cluttered sideboard peeking out from an equally cluttered dining room.

"Anyway, I got Gran to give this to me when I told her that you were going through your uncle's effects. She can't see to enjoy it anymore, and I certainly don't want it willed to me with all the other rubbish in her house." Pansy plucked a stiff piece of cardboard the size of an index card from a pile of papers and walked over to me. I realized that I was still standing. I plucked the lamp's smoking cord from the wall socket and sat back down in my chair. Pansy handed me the cardboard.

"You can have it if you'd like. Gran snapped it herself one summer when she was just a girl. Sixteen, I think she said she was."

I looked down at the sepia snapshot in my hand.

Pansy went back to the sofa, stepped over Lotus, and sat down. Lotus rolled over, rose to his hands and knees, and began to burp up his milk, managing to hit the toe of Tamsin's shoe like a llama spitting at a tourist.

"Gran said the photo was snapped at the beach just west of the village. It doesn't look like it to me, but it just goes to show how much can change in that many years. Even nature, apparently. I think she's misremembering. Near to seven decades it was, she said."

A slender young man in an old-fashioned bathing costume stood stiffly facing the camera, a snorkel in one hand and a pale towel in the other. His hair was thick and dark with curling sideburns, and a luxuriant moustache overhung his strong jaw. His torso was covered with what looked like a wet patch of bear fur, and his sinewy shanks were as hairy as his chest.

"That's your great-uncle, that is." Pansy nodded at the picture in my hand.

"Great-uncle Desmond?" I said, startled, remembering the aged fly that had spouted curses at me.

"Gran said that he could swim like a fish and shoot the pit out of a cherry . . . Cherry. Now that's a nice name. If I ever have me another baby, that's what I'll name it. Cherry Rave Bliss. Has a nice ring to it, don't you think?"

"Sounds like a dessert, that does," Lark Midnight Bliss told his Mum from the top of the table where he was carving his initials into the veneer with a pen. "When's tea?"

After the study with Pansy, Tamsin and I went to have midmorning tea with Arabel Bunt and her sister, Zinnia. Tea at the boardinghouse where Tamsin lived was far more entertaining than I had expected. And much more informative. Arabel Bunt made MI5 look like drunken Alzheimer patients.

The boardinghouse where Tamsin lived was a tall narrow three-storied stone structure in the middle of the village. It had bow windows on either side of the front doors, and it reminded me a bit of Bath, all white and gold stone, elegant windows and Regency embellishments. It was charming and as out of place in the more rustic part of the village as a frosted bonbon in a cat's litter box.

Arabel escorted us out to the teeny back lawn where the tea things were laid out on a white iron table, telling me as she led the way that, if I would like, I may call her Arabel since we very nearly were related. I looked at Tamsin, who shrugged.

Already seated around the tiny iron table were two others. Her younger sister, Zinnia, and an elderly gentleman whom she introduced as Colonel Robert Malthus made up the rest of our party.

Colonel Malthus struggled to his feet as we approached, using his battered hawthorn cane like a ski pole to lever himself out of his wee chair. All the chairs were wee. Made of fine white filigree, they looked too frail and feminine to prop up anybody. I noticed that Arabel's chair had a fat cushion on its seat, which made sense since Arabel was so stout I had a feeling that she would extrude through the lacework clear to the grass if she rested her full weight on it.

Tamsin obviously knew Colonel Malthus from somewhere else, possibly from the boardinghouse since he seemed to be an intimate friend of the Bunt sisters. He nodded happily at Tamsin as he struggled to his feet, and, once standing, he bowed to me.

"Robert, may I present dear Desmond's great-niece, Isabella Wildeve. Isabella, this is Colonel Robert Malthus."

"You don't look like him," he barked out and took my fingers in his raspy clasp. "Which is a jolly good thing, if I may say so. Call me Robert, my dear."

"And I," Zinnia said dramatically in her phony French accent, "am Arabel's baby sister, Zinnia Bunt-Joliet. You may call me Madame Zinnia."

I murmured my greeting and looked to Tamsin for what to do next. Tamsin merely waited for Arabel to sit on her cushion before selecting a seat for herself. I sat on the only chair that was left, which put me between Madame Zinnia and Colonel Malthus. They both turned to face me, and I suddenly felt like a newly discovered species of dung beetle being pinned to a card.

"You are right, Colonel Robert." Madame Zinnia arched her kohl-darkened eyebrows at me and flared her nostrils. "She does not look like dear Desmond. Dear Desmond was an English gentleman. This girl child looks exotic."

Exotic? My eyes widened involuntarily.

Madame Zinnia was draped in a lime green caftan the size of a parasail. Ropes of Murano beads cascaded down her bosom, tinkling like wind chimes every time she moved, and jeweled clasps held back the long hair she had dyed the color of Bing cherries. Deep scarlet lipstick enlarged her age-thinned mouth, and false eyelashes ringed her eyes like squatting tarantulas. She was spectacular enough to suck the breath out of my lungs at first sight, and I kept expecting her to tell me how she had danced naked one moonlit night in a fountain with Rudolf Nureyev.

If Madame Zinnia thought of me as exotic, I was going to have to go home and shoot myself.

"A bit," barked Colonel Malthus, "a bit. It's in the eyes and the cheekbones. Eye-tie. Take after your mother, do you? Did she favor Mussolini?"

I assumed that he was referring to her political persuasion and not to her profile.

"She wasn't born yet," I said neutrally and smiled. I wasn't sure what was expected of me. I accepted my wee cup of tea and a ginger biscuit from Arabel and tried to look less exotic, whatever that was.

"Of course not," Arabel tittered and handed a cup to the colonel, who balanced it neatly on his bony kneecap. "Zinnia, dear? The usual?"

"Of course," she replied wearily and watched as her sister poured a generous tot of cognac into her cup. Tamsin, who had already been handed her tea, took a quiet sip, put the cup back in the saucer, and gave me an unreadable look.

"The cognac is for Madame Zinnia's pain," Tamsin said.

"Eet ees for my aches, *oui*," Madame Zinnia agreed and accepted her medicinal refreshment. "I am zee lover of zee heat and zee light. I should be wis zee sunshine. But, no, I live here wis my sister. She is getting too old and too fat to be alone. I sacrifice myself for love."

"You live here, my dear Zinnia, because your pretty French husband died and left you with a garret of unlovely paintings. What you insist on calling 'abstract' are nothing more than giant blobs of muddy color that you cannot sell. You were penniless, my dear, and I am the one who sacrificed myself for love." Arabel looked pointedly at me. "Jean Baptiste was an artist like your strapping Irish father."

I felt myself blushing. I shouldn't have bothered. As teatime wore on, I realized that I was watching a competition that had been raging between the two siblings for the last eighty years. They enjoyed themselves as much as sumo wrestlers performing in a ring before an audience.

"Humph!" Zinnia snorted in return, took a sip of tea-diluted cognac, and plotted a comeback.

"Of course, dear, your father is very, very good." Arabel turned twinkling blue eyes on me, ignoring her sister's calculating pout, and set her own cup and saucer on her corseted bosom next to the plate-sized brooch, closed fan, and snowy napkin already reclining there. There was room on her enormous bosom for a sleeping cat as well, but I was glad she was petless for the moment. It was hard enough to keep my eyes from straying to the impressive shelf as it was. "So powerful. Even a little frightening. Such masculine paintings. I had once seen an exhibition of his work in Florence over thirty years ago. I assume that the lovely blonde in his early work is your mother?"

Even Tamsin doesn't know that particular secret. We have all been sworn to secrecy. My mother is morbidly phobic that Circuit Overseers will spot her nude teenage likeness hanging from a Bible student's walls someday.

"I haven't seen all his work," I said truthfully, thinking fast.

"I am aware now, of course, that he paints more conventional portraits and landscapes. I understand that he is quite well-known internationally. Isn't he, Zinnia, my dear?"

"Ah, Bryn," Madame Zinnia breathed out my grandmother's name as if we had just mentioned her. Which we hadn't. "Yes, Bryn. A lovely girl wis zee green eyes of zee cat. She was much more popular zan Arabel. Me? I was still an *enfant* zen."

I could see Arabel wince.

"Perhaps," Arabel said, recovering quickly, tittering, and taking a genteel sip of tea while she worked out her return serve. "But, Zinnia, my dear, you were hardly a baby. You were old enough to try to snatch Finghin from her."

"You knew my grandparents before they were married?" I asked. Colonel Malthus decided to reenter the conversation.

"Lovely girl, Bryn. Lovely." He smiled at the rosebushes and then caught himself as Arabel and Zinnia turned in unison to glare at him. "Of course, the Bunt girls were every bit as lovely."

"*Oui*, I knew zee Wildeves. All of zem." Zinnia pulled a jeweled clasp from her hair and reattached it to the low neck of her caftan. It twinkled frantically in the light like a hummingbird that had gotten trapped in her wrinkled cleavage. She slanted a malevolent look at Arabel. "Even Desmond. I knew him well."

"Did you know my great-grandparents?" I asked. Arabel nodded at me.

"Yes, I did, my dear." Arabel smiled complacently, ignoring her sister's glare, and took a sip of tea. "Zinnia's memory is going south with the rest of her, so I doubt if she can remember that far back."

"I can!" Madame Zinnia threw her sister a fierce look and flared her nostrils.

"However," Arabel went on, ignoring her, "I can barely recall Destiny. I was quite young when she died."

"What do you remember of her?"

"I remember her!" Madame Zinnia leaned over to catch my attention, tapping my hand with a long crimson fingernail. "She was very beautiful."

"You can't remember her, dear. She was very rarely out." Arabel frowned at her younger sister and then gave me a coy look from under her lashes. "It seemed as if she was always expecting. And well-brought-up women didn't go out in those days when they started showing. It just wasn't done. Not here in the village, anyway."

"But she did, Arabel." Madame Zinnia smiled triumphantly at her sister. "She did. I would see her riding her huge black horse."

"Not in town, dear."

"No." Madame Zinnia shrugged, and the clasp above her cleavage was temporarily swallowed up. "Not in zee village. But I see her wis her daughters in zee cart. And on her horse."

"What was my grandfather like?"

"Finghin was handsome," Madame Zinnia said simply and cast her eyes heavenward. I looked at Arabel, who was regarding her sister with an unreadable stare.

"Well," Arabel conceded and peeled her eyes away from Zinnia's blissful expression to peer at me, "he was certainly that, but he was more than a bit of the rogue, if you understand me. Father found him with Zinnia and tried to take a whip to him."

I felt the biscuit in my hand crack, and small pebble of it plopped into my cup.

"But he was so much more powerful than father. He just took the whip from him before he could strike and tore it in two. Just put the leather thong under his boot and ripped the handle free. Then he tossed both pieces on to the roof of the stable and left, never looking back."

"I was heartbroken." Madame Zinnia peered soulfully at me through her jungle of false eyelashes. "I never saw him again."

"Oh, Zinnia never even had one petal plucked. It didn't go as far as that," Arabel twittered coyly, setting the matter straight in case Colonel Malthus minded. "Just frustrated that she couldn't hold his attention."

"Arabel!" Madame Zinnia huffed and turned in her wee chair to look at something else besides her sister's hated profile. "Zat ees enough talk of my Finghin! Or I will tell zem many zings about Desmond!"

"There's a chap for you," Colonel Malthus barked out and thoughtfully ran a gnarled finger over his top lip. He stared down at the delicately scrolled tabletop in front of us. "Not right all the way. Not by any means. Had a thing for apple pips as a boy. Would eat the core right out of your hand before you were even through with it. He didn't go away to school like the rest of us, though. Didn't get sent away. Sir James had some sort of tutor in, so he wouldn't have to leave."

"Someone gave me an old photograph of him. Her grandmother had taken it when she was a girl. She had told her granddaughter that she had been sweet on him, but he wouldn't have anything to do with her because he was afraid of girls," I said and took a sip of tea. I could see the biscuit chunk in the bottom disintegrating like a lump of sugar.

"Oh no, my dear, he was not afraid of girls." Arabel's look became coy again. "Oh no, to the contrary. Dear Desmond was my fiancé. He was my first love, and we were betrothed to be married."

Tamsin sprayed a clot of dry crumbs from her mouth, I choked on the sip of tea I had inadvertently inhaled, and Madame Zinnia crossed her arms theatrically over her bosom in a "now you've done it" gesture. Only Colonel Malthus was unaffected by Arabel's statement.

"Oh yes, we were betrothed," Arabel went on, seemingly unaware that I continued to cough warm Darjeeling from my lungs. "I was barely seventeen, and he was not yet twenty."

"The young idiot threw you over, didn't he?" Colonel Malthus barked and peered upward through his bushy eyebrows at Arabel. "Seems I remember something about that."

"No. No, it wasn't like that, dear. We both agreed. You know. It was because of his mother."

"His mother?" I hesitated and then took a chance. There was no way that I would know something that Arabel didn't. "You mean Sarah?"

"Yes. Sarah, poor dear. He had just found out. His father told him just after Destiny died. None of us knew. None of us younger ones, that is. Father and mother knew. They were against our betrothal from the first."

"Load of rubbish!" Colonel Malthus barked. "No need to have broken off the engagement, you know. Fellow was an idiot, but harmless."

"He may have been zee idiot," Madame Zinnia surged back into the conversation, throwing her hands in the air like she was shooing cows, "but his mother, she was stark raving mad. She was insane."

I couldn't help throwing a startled look at Tamsin. Colonel Malthus noticed.

"No shame in that!" he countered. "Most of the best families have a few loonies in the attic, you know. Very common, unfortunately. Even the royal family tree has more than a few of those barking in the branches."

"Tyne Hospital," I stated. Colonel Malthus shot me a shrewd look from his rheumy eyes.

"Was an asylum, my dear." He tapped his cane against a table leg. "I remember Auntie Sol was a nurse there. Trained in London and went out to India with my uncle Chuffy. Had to come back when he died. Went to work at Tyne. Of course, Tyne was the best. Patients there had private rooms and doctors to see to them. They weren't big on restraints, hoses, or force-feeding as a rule. Even that fellow Freud spent a summer there, observing. Auntie Sol couldn't stop talking about him."

I gathered my thoughts together while he reminisced.

"When was Sarah committed?" I asked when the colonel fell silent. Arabel looked deeply into her cup and then set it down.

"I don't remember Father ever saying when I told him that Desmond and I had broken our engagement."

"I know!" Madame Zinnia said triumphantly. "I heard Mother and Father talking. Zey do not zink to pay attention to me because I was an *enfant*."

We all looked at Zinnia expectantly, who paused dramatically to take a slow sip from her cup. Then she delicately nibbled a ginger biscuit.

"When, dear?" Arabel asked grimly when her sister stretched the expectant silence as long as she dared.

"I do not know when. I only know zat she cut herself wis zee knife, and zee doctor, he put her in."

I remembered Destiny's entry in her journal about Mrs. Leyeland.

"I believe it was an ornamental letter opener," I said slowly and then realized uneasily that I had spoken out loud.

"Perhaps," Madame Zinnia conceded. "But eet did not happen, Arabel, and you did not marry zee pretty Desmond. You are here wis me and not in zee big house."

"More's the pity," barked Colonel Malthus, and he shifted his rheumy gaze from Arabel to me. "I hear he has some interesting souvenirs. Been everywhere. Ceylon, Thailand, Egypt, Japan, New Guinea, America. I heard in 1954 that he was smuggling a mummy into England."

I didn't say anything.

"Pity the fellow didn't marry you." Colonel Malthus put his rheumy stare back on Arabel. "A pity."

"Yes, eet ees a pity," Madame Zinnia pursued. She had her sister in verbal headlock and was making the most of it. "Zee house, and all eets treasures, zey go to Astrid and Aurora. Zere is no wife for Desmond. He died alone."

Arabel may have been in a headlock, but she could still bite.

"At least he died relatively well-known." She smiled sweetly.

"Poor Desmond. He knew zat insanity is hereditary," Madame Zinnia verbally pummeled her right back. "We all did. No one else would have married him."

Were the members of my family the only ones who had no idea that Great-uncle Desmond was merely a half brother? Did everyone in the village over the age of sixty know? I was willing to bet that the ones who knew Desmond's precise relationship to my grandmother and my great-aunts also knew about Sarah's insanity. Except, perhaps, for Pansy's gran who assumed that Desmond avoided girls because he was a shy wallflower. A shrinking violet that could shoot the pit out of a cherry.

"Arabel"—I paused, getting her attention, and she switched her attention from Madame Zinnia to me—"do you know of any relative in our family named Clarisse De Mornay?"

"Ah!" Madame Zinnia was quick to show her advantage over her sister. "You have a relative who ees French?"

"French?"

"Clarisse De Mornay, you say?" Madame Zinnia tilted her head at us. "*Oui*, zat ees French."

"No, dear." Arabel ignored her sister's contributory nugget. "I can't say that I have met her. Is she coming to visit with Astrid and Aurora as well as dear Bryn?"

How did she know that my grandmother was due any day from Ireland?

"Not this time," I faltered, excited, and decided to drop the question now that Madame Zinnia had inadvertently given us a lead. I wasn't about to tell the omniscient Arabel that we had gotten the name off an urn of charred chicken bones.

I glanced at Tamsin, and I could see she had caught the same idea that I had. If Clarisse had been French, then that was why she didn't come up in the library's computers. Tamsin had never thought to cross-reference her research. Excited at our new lead, trying to fit it in with the other clues, I barely heard the sudden turn in the conversation until Zinnia shouted. The one-word comment penetrated my thoughts, and I hurriedly tuned in to the words flying around me.

"Rubbish!" she yelled with her nostrils flaring like a stallion's. Arabel was quick to talk over her.

"Zinnia, as you've just seen, thinks that it's all rubbish. She doesn't believe in heaven, I'm afraid. She really doesn't believe in death, come to think of it."

"Wish I didn't," the colonel said morosely and stared at the teacup on the point of his bony knee. Arabel continued as if he hadn't spoken.

"Zinnia believes that Desmond is back among us. That his spirit regenerated itself into a crab. Or perhaps an eel. He always loved the water." She looked at me expectantly as if waiting for me to disagree with such an outrageous assumption. I stared at her and searched my mind vainly for a coherent thought, but all I could do was recall the crab legs I had for dinner the day we had learned of his death. Tamsin suddenly stood up and smiled brightly at Arabel.

"Thank you very much for the tea. We'll have to be going—"

"Wait, dear, I have a present for you and Isabella." She struggled out of her chair, and the cushion fell to the grass behind her. "I have that great ginger tom in a box for you. The manor must need a good mouser, and at least it gets him off the streets and out of everybody's trash."

How did she know that we had wanted to transplant the tomcat?

We were on the way to the kitchens to collect the boxed feline when Arabel let go of one more surprising nugget.

"By the way, dear," she threw over her shoulder at me as she waddled ahead of us, leading the way, "you might want to talk to Liza Weebs, Len Weebs's grandmother. I believe she used to sit with your uncle Desmond when he was a baby. She knew your great-grandmother."

Len Weebs is Halfmoon's aging punk rocker. He is older than my parents, sports a crusty mohawk on his freckled head, dresses in black leather, and has more studs that a set of snow tires. I had once seen him peel a wad of gum from the bottom of his combat boots and pop it into his mouth for dessert.

"His grandmother is still alive?" I gasped thoughtlessly. Arabel nodded.

"She's over a hundred, I believe, but is still sharp enough in her mind. She lives by the Moonstone in that little cottage with the wheelchair ramp. Go see her. Tell her I sent you."

The ginger tom turned out to be mostly ginger cat and part Scottish Highland wildcat, which meant that the giant rats in the manor were mere *hors d'oeuvres*. The cat was the size of a puma, had teeth like a crocodile, claws like a sloth, and the lumpy head of a street survivor. The box moved and yowled with a life of its own, and it took both Tamsin and I to carry it to the car. It continued to thump and screech all the way to the manor, and I was beginning to wonder how Arabel had managed to imprison it without losing a limb. Frankly, Arabel scared me far more than the tom did.

We dragged the struggling box through the manor's back doors and into the kitchens where we wedged it in the open door leading down to the cellars. We tilted the box on its side so that, once freed, the angry animal would dash away from us and not leap onto our heads to exact retribution. We pulled the slipknot that Arabel had tied in the cords encircling the container and jumped back. The tom sprang free, yowling, and tore off down the stairs like a rabid badger. I jerked the box from the threshold and slammed the door shut.

"Why did you do that?" Tamsin asked as I tossed the clawed box on top of the table with the test tubes and the other rubbish.

"I can't think of anything worse than coming in here in the dark and being attacked by that cat. At least I know he's in the cellars, and I can avoid going there unless I'm armed. And I can get Michael to free him later once the cat is calmed down from being in the box."

"Good point," she sighed. "And there's plenty of water for him pooling under the boiler."

After depositing the starving tomcat in the cellars, we left. Tamsin took me to Liza Weebs's picturesque cottage on her way to work and dropped me off.

I ducked under the profusion of roses framing the door and knocked, wondering what on earth I was going to say. At over a hundred years of age, I pictured Liza Weebs to be a frail prunelike creature that smelled like talcum and cheese, someone who needed assistance going to the bathroom. I was completely unprepared when the door suddenly opened on well-oiled hinges, and I found myself looking down at an ancient gnome in a dress and an apron.

If you look up the definition of "gnome" in the dictionary, you get two things. The first definition says that it is a fabled creature that lives underground and guards treasure. The second is what I seemed to be looking at—a shriveled old man. Poor Liza Weebs looked a bit like Great-uncle Desmond in a dress.

"I know who you are, and I don't want any," she cackled in a rude voice and started to slam the door. I put out a tentative hand as if to halt her.

"Wait, please. Arabel Bunt sent me. I'm interested in certain parts of local history."

She stared up at me with eyes so faded they were nearly transparent. Huge faded orbs magnified to translucent golf balls behind lenses as thick and as blurry as ice cubes.

"I'm Isabella Wildeve," I said.

"I know who you are. You're that fifth child of that foreign artist over at the Iron Rose. You also go to people's houses and try to convert them." Her golf ball eyes narrowed into slits. "But you say Arabel sent you."

I nodded.

"For what?" she asked bluntly. "I'm Church of England when I bother to go, and I won't change even for Arabel."

"I just wanted to ask you some questions about my family. We had just moved here two years ago, and I would like to know more of my family history from this area."

"Stay here, girlie," she cackled grudgingly. "I'm calling Arabel to make sure this isn't some kind of trick to get in my house and steal my Hummels."

She slammed the door, leaving me on her doorstep with my reassurance dying before it could leave my lips. I now knew where her punk rocker grandson got his talent for antisocial behavior. The door opened a moment later.

"Come in," she said without preamble. "I couldn't get Arabel. That idiot sister of hers wouldn't get her. But Zinnia said you're harmless if a bit exotic."

Liza Weebs led me into a tiny dark sitting room with a slanting floor that had the disconcerting trick of going uphill no matter which direction you were heading. She plopped her wizened frame on a rocking chair by the hearth and gestured me toward an upright wingback.

"Sit, girlie. Since you're only here to ask questions, I won't bother with making tea. You can pour yourself a homemade beer if you'd like. There's some in the cabinet. Or some scotch."

"No, thank you."

"Well, get up anyway and pour me one." She stabbed a finger at an array of bottles on top of a low sideboard. "A large scotch, mind you, and not a thimbleful. Well, go on. Get up, girlie. You know what scotch looks like, don't you?"

I got up and did as I was told, finding the pale liquid in a decanter wedged behind what I guessed to be sherry. I poured a great whopping tot of the stuff into a brandy snifter the size of her head and brought it to her. She accepted it from me and frowned.

"Well, get on with it. Get on with it. I have a batch of scones baking, and once they're done, you'll have to leave. Ask your questions."

"How well did you know my Great-uncle Desmond Wildeve?"

"Well enough. I babysat him enough times, what with his mother going loony and dying like she did. I babysat him in between servants. Your great-grandfather had quite a time keeping servants on with Sarah like she was. I kept him until your great-grandmam Destiny came along and snatched Sir James from all the village maidens."

"What was my great-grandmother like?"

"What's the matter? Doesn't your own grandmother know?"

"She died when my grandmother was only eight years old. She doesn't remember much."

"Your great-grandmam was exactly what Zinnia Bunt-Joliet wishes she was," Liza Weebs said with brutal satisfaction. "French, beautiful, artistic, exotic, and smart."

"She was French?" I said a second later, trying not to sound too gobsmacked. But Liza Weebs was too shrewd.

"Didn't know that, did you? Don't get so excited. She wasn't all the way French. French English. Her father was some Cornishman named Henry. Or was it Harry? Anyway, he had married some French beauty visiting here with her family and went back to France with her. She had a sister who had married some banker just outside of London. The sister stayed. Destiny's mother went back with her parents, taking Harry with her. They had Destiny somewhere in France."

I thought back to the entries that I had managed to read in Destiny's first journal.

"Was Jeanine the name of the sister who stayed in England?"

"Could be." She frowned at me. "Could be. I know when her banker husband died in London she sold everything and retired here. Destiny came over here during the Great War to live with her."

"Can you remember the maiden name of Destiny's mother?"

"No," she snapped, taking a sip of her rapidly dwindling vat of scotch. "I'm not magic, you know."

"Is there any of Destiny's family on her father's side still here?"

"Goodness, girlie, you are probably the closest relative of Harry left. He was an only son, and as far as I know, Destiny was his only spawn. Wait a minute. I tell a lie. It was Wycliffe."

"What was?"

"Pay attention, girlie! Your great-great-grandmam's maiden name. She was a Wycliffe. I seem to remember hearing that. And she married a Wildeve."

"My great-grandmother Destiny married Sir James Wildeve. Is that who you are talking about?" I asked, getting rapidly confused by her overabundant use of pronouns instead of proper names.

"You don't know your own family tree, do you? Open your ears, girlie! Your great-grandmam Destiny was already a Wildeve when she got married to the one up in the manor house on the hill. Sir James was a distant cousin of her father. Destiny's mother, your great-great-grandmam, was a Wycliffe who married a Wildeve. The first Wildeve. Sir James was the second in your family tree."

I sorted out her garbled genealogical lesson out loud.

"So you're saying that Destiny's mother married a Wildeve, and her daughter, Destiny, married one. Her own father's distant cousin."

"Very distant, girlie."

"So Destiny's father's name was Harry Wildeve." I frowned thoughtfully at her, remembering the obvious clue I had overlooked the first time in the diary. She had written the first journal before she had even married my great-grandfather, Sir James, yet she had personalized the journal with the name of Destiny Olivia Wildeve. I should have noticed that for what it was. And I should have noticed it when I read the marriage lines between Destiny Olivia Wildeve, spinster, and Sir James. She was a Wildeve before she married, and even with those two clues, I never noticed that fact until Liza Weebs informed me of it.

"Very good," she cackled sarcastically and took another mouthful of scotch. "Any other questions, girlie?"

"Have you ever heard of Clarisse De Mornay?"

"No," she snapped. "Next?"

"Can you tell me what region in France Destiny was from?"

"No, I can't. Wait." She paused, and her eyes seemed to pucker at me from behind her glasses. "I tell another lie. Somewhere just outside of Paris. A day's journey, perhaps. Not by the automobile, but as the horse trots."

"What happened to Destiny's parents? Did you ever see them after they went to live in France?"

"No. They were long dead." She paused, upended her snifter, sucked noisily, and then slapped the empty glass onto a side table beside the rocking chair. I was surprised that the snifter's squat stem didn't snap. "I can still remember the day she arrived with her belongings. She had said that her stay was temporary, but I had a feeling that she wasn't going back to France no matter how much she liked to think she was. She had pretty much escaped with what was left of her parents' things. The house ended up destroyed. I can still see all the bits and bobs of furniture she had managed to ship over with herself. Nothing but a big jumble tied to the carts."

Her giant eyes puckered closed as she demonstrated reminiscing to me.

"What did she look like?" I asked after a second of watching her.

Liza Weebs' eyes popped open, and she stared at me.

"You mean you don't even know that, girlie?" she demanded. "A bit like your grandmother. A bit like you, come to that. You have her look about your mouth. Except her hair was so black it looked blue in the sunshine. Not blond like yours. And a bit more bosom. But, of course, that could have been her corsets. The corsets back then bunched up what you had into one big lump like a goiter. I never could stand those things. Never wore them. Never will, girlie. I'm as free under this dress as the day I was born."

"What was my great-grandfather like?" I distracted her before she could raise her muumuu and show me.

"Big, with a great mop of chestnut hair. Beard, moustache, barrel chest. Everything needed to set female pulses back then to racing. I don't know how handsome he would be reckoned now."

Dismayed, I pictured a huge man with an expansive gut, a loud voice, and bits of biscuit and jam stuck in his beard.

"No, girlie, you have it wrong," she laughed, reading my face. "He was a fine-looking man to us in the village. Strong and—"

The sound of a timer going off echoed tinnily in the back of the house. She may have been a hundred years old with beer mug glasses, but there was nothing wrong with her hearing. She slapped the arms of her rocker.

"There're my scones. Off with you, girlie. Next time if you have any more questions, bring a cake or something. Or oysters. I'm partial to oysters. They don't take teeth."

I stood up, thanked her for her time, tried to ignore her flapping hands shooing me out of the front door as if I was a stray chicken, and left. She slammed the door behind me, and it wasn't until I was walking away that I wondered what the wheelchair ramp was for. It certainly wasn't for Liza Weebs unless it was for rolling her home from the pub.

# 8

I finished with Liza Weebs earlier than I had expected to, thanks to the quickness of her scones, so I decided to walk back home instead of calling for a ride. The late-morning air was like a fall apple—crisp, wet, bright, with an aftertaste of cider—and the water was equally dazzling with millions of sunshine chips strewn across its surface. The walk home was uphill all the way, but it only took me a little over half an hour even though my book bag got heavier with every step.

Feeling battle worn from my morning and somewhat disheveled, I entered the dining room after I arrived at the inn, checked my skirt for Buzzer stains, and found a mashed piece of chocolate stuck to my hem like a parasite. I pried it off with a tissue, folded it chocolate side in, and tucked it into a side pocket of my book bag, then found a table by the kitchens, waving a greeting to Rayvyn who was waiting on the other diners in her usual eccentric fashion.

After a second, Rayvyn darted to my table, weaving her way around the tables and chairs as if she was being timed running on an obstacle course. Her free breast couldn't decide which way to go under her gypsy blouse, and it was a bit more disconcerting than usual when she hitched the waistband of her skirt up to her armpits and imprisoned it impatiently under the elastic.

"I've been waiting for you to get here," she hissed. "I've got Michael's gift."

"Where is he?"

"He's not due for another half hour yet." She pulled a Fisherman's Friend from her skirt pocket, plucked off a piece of lint, and popped the cough drop into her mouth. "His gift turned out beautifully. Astra made a true work of art. I went all the way on the nozzle and got the deluxe settings."

"Nozzle?"

"A bag. You know, for colon cleansing. He keeps eating flesh in spite of my warnings."

I stared at her face for a minute, willing myself not to laugh.

"What color did you make it?" I finally asked.

"Silver. All glittery with his name in giant pink letters. I didn't have time to wrap it. Do you think he'll mind?"

"I don't even think he'll notice," I said truthfully. "When you give it to him, do it out here behind the screen. That way I can watch."

"I'll bring him to your table when he arrives," she said, spotted a chunk of girls standing in the doorway waiting to be shown to their table, and sighed meaningfully. "It's those Americans again. They took pictures of me at breakfast, and I wasn't even doing a pose."

She sighed again and left to seat them, forgetting to take my lunch order. I left my book bag by my seat and went into the kitchen to serve myself. Pete was standing over one of the huge vats on the stove ladling up bowls of thick Irish stew.

"Whatcha know, doll?" Pete gave me the usual greeting he reserves for every female except Rayvyn and my mother. He ignores Rayvyn like a rash that he can't reach, but when my mother is in the kitchen, he merely stands mute like a stag caught in a car's headlights.

"Can I have some of that?" I asked. He handed me a full bowl. "Thanks."

"Rayvyn is driving me nuts," he growled and swiped a forearm over his eyes, the dripping ladle in one hand and another empty bowl in the other. "The next time her braid drops into another pot of my soup, I'm going to hack it off with the cleaver."

"I heard that!" Rayvyn came into the kitchen behind me as I was grabbing a spoon and a napkin from the tub by the doors. "I told you if you'd eat bran and greens for breakfast, you'd be in a better mood!"

"I am not a horse!" Pete bellowed. I ducked out before I was forced to stay in the kitchen to mediate. I was hungry, and I wanted a look at the journal. I had taken the diary that Dante had found in the riding boot and had stashed it in my book bag that morning, hoping that I would have a free moment to look through it. I sat down with my stew and opened the journal beside my bowl.

Thirty minutes later, I had finished both my food and the slim volume. It was as full of interesting bits about my great-grandparents as the first journal I had read, but I couldn't spot anything out of the ordinary. There didn't seem to be anything that would make Great-uncle Desmond cull this journal from the others except two sentences that didn't make sense.

I opened the journal and relocated the entry dated sometime in midsummer, wondering if I had found the clue. The first part was printed in capital letters. That alone was uncharacteristic of the rest of the diary, and the words themselves didn't make sense to me.

> *TODAY I FOUND ANOTHER DESTINY. If it had gone properly, I would not be here today.*

I carefully marked the page and set it beside my empty bowl, looking up in time to see Gabriel and Jude enter the dining room. Jude had a hold of Gabriel's shirt collar like he was trying to leash-train a puppy, and my baby brother was waving at me as if he were trying to flag down a rescue boat. I held out my arms, and Gabriel broke free to dash toward my table. Smiling, Jude followed at a less-exuberant pace.

"I missed you, Bella!" Gabriel said in his usually affectionate fashion and swarmed me. I wrestled him down across my lap and showered noisy kisses all over his face. Gabriel giggled delightedly while Jude sat down in one of the chairs around the table, leaving a chair between us for our little brother once I was done with him.

"I shouldn't have let him have sugar before lunch," he said, eyeing me as I pretended to eat my little brother's neck. Gabriel began to scissor-kick. "People are staring, Bella."

I came up for air.

"Since when has that bothered you?" I grinned at him.

"Since they seem to be three pretty females," he murmured back and ran a hand over his blond hair in a ruefully self-conscious gesture.

"Where?" Gabriel sat up with alarming alacrity and put a finger up his nose. I jerked his hand down and looked behind me at the group of women that Rayvyn had complained about earlier. The young American women sat together in a friendly tangle of tanned skin and dazzling teeth, which they were all showing in wide giggles. I waved a friendly greeting at them and then looked back at Jude.

"They're not staring at me. They're staring at you."

"No they aren't," he said with characteristic blindness. I laughed and planted Gabriel in his seat. He wriggled around until he was on his knees, his chin higher than the edge of the table, and held still as I unclipped his necktie and folded it, inserting it in his pants pocket. Jude loosened the knot on his own tie and reached past Gabriel to pick up the journal by my bowl.

"What did you find *poca*?" he asked, noticing the strip of paper I had inserted between the pages. He opened it up, and I watched his green eyes skim the words. He seemed to be able to decipher the flowing cursive faster than I had.

"What do you think?" I asked once he finished. He shook his head.

"I don't know," he admitted with a short laugh. "At first reading it sounds like she had somehow cheated death. But what an odd way to put it." He paused and flipped through the other pages, stopping now and then to read another entry. "If that is what happened, you would think she would have written more than two sentences about it."

"It must refer to something else, but I have no idea what it could be," I said and watched Rayvyn as she glided by us on her way to a far table. Her breast, still imprisoned under the elastic, looked like a bun in her skirt pocket, and I noticed the older couple she was speaking to stare at it in puzzlement. She took their orders and began to glide back toward us. Jude stopped her before she could push through the swinging doors and disappear into the nether regions of the kitchens.

"Rayvyn, be a good sport and get me a coffee and a roast beef sandwich, please." Jude smiled and laced his fingers over the journal, resting his hands over it. "And Gabriel will have a cheese-and-tomato sandwich and a glass of milk."

Rayvyn lowered her eyebrows or, more accurately, her one unplucked brow and gave Jude a stern look.

"Dead cows give people gas," she stated flatly. Gabriel looked up with interest.

"I'll risk it." Jude grinned. "With horseradish, please."

"Maybe I should get him one as well," she murmured pointedly at me and moved off with her nostrils flaring.

"One what?" Jude asked. I glanced at my watch.

"You'll see if you hang around long enough to eat your sandwich." I heard a fresh peal of American giggles erupt behind me, and I turned to see Dante and Brandt enter the dining room. Rayvyn burst out of the kitchens before I could say anything else.

"The sandwiches will be out in a moment," she informed Jude and then clasped her hands over her sternum in pantomimed ecstasy. "Michael just came in. Are you ready?"

"Wait a moment for Dante and Brandt," I suggested as my two oldest brothers sat down beside us. Rayvyn lowered her clasped hands and waited impatiently for their orders.

"I'll just have some dead cow on rye," Brandt told her, grinning, and was rewarded with a flick of braid in his eye when Rayvyn tossed her head back, her nostrils flaring. He chuckled and rubbed a fingertip over his eyelid. "With hot mustard so it can process unassisted."

"And you?" Rayvyn turned to Dante, her tone icy when he made the mistake of smiling at Brandt's choice of words.

"The same for me. With a cup of coffee, please," he said, obviously amused. Rayvyn whirled away into the kitchens, the picture of organic indignation. I looked at Brandt, who was still laughing.

"She'll probably spit on it," I said.

"Like that's new," Gabriel sighed and rested his chin on his forearms. He blinked owlishly at the candleholder in front of his face. "I sure wish she would bring my milk soon."

I slid the journal out from under Jude's hands and pushed it toward Dante and Brandt.

"Read that and tell me what you think," I instructed. Dante picked it up, holding it out where Brandt could read along with him. When they had finished scanning the page, Brandt tapped the sentence in printed capitals.

"Are you talking about this?" He raised his eyebrows at me, and I nodded. They reread the entry and handed the journal back to me.

"It's odd, that's for sure," Dante sighed and loosened his necktie. "Is she talking about 'destiny' as in 'fate,' or is she using it as a name?"

"A name?"

"Today I found another Destiny," Dante repeated her entry. "It sounds like she found a twin."

"A doppelganger," Brandt supplied, running a hand over his chin. "Another person like herself."

"If it had gone properly, I would not be here today," I repeated the second sentence of the entry. "What would that mean?"

"I'm not touching that until I get my coffee," Dante laughed. Suddenly the kitchen doors swung open with the drama of a showdown at a cowboy saloon. Rayvyn stood in the threshold, her arms full of food-laden tray, and hissed like an excited goose defending her territory.

"He's in the larder," she said theatrically, plunked the plates down in front of my brothers, and shot back through the kitchen doors.

"What's with Rayvyn?" Dante asked, puzzled. I noticed the kitchen door opening again with Michael's large brown hand holding the edge. He seemed to be in consultation on the other side.

"Cabaret," I said and slipped the journal back into my book bag.

A few seconds later, Michael emerged, having been dragged from the kitchen by Rayvyn, and a wary look crept into his eyes when he saw our expectant faces.

"Michael," Rayvyn began formally and fidgeted nervously with her braid, running her hands down it repeatedly as if she was smoothing a frayed rope. "The mucous membrane of our colon is a delicate microcosm of warring bacteria, battling germs, and sometimes old tomato seeds if we don't eat enough fiber."

Michael blinked at her, saying nothing, wisely realizing that there is no rational response to someone who chooses to utter that sentence aloud.

"Dead flesh can cork us up"—she paused to glare at Brandt—"with or without hot mustard!"

Michael looked suitably confused at her declaration to our table.

"And poop is like feelings. You cannot keep it bottled up and stay healthy. So I would like to give you the gift of art and good feelings."

She reached behind her and opened the flap of a small box that had been sitting on a spare dining chair behind the screen. Gabriel gasped at the glittering vision of silver and hot pink that emerged, its long flexible hose whipping around like an elephant's trunk in search of popcorn.

"I've had this made especially for you. Something personalized that no one can mistakenly use as their own. It comes with its own illustrated instructions and a travel bottle of mint chlorophyll."

"You can flavor your tea with it as well," I called out, inadvertently sounding like a music hall heckler.

"Isabella told me that your favorite color is hot pink." She paused, blushed, and held it out to him draped over her arms like a dead baby. "For you. With love."

Michael looked down, stupefied, the shock of black hair falling over his forehead making him look like Lord Byron with poet's block.

"Speech! Speech!" I pounded on the table.

"Can I have it?" Gabriel asked innocently, tomato on his cheeks as he chewed a bite of his sandwich. Michael glanced at him and then looked back at the bag, slowly taking it from Rayvyn's hands. A grim smile crept over his face when he realized that it was full and sloshing.

"It's already full of diluted molasses. I'll cover for you in the kitchen if you want to try it out."

"Thank you, Rayvyn. It was very thoughtful of you." He gave her another smile and then turned to look meaningfully at me. "And of you too."

I fished under the table and found the handles of my book bag.

"You're welcome, Michael," she said, still blushing, clasped her hands in front of her chest, and then seemed to realize that her skirt was still hiked to her sternum. She yanked it down impatiently, squirting her breast free like a tiddly wink from its elastic restriction. "I'll just go and get the other orders, shall I?" She turned and passed through the swinging doors of the kitchen.

"Excuse me." I stood up and proceeded to weave my way through the tables to the doors leading to Reception. It's nearly impossible to achieve that very quickly with any great dignity. We didn't break into a run until we had left the dining room.

Of course, he caught me. Right out in front of the front desk. Besides being nearly a foot taller with fifty more pounds of leg muscle, Michael was not wearing a skirt, dress shoes, and carrying a loaded book bag.

Every time I leave Pansy's study, I always look like something that a cat had coughed up. I was in my bedroom picking glue off my arm when my father found me. At least I hoped it was dried glue on my arm and not the substance that seemed to run freely from Buzzer's button nose every time he drank milk.

"What are you doing this afternoon?" My father leaned a shoulder against my vintage photograph of Einstein, his eyes amused. He knew where I had been.

I had changed into jeans and a tee shirt, but I had yet to shake Fiesta's cookie crumbs from my hair. I walked to a window, cranked it open, and leaned my head out, shaking my hair like a wet dog. Gingersnap bits went flying everywhere, hitting the panes like grapeshot, and I waited until I was bodily back into the room before answering.

"I thought about asking Dante to go to the manor with me," I said, finger-combing my hair and searching for something to use to tie it back from my face. Snatching a satiny ribbon the color of raspberries, I slipped it under the sweaty coils at the nape of my neck and brought it up and out, tying it with the ease of long practice. I regarded my reflection with resignation and sighed. I suddenly realized that my father was still watching me. I turned to look at him.

"Would your mother and I do instead?" He grinned, his eyes crinkling at the corners. I grinned back at him as he uncrossed his arms from his chest and leaned over to pick a raisin from my hair. At least I hoped it was a raisin. Buzzer's and Fiesta's lips never touched fruit, although I couldn't say with any certainty whether Lark's ever did. "How about a walk on the beach, daughter, an ice cream, and then we'll go look for the entrance to the secret garden? Violet will keep an eye on Astrid and Aurora while they rest."

Which was how, less than thirty minutes later, the three of us ended up on the Low Street inside the village's only confectionery shop.

Unimaginatively named Penhaligon's Candy, the shop had expanded to carry a tiny coffee bar to accommodate the tourists that straggled in from the beach every summer. Penhaligon's had been the local sweet shop ever since Victoria had been queen, and now the fourth generation of Penhaligons stirred the chocolate and turned on the taffy machine in the front window while the fifth generation manned the counters.

I was nibbling chunks of chocolate ice cream from my loaded cone and wandering outside while Bertie, a fifth-generation Penhaligon, was busily scooping out peach gelato for my mother. A year older than I, Bertie did everything with the overdone flourishes of a performer. He habitually garnished everything he ever sold to me with cherries that had love knots tied in their stems. I had even found a cherry in my soda bottle once with the plastic hors d'oeuvre fork still attached to it.

Liza Weebs passed me on the walk. She was toddling out of the neighboring grocer's and heading back toward her cottage carrying a hemp tote. A bunch of carrots stuck out of its webbing like orange udders.

"Hi, girlie!" she cackled, acknowledging my greeting as she passed. She made it a few steps past, then stopped, and turned to face me, teetering from side to side like a wind-up toy with a fresh battery. "There's something I forgot to tell you about your family."

I paused, an icy lump of chocolate melting on my tongue, and raised my eyebrows at her.

"What was that?" I asked, swallowing. She put a finger to the side of her chin and squinted up at the blue sky. The sunshine reflected off her glasses, and she looked like a praying mantis in a chintz dress and sandals.

"You haven't descended from the original Wildeves. You inherited the estate by default," she cackled again. "Betcha didn't know that, girlie, did you?"

"What do you mean?" I asked, genuinely curious. She grinned, clacking her false teeth like castanets.

"Can't say exactly. That's all I know. That was way before my time, girlie. Way before my time." She spun around, rocking from foot to foot, and toddled away. "Bye, girlie. Give my regards to your grandmam when she comes."

My parents came out of Penhaligon's and watched Liza Weebs as she tottered away.

"Poor dear," my mother murmured, watching as Liza tottered to the middle of the cobblestone lane and proceeded to walk down the center of the street as if she were leading a parade. "She'll get hit one of these days."

"No one would dare," my father laughed, watching with interest as a motorcyclist came to a dead stop behind her before inching past with the delicate horror of an anorexic skirting a pizza.

We walked down to the sandy beach fronting the road and strolled close to the scalloped edge of the outgoing waves. The tiny sparse clouds scudding overhead were as perfectly opalescent as a newborn's fingernails, and the water beside us was lazy, sparkling with the same diamond chips I had seen earlier that morning. The docked fishing boats were on the curve of beach behind us, and ahead stretched the rest of the wavy shoreline, empty save for the village's dwindling supply of tourists catching what sun they could. A little girl in a frilly polka-dotted bathing suit was tossing handfuls of smooth pebbles at her brother, missing by miles as he laughed and dodged.

After a moment of easy silence, I told my parents what Liza Weebs had told me.

"She said the estate had been inherited by default?" my mother repeated curiously and put a tiny scoop of gelato in her mouth. "Did she explain what she meant?"

"No. She just said that it happened way before her time."

"It probably wasn't the first time in the family's history," my father remarked calmly. "Family lines back then died out frequently, and more distant relatives inherited. Having children didn't always come easily, especially sons, and for most of her history, England had enforced the law of primogeniture."

"Primogeniture? I had forgotten all about that." I frowned at the dazzling waves as a breeze sprang up from the water and swirled around us in a salted eddy. "Only males of the family could inherit."

"So if a man only had daughters, his property and wealth wouldn't go to them?" my mother asked and took another bite of gelato.

"It would have to go to the nearest male relative unless there was a special consideration from the king," my father answered. "I would have been more surprised if the family lineage had gone through five hundred years of wars, diseases, and the frequent infertility without being interrupted."

On the way down from the inn to Penhaligon's in the Range Rover, I had already told my parents about the latest things that I had discovered. They had reacted with predictable surprise at finding out about our French heritage, with horrified sympathy for Sarah Wildeve's insanity, but with a harder-to-understand amusement when we discussed the meaning of my great-grandmother's monogram that had been popping up everywhere. They were amused last night, as well, when I had told them about our solution to the mysterious figures the first time.

After a few minutes, I finished my ice cream and tossed the point of the cone to a lonely-looking seagull. He snatched it in midair and flew away screeching.

"There's something that keeps bothering me, but I can't seem to figure out what it is," I said as my mother broke away from us to toss her empty paper bowl and tiny plastic scoop into a nearby trash bin.

"What do you mean, *bocciolo*?" she asked. Up ahead of us the cliffs rose in pieces from the sea. They were the same cliffs that ran inland in a craggy line to cup the tiny fishing village behind us, leaving only the thin pebbled trail that emerged at low tide. This thin pebbled trail was also the same trail that had been traveled during low tide by the trespassers who had discovered Great-uncle Desmond's body only a few weeks earlier.

"Every time I hear the clues, I keep feeling that I'm missing an obvious connection to them, but when I try to grasp what it is, I can't. It seems like it is right there, and every new thing that I learn connects to it in some way, but I'm just not calling it up. It's driving me crazy."

"Let's try this then." My father took my arm and made his way to a low outcropping of rock. He perched on its ledge and turned me around until I stood between his knees. I leaned against him and faced the tide. "Let's go over the clues again and what we know. Maybe we can jog something loose."

My mother sat on a sunny flat of rock beside us and leaned back a little, facing the sky as she listened. One by one, we reiterated the clues.

"Men aren't the dead," I began, closing my eyes to feel the late-summer sun on my face. "That was in the sarcophagus with the fake mummy. I found the real mummy with Great-grandmother's journals. The only part of her journals I don't understand was the part written in the one hidden in the riding boot. 'Today I found another Destiny. If it had gone properly, I would not be here today,'" I quoted. "Then there was the first clue that we would never find the treasure unless we knew Great-uncle Desmond and Aunt Astrid and Aunt Aurora better."

"What else?" my father prodded, his voice rumbling through me.

"Great-uncle Desmond scratched Destiny's monogram on each clue."

"What else?"

"The urn with the name Clarisse De Mornay on it."

"The supposed remains of Clarisse De Mornay," my father clarified thoughtfully. "It must have something to do with her death. An inheritance? Something stolen?"

"I also think that the inscription we found outside on that slab of stone and the inscriptions over the boiler and in the hearth of the fireplace are important, but I don't know how. I know they aren't clues from Great-uncle Desmond."

"The armoire," my mother supplied. "Don't forget that the monogram was scratched on its back panel."

"Perhaps it was to lead someone to the urn," my father suggested and wrapped a heavy arm around my middle, pinning me in so he could rest his chin on the top of my head. "The back panel was the door to the secret passage. I don't think Uncle Desmond counted on someone stumbling in from the other way. He probably intended for his sisters to push their way through to the secret passage in the way that they remembered."

"Then there are the fake tombstones planted by Great-uncle Desmond in the Great Hall," I added. "Tamsin is looking up the names to see who they are. Maybe that will tell us something."

"What else?"

I thought for a moment, listening idly to the waves. The sun on my face and the familiar childhood security of my father's arm made me feel somnolently content. A few more minutes of this and I knew I would drift into a pointless nap. I opened my eyes and squinted into the sun's dazzle in an effort to refocus my thoughts.

"I don't know," I admitted. "I can't think of anything else."

"It must mean something that Destiny is French since Clarisse De Mornay is a French name," my mother murmured. And once again, I felt that frustrating glimpse at something I couldn't quite see.

"Say that again." I closed my eyes and willed my mind to empty itself from the chaotic jumble of clues. Perhaps the connection could be made if the spark that kept igniting and blowing out wasn't crowded. "It has to do with that."

"There is a French connection," my mother said thoughtfully. I could hear her shift on the rock. "Destiny, the urn, Napoleon in the bathtub. He has to be a clue. Rawlings must have placed the mannequin there after Uncle Desmond died."

"What about Confucius?" I asked. My father laughed.

"It could have also been merely a commentary from Rawlings on his view of philosophy. Don't forget, there are mannequins scattered throughout the whole house, and they can't all be clues."

"Elvis," I said suddenly and sat up. "French." I looked over at my mother, who was regarding me out of questioning eyes. "You said there had to be a French connection. What was I thinking of? Of course, there is a French connection." I shifted to look up at my father. "That's it. It's everywhere."

"Slow down, child," my father laughed. "Explain."

"That whole passageway. That first one." I took a deep breath and let it out slowly while my mind vacuumed up the bits and pieces that had fallen into place. "There is Destiny, who was from France. Then there is Clarisse De Mornay, who is probably French. The passageway where the urn was is full of nothing but French artifacts. French underwear. French wigs"—I stopped.

"What is it?" My father gave me a gentle shake.

"That's it," I said slowly. "That's it. It's not just French. It's the date of it all, as well. Those wigs. Everything dates from the French Revolution. Everything." I felt the pit of my stomach flutter, and I whipped out of my father's niche to face my parents. They were regarding me with open amusement and curiosity.

"I knew that those wigs were French because they were styled the same way that Marie Antoinette wore them. In addition, they were all displayed on mannequin heads. Mannequin heads without bodies. Heads on spikes like the French Revolution. The underwear and the shoes and things spilling out of the crates in the passageway were all from that era."

"Go on." My father smiled, and my mother slowly unfolded herself to sit up.

"So what was Elvis's shoe doing in there?" I asked. And then I answered my own question, "To lead us to his figure. Great-uncle Desmond had placed a mannequin of Elvis by that fireplace that had the inscription in the hearth. The inscription that said 'I wait beyond the flames.' Also, above the mantel was a painting. I remember it because it looked truly old. It was of Marie Antoinette."

"Does Napoleon fit into it?" my mother asked, smiling. I bit my lip.

"Just part of the French connection?" I hazarded. "The date is appropriate. Wait!"

"What, child?" My father raised an eyebrow at me.

"The chocolate box on the rim of the tub. The chocolates were French. And so was the book."

"What about the French wines that Basil found, *bambina*?" My mother shifted to clasp her arms around her knee.

"That's right." I stared at her. "He found them by the boiler with the other inscription. The inscription that said, 'I wait beyond the grave.' And the date is right. At least it's close."

"What date, child?" my father asked.

"Seventeen eighty-eight," I answered. I was rewarded with a raise of his slanted eyebrows.

"Seventeen eighty-eight?" he repeated, and a slow smile spread over his features. "That would bring us to the time of the French Revolution as well."

"How's that?" my mother asked.

"Most wines are usually made in vats and then bottled with the date it was made on the label. Some estates, however, had a secondary label with the date that it left the estate, and the better estates would have sold their wine about five years after it was made."

"That would mean that the wine was bottled in 1793," I said excitedly, doing the math.

"The middle of the French Revolution," my mother remarked thoughtfully. "So what on earth did your French grandmother have from the French Revolution that was of value?"

"Do you think that's what the treasure is?" I asked. But before she could answer, I was struck by another connection that nearly sucked everything else from my brain. "That's it. That's it. That is who Clarisse De Mornay is. The date she died. The date on the urn."

"The date, child?" My father dodged a wayward tendril of my ponytail.

"Seventeen ninety-two," I pulled in a deep breath. "She was executed during the French Revolution."

"How do you know, *bambina*?" my mother asked reasonably.

"By the words etched underneath her name. It wasn't 'terrier' like we'd thought. But," I said simply, "the Terror."

"The Reign of Terror," my father said quietly after the pregnant pause of silence that had greeted my statement. "That's what it was called."

"The French Revolution?" my mother asked. He nodded. Another silence descended on us, and I turned around to look out at the sea. I knew that in spite of the tourists we had left behind on the more populated end of the beach, the water would be too cold for bathing. I could smell an early autumn in the air and see it in the wetness of the sunlight.

"That's what was bothering me," I said and turned back. "I guess my subconscious put it together, but the weirdness of Great-uncle Desmond's clues kept distracting me. It's even in the date that the armoire had been built. Basil said that it predated the Regency period by about twenty years. Wasn't the Regency period around the early eighteen hundreds?" My father nodded.

"Around 1811 to about 1820," he answered thoughtfully. "That is if my memory of history is accurate."

"Twenty years or so before the Regency period would make it close to the time of the French Revolution as well."

"What armoire, *bocciolo*?" my mother asked. "The one in the bathroom?"

I nodded.

"That bothered me too, but I couldn't think why," she went on, her voice unaccountably amused. "I think there is something about that armoire being built hundreds of years after the passageway. I wondered what had been there previously."

"Dante said that he had found copies of the house plans in the library," my father said thoughtfully. "They were drawn up on the same old parchment that he had written Basil's translation on."

"What translation?" my mother asked.

"The Latin words Bella and Tamsin had found on a stone slab. Dante wrote Basil's translation down for them on a scrap of old parchment he had found in the manor's library. The blank scraps were all jumbled together with parchments of the manor's floor plans," my father reminded her and laughed dryly. "Of course, we have no way of knowing whether or not they're authentic floor plans or clues fabricated by Uncle Desmond. It wouldn't make much of a difference either way."

"How's that?" I asked.

"Look at it this way," my mother said calmly and stood up from the rock she had been sitting on, brushing down the seat of her pants. "If they are authentic, then we might learn something about the passageway. If they aren't, then they must be another one of Desmond's clues. We would just have to guess which one when we see them. Either way, it would be good to examine them. Ready to go look?"

Thirty minutes later, we were in the manor's library navigating the maze of stacked curios. The wall shelves covered at least two-thirds of the cavernous room and went from mahogany skirting to ornate ceiling. The plastered ceiling had to be over twenty feet from the dirty rug-covered floor. Each wall had its own wooden ladder on rails and rusted wheels, but after looking at them closely, I decided that no one had used them within the last lifetime. Perhaps the last human to scale the ladders had been Great-grandfather James. That is, the last person to get a book to read. Great-uncle Desmond and Rawlings had used the ladders since, but only to climb up to remove books and replace them with curios. Only a handful of books were left, and I could see the mold on the spines from where I stood.

The room carried the pungent choking scent of a neglected tomb. In between the short bursts of mold, I could smell damp rotting leather, dust, and stagnant age. Light streamed in from the tall windows, creating sunny slabs of dust motes alternating with shadows among the piled souvenirs. The room looked like a giant curio shop that had died long ago and was beginning to decompose.

High on the shelves and stacked throughout the room I saw primitively carved wooden masks, stuffed birds, including hummingbirds on strings, ornately nicked brass whatnots, cowbells, porcelain figurines, black iron candlesticks (some over six feet tall), earthenware pottery from dead civilizations, tiny Chinese shoes, mounted dioramas, surfboards as wide as our dining table, carved coconuts, velvet paintings of matadors, fringed evening bags, shields, daggers, tattered medical charts, tooled leather (from belts to book marks), ancient navigational instruments, false teeth labeled with the names of famous people who had passed on, vintage buttons in jars, rusty dental instruments, dead bonsai trees in clay trays, and on and on and on. Second only to the Great Hall and the ballroom in bizarre curios, and first in smell and dust, it was one of the worst rooms in the house.

"*E' tremendo!,*" was my mother's comment when she entered the room. "Poor Desmond!"

My father grinned and found the enormous table and desk by one of the huge fireplaces, pulling free the rolls of parchment that were weighted across its surface. The scattered paperweights consisted of two huge fossilized shark's teeth, a chunk of stone, and a snow globe of the Sydney Opera House. I picked up the latter and shook it vigorously. The roof broke off and floated free. I put it back.

"Let's clear this table a bit and see what we have," my father said and began to stack the miscellaneous music boxes and mannequin heads on the floor below the table's expanse. My mother picked up the chunk of stone pinning the parchments to the table and traced a finger over its cut edges, smiling as she watched my father spread out the papers. There were four sheets of parchment, each the size of the Range Rover's hood and covered in faded ink. We bent over the table to decipher the lines, letters, and numbers.

After a few minutes, I gave up and leaned back against a stack of shrouded boxes. The rooms were labeled, not by name such as the morning room, the dining room, the kitchens, but were labeled by numbers, deciphered only by a miniscule key on a corner too far away for me to read.

"Child, tell me which room had the inscription in the fireplace," my father said thoughtfully and ran his fingertips down the middle of one of the floor plans as if he was speed-reading Braille. "Can you remember how to get there from the main stairs?"

"Not from that," I said helplessly. "I can take you to it, though."

"Let's go," he said and gestured toward the door to the hallway. "I'd like to locate it on the floor plans."

After a few false starts, I found the correct hall and the correct room. It took only a few minutes. My parents bypassed the mannequin of Elvis and knelt next to the fireplace beside me. I felt along the sooty stones and located the incised letters in the hearth wall.

"It's up here," I said and looked at the smoky light struggling past the crusty windows. "If we had a torch, we could see it better."

"Is that the painting?" My mother stood up and peered at the ornately framed canvas above the mantel. Marie's flat eyes looked unseeingly into ours.

"That's the one," I said, nodding, and turned my attention back to my father who was studying the hearth and giving the stones an occasional prod. After a few minutes, he reached up into the flue to trace out the Latin words. Frowning, he withdrew his hands and shifted to lie on the floor, reclining on one shoulder and turning to look directly up into the chimney.

"What is it?" my mother asked curiously. My father's only reply was a thoughtful grunt as he sat up again and reached a hand back up into the flue. I could see the muscles of his forearm rippling. He seemed to be doing something in the fireplace's upper regions. After a few seconds, he got to his feet and wiped his hands thoughtfully on the back pockets of his jeans.

"There seems to be a piece of the inscription missing," he said, turning to look at the cluttered mantel, his eyes moving quickly over the discarded curios that tumbled about the stone shelf. "You can still read it, but a corner is gone. Part of the border."

"The whole house is falling apart, Luc," my mother said, her voice questioning even though her words were in the form of a statement.

"I know, love, I know." He smiled as he continued to search the fireplace's surroundings. "But it doesn't seem as if it was broken off. It seems as if it had been chiseled free and removed."

"What does it look like?" I asked and peered down into a large Chinese jar beside the stonework. "Maybe it's still somewhere in the room."

"It's a piece of Greek key." He held out his hands in the shape and size of a kitchen tile. "I don't think it's very deep."

"A Greek key?" My mother stared at him. Something in her tone made both of us pause. "There was a piece of Greek key on Desmond's table in the library. I was just playing with it."

My father's handsome face creased into a slow grin, and my mother laughed as instant understanding passed between them. Their amused eyes skewed to me, including me in their silent communication, but I frowned in puzzlement.

"Are you telling me that piece of stone I saw you holding is the clue left by Great-uncle Desmond?" I asked and knelt to peer once more up into the flue. "Why would he chisel a piece of the inscription off and put it in the library?"

"That's not it, *bambina*," my mother said gently. "It's a play on words. It's a key."

"A key?" I stood up and looked back at them. "So the key to something is back in the library written on the parchment?"

"Not necessarily, *coca'n ro'is*," my father laughed. "Desmond didn't chisel it off. It's much older than that. It's part of the design. It has been cut in such a way that the missing piece can be detached."

"So what came first?" I asked. "Is Great-uncle Desmond using the key to draw attention to the parchment, implying that the drawings hold a key, or were we supposed to find the plans first and then be led by the key to the fireplace?"

"Let's go see." My father smiled and motioned us toward the door. "I want to look at the parchment again and then bring the key back here."

Once we were back in the library, my father bent over the first parchment we had looked at and traced a route from the stairs to the room we had just left. I peered at the drawn rectangle, but it looked exactly like the other rooms, even down to the outlined space for the fireplace. My father frowned as he studied the drawing.

"I wonder what's up," he said, jabbing a finger at what looked like a meandering hallway drawn into the plans. "There's the secret passageway you and Tamsin had stumbled into on your first night here."

"They drew the secret passageway into the floor plans?" I frowned. "How secret is that?"

"Why not?" my father laughed. "No one would see these except the master of the house." He traced a line to the tower room that had been Great-grandmother Destiny's bedroom. "The secret room that Desmond had stashed the mummy in is drawn in as well."

"Does that mean that we can find all the secret passageways by the floor plans?" my mother asked. My father shrugged.

"Possibly." He looked back at the outline of the room we had just left behind, the one with Marie and Elvis and the missing Greek key. "I wonder what's up with this room, then."

"What do you mean?" My mother turned to look up at his profile. He glanced at her and then picked up the loose chunk of stone that my mother had been playing with earlier.

"The plans don't show a secret room or passageway like it had done with the rooms. Let's go see what this thing does once it's put back in its place," he said and looked thoughtfully at the stone in his hand. "I keep feeling that the key is in the room with the fireplace. Not here in the library."

Once more, we made our way back to the room with the Latin inscription in the hearth wall. Examining the front and back of the chiseled piece of stone, my father got down once more on his knees and felt in the flue for the incisions. Finding the right spot with the fingers of one hand, he reached up with the stone in the other and inserted the chiseled tile into place. I held my breath, watching the muscles of his arm shift as he manipulated the tile first one way and then the other. We didn't have long to wait.

There was a loud grating noise, and a piece of the fireplace began to move. I felt a gasp catch at the back of my throat as the wall moved in front of my father's knees, and a black hole opened up in front of him. The back of the hearth had shifted, and beyond the squat portal, a flight of stone steps led downward into blackness.

"Bingo," my father said softly.

"*Incredibile!*" my mother gasped. And I echoed her, letting loose the breath that had caught in the back of my throat. My father laughed at us.

"I have a couple of torches in the Range Rover." He stood up and dusted his hands off on each other, then on the seat of his jeans. "Let me get them."

"Are we going down?" I asked as we followed him out of the room and to the Great Hall.

"I'm going down," he said and led the way to the front doors. "And if it's safe, I'm coming back and taking both of you down if you would like."

"I would," I said, wondering if we were actually going to discover what, if anything, was waiting beyond the flames.

Probably spiders.

# 9

My father had been in the hidden space behind the fireplace for only twenty minutes.

While my mother and I had waited for his return, I had spent the time fidgeting about the curios—picking up a boomerang, putting it down; picking up an ornately carved dagger, putting it down; picking up an ivory carving, screeching and flinging it across the room when it turned out to be the tiny skull of a mouse. My mother just sat in a smoky sunbeam like a patient Madonna, her silvery blond hair lighting up in a dusty nimbus.

"Why don't you sit here with me, *bocciolo*?" she said when the tiny mouse skull pinged off an ormolu clock like a ricocheting pellet from an air gun. Before I could move, we heard a rustle from the dark hole that had been the fireplace hearth, and my father emerged, grinning and running a hand over the cobwebs smeared over his black hair like a gummy hairnet.

"What did you find?" I blurted out, watching as my mother began picking the webs from his hair while he swiped at his shirt.

"Where did it lead?" she asked as he bent his head.

"You'll need to see for yourselves." He grinned, winking at me, seeing my obvious impatience. I picked up the spare torch that he had left on the mantel and hefted it in my right hand like a squat baton.

"You'll take us in?" I asked and handed the torch to my mother, who promptly handed it back.

"I'd rather you keep it, *bocciolo*. I'll be fine with your father's." She smiled and dusted her hands over her slacks, putting minute smears of web down her thighs.

"I'll take you in," my father laughed. "But be careful. Part of it will have to be single file. And don't worry about the cobwebs. I've already blazed a trail." My father turned back to face the hearth, looking over his shoulder at us as we queued up behind him. "Are you ready? Stay close."

We bent low and entered the passageway. I went in last since I was carrying the second torch. Once past the hearth's threshold, the ceiling opened up several feet high, and we could stand. My father paused to let our eyes adjust to the gloominess.

We were on a landing with a skinny flight of roughly hewn steps descending into darkness so devoid of light it looked like we were in the inner tomb of a pyramid. The smothering stillness was dark, thick, and stale, and the stone underfoot was gritty with dust. Rusty spirals of iron were set at intervals along the high walls, and I felt a giddy mixture of excitement, apprehension, and intense curiosity when I realized that the spirals had once held a procession of lit lanterns and torches hundreds of years ago.

"Ready?" my father asked and began taking the long flight of stairs tumbling away from the ends of our torch beams. "It's quite a long staircase. Be careful."

We carefully descended the treacherous-looking steps, my father in the lead to stop the domino effect that would happen if one of us slipped. The steps were crooked and rough, tipping drunkenly in uneven treads full of dips, unexpected ridges, and slick hollows. I wondered how many pairs of feet through the centuries had trod the stones under mine and realized after nearly stumbling on one sharp protrusion that there couldn't have been many. I wondered if my grandmother even knew of the tunnel's existence.

"How much longer?" my mother murmured curiously. The combined beams of our torches showed nothing but steps and more steps.

"Not much," my father answered her cheerfully, still descending step after careful step. "There are seventy steps. We've done close to forty already."

"That's over three stories," I exclaimed, then recalculated. "No. Maybe only two with a house this size. I don't know. It's hard to tell since the ceilings are so high."

"It's a good thing the steps are shallow," my mother said.

We fell silent again as we finished the steep staircase down into the earth's bowels. The air had changed subtly from musty closeness to the more earthy scent of salt, dirt clods, and dank stones. The bottom of the stairs had abruptly widened into a large room the size of one of the manor's smaller bedrooms, and my father stopped to let us look around at the unexpected cavern.

"It's empty," my mother said, letting her torch beam drag over the rough walls. "But this isn't all, is it?"

On the far wall was a door that looked as large and as solid as an Elizabethan dining table. Its iron bands and hinges had once been thick and heavy, but the salty air of Cornwall had long since reduced the iron into ponderous filigree. There were iron hooks as well and a shaft the size of a battering ram that could be lowered to bar the door.

"Ready?" My father grinned and made his way across the room. "We haven't reached the surprise yet."

"There's a surprise?" I asked as my father pulled the heavy door open. The rusted hinges screeched like a tortured monkey. The tunnel ahead was just as dark as what was behind us, but with slight differences. Instead of roughly hewn gray walls with a high boxlike ceiling above, the tunnel was much wider and arched, and the stones underneath were as smooth and as even as the flagstones in the Great Hall. We started down the passageway. It looked endless, the torch beams touching nothing but blackness and straight tunnel walls.

"We must be outside the house and under earth," my mother stated and turned to look over her shoulder at the blackness behind us. "We're going in the opposite direction of the cliffs, aren't we?"

My father pulled her close with his free arm and grinned.

"You'll see."

My mother looked past his chest at me on his other side and laughed.

"What is your guess, *bocciolo*?"

"It's not leading us to the village, that's for sure," I said and hooked a finger into my father's belt loop. In view of my recent success in falling into secret passageways with no visible way of falling back out, I should bring some books, a snack, and maybe a chamber pot the next time I ventured into the manor. "It's miles to the next house."

"I suppose this passage isn't leading us to the treasure," my mother said and touched the wall. "The stones are cold, like cave stones. Is this leading to a cave?"

My father laughed.

"We're almost there."

Just ahead was another closed door. I could barely make out a rectangular seam joining dark planks with dark stones.

"So have we arrived now?" my mother laughed as we drew near. My father nodded.

"We're here," he said and pulled open the door.

We were at the threshold of what looked like a small cave that ascended up and out into the sunshine. The cavern was no larger than a small tomb, and a drapery of vines rustling gently in the breeze obscured its exit.

"Flowers," my mother said, sounding astonished, and inhaled deeply. "It smells like home."

I knew that she meant her parents' home, where my grandmother tended a garden the size of a small village. It was constantly profuse with blooms, color, and perfume.

"The garden!" I screeched suddenly. The sound bounced around us in the enclosed space like berserk Ping-Pong balls. "It's the way into the hidden garden!" I darted forward and parted the dense drapery of leaves, barely aware of my father's fingers relieving me of the torch in my hand before I could drop it.

"So I see, *bocciolo*," my mother laughed and joined me to peer out of our hidden place in the stones.

Framed in the green fall of leaves was a fantasyland of twisted trees, rioting shrubs, and unruly, cascading, exploding blooms of every color of the rainbow. Vines climbed trees, snaked along the ground like gnarled roots, encircled shrubbery, and hung off statues. It was exuberant, neglected, wild, ancient, and breathtaking.

In front of us, as if framed, stood a fountain of a marble man and woman, their bodies bare, their hands touching, her wild hair brushing his body in stylized waves. They were dancing in the empty marble basin in true Renaissance fashion, looking indolent and slightly martyred, with weak sloping shoulders, swanlike necks, long crooked fingers and enormous feet. Obviously, they were Adam and Eve before the sin, innocent and perfect.

My father slipped past us, parted the vines farther, stepped out of the tiny cave, and then turned to offer us a hand up into some Wildeve ancestor's version of Eden.

"*E' bella!*" my mother exclaimed in breathy Italian. "*Bellissima!*"

I turned to look at the low cave we had just climbed out of. The vines hiding the entry were as dense and as uninviting as a bramble wall, swinging completely closed once my father released the heavy curtain of leaves, and the roof of the cave was nothing more than a hump of undulating ground topped by a bank of weeping shrubs. You would never guess that it masked an entrance to the manor.

I spun around, trying to take it all in. Butterflies flitted about the flowers like blown petals, flickering in the sun. Climbing roses cascaded from the massive branches of the trees, along with late-summer wisteria, white-veined ivy, honeysuckle, jasmine, and other perfumed flowers I couldn't identify. The sunlit grass was long, golden, and interspersed with statuary, scarlet and purple poppies, flowerless snapdragons, moss-covered stones, and wild blackberries gone to seed. The buzzing of bees filled the cloistered silence, and the occasional warble of a songbird came from the greenery around us.

Spellbound, I walked over to a white archway of wisteria and looked through to the path twisting away and out of sight. I ducked low to follow it, and a shower of white petals fell about me like snow. A petal hung on my eyelashes, and I picked it off absently as I followed the path, passing a hidden statue of a child tucked in a tangle of vines that had taken decades to grow. A little boy turned to stone in a cage of wisteria.

I kept to the tangled overgrown path, tripping over the occasional piece of broken statuary and catching myself on tree boles, shrubbery, and vines. I passed a small glade of tiny blue flowers around an exuberant thatch of pink roses growing in the only patch of sunlight. The outer petals of each fat blossom lit up fuchsia red in the light, and their heady perfume filled the glade with the scent of green apples.

Up ahead was a low branch of a tree curving downward in a graceful curl, beckoning me to clamber up in its arms. I hadn't climbed a tree since I had been a child. I ran to the branch, jumped, and pulled myself up like a gymnast flipping up onto a beam, getting a tiny splinter in my hand as a predictable reward for my burst of spontaneous childhood regression.

I clambered up a bit higher and wedged myself in a fork to nurse my thumb, looking around to see what I could see of the garden as I sucked ineffectively at the splinter. The foliage of other trees blocked my view, and all I could do was peer at the gaps in the greenery. To my right was a flash of something that looked like a high wall, and I wondered if a Wildeve ancestor had built a folly in the confines of his garden. Then I remembered the insects I had seen and wondered if there was also a small pool of water. The garden was certainly large enough to hold more than a few surprises.

I heard a faint murmur in the distance, and I wondered if my parents were following the same trail that I had. I frowned at the splinter, picking it out, and listened to the murmur of voices growing slowly louder and louder until I recognized the quivery timbre of Great-aunt Aurora. I jerked my gaze up and looked about me, trying to pierce the green mass to see where she was but couldn't make out anything except a tiny patch of moving pink. In the garden, pink could be anything from a rose, to wisteria, to one of Aunt Aurora's dresses.

How did she get in here? I couldn't see her following the stygian tunnel even if she had happened to wander in right behind us. The garden must have another entrance, one used more frequently than the web-encrusted tunnel my father had discovered. Did that make his tunnel a truly secret one, one that my grandmother didn't even know about? I pondered that question and the unfathomable puzzle of what Aunt Aurora was doing here. I wondered if she had shaken off Violet Pengarth, who was supposed to be keeping them company.

I was shifting on my perch, getting ready to slither down the tree, when Michael wandered into view and stood under the branch I was balanced on. Even though his back was to me, I wondered why he hadn't spotted me yet. I hadn't made a sound, true, but I thought I was visible behind all the waving foliage.

You could blame what happened next on whimsy, or on another burst of spontaneous regression, but it would be more accurate to blame it on thoughtlessness and a knee-jerk reaction to older brothers. I dropped the flake of bark in my hand and launched myself into the air. I screamed as I sailed, earning a split-second flash of astonished surprise from Michael as he looked up. I landed on Michael's back, wrapped my arms and legs around him, and clung to his shirt with my fingers.

"Get off, you lunatic," Michael gasped. "How did you get in here?" He reeled and tried to scrape me off on the bole of a nearby tree. "Where are Mom and Dad?"

"They won't help you," I grunted, having no idea where my parents were. "Scream. They won't hear you."

Michael started laughing. I started laughing. Then we both abruptly stopped when Aunt Astrid suddenly charged into the clearing, brandishing a large stick. She landed a great wallop across Michael's chest. She was trying for me, but my brother spun around at the last minute and caught the blow right under the clasp of my hands.

"Ow, Aunt Astrid," he gasped and spun around again, calculating her aim so he could put his body between the wildly arcing weapon and me.

"It's me, Aunt Astrid! It's only me!" I yelled, ducking my head into the back of Michael's neck. The club whistled by my ear. It wasn't that it didn't occur to me to let go of my brother and defend myself. Or sprint to safety. I couldn't. My fingers were convulsed, and the Jaws of Life could not have pried my legs loose at that point.

"Run!" I screeched as another blow barely missed our heads. "Run! Run! Run!"

"Stop, Aunt Astrid!" Michael gasped and swung around to face her, backing away. "It's okay! It's just Bella." His hands were scrabbling at my arms, unhooking them from his shoulders as he tried to drop me behind him. It was a good move, except that in ducking from Aunt Astrid we had completely forgotten about Aunt Aurora.

There was an unintelligible shout in Spanish from behind as Michael successfully pried my fingers open, and a great whacking thump of leaf-laden branch came crashing down on my head, severing me from my brother's shoulders as cleanly as a machete severing a python's head. I flipped backward into the rosebushes behind us. The blow on my scalp was cushioned by my hair, but I felt every thorn on my way through the mass of roses. I landed on something rock hard, and every vestige of breath left my body.

"What's going on here?" my father's authoritative voice cut across everything. I barely heard Aunt Aurora's keening over the ringing in my head.

"Oh, Luc!" she wailed. "I think I've killed it!"

"Bella!" Michael's worried voice floated overhead. The wall of roses around me quivered and parted. Michael's face swam into view as I fell back and closed my eyes. "Are you all right?"

I thought for a second, sucked in a ragged gasp of air, and started laughing. I could see Michael wondering if I was hysterical. I held up a hand to stave off any slap he might have been contemplating, my laughter genuine if a little convulsive, and my father's anxious face swam up beside Michael's.

"Bella!" He frowned and began pulling the thorn-encrusted branches free from my clothes and hair. "Are you all right? What on earth just happened?"

"Luc?" my mother's worried voice set off a fresh wail from Aunt Aurora. "Is that Bella? Is she all right?"

"She's fine," my father said reassuringly and freed me from my bed of thorny branches. He set me on my feet, and Michael let the wall of roses spring back into place. I rubbed my tailbone and peered with interest back at the clump of rosebushes with the unexpected heart of stone. Before I could say anything, however, Aunt Astrid and Aunt Aurora darted to my side and enveloped me in a group hug, burying me in tears and bosoms.

"Bella!" Aunt Aurora wailed. "Did it get you too?"

I hugged her back and would have thrown a helpless look at my father if I could have seen anything past all the flowered fabric. I clawed a floating sleeve from my mouth.

"She's all right, Aunt Aurora. Here, let go. Let me see her," he said soothingly. I felt my mother's presence hovering outside my aunts' comforting wall of flesh.

"Your poor arms," my mother cried out disapprovingly, and she seized the hand I was using to pat Aunt Aurora's shoulder. "Thank goodness those thorns missed your eyes, *bambina.* How in the world did you end up in the bush like that?"

"Am I missing something?" Jude's unexpected voice entered the glade a split second before he did. I started in surprise. "Gabriel and I could hear the commotion from the maze. Who was that screaming?"

"Bella!" Gabriel yelled enthusiastically, unknowingly answering him, and darted into the tiny clearing like a seed squirting from a lemon. "Hi, Bella!" He ran toward me and added his body to the melee, somehow inserting himself into the center. I could feel his sharp little chin gouging my hip enthusiastically, and I wondered if once we separated we would find him popped between Aunt Aurora's ample thighs like a squashed grape.

"Help," I gurgled. Coming to my rescue, my father gently pried Aunt Aurora and Aunt Astrid from my neck, hiding his smile as he peeled me free.

"What happened to your arms, *poca*?" Jude asked with interest and walked up to lift one closer to his eyes. He jerked his head toward the enormous clot of ancient bushes. "Don't tell me you crashed into those roses. How?"

My mother pulled a handkerchief from my father's pocket and began to swipe at the tiny scratches going down my arms, cleaning off the tiny bubbles of blood. Gabriel continued to hug my thighs, digging his pointed little chin into my hip as he gazed up at me.

"I'll tell you later."

"She ambushed me out of a tree," Michael answered him, satisfied that I was intact, and grinned as I gave him a dark look. "Aunt Astrid and Aunt Aurora didn't know what was attacking me, so they whacked her off my back and into the roses with a stick."

"Bella!" my mother wailed at the explanation and stopped swabbing my scratches long enough to grab my cheek and peer into my eyes for signs of brain damage.

"My dear, that was you?" Aunt Astrid pressed a hand to her heart and staggered backward, sitting heavily onto a moss-covered bench. "Oh, my goodness. I'm so sorry, dear, I'm so sorry. Did I hurt either one of you?"

"That's all right," I said hastily and held my hands up to forestall the horrified exclamations I saw trembling on my great-aunts' lips. "It wasn't your fault. It was mine. I'm really sorry."

"Oh, my goodness," Aunt Astrid continued to press her hand to her heart. "Oh, my goodness."

"It's okay, Aunt Astrid." Michael put a steadying hand on her bony shoulder. "Are you all right?"

"Oh no, dearest, I'm fine. Oh, my goodness. I could have seriously hurt you. Remember, Aurora?"

"I remember, dear," Aunt Aurora answered her sister and patted my face with a shaky hand. "It wasn't you, Bella. I believe Astrid flashed back to that enormous snake. She killed it with the oar, then, too."

"Enormous snake?" Jude grinned. "What snake did you kill with an oar, Aunt Astrid?"

"In the Amazon," she barked and gave a shaky laugh. "It swam right by our canoe. One of those big ones that eat goats."

"You killed a python with an oar from a canoe?" my father asked incredulously, his brogue pronounced. He sounded like he was trying hard not to laugh. My mother was rubbing a palmful of fiery sanitizer on my arms, where the scratches crisscrossed each other. Trust my mother to have sanitizer in the pocket of her linen slacks.

"It wasn't fully grown," Aunt Astrid said sounding embarrassed. "It was only about seven feet long. That was years ago."

"It was much the same," Aunt Aurora explained somewhat cryptically. "She knocked Brother Celestino unconscious as well. The oar was rather large and unwieldy. There was water everywhere, and my literature was ruined."

Gabriel suddenly let go of me to twist a full-blown rose from the mass of bushes beside me. He walked over to Aunt Astrid, who was still sitting on her moss-covered bench and presented the flower to her, his eyes enormous with solemn admiration. She took it from him with a shaky smile of amusement.

"Thank you, *niño*," she laughed. He scrambled away to get a rose for Aunt Aurora.

My mother capped the tiny bottle of sanitizer and dropped it back into her pocket.

"Better, *bambina*?" she asked, smoothing the stray tendrils from my face, checking the back of my head for a bump. But before I could thank her, Gabriel's voice rose curiously from the edge of the rose bushes.

"There's a box in here."

"A box?" my father asked. I froze, my hand involuntarily straying to the answering twinge in my bruised tailbone.

"A stone box," my baby brother amended, his face buried in the petals and leaves, his hands holding the thorny branches aside. "A great, big stone box."

We darted over to his side. Nestled in the enormous bank of roses underneath all the foliage and petals was what looked, at first glance, like a stone bench. My father leaned over Gabriel and moved a heavily laden branch aside, exposing a chiseled letter on its flat top.

"It's not a box, son," my father said thoughtfully. "It's a grave."

"A grave?" my mother gasped. I looked up at Michael and Jude. Jude saw my look and raised a suggestive eyebrow. They leaned into the roses and helped my father clear the top of the stone, holding wads of thorny branches in their hands. We looked down at the inscription chiseled into the lid of the long squat tomb.

"Destiny," my father read aloud. I felt a chill pass gently down my body.

"Destiny?" Aunt Astrid sounded mildly perplexed. "It can't be."

We looked up from contemplating the tomb's lid and stared at her, uncomprehending.

"It can't be," Aunt Aurora supplemented. "Mother was never buried in the garden. She's over in the village cemetery."

"Are you sure?" my father asked. They nodded.

"The men aren't the dead," Jude said softly, quoting from the clue we found in the sarcophagus along with the repulsive wax mummy. "I wonder if this is your grave, Bella. The one you want to open."

"Oh, my goodness," I exclaimed and put a thoughtful hand on my mouth, backing up from the thorny foliage to stare at the mass of flowers.

"What is it, child?" my father said softly, his thick black eyebrows coming down in a sudden frown.

"That's it." I took the hand from my mouth and pointed at the trampled blue flowers around the ancient clump of dark pink roses. "How stupid could I get? It's the rhyme."

"What?" my father repeated. I looked up at him, grinning.

"Roses are red," I quoted, "violets are blue. It belongs to Destiny, and so do you."

"Oh, my goodness, Luc," my mother exclaimed and then looked over at my bemused great-aunts.

Aunt Aurora had magically produced a hankie the size of a pillowcase from the neck of her pink dress and was sniffling daintily into it, her eyes as round as snooker balls as she stared at the roses. Made of sterner stuff, Aunt Astrid rose from her stone seat and walked over to look down at the slab.

"No, that's not Mother's grave," she said flatly. "Dear Bella is right. Desmond's silly little rhyme seems to make more sense now."

"Can we open it?" I asked eagerly and was rewarded with a horrified exclamation from my mother. I looked over at her. "But it's a clue from Great-uncle Desmond."

"He didn't plant that grave in the middle of those bushes, *bocciolo*. He couldn't have. Those bushes took a long time to grow that way," she replied reasonably. "I'm sure that box is someone's grave."

"Are there any dates on it?" Jude asked and shifted another swath of roses from the lid. "I don't see anything, do you?"

"Wait a minute. Hold it steady, son." My father suddenly frowned and reached a long arm down into the clutch of thorns. "What's this?"

We watched as he lifted a small metal box from the tangled heart of the bushes. It was the size of a shoebox and new, its gray surface without gouges or rust.

"Is it locked?" I breathed. "Can you open it?"

Holding the box in one hand, he gently tried the lid's clasp with the other. It opened easily. We all leaned forward. My father looked into the box, grinned, and pulled out another piece of parchment. He read Desmond's words aloud.

"I told you roses were red, and that the violets were blue. See where this led? You understood my clue."

"What does it say on the back?" I asked. "He always puts something on the back."

My father flipped the paper over and read the added words.

"You are on the right track."

"I wonder what he means by that." My mother looked at my father while I danced a jig on the carpet of violet-colored flowers.

"No one knows," I laughed. "But we've done something right."

"That certainly can't be dear Desmond's way of telling us that the hidden treasure was Mother's," Aunt Astrid said briskly. "I thought we already knew that."

"Maybe this isn't about Destiny. Maybe Uncle Desmond wanted to draw our attention to graves." Jude folded his arms over his chest. "This isn't the first reference to graves. There are those fake tombstones in the Great Hall."

"Maybe it has something to do with this garden," Gabriel said innocently, his back to us as he wandered over to a thick vine of ivy and began to swing on it. "He said, 'See where this led.'"

Jude looked speculatively at my great-aunts.

"Aunt Astrid, Aurora," he said, looking from one to the other, "is there a family burial plot in the garden?"

"I believe so," Aunt Astrid said slowly, glancing at Aunt Aurora for confirmation. "Only a few headstones, though. All behind a prickly fence."

"Can you show us?" he asked.

"Certainly," Aunt Astrid answered. "It really isn't far from here. Aurora and I never played near it, though. The burial plot was too atmospheric even though one of the hired boys always kept it up."

"It was absolutely frightening," Aunt Aurora breathed. "Even though we knew that the ones who had passed away were only sleeping."

Cemeteries usually give me the willies. All that walking on dead people. I find it especially nerve-wracking when I have a foot sink into soft earth where somebody and their casket had biodegraded into an earthy pudding. I shook off a shiver.

"It's this way." Aunt Astrid pointed to a spot behind us and began walking away with the intrepid strides of the lead Sherpa on an expedition. "I think."

"I believe you're right, dearest." Aunt Aurora toddled off after her. "It's somewhere near the maze."

That was the second time I had heard of a maze being in the garden.

"Is there really a maze?" I asked as we circumnavigated trees and shrubs toward a denser part of the garden. "What is it like?"

"Overgrown, I imagine," Aunt Astrid snorted. "It used to take a battalion of gardeners to keep this place trimmed and landscaped properly. There was always a boy in the maze clipping and scything. Every house of any size back then had a maze on the property."

"Was it easy to find your way through?" I persisted and felt Gabriel's warm little hand steal into mine. I glanced down, and he grinned up at me. "Do you remember how to get into the center?"

"I don't," Aunt Aurora sighed after a moment. "It confused me as a child even when I knew the key."

"I don't believe that I remember, either, dear." Aunt Astrid smiled apologetically at me. "We never went in there much. It was a bit dark."

"What's in its center?"

"A plain little folly," she answered and glanced at me thoughtfully. "There are curiosities all over the place in here, but I will tell you what I found to be the most fascinating part of the garden."

"What's the most fascinating part of the garden, Aunt Astrid?" Michael came up alongside me and grabbed Gabriel, breaking our hands apart as he swung my baby brother up onto his shoulders. My older brother glanced at me with a grin. "It's better than a leash."

"Much better," my baby brother agreed solemnly, looking around with interest from his new vantage point.

"There's a ruin built in the center of the garden," Aunt Astrid went on as if we hadn't spoken. "People did that back then, you know."

"What?" my mother asked. "Build ruins into their gardens? I had heard of that."

"It gave the estates a false history." My father grinned. "The newly rich tried to look like the old rich."

"Italy does the opposite," my mother laughed. "There are entirely too many ruins. Italy is a very old country. And thrifty. They repair the ruins and use them again."

"There, Astrid, dearest," Aunt Aurora suddenly gasped, cutting off the rest of our speculation. "I see it there. See the spiky fence?"

We had come within sighting distance of the family's burial plot. Ancient trees with twisted arthritic-looking branches ringed it about. The tombstones were squatting in green, luminous air under the foliage, and as we drew near, I felt my toes try to curl up in my shoes.

The wrought-iron fence was rusted and high with lethal-looking spikes along its top like soldiers' spears held aloft. We looked through the bars at the tombstones leaning drunkenly against each other. There were only four, and the letters chiseled into them were covered in lichen and scoured by decades of weather. I gasped when I slowly deciphered the name on the one closest to where we stood.

"That one there." I pointed, realizing that I would be the only one in the group to recognize the inscription. "Henry Bertrand Wildeve. His name was also on one of those tombstones in the Great Hall."

"On those fake tombstones?" Jude asked. I nodded.

"This one must be the real grave marker." I frowned and tentatively tried the gate. It was as unmovable as if it had been welded onto the fence. "I wish I could see the other names. One's missing."

"Missing from where?" my father asked as I crept carefully around the burial plot and its screening fence.

"From here. There are four headstones here, but there are five in the Great Hall."

Michael and Jude looked at each other and split up, going in opposite directions around the fence. I looked over at Michael and Gabriel on the other side of the wrought iron and at Jude, who was walking behind me.

"Read the names if you can see them," I said. Jude raised his eyebrows at me.

"You had only caught a quick glimpse of Uncle Desmond's fake tombstones last night. You can remember them all, *poca?*"

"Maybe."

My parents watched us with amusement while Great-aunts Astrid and Aurora watched us with perplexed frowns.

"Henry Hubert Wildeve," Michael deciphered carefully.

"Henry Hubert Wildeve II," Jude murmured and pointed to one on the far side of the row.

"Hubert Aloyoisius Wildeve," I said, finally making out the name on the last unread marker. I closed my eyes and tried to think back. "Actually," I said slowly, "I think all those names are on the tombstones in the Great Hall, but one is missing, and I don't remember his name."

"It wasn't a Hubert?" Jude laughed. I opened my eyes to shake my head.

"No, he was only one besides Henry Bertrand, not a Hubert."

"So what does it mean?" my mother asked. I looked over at her standing beside Aunt Astrid, who was busily poking at the locked gate with a stick.

"I don't know," I sighed. "I'm stumped. I don't even know who these people are until Tamsin looks the names up at the library."

"So what do we do now?" Aunt Aurora sighed. Aunt Astrid propped her stick up against the bars of the fence.

"It looks like Desmond's silly clue in the rosebushes is at a dead end for now." Aunt Astrid brushed her hands off and looked around. "Why don't we go up and look at Mother's room? That's why we came. That and to see the garden again."

"Where's Violet?" my mother suddenly asked. Jude grinned.

"She's fine. She went back home when these two insisted on coming to see the house again."

"It was pure chance that Jude and I intercepted their phone call to Patrick," Michael laughed and lowered Gabriel from his shoulders. He ran to my mother and took her hand. "They were planning on taking his taxi over here by themselves."

"*E' tremendo,*" my mother murmured under her breath.

"Ready?" Aunt Astrid grinned at her sister. "Let's go see Mother's room." They set off.

"How did you get in here?" I asked Jude as we followed Aunts Astrid and Aurora through the garden. "Through the tunnel?"

"What tunnel?" Jude grinned at me and raised an eyebrow. "Don't tell me you found another tunnel."

"Dad did," I said defensively.

"You found a tunnel to the garden?" Michael heard us and dropped back. "Where? We came in through the gate."

"The gate that Grandmother said is always locked?" I asked. Jude shook his head.

"If you're referring to the huge iron ones in the back, no. Aunt Astrid took us to a small wooden one set into the wall behind the hedge. Apparently that was the one that they used as children."

"What tunnel?" Michael persisted.

I told them about the inscription and moving hearth. My father heard us and turned.

"I'd rather not show it to your great-aunts, just now." He grinned. "Later I'd like one of you to go back and close it up. Bella can show you how."

"After dinner?" Michael asked. My father nodded. Up ahead of us, Aunt Astrid yanked at a low vine in her way, and it came loose from the branches overhead to fall on her sister. Aunt Aurora squeaked, jumped free like startled goat, and kicked at it with defensive vigor.

"We'd better close it up before Astrid or Aurora finds it," My father said quietly, watching the tableau with a grin.

We eventually came to the edge of the garden. An unruly high yew hedge concealed a thick stone wall. Aunt Astrid unwaveringly led us straight to a slender gap, pushed through the prickly branches, and reached a long tanned arm into the greenery. I heard a latch click, and a door made of thick planks swung inward on well-balanced hinges.

"That's the secret way in?" I asked stupidly once I saw what waited for us beyond the portal. We slipped out onto the last flagstone of the rose-bordered path that Tamsin and I had discovered between the house and the garden. I toed the ground and noticed the naked dirt where Tamsin and I had shoved the inscribed slab of stone into the sunlight where we could read it. "Tamsin and I passed by this door several times, and we never even saw it."

"Even when we were girls this door was well hidden," Aunt Astrid answered and slammed the door behind us once we had all exited the hidden garden. She dusted her hands together and then ran both palms through her hair and down the front of her dress. "Well, are we ready to go see Mother's room?"

"Mother's room. After all these years. Oh, Astrid, dearest, I think I'm going to cry."

"No, you aren't, dear. Come on." Aunt Astrid led the way to the back of the manor house. We hurried behind them, following Aunt Astrid as she led the way unerringly through the manor's back doors and upstairs toward her deceased mother's bedchamber.

The door stood open, and we paused at the threshold, giving Great-aunts Astrid and Aurora space to enter alone. I heard a sniffle coming from one of them, guessing it was from Aunt Aurora when Aunt Astrid gave her a brisk slap on the back. It jarred a watery hiccup loose, and Aunt Aurora sniffled again.

"Brace up, dearest," Aunt Astrid barked kindly. Jude grinned, his green eyes kind, and leaned into the room, bracing himself with a hand on the ornate doorjamb.

"Watch out, Aunt Astrid. You're about to step on a spider."

My great-aunt looked down at her sandaled foot and then casually nailed the eight-legged blob to the floor with a quick stomp. She wiped her sole on the edge of the elegant rug.

"You should see the jumping creatures that Peru offers," she said dryly.

"Desmond was forever smearing preserves in the corners," Aunt Aurora breathed enigmatically. Aunt Astrid looked over her shoulder at us and snorted.

"To trap them," Aunt Astrid explained her sister's cryptic comment with a roll of her eyes. "Jam in the corners in tiny little smears. So the bugs would be stuck and die. Silly man. It pretty well brought them indoors."

Knowing Great-uncle Desmond, the man who ate chalk, he was probably aware of that fact and was really doing it to harvest a bit of crunch for his morning muffins.

My father stepped into the room and walked over to a framed watercolor hanging on the wall beside one of the windows. He studied it, frowning. It was of green waves and white foam under a storm green sky.

"Grandmother did this?" he asked, noting the tiny signature of "Destiny" in the corner. Aunt Astrid smiled.

"She did. It must be where you got your talent." She went to stand beside him, and we all flowed hesitantly into the room. "Did you pass any of it along to the children?"

"They all have a fair amount, even Gabriel." My father smiled.

I thought of one of my first attempts with oil paints and the lopsided faintly blue portrait of my mother that was the disappointing result. I could claim that I had been influenced by Picasso, but that wouldn't be even near to the truth. It had been a school project when I was nine. I can still hear my tutor's voice as she lurched expressively around the studio with her arms outstretched like an inebriated seagull, trailing her sleeves over my paint-loaded brush. 'Fly, my dears. Let your feelings soar into the colors.'

"Aurora and I can't draw a straight line, and that's the truth." Aunt Astrid rolled her eyes. "Mother's talent completely passed us by."

"What about this oil painting? This one over the mantel?" Michael interrupted. We turned to look at him. He was standing under the huge canvas suspended over the fireplace. "It looks like Destiny did this one too."

"Mother?" Aunt Aurora wrinkled her powdered brow. "I don't recall mother ever doing oils."

"I don't think she did," Aunt Astrid barked and squinted at the painting of a floundering ship. "But I remember that picture. It always made me feel uncomfortable."

"It is a bit overpowering," my mother murmured and lifted Gabriel to her hip. He wrapped his arms around her neck and stared up at the painting alongside her, his cheek pressed to hers.

"It looks pretty grimy," Jude commented and went to stand beside Michael. Curious, I went to join them, standing in the middle where I could see it better, and I felt a sudden rush of goose bumps domino down my spine.

There was a definite feeling of fear in the brushstrokes.

"Dad?" I said and looked back at my father, who was frowning at the painting above my head.

"Let's take it down," he said abruptly. "I need to see something closer."

Michael and Jude maneuvered the massive frame and managed to unhook the stiff wire from the picture rail high above the painting. They carried it to the flour-laden bed and laid it on the coverlet. A cloud of white rose up around the edges and dispersed gently into the air, making Gabriel sneeze. My father bent over the painting to study it, occasionally running his fingertips over its surface, his face intense.

Even though I watched him with fascination, I had no idea what he was doing. We all held our breath and waited quietly. After a few moments, he stepped back and frowned.

"I've never seen a painting like this before from a woman." He crossed his arms over his chest and continued to stare down at the canvas. Jude was right. It was grimy. It was easy to see the foundering ship under all the layers of soot and dust, but it was harder to make out what the dark blobs were that were scattered all over the shoreline. I leaned down and touched one.

"What are these? Brushstrokes?"

"No," Jude said slowly as he bent over the edge of the bed beside me. "Bella, I think those are men."

"Men?" I echoed and bent closer to a blob next to the signature. I could barely make out the outstretched limbs of a torso. I blinked and bent closer. "They're drowning," I said incredulously, looking back at my father. "Those dark pieces are drowning men."

"I know," he said quietly. "But for all that, it isn't a psychotic painting."

"Oh, my goodness, no," Aunt Aurora breathed and touched her fingertips to her mouth. "Mother certainly wasn't that."

I expected my father to smile at Aunt Aurora's misunderstanding, but he didn't. He continued to stare down at the painting thoughtfully.

"Oh no," he said quietly. "Your mother didn't paint this. It's far too old."

We all turned to stare at him.

"There is a sense of trauma, but no psychosis."

"Say that again, Luc," my mother said, letting Gabriel slip from her arms. He came over to me and wrapped his arms around my hips to press his face into the back of my jeans. I swatted at him.

"There's a sense of trauma, but no psychosis."

"No," Aunt Astrid breathed, sounding more like Aunt Aurora than herself. "The part before that. Are you certain that Mother never painted this?"

"I'm sure Mother never did oils," Aunt Aurora said and stared at the picture.

"I'm certain," my father answered. "This painting is at least two hundred years old." He gestured vaguely toward a glowing brushstroke of yellow. "That color hasn't been made for at least that long."

"Then what about the signature?" Michael asked quietly and ran a fingertip across the black letters in the corner. "Destiny signed it."

"I don't know about that." My father frowned again and reached down to wrap a hand around the side of the frame, lifting it to stand upright on the bed. "Let me look on the back. Sometimes a framer put his mark and the date on the back of a frame with chalk. You'd be surprised at how long that mark lasts."

Jude went to the other side of the painting and held it upright while my father let go of the frame and walked around the bed to look at the painting's back.

"Seventeen ninety-two," he said, his somber expression breaking into a grin. "I was right."

"Seventeen ninety-two, Luc," my mother gasped meaningfully. I felt Gabriel begin to gnaw on my butt. I pried his jaws off my jeans with the heel of my hand against his hard little forehead. It wasn't the first time he had done that to me. I hoped he wasn't going to make a habit of it. Worse yet, I hoped that he wasn't going to greet anyone at the meetings that way. I could think of plenty of elderly sisters whose hearts would never survive it. We would end up plucking baby teeth from corsets with pliers, rather like the time Dante had to pick cactus needles from my hand when I was ten.

I jerked my bored little brother around from behind me.

"Seventeen ninety-two," I repeated. Now it was my turn to frown thoughtfully. "That was the date on the urn."

"Could this be the treasure?" my mother asked, looking dubiously at the canvas. "Is the painting valuable?"

My father shook his head in answer.

"Maybe there's another painting under this one," Michael remarked as my father helped Jude lay the painting back onto the bed. "Perhaps someone painted over a more valuable canvas. Why else would Great-grandmother's name be on it when she hadn't painted it? Maybe Great-uncle Desmond signed the picture with Destiny's name so we know the canvas is significant. He'd already put her monogram on the clues he had planted."

"That makes sense. The clue did say that the treasure belongs to Destiny," my mother murmured and reached out to pull Gabriel back to her side, stilling his restlessness.

"I don't know," my father sighed and looked over at his aunts. "If it's all right with both of you, I would like to take this to my studio and clean it. At the very least I should be able to guess if anyone had painted over something else."

"Oh, my goodness," Aunt Aurora breathed and eyed the massive painting covering the surface of the huge bed. "Will it fit through the doors?"

"Of course," Aunt Astrid barked. "Are we going now?"

"We took Michael's Saab, but we can go back and get my van." Jude shrugged and glanced over at Michael. "Then Michael and I can bring it over and carry it up to your studio."

"That's our cue, dearest." Aunt Astrid rubbed a tired hand over her temple. "I think we'd better be getting back. I feel a slight headache coming on, and I certainly wouldn't object to another quick nap."

"And maybe a wee tot of brandy." Aunt Aurora turned huge blue eyes to my father. "For my aching knees."

"Of course." My father grinned and checked his watch. "It's time we were getting back as well. Maybe I'll have a sip of brandy with you before I start cleaning the picture."

"That would be lovely." Aunt Aurora beamed. "And perhaps a sherry for Astrid."

"Oh no. Not if both of you are having a wee tot of brandy," Aunt Astrid said grimly.

It suddenly occurred to me that neither one of my great-aunts knew about their French heritage. I had just found out that morning, and I had just told my parents on the way to get our ice cream. I wondered when my father was going to tell them. Probably somewhere after their first sip of brandy.

# 10

My father came down from his studio while I was helping my mother prepare dinner.

Great-aunts Astrid and Aurora were already in their tiny suites sleeping off their fatigue, and Gabriel was in the tub taking his bath, happily surrounded by a flotilla of bobbing toys while he made islands of the soapy bubbles. Michael was in his room preparing for the meeting tomorrow, and Jude was back at his cottage finishing up one of the "talks" he had been assigned to give. I had no idea where Dante and Brandt were. Probably still tunneling their way out of Mr. Peevey's sewer with Brandt's phone in their tool bags.

My father came into the kitchen, smelling faintly of solvents, and wrapped his arms around my mother as she tried to roll meatballs in the bowl of herbed breadcrumbs.

"I want both of you to come see the painting," he said, kissing my mother on the neck before reaching around her to steal a shiny olive from the salad bowl.

"Is it Desmond's treasure?" She raised an eyebrow, and he kissed her again.

"No."

"In that case, let me wait until the lasagna is in the oven before I traipse up those stairs with you and Bella."

"So I can go ahead and see it?" I asked and pulled the wooden spoon from the pot of tomato sauce that was simmering on the stove.

"Go ahead, *bocciolo*." My mother smiled. "But when you and your father are done, can you see to Gabriel? He needs to get ready before Albert and Violet come for dinner."

"Sure," I said and took off my apron to hang it on its hook by the larder.

"Come on, *coca'n ro'is.*" My father grinned and held out a hand, waiting for me to join him. "I'd like for you to tell me what you notice about the painting."

My father's art studio is a large attic room over the family apartments. It's huge, lit by skylights and dormer windows, and smells of oils and turpentine. The floorboards are speckled with blobs of color, and a large dais with a model's throne sits under the glow of a skylight. There are various drapes, tables, pictures, photographs, spotlights, props, and even a couple of life-sized artist's mannequins. Easels are scattered in various places, along with blank canvases and pieces of artwork in different stages of completion. The canvases, the easels, and the tables are huge since my father's art has never been small.

Destiny's painting was lying on one of the larger tables, a spotlight trained on its chemically lightened surface. The white light skimmed over the glazed paint, highlighting the cracks and fissures of age, and I could see the swipes where my father had carefully applied the cotton soaked in the cleaning solution.

Mesmerized, I walked over to stand at the base of the painting to stare at it. I felt the goose bumps slide up my body again.

"There's energy in this painting, *leanbh.*" My father came to stand beside me, his fingertips shoved into the pockets of his jeans. "Technically, this painting isn't accurate, but it does carry emotion."

"Fear." I thought about it, looking at the tiny drowning figures, the tempest in the air around the ship, the unmoving rocks. And I touched the jagged hole in the ship's hull. "The artist must have been an eyewitness."

"Perhaps," my father agreed and put a hand on my shoulder. "Do you recognize anything?"

"Recognize anything?" I murmured, glanced up at his profile as he studied the painting in front of us, and then looked back down at the canvas to study it closer.

The cliffs looming over the shoreline were rough, broken, and with a zigzag of forgiving ledges. The ship itself was streamlined, smallish, built for speed, without any kind of ornate figurehead, and its masts were closed tight against what must have been a gale forcing it sideways toward the shore. I looked closer and could see tiny figures scurrying about the sliver of beach. I knew that the sea was on its way to high tide and that the people only had minutes to find higher ground.

"Wait a minute," I said, surprised and stepped back to stare at the whole picture. How did I know that the tide was turning and that it would only take minutes to cover the sandy shore completely? "That's the beach under Tanglewood Manor!"

"It certainly looks like it," my father agreed. "That's what I think too."

"A Wildeve painted this!" I exclaimed. "It has to be another clue from Great-uncle Desmond. He put Destiny's name on it, but a Wildeve from two hundred years ago must have painted it. Whoever it was must have seen a shipwreck on the rocks below the manor."

"Probably."

"Maybe I should have Tamsin look this up in the local history section," I suggested excitedly. "That could be what Great-uncle Desmond was looking up when he went to the library. Maybe he wasn't looking up our genealogy. Maybe he was looking up shipwrecks that happened two hundred years ago." I had a sudden unpleasant thought and stepped closer to the painting to look more closely at the scurrying figures. "Do you think this one was the work of wreckers?"

Wreckers were infamous along the Cornish coast. They used to lure unsuspecting ships on to the rocks with confusing lights; then, once the ship foundered, they would go out and scavenge the ship's cargo, or whatever they could strip from the victims, as well as claim what washed to shore.

"I don't think so." My father frowned, thinking about the less-pleasant history of Cornwall. "It seems too chaotic. I think it was a real shipwreck with survivors."

"That looks like a keg there." I touched a tiny figure, pushing something along the pebbled beach. "Or perhaps a chest of some kind. A trunk."

"Probably saving what cargo they could."

"What's the name of the ship?" I asked, searching the hull for lettering or an insignia.

"There isn't one," my father said. "She didn't paint it in."

"Even though we know this wasn't painted by Great-grandmother Destiny, you still keep saying 'she.' So you still think this was done by a woman?"

My father nodded.

"It's just a gut feeling," he said and gently ran a finger over a brushstroke. "I think it was."

I leaned against him, and he bent to give me a quick kiss on the top of my head.

"There's one more surprise," he said quietly. "I don't believe that the signature was added much later than the time this was painted."

"What?" I stared up at him and he laughed at my expression.

"Whoever painted this over two hundred years ago," he said carefully, "was the one who signed it Destiny. It wasn't your great-uncle Desmond. This is a legitimate two-hundred-year-old signature."

I felt my third rush of goose bumps that day.

"Today I found another Destiny," I quoted softly from my great-grandmother's lost diary, the journal that Great-uncle Desmond had separated from the others to hide in the riding boot. "Great-grandmother must have found this painting." I tried to remember the rest of the quotation, but was lost without having the journal in front of me. Something about her not being there if it had gone properly. I frowned. That didn't make a lot of sense yet.

I traced my fingers over the ornately scrolled letters on the bottom of the painting.

"Do you think that *Destiny* is the name of the painting?" I asked thoughtfully, trying to piece the nuggets together into a coherent chain. "Not the name of the artist?"

"Could be." My father nodded and propped his hands on his hips, looking down at the puzzling painting with one Dali-esque eyebrow raised skeptically. "I had considered that as being as probable as a signature."

"It does seem to be appropriate," I said dryly, renaming the painting of the floundering ship caught in the unexpected storm. "Fate. Destiny."

"Of course, *Destiny* might even be the name of the ship even though the artist didn't paint it on the hulls."

"You both look as if you're in the middle of plotting something together," my mother's amused voice floated into the vast studio. "So tell me about the painting." My father and I turned in unison, and my father laughed.

"Uh-oh," I gasped, suddenly realizing the time. "The lasagna must be in the oven. I'd better go scrub Gabriel and get him presentable for company."

"No rush, *bocciolo*," she said, smiling as I passed her. I rolled my eyes.

"Gabriel isn't the only one who needs to be cleaned up," I said and pulled the ends of my ponytail around to my face, sniffing, finally locating the invasive smell that seemed to be hovering around me in a faint cloud. "I smell a bit like Great-uncle Desmond."

As I went down the attic stairs, I suddenly thought about the framer's date on the back of the picture. Seventeen ninety-two. And then I thought about what we had surmised from the clues that seemed to point to the French Revolution.

Was the treasure something that had been stripped from this shipwreck?

Abruptly I rejected the idea. How could it have belonged to my great-grandmother who was born a hundred years after the wreck?

But then, perhaps *Destiny* really was the name of the ship, and whatever Great-uncle Desmond had found had been washed up from that wreck. Or found in the rocks under the water. I remembered Pansy Bliss's old photograph of my great-uncle in bathing costume with a snorkel in his hand. According to Pansy's gran, he could "swim like a fish." I also couldn't forget that his body had been discovered on the shore below the cliffs, complete with a Speedo compressing his knobby hips and a snorkel in his stiffened fist. But if the treasure that "belonged to Destiny" was something from an old shipwreck that Great-uncle Desmond had found while exploring, then why hadn't he sold whatever it was? He had already done that with all the other valuable bits of the estate.

Nothing was making complete sense yet, but I was seeing glimmers.

Albert Pengarth and his wife, Violet, sat across the table from me.

My parents' dining table is the size of a runway. I think the Italian genes in my mother chose it. Visions of grandchildren were probably dancing in her head along with family reunions and get-togethers. It's definitely large enough to entertain nearly everyone in Halfmoon at the same time.

Okay, that may have been a bit of an exaggeration, but we did have thirteen people squeezed around it along with enough cheesy lasagna to set Ethiopia back on its feet.

Eli, the Pengarths' great-grandson, sat beside me along with Gabriel and kept throwing me bashful looks from under his long eyelashes. Next to my more exuberant darker little brother, blond Eli seemed as ethereal and as fragile as an insect's wing. I gave Eli a smile for every bashful glance.

"Bella," Gabriel had whispered to me after we had seated ourselves at the table, "I told Eli he could marry you if it was all right with Dad."

During the meal, Albert caught me staring absentmindedly at him and gave me a wink, his handsome old spy's face looking amused.

"You're certainly deep in thought, Isabella. I hear you and Tamsin have been looking for treasure."

"Oh my, yes," Aunt Aurora breathed. "They've been very busy. So far they found out that I'm French."

Albert blinked at that, turning to his wife for a translation.

"Your great-aunts have been telling me all about it this afternoon," she said, smiling her cheerful smile at me, and then looked questioningly at Aunt Aurora. "But I don't believe I know what you are referring to, my dear."

"It's true. Dear Astrid and I are half French."

"It seems that our mother was from France. She had an English father, though," Aunt Astrid clarified, holding a forkful of salad. "We have no knowledge about our family on either parents' side, especially Mother's. Seems that Bella talked to an old lady that knew us as children. She remembered Mother and said that she was half French."

"Bella," Gabriel whispered urgently from the other side of Eli and picked a mushroom from his salad bowl, holding it aloft with a forefinger and thumb. "These grow in doo-doo."

"What old lady is that, dear?" Violet asked me, distracting me from answering Gabriel. I reached around Eli to flick at my little brother's ear. He grinned and put the offending fungus down on Eli's plate. Eli stared at it.

"Liza Weebs. She babysat Great-uncle Desmond."

"Ah, Liza," Albert said thoughtfully. "Isn't she that tiny little woman who lives by the Moonstone pub? A cottage covered in roses with a wheelchair ramp?"

I nodded, and Violet rolled her eyes heavenward, looking speechless for a moment before pressing a dainty birdlike hand to her sternum.

"She used to be Elsie Schnitzler's return visit."

Elsie Schnitzler is an eighty-one-year-old Austrian sister in the Halfmoon congregation. Extremely hard of hearing and too stubborn to wear a deaf aid, she has a tendency to shout her words loudly in a Viennese accent so thick it sounds like she's coughing up barbed wire. The microphone attendant just discreetly turns off the microphone when she speaks into it so she doesn't blow a speaker.

I could understand Violet's expressively rolled eyes, picturing the discussion that must have raged between Elsie Schnitzler shouting her thick phlegmatic consonants and Liza, fortified with a fishbowl of scotch, staunchly refusing to be anything but Church of England.

"I wanted to know about our family history," I said, explaining my visit to Liza. "Arabel Bunt sent me to her."

"If you want history, do you know who is a good person to try?" Albert asked. "Try Bunny Dawlish."

Bunny Dawlish is the Pengarths' neighbor and my only remaining Bible student. I taught her on Thursday mornings. I had two other people who had been studying with me, but one had recently moved to London, and the other had quietly died just two weeks ago while waiting for her tea to steep.

Bunny is a befuddled energetic seventy-something, and her passions are gardening, gossiping, and her best friend and neighbor on the other side, Ginger Tregaren. Ginger is an equally befuddled and energetic elderly man who usually sits in on her study. Bunny and Ginger share a thing about miracles. Only last week she showed me a bunion on Ginger's gnarly foot that she swore looked like Saint Francis of Assisi gathering herbs. It looked more like a cross between a Brillo pad and the budding of a sixth toe to me, but she wanted me to touch it for a blessing anyway. I had to think quickly to find a tactful way to refuse. We hadn't covered modern-day miracles with Bunny yet.

"Bunny knows about history?" I asked, and I noticed Michael's hastily covered grin. I had told him about the miracle bunion.

"I don't know how much she carries in her head," Albert said, glancing over at Aunts Astrid and Aurora, "but I know she has quite an extensive library on the subject. She has personal papers and letters from other families that her historian grandfather and her father had gathered and bound together. She might even have something that had been written about your family."

I thought of the shipwreck that seemed to have occurred below the family's manor house, and I thought about the names on the tombstones in the garden, not to mention the extra tombstone propped up in the Great Hall.

"Thank you." I smiled. "That's a good idea. I'll ask her tomorrow at the study."

It wasn't until the Pengarths had left and we had finished our own family study that evening that I was to decipher a major part of Great-uncle Desmond's clues.

It began with Tamsin's phone call from work while my mother and I were washing dishes. My mother had handed me the receiver, trading it for the dishtowel in my hands.

"It's for you, *bambina*. It's Tamsin. I think she's calling from the library."

I took the receiver and could hear Colonel Arbuthnot shouting in the background.

"Hi," I said informally. "What did you find out?"

"I don't know which part to tell you first," she said, sounding breathless. I heard a sudden crash after her pause and Ms. Dilly's voice shouting over Colonel Arbuthnot. "I had just found out who Clarisse De Mornay was."

"Wait a minute." I put my hand over the mouthpiece and looked over at my mother who was quietly drying the lasagna pan it had just taken me fifteen minutes to chip clean. "Can I meet Tamsin at the manor?"

"Tonight?" My mother raised a delicate eyebrow at me, looking worried as she paused in mid swipe. "I don't know, *bocciolo*. Why?"

"She said she found something out. I want to take her to the manor and show her the tunnel and the burial plot in the garden." I bit my lip. "It's not even cloudy tonight, and I'll take Michael."

"Take Michael where?" my brother asked cheerfully, stepping into the kitchen with an empty soda glass. He leaned past my mother at the sink and began rinsing the glass in the suds.

"Will you be willing to take Bella and Tamsin to the manor tonight?" my mother asked, still sounding unsure. My brother looked at me with raised eyebrows.

"Why? Didn't you get enough of the place this afternoon?" He grinned.

"Please?" I pleaded. "I'll show you the tunnel to the garden."

"That's right. You never showed it to us today. Dad did say he wanted one of us to go back there and close it. He said those stairs are pretty treacherous."

"Go ask your father." My mother suddenly capitulated with a roll of her eyes and a smile. "If he says it's all right, you may go."

Twenty minutes later, we were in Michael's Saab bouncing over the cliff lane potholes on our way to meet Tamsin at the manor. She was in her cherry red Mini waiting for us when we bobbled around the sweep to park beside her, getting out of her car when Michael cut his engine.

"So tell me." I grinned at her as I got out of the car, handing her a torch. "Who is Clarisse De Mornay? I'm dying to find out." We had hung up after we had made arrangements to meet each other at the manor, deciding to see each other face-to-face to share our news.

"First things first." She grinned as Michael got out of the car. I left my rucksack in the floorboards, grabbed the third torch in our trio, and slammed the passenger door. Tamsin clicked on her light. "I looked up all the names on the fake tombstones in the Great Hall."

"We found the real ones in the garden," I said as we trooped up the wide sweep of stairs to the front doors. "There's a burial plot out back."

A wind sprang up from the cliff and rustled something in Tamsin's hand. I looked down and saw a rolled sheaf of papers. Overhead a lone cloud sailed under the stars, moving rapidly inland. I could smell salt and a hint of ozone.

"Summer's moving out," Michael remarked calmly, firmly clamped the heavy torch under his arm, and unlocked the massive manor doors. They opened with a groan worthy of Hitchcock. We stepped inside, and Tamsin walked over to the row of leaning tombstones. All were still facing outward where Dante and Brandt had left them. Curious to see if I had identified the stones in the burial plot correctly, I shined my torch beam over their inscriptions.

"That's the one!" I said excitedly and let my beam rest on the tombstone of James George Wildeve, born in 1760 and already dead by thirty-three years of age. I blinked at the date of his death, suddenly noticing its significance.

"The one what?" Tamsin asked, clamped the torch between her jaw and shoulder like a phone receiver, and hurriedly unrolled her papers to shuffle through them.

"James George is the one that's not in the garden's burial plot."

"You mean you found only four of the graves? Only four were in the plot?" Tamsin's head jerked up with interest, and she caught the torch in her free hand. "But not him?"

"He's the only one," I said, still staring at the date of his death chiseled into the stone. "Why?"

"These ones," she said, giving up rifling her papers for a moment to shine her torch over the names on the other tombstones, leaving out James George, "are all related. Father and son down through four generations. I have their birth certificates and death certificates here." She let her beam linger on the last tombstone. "This one, Henry Bertrand Wildeve, is your great-great-grandfather. He's Sir James's father."

"Sir James who was married to Destiny?" Michael asked and went to stand at the tombstone, looking down at it like he was actually standing at his great-great-grandfather's grave. "So that's why they're in the garden."

"Garden?" Tamsin suddenly noticed what we had been saying. "Wait a minute. You've been saying 'garden.' You found the way into the garden?"

"That's my other news." I grinned at her. "We found another passageway."

"Another one?" Her mouth dropped open slightly as she frowned at me. "How many passageways does this place have?"

I suddenly thought of the floor plans unrolled on the table in the library and realized that we had never looked. Not that it would make a difference. The truly secret ones were never drawn in, and I didn't know the layout of the house well enough to read what I was looking at. I thought about taking the floor plans home to let my grandmother look them over when she came. She would be able to point out the secret passages. I wondered if there were more clues left in the other hidden rooms and passageways. That is, if there were others, and we hadn't actually discovered all the secrets already.

"Dad found it," I said. "Remember the fireplace with the inscription on it that said, 'I wait beyond the flames'?"

"Elvis and Marie Antoinette?"

"Oh, that's right." It was my turn to stare at her openmouthed. "You don't know yet. We figured out what some of the clues mean." I told her about our surmises about the French Revolution, the fireplace, and its secret tunnel, and ended with having landed tailbone first on the grave marker with Destiny's name on it. "I'm guessing that whatever was on the grave's lid was so weathered that Great-uncle Desmond could chisel his clue of 'Destiny' on it so we would find the box he had stashed in the roses."

"Wait. Wait. Wait." Tamsin crushed the papers in her hand and clutched a fistful of her dark hair, making it stand up over her scalp like a feather duster. She clenched her eyes shut. "So you are French."

"Barely," I said, wondering why she picked that random nugget from my recital. She opened her eyes to stare at me. They gleamed spectrally in the glow from my torch.

"Then you're going to love what I had found out at the library. First, let me tell you about James George, the one born in 1760." She grinned and flashed her beam over his tombstone.

"Who is he?" Michael looked at both of us, his torch beam shining on the floor at his feet. "Is he even related to the others?"

"He's a cousin."

"Of whom?" I said blankly.

"Of Hubert Aloyoisius, here," she said and trained her beam on the tombstone dated from 1770 to 1840. "James George was the owner of

Tanglewood, and he had died without issue. His cousin Hubert Aloyoisius inherited. If James hadn't died, your family wouldn't have originally been from Halfmoon."

"That's what Liza Weebs had said. She said that we weren't the original owners of Tanglewood." I looked at Michael. "Now why do Tamsin's words remind me of something else? I can't think what."

"What words?"

"That last part. If James hadn't died, we wouldn't be from Halfmoon." I knew that she had meant that we wouldn't be standing in the manor. It would have never been in the family. Michael merely raised his eyebrows.

"I'll think of it eventually," I said, frustrated, and looked back at Tamsin. "What did he die of?"

"James George?" Tamsin slowly widened her eyes until they were shiny black pools. "This is the interesting part. He drowned at sea. He was a smuggler."

Her low voice echoed weirdly in the vast hall, and I felt the hair on my neck stir. I reached back and touched my nape, stilling the involuntary goose bumps that rose when I immediately thought of the painting of the foundering ship.

"That can't be," I murmured, speaking to myself as I looked back at the date of James George's death. "Seventeen ninety-three is when he died. That's a year after the shipwreck was painted, not a year before. So that can't be the shipwreck."

"What are you talking about?" Tamsin asked curiously. I blinked back at her, thinking.

"How did you find out he had been a smuggler?" Michael asked. Tamsin shrugged.

"It's pretty much local legend. He was never caught, but local historians had written about him. He had his own ship, and every time the moon was dark, he went to France and smuggled brandy and whatever."

"Brandy." I looked up. "Those wine bottles."

"French wine." Tamsin's eyes widened again into shiny black pools. "The bottle Basil found had water stains on the label. Those bottles of wine are probably some of his contraband."

"So I wonder why Great-uncle Desmond made a fake tombstone for James George," Michael murmured, listening to us with only half of his attention. "If he drowned at sea, he certainly wouldn't be buried anywhere. Unless"—he looked at Tamsin—"he was washed up somewhere. Was he?"

Tamsin shook her head, her eyes still enormous.

"He was too far out to sea. There were eyewitness accounts, though. His ship and all the men sank in a storm, and there were only two survivors. They were washed up in France. Apparently they were close enough to the French coast when the boat went down, and two men managed to make it to shore a day later after the storm abated."

"Then why did Great-uncle Desmond make a fake tombstone?" I repeated Michael and bent over it, studying the chiseled name as if it could tell me the answer. "He obviously wanted to draw attention to James George. Did you find out anything else about him?"

"No." She paused. And when I turned to look over my shoulder, her eyes went from enormous black pools to puzzled slits. "You were talking about a shipwreck painting that was done the year before James George died. Seventeen ninety-two? What painting?"

"It's in Dad's studio now. It was the painting of the foundered ship hanging over Destiny's mantel—," I jumped when she interrupted me with a sudden loud gasp.

"I forgot! That's the best part!" She clamped her torch between her jaw and her shoulder again and began to rifle feverishly through her papers. Abruptly stopping on one sheet, she stripped it from its slot and handed it to me with a flourish. "Read that."

I stood up from crouching by James's tombstone and went over to where she stood holding out the crumpled paper, taking it curiously. Michael came up behind me and shined his torch beam on it so we could read it together. I felt my heart race in giddy thumps as I realized the significance of what I was reading.

It was a copy of Destiny's birth registration. Not my great-grandmother's birth registration. It was the birth registration of another Destiny who was born in 1776. For the second time, I felt goose bumps swell over my skin.

"Today I found another Destiny," I quoted softly from my great-grandmother's journal.

"Bella," Michael said quietly, his voice right above my head, "look at her mother's name."

"Clarisse De Mornay," I gulped. "How did you find this?"

"I got into the French records and found it under Clarisse De Mornay."

"Did you find anything else?" I looked up at her, feeling my own eyes grow wide. "Did you find out who Clarisse herself was?"

Tamsin shook her head, and I could see a glimpse of frustration on her face as she frowned.

"If she had been executed during the French Revolution, there is a good chance that her papers had been destroyed," Michael stated thoughtfully and moved away to train his light on the rest of the sheaf of papers in Tamsin's hand. "Do you have anything from Clarisse's daughter? The first Destiny?"

Tamsin shook her head.

"That's all I could find. She must have died in the French Revolution with her mother." She frowned. "I'm going to try to do more research later. I had just found this last bit right before I called you."

"Thanks for looking all that up." I accepted the rest of the sheaf of papers from her hand, realizing that they were copies of the information she had found that day. I rolled them up and shoved them deep into the hip pocket of my jeans. "Come on, let's go ahead and shut the entry to the tunnel."

"When do I get to see the garden? What's it like?" Tamsin asked, her voice breathlessly curious. I considered her question, took a deep breath, and turned to look at her before feeling the words abruptly abandon me.

"I can't describe it," I finally said and shrugged helplessly. "It's unbelievable. You'll have to see it for yourself."

"In the dark?" Michael laughed.

"I hadn't thought of that." I raised my eyebrows as I regarded Tamsin, trying to picture the ancient and wild greenery in the moonlight. "But, you know, that might be an experience in itself."

I led them to the 'Elvis' room where the tunnel began and shined my torch up into the fireplace, picking out the inscription with the strong beam.

"See that piece of stone with the Greek key on it?" I asked as Michael knelt beside me, bending lower so that he could see it clearly. "You turn it counterclockwise if you want to open the wall to the tunnel."

"And the other way to close it," Michael supplemented the rest of the instructions and reached up to grasp the stone. I put my hand on his forearm to stop him.

"Let's go through the tunnel to the garden, first. We'll close it up when we get back out."

"And not take the much easier way through the hedge door that Aunt Astrid had taken us through?" He grinned. "You're right. I would like to see the tunnel myself, and it shouldn't take us too long."

# 11

We parted the veil of vines, stepped out under the starry sky, and the garden shimmered before us in the silver light, all spectral blooms gleaming in black shadows. Tamsin gasped. So did I, and I'd seen it before.

The white wisteria glowed and moved like misted breath, making Adam and Eve dance in the flickering shadows. A cool breeze was rustling the leaves around us, stirring our hair, and then moving up and out into the treetops.

"I wonder where the ruins are," Michael murmured. A windblown leaf floated in front of us, swaying from side to side until it landed on a ghostly hump of stone.

"Somewhere in the center of the garden," I said, remembering Aunt Astrid's words. "Do you want to go see it in the moonlight?"

"Ruins?" Tamsin shifted her beam to pick out the tops of the trees around us in a slow sweeping arc. "Ruins in the garden? Of what?"

"Aunt Astrid and Aunt Aurora didn't know. They said that they would play with Grandmother there when they were children, but that no one had ever told them if the ruins were real or just some kind of gothic reproduction."

"I'd like to see it," she said. Another soft breeze lifted her hair, blowing a short dark tendril across her eyes. She brushed it away and shined her beam at me. "Can you find it?"

"We can try." Michael grinned and looked up at the deep sky.

"What are you doing?" I asked as he spun around slowly, his face to the heavens.

"Trying to get my bearings." He pointed to a spot over my shoulder. "I think that way is toward the center of the garden."

"I wish I could do that. Then I would be able to read my territory cards," Tamsin muttered, watching him. And we began our surreal trek toward the center of the garden, following Michael who paused every now and again to look at the sky above us.

The garden was silver with tarnished starlight. Tree branches raised and dipped in angles and curls, their foliage moving in the sporadic breeze and tossing flower petals with every fresh wave. I felt like I was walking through a dream.

We eventually wandered into a tree-rimmed glade and stopped dead. We had found the ruins. The broken walls rose up in places as high as twenty feet, and ancient climbing roses twined thorny arms over the stones and through paneless windows like Sleeping Beauty's castle. I staggered backward and sat down heavily on a conveniently placed stone bench.

"Oh, my goodness," I breathed my only comment, feeling speechless. Tamsin and Michael were frozen in front of me.

Starlight glittered on the ghostly pink roses, making them look as if they were made of ice and smoke. Clouds of blooms hung in clusters, and a carpet of scattered petals rested on ledges, sills, and grass in drifts of ethereal confetti. The whole structure was in the shape of a squat broken tower with several crumbling antechambers rimming the round curve of stone. Michael was the first to break the spell. He walked to one of the large antechambers and peered over a windowsill into the ruin's rubble-strewn center.

"You have to see this," he said quietly. I reached for Tamsin's hand as I stood up, and together we crept up to Michael to peer over the sill.

Flowers of every shape and moon-bleached color carpeted the darkened inside. Wildflowers. Flowers from the garden. Decades of seeds had collected and grown inside the protection of the broken walls. Vines and thinly scattered trees as slender as whips grew toward the sky, and on one wall I could make out the enormous arched lintel and hearth of a stone fireplace.

A wind swept through, rustled the vines, and a shower of rose petals fell in glittering butterfly movements around us. Mesmerized, I clambered over the sill, picked my way delicately over the thorns, and dropped down on the other side.

"Bella," Michael warned quietly, "you might want to wait until daylight."

"I have a torch," I said reasonably and shined it toward the enormous fireplace on the other side of the antechamber. "I won't go any farther than this room." I crept carefully into the room's center, and the tall flowers released their fragrance as I waded through them.

"What about mantraps, Isabella?" Tamsin breathed from her place behind the windowsill. I froze, looking over my shoulder.

"Mantraps?" I stared at her incredulously. "But this is in a walled garden."

"You're scaring me," she said plaintively. But before I could reply, I heard a stealthy rustle behind me in the tall grass. I swung around with the torch's beam and saw nothing.

"Bella," Michael's order was implicit in his tone. "Listen to me. Get out and leave it for the daytime." Before I could obey, I heard another ominous rustle, this time closer. I swept the area with my light, frowning.

"Did you hear that?" I whispered and held still, straining my ears. I wasn't moving until I identified the sound. Or at least figured out where it was coming from so I wouldn't inadvertently step on it, whatever it was.

"Hear what?" I could hear the impatient frown in Michael's voice. The grass rustled again, this time by the ruin's outer wall, and I backed away from it as carefully as I could.

"That rustle," I whispered back, freezing when the rustle suddenly came from the grass at my feet.

"Bella, if you aren't coming out, I'm coming in and getting you," Michael said a bit grimly. Ignoring him, I jerked my torch beam to my feet. Three bulbous pairs of glittering eyes stared back up at me.

"Rats!" I screamed lustily and took off running, bounding over the thigh-high flowers like Julie Andrews in the *Sound of Music.* The flowers around me burst into sudden terrifying life. Loud squeaks and rustlings came at me from all sides, and I took off toward the open doorway on the far side of the antechamber. I didn't know where the open doorway led. I didn't much care. I was getting out of there somehow, but I wasn't going to step on the rats between Michael and me to do it.

I left one long trail of a scream as I vaulted over the broken stones in front of the threshold, half-expecting to land on a squirming mass of furry squeaking rat bodies. I didn't. I landed on something else. Whatever it was, it yowled like a puma. My knees buckled in surprise, and I pitched facedown into the prickly flowers, pinning whatever was screaming under my stomach. It writhed in a mass of furious muscles, and claws punctured my belly. I screamed, flipped myself over, and the furry mass bounded off, puma-screaming all the way. Hands descended on me, and I screamed again.

"It's me!" Michael's exasperated voice boomed. And the hands hauled me unceremoniously to my feet, shaking me a little before sliding to my knees. "Hold on to your torch!" he commanded. I grunted loudly as I was suddenly hoisted aloft and slung over his shoulder like a duffel bag.

"Put me down!" I gasped stupidly. An arm clamped on my knees, stilling my kicking.

"Hold still, or I'll leave you to the rats."

"No!" I screeched unreasonably in alarmed protest and began struggling again. "The rats will eat me!"

"Bella!" He landed a stinging slap on my backside. I gasped and shut my mouth. "Stop fighting me, you little idiot! Bella, how could you do something so stupid! Anything could have happened." I bobbled helplessly over Michael's shoulder, my face slapping jarringly on his back with every stride. "What possessed you to run blindly into the ruins?"

"I'm telling Dad," I said childishly, still rattled, my posterior stinging with the imprint of my brother's hand. Michael's annoying chuckle rumbled under me. I was deposited over the sill to land ignominiously on the other side beside an agitated Tamsin. Michael climbed out behind me.

"No you won't," Michael laughed again, running his hand through his hair. Rose petals floated down like confetti. He was right. I wasn't about to tell my father that I had climbed into the starlit ruins against Michael's better judgment.

"Bella, are you all right?" Tamsin fell on me in a hug and then stepped back to brush off the crushed bits of flowers that clung to me. I felt my toes curl up in my shoes at the thought of the rats. I grabbed her hands and edged away, dragging her with me.

"I'm fine, but let's get out of here. This place is crawling with rats."

"They're more afraid of you than you are of them," Michael said reasonably and picked a leafy twig from his thick hair.

"They were chasing me!" I declared, contradicting him as he laughed. "Didn't you hear them?"

"I heard them scatter. They were trying to get away from you."

I gave him an exasperated look, lifted the hem of my tee shirt, and looked at the scratches on my stomach. The beam of my torch picked out tiny drops of blood that looked black in the yellowed light.

"What happened?" Tamsin gasped. I made a face as I ran a finger over the row of scratches.

"I fell on that nasty cat." I stopped and blinked, hearing myself, then jerked my head up to stare at her. "The ginger tomcat. He's outside! How did he get outside?"

"What ginger tom?" Michael asked and brushed his hands off on his shirt.

"Tamsin got a stray tomcat from the boardinghouse, and we brought it here to chase away the rats. It was so angry at being boxed up we tipped it out into the cellars and closed the door behind it. We were going to ask you to let it out later."

"I forgot about him!" Tamsin put long fingers over her mouth, looking horrified at her lapse. "Poor thing."

"I know." I dropped the hem of my shirt over the scratches and scrubbed vigorously. They were already starting to itch. "I did too. I daresay I would have remembered in the morning."

"Well," Michael said dryly, "no need to worry. He's out now."

"Yes, but how?" I said and stared up at him. "Michael, this means there is another way from the house to the garden. A tunnel from the cellars."

Tamsin and Michael looked at me wordlessly, and I could see the cogs turning in their brains. Unfortunately, my cogs were still jarred out of sync from my rat encounter. I watched them, feeling a bit gobsmacked that there had to be yet another tunnel. In the words of Tamsin, I voiced my last question out loud, "Just how many passages did this place have? And why?"

"Bella," Michael laughed. "Of course, there are tunnels. Two hundred years ago a smuggler lived here."

"Do you think he built them?" I countered, not being able to make sense of his unspoken reasoning. "This house was here three hundred years before he was."

"Bella," Michael said dryly, "haven't you heard of remodeling? He could have had some workman and stonemasons in to build fireplaces and false walls over some of the servants' back passages. All he had to do was block the ways in and out with hidden doors."

"What about the tunnels underground?" I asked, noticing Tamsin's gaze bouncing back and forth between us like she was at Wimbledon.

"That's easily done if you had enough time and manpower."

"Oh, my goodness!" Tamsin suddenly blurted out. "The tunnel we just came through. There was a large room in the middle of it. James George could have used it for storing the contraband until he could sell it or get rid of it."

"That's an idea," I said slowly, rubbing a hand over the scratches. Tamsin looked down at my stomach.

"I still have sanitizer in my pocket," she said, grinning, and fished it out to hand it to me. I squeezed a blob on to my fingertips, smeared the icy goo over my scratches, and felt a flush of chills from the sting. I handed the small bottle back to her.

"Thanks," I said. Michael was watching the procedure with his arms crossed over his chest, the torch in his hand shining its long beam into a treetop behind him. I looked up into his shadowed face. "So how did the tomcat get out? Any ideas on where to start?"

"I have one," Tamsin said timidly and gestured behind us in the vague direction of the manor house. "What about behind the boiler fireplace in the cellars?"

"Why the boiler?" I asked. Michael raised both eyebrows and answered my question.

"The inscription. There was an inscription over the hearth of the fireplace we just came through. They obviously direct us to the tunnels. Perhaps the one over the boiler directs us to a tunnel as well," he said. He quoted the inscription that Basil had discovered in the cellars, "I wait beyond the grave."

Both fireplaces, the one in the cellar behind the boiler and the one in the house with Elvis as sentinel, had the same stonemason's mark of the Greek key and the two different inscriptions. We knew what "I wait beyond the flames" meant. It meant that a tunnel was behind the hearth. But the boiler's inscription of "I wait beyond the grave" must only mean one thing. It was another way out into the garden from behind the boiler, via a grave. The only grave I knew of above ground where one could actually pass through to freedom was the one with the slab bearing Destiny's name.

Tamsin and I suddenly looked at each other, our minds obviously following the same train of thought. I felt my eyes growing wider and wider.

"The Destiny grave. That must be the tunnel's entrance," Tamsin gasped.

"Great-uncle Desmond's clues," I gasped back.

Michael was looking at both of us, his eyes pools of shadow below his lowered eyebrows. I could tell by the grim set of his mouth that he was way ahead of us. I looked up at him pleadingly.

"Oh, all right," he said a moment later and sighed heavily, pulling his mobile phone from his pocket.

"Who are you calling?"

"Dante. If there is a tunnel under that slab, I'm not letting you go in without me, and I'm certainly not going in that thing without someone on the outside knowing where we are in case we get shut in."

"Good idea," I said dryly, remembering the other passageways I had managed to get into without discovering how to get back out.

"And there's something else you haven't considered," he went on, placing the call to our eldest brother. "Unless the cat tripped some inside mechanism that moved the slab, there is no way that cat got out through there. If that slab is still in place, there has to be another way that the cat used to get out."

"But it still makes sense to check," I protested. "Somewhere there is another tunnel, and it's the only place we can think of that has a grave to fit the inscription over the boiler."

"I agree, *poca*. We should at least look to see if the slab has been moved." Dante must have picked up the phone at the other end. Michael turned away from us and began talking. We listened to the one-sided conversation as he made arrangements with Dante to meet us by the fountain of Adam and Eve, telling our older brother where the manor's entrance to the tunnel was. After a few minutes of instructions, he hung up and shoved the mobile back into his pocket.

"Let's go ahead and check that slab to see if the cat triggered it somehow from the inside. Goodness knows he's heavy enough if those lion's screams were anything to go by."

As we waded back through the shadowed garden toward the Adam and Eve fountain, I thought about the inscriptions over the fireplaces and about the smuggler, James George Wildeve, who must have been responsible for putting them there. We were passing by a spectacular cascade of honeysuckle when I had a sudden thought.

"Tamsin," I said after a moment, "remember that slab we found outside the garden? The one that I said looked like a grave marker?"

"The one with the long inscription?"

"That one." I frowned in concentration, trying to remember the exact wording. "I wait beyond the flames. Where I dance above light, silver are my feet, and black is my crown."

"What about it, *poca*?" Michael asked amiably.

"What if that was the original slab over the 'Destiny grave'? We thought it was a grave marker when we first saw it."

Tamsin and Michael suddenly stopped and looked at me.

"Go on," Michael said, quietly curious. And I fiddled with my torch, rubbing my fingers over the lens while I formulated my thoughts.

The beam rippled eerily, and I watched the play of light behind my fingertips.

"What if that slab was the original slab, and Great-uncle Desmond had changed it for one he had made with Destiny's name on it. A fake grave marker just like the fake tombstones in the Great Hall." I looked up from my torch and frowned at Michael. "It would be the only way we would know that the grave was a clue. Great-aunts Astrid and Aurora played in that glade as children. Given enough time, they would have remembered that grave was there with the slab, and they would have never given it a second look. But change the slab to something more in keeping with the clues, like exchanging the slab for one with Destiny's name on it, and then their attention would have been drawn to it. Remember, he put Destiny's monogram on everything that he wanted us to see as clues."

"That's possible," Michael said. "Go on."

"So why would he go through that much trouble to plant a clue there unless it was important for the clue to be found there? He could have just hidden the metal box that Dad had found in any room of the manor."

"I get it," Tamsin breathed.

"Good point." Michael nodded and started walking again. "He did say on the clue in the box that we were on the right track. So it may not have been referring to the garden's burial plot like we had thought. Being on the right track, according to Great-uncle Desmond, may have been the actual grave the clue was on."

"Great-uncle Desmond did say, 'See where this led,'" I took a deep breath. "What if he meant for us to look behind the slab and follow a tunnel?"

"It's possible, but"—Michael agreed and then paused, a slow half-smile quirking up one corner of his mouth.

"What?" I asked, frowning at his profile. He turned to look down at me, and I could see one of his eyebrows lift.

"What if we are completely wrong, and it is someone's grave? And the word 'destiny' is the original inscription?"

"Oh, I wish you hadn't said that," Tamsin wailed behind me and darted forward to wrap long fingers around my elbow.

"Never mind." Michael began walking again. "Let's go see if it's open before we start imagining caskets and skeletons inside."

We made our way past Adam and Eve and through the winding wisteria tunnel until we came to the small glade. Glowing starlight fell into the center of the clearing and lit up the thick cluster of rosebushes in a spotlight of silver. The pink petals looked like pale butterflies in the dim light, and the leaves rustled suggestively in the breeze.

As Tamsin and I squeamishly hung back, Michael went up to the rosebushes and carefully parted a handful of the gnarly branches from the tangle to peer inside. A huge ball of fur suddenly exploded from its shadowy center, shooting straight up and outward, and Michael's whole body jerked as he leapt backward. An unearthly yowl rent the night, and Tamsin and I screamed.

I would have bounded away into the darkness except Tamsin's hand wouldn't let go of mine. Her knees crumpled, and I ended up dragging her along behind me for a good three meters before I realized that she was still attached. The resultant boomerang effect spun both of us around in a circle, and I tripped over her recumbent body, jarring a loud grunt from both of us as I fell across her thighs. I could feel Tamsin's body shake with laughter under me, and I heard her snort into the grass. I groaned and let my face drop back down in the prickly tufts, but not before I caught a glimpse of Michael laughing so hard he had dropped to one knee beside the rosebushes.

"Where are Aunt Aurora and her tree branch when you need her?" I intoned feelingly into the scratchy grass as the offended tomcat sailed over our recumbent bodies, screaming, spitting, and snarling as he bounded away.

I struggled to my feet and pinned the torch's beam on my brother as he stood up, wiping his eyes with the knuckle of his thumb. I turned and extended a hand to Tamsin. She spit out a long shaft of grass and put a hand to her stomach, groaning and giggling.

"Well?" I looked questioningly at Michael. "Is it the way the cat used?" He nodded.

"It's open."

"It is?" I bleated excitedly, dragged Tamsin to the clot of rosebushes, and leaned against Michael as he parted the branches. He shined his light on to the misplaced slab.

"We've found the second tunnel, *poca*."

The slab had skewed itself sideways, as if it had been attached to a pivot on one side midway down, and as it had moved, it had opened up the top half of the grave. The beams of the combined torches showed a flight of steep steps descending into utter blackness.

"Where's the trigger?" Tamsin asked curiously and waved her light over the inside walls of the grave, exposing nothing but gouge marks. Michael leaned over the edge and gently pushed against a small stone ledge against the inside wall. The slab shifted another inch and then clicked grittily to a complete stop. The tomcat had obviously been hefty enough to shift the delicate mechanism. He must have stood on it or jumped from it in pursuit of a rat.

"How do you close it?" Tamsin wondered out loud and leaned down to touch the lid with the tips of her fingers, feeling its rough surface. "I think there are casters under this thing."

"And how do you trigger it from out here?" I shined my torch over the top of the slab. "That's what I'd like to know. If James George was a smuggler, then he would have to have a trigger to shut it back up behind himself, wouldn't he?"

"Maybe he just shoved it back into place," Tamsin murmured and withdrew her arm from the open grave. "I'd like to know why he needed two tunnels. One from the house to the garden and one from the cellars to the garden."

"Frankly," Michael said dryly, "I don't see why he'd need any of them to go to the garden anyway."

"Maybe he needed two different tunnels to get into the house, not to get out from the house to the garden. Maybe that's what the ruins are," I said thoughtfully. "Maybe they doubled as a sort of storehouse for contraband."

"In full sight of Customs and Excise?" Michael laughed. "I doubt it. Anyway, we really can't speculate until we see where the tunnel leads to begin with. All we know is that the cat could use it to get out of the house."

We fell silent at that.

When we arrived back at the fountain, Dante and Jude were waiting for us.

"How did you get here so quickly?" I asked and clambered up on the rim of the fountain to peer down at my much taller brothers. I put a hand on Tamsin to steady myself.

"We were up at Lamond's place going over the congregation's accounts," Dante answered, flicking his torch beam at my feet where I stood unsteadily on a crust of damp lichen. "We were just leaving when you called."

Lamond Makumba was originally from Nairobi's business districts. He lived at the top of the village in the basement flat of what used to be a boarding house. He was spending his summer in Cornwall to polish up his English. He intends to go back home and pioneer in the English-speaking territory in his native country. He's a twenty-four-year-old ministerial servant and Albert Pengarth's book study assistant. His skin is blue-black, his teeth are golden, and the hair on his perfectly shaped head has the same stylized waves as the fur on a kitten's nose.

He likes to practice his English idioms on me. At the last meeting, he told me that my "white" hair is beautiful, but always "amiss" and "awry." Jude had overheard and had teasingly supplied the word "unruly" as a correction. So Lamond went around before the meeting telling everyone that I wasn't amiss and awry, that I was merely beautiful, white, and unruly.

Clive Chaucer had eyed him at this, grinned, and then quoted a poetic line from the "Banks of Claudy," an obscure Irish ballad, "Oh, it's when she heard this dreadful news she flew into despair, by the wringing of her milk white hands and the tearing of her hair."

I decided then that it was a good time for me to hide in the bathroom with Tamsin until the meeting started.

A cloud moved over the starlight above us, and another breeze rustled the greenery. I jumped off the fountain's edge, and we led them back through the wisteria to the open grave. Jude shined his light into the black portal.

"So who's going down, and who's staying aboveground?"

"I want to go down," I said hastily in an effort to forestall any excessive brotherly caution. "And Tamsin."

"I'll stay aboveground," Dante volunteered, testing the stability of the shifted slab with a firm hand. "I don't think it will take more than one person up here in case anything goes wrong."

In the end, we decided that Dante would stay out and that the rest of us would lower ourselves into the grave. Michael went first while Jude and Dante held back the wild tangle of thorns from the edge of the coffin, clearing the way for Tamsin and me once Michael called for us.

The steps were as steep and as narrow as a fire escape and as musty and as stale as one of Great-uncle Desmond's lumpy bed pillows. Consisting of only one flight, the steps descended a mere fifteen feet under the soil and led to the mouth of a widened tunnel that looked a bit like the one we had traversed to get into the garden. Jude came in behind us, bringing up the rear.

"Look," I said and shined my beam along the walls at the iron rings. "Torch holders."

"They would have had to work fast," Jude commented, touching one. It left a greasy smear of black on his fingertips. "Too much fire, and they would be a bit oxygen deprived unless they left both ends open while they worked."

"I hadn't thought of that," I murmured and felt Tamsin's fingers intertwine in mine. She sidled up to me and pressed her arm against my shoulder in nervous excitement.

"Come on. Let's see where this leads." Michael began walking, moving his torch beam from wall to wall and from floor to ceiling. "Keep an eye out for anything that looks weak."

"Are you thinking this place could cave in?" Tamsin whispered. I felt her fingers spasm in mine.

"Not particularly," Michael said reassuringly. "It must be relatively safe, or Great-uncle Desmond wouldn't have directed Aunts Astrid and Aurora to go down here."

"Michael is just playing it safe," I murmured to her even though I felt my skin crawl at the thoughts her words had invoked. The rocks forming the arch above us looked suddenly very heavy. I glanced at her walking beside me. "Are you claustrophobic?"

She shook her head, but her eyes were enormous as they tried to take in every foot of the ceiling and walls as we walked.

"Are you?" she whispered.

"Not until a minute ago," I whispered dryly and shined my beam up above us, noticing the way the stones interlocked in an arched pattern that resembled the stonework above the manor's gothic windows. My light passed over what seemed to be a blemish in the hewn stones, and I stopped dead as if my beam had snagged on it. Jude bumped into me, and I staggered before he caught me with a hand to my shoulder. "Wait a minute! What's that?"

"What's what, *poca*?" he asked amiably and looked up at the mark my beam had picked out. "How odd."

"What?" Michael had turned around and added his beam to ours.

"It looks like it's been etched in," Tamsin breathed, let go of my hand, and shined her torch on the crude figures.

Scratched into the stone above us, just right below the ceiling's curve, was a circle surrounded by a round band of cross marks. Jude reached up and traced the marks with his fingertips.

"It's not cut very deep," he said and stepped back to let Michael run his fingers over the markings. It was no bigger than his spread hand.

"What do you think it is?" Tamsin whispered and then cleared her throat. "Is it old?"

"It's hard to tell." Michael frowned and shined his light on the ceiling behind us, illuminating the part of the tunnel we had just taken. "Did we pass other markings?"

"I didn't see any," I said. "But on the way back we can look."

"I wonder what they mean," Tamsin whispered eerily.

"Maybe Great-uncle Desmond added part of it later," Michael suggested and then shrugged, looking at Tamsin. "Maybe you can look it up at the library."

"That's a good idea," Tamsin said. I could see her carefully count the number of cross marks bordering the circle. "Ms. Dilly has a program on her computer for symbols and marks like that. It has everything from silversmith's marks to old banners. It comes in handy for family crests and collectors."

"Come on," Jude said and gestured toward the unexplored end of the tunnel. "Let's see where the rest of this goes."

Leaving the curious etching behind, we continued our trek through the long straight tunnel, passing no other carvings in stone and going for at least another hundred feet before coming to a partially opened door.

We entered a large room just like the one hewn underground in the other tunnel. On the far side was another open doorway, and at first glance the room we had entered looked as empty as the other one that my father had discovered. And then Michael bent down and picked something small and metallic out of one of the stone's seams, shining his torch beam on the tiny object in his palm. We crowded around to get a better look as he rolled it thoughtfully under his thumb.

"What is it?" I asked, staring at the tiny round object that glittered, a dull yellow in our torch beams. It was no larger than a penny and would have been flat if the years in the stones hadn't bent a small crook into it. "It looks like it's gold."

"It is," Michael said and rolled it over to touch a tiny nub formed in its back. "It's an old-fashioned buckle."

"For a belt?" Tamsin asked, sounding baffled. Jude shook his head.

"No, not a belt. Perhaps a shoe. Or a clasp for a purse."

"A purse?" I rolled the tiny object over to look at the design chased on the front. It was formed into the shape of a stylized rose.

"Not a woman's purse, *poca*," Jude answered. "A purse for valuables."

"It's old," Michael said and looked up at Jude, his eyes shadowed in the peripheral glow of the torches. "Nineteenth century?"

"Or older," Jude agreed. And I felt a shiver of goose bumps suddenly touch my scalp. I looked at Tamsin and could see that she was thinking the same thing.

"James George," I whispered a bit dramatically. "The smuggler."

"Who?" Jude looked at me, and I realized that he hadn't heard about the results of Tamsin's latest research.

In somewhat jumbled sentences, Tamsin and I told him about what she had found out. I added our surmises about the newly cleaned painting that we had taken down from Destiny's mantel and pointed at the ornate buckle in Michael's hand.

"Maybe the clasp came from some contraband. Or perhaps the rose had been James George's insignia."

Michael bent down at my words and touched the space between the fitted flagstones where he had first pulled the buckle free.

"There's something else in here," he said, pulled a penknife from his jean pocket, and crouched, opening the sharp middle blade to dig into the tight slit between the stones. I held my breath as he worked a small coin free. He stood and held it up.

"A penny!" I exclaimed, disappointed at the sight of the modern coin.

"It's only about ten years old," Jude laughed, squinting at the date. "The insane old sot."

"You mean Great-uncle Desmond planted this?" I took the penny from Michael and rubbed my thumb over it, holding it up in my torch beam to see the date for myself.

"So the buckle is another clue." Michael grinned, closed his penknife, reinserted it in his pocket, and looked back at the buckle in his palm. "He may have planted this bit of gold as a clue, but I still think it's authentic. It might have belonged to the smuggler."

"So James George is as big a clue as Destiny," Tamsin said thoughtfully and then nudged me with her elbow, adding emphasis to her next words. "I'm willing to bet that the treasure is something he stole from Destiny when she was executed during the French Revolution. He found it during one of his smuggling trips into France and brought it back."

"That's what I think too," I said, agreeing with her. "But it still doesn't answer the question of why Great-uncle Desmond didn't use the treasure himself."

"Maybe that's his great joke," Jude said and shrugged. "Perhaps it really is stolen, and he couldn't sell it. Maybe it's something we'll have to return."

"He did say that it was valuable," Michael added quietly. "He never said it was his. He said it belongs to Destiny. We didn't know yet about the Frenchwoman named Destiny. We had thought that he had meant Dad's grandmother. Whatever it is, he had already hinted that it belongs to this Frenchwoman named Destiny."

"That certainly sounds like his parallel thinking," I sighed. "If all that is true, at least no one has to worry about the enormous death duties. The National Trust is willing to take care of those in a couple of months."

I suddenly felt depressed. Jude felt something of my mood and nudged me playfully.

"It doesn't matter, *poca*. It's been fun, and Aunts Astrid and Aurora are still taken care of."

"I know," I said and gave the penny back to Michael. He pocketed the coin and the buckle and then shined his torch beam toward the open doorway on the far wall.

"Let's see where this goes," he said and moved forward as Tamsin clasped my fingers in hers, obviously still unnerved by the unknown. "We have more tunnel to explore."

The doorway led to another tunnel, but this short passage was disappointing, leading nowhere. It ended in a blank wall with a rectangular opening near the floor that presumably led to the hearth behind the boiler. I had a feeling that the exit into the cellars had been cemented up years ago when one of my male ancestors had decided to install the boiler. Or perhaps it was Great-uncle Desmond when he converted it. I knew we would have to go back the way we came. Unless there was a trigger that we had yet to discover. The wall looked blank except for the small hole.

"This must be the way the cat got out," Michael said and bent to shine his light into the deep aperture. "Wait a minute," he said and shifted to drop on one knee by the exit. "There's an envelope in here."

"What?" I said, startled. "From Great-uncle Desmond?"

"It's wedged in the stones between the side and the floor seam," Michael grunted. We heard the scrape of something against the rock as he gently worked the paper loose.

"Silly sot," he grunted a moment later. "He put it in the puddle under the boiler." He stood up and brandished a slightly wrinkled envelope in the combined beams of our torches. He handed his torch to Jude and turned the yellow legal-sized envelope over in his hand. One corner had blotted up the metallic water that had pooled under the boiler, and the wetness had spread down the edge in blotches. He carefully opened the sealed envelope and extracted another sheet of parchment.

"Thank goodness for that," Michael chuckled and unfolded it. "This stuff is impervious to damp."

"Read it out loud," I suggested.

Michael grinned as he read the silly-sounding verse to us, his deep voice quietly echoing in the short tunnel, "Roses are red, violets are blue. You went where this led, and you found the main clue."

"The buckle?" Tamsin murmured, her hushed voice slightly incredulous. "How on earth is that a main clue?"

"Is there anything written on the back?" Jude asked and waited as Michael turned the torn piece of parchment over.

"There is," he laughed. "But as usual, it's very faint."

We held the torch beams closer to the parchment so Michael could make out the words.

"It seems to say"—he frowned and tilted the parchment toward the light—"put it all together and look."

"Put it all together and look?" I repeated and let go of Tamsin's hand to rub my eyes. "How do we know if we've found all his clues?"

"We don't," Jude said and rubbed a hand over my shoulders. "The insane old sot."

# 12

The next morning, I took the newly affianced Chloe O'Rourke with me to Bunny Dawlish's house for her Bible lesson. Tamsin had to fill in for Ms. Dilly at the library, which was convenient for our treasure hunt since she had planned on searching through the computers for more information.

Bunny Dawlish met us at her front door with her friend and neighbor, the equally elderly Ginger Tregaren, at her elbow. He was holding a tray of burnt cakes in one oven-mittened hand and his floppy King James Bible in the other.

"Come in, my dears, come in!" Bunny trilled enthusiastically as I helped Chloe from her car. Chloe had no problem maneuvering her ancient Volvo wagon around the village. She just had a problem straightening out her knees once they were bent. I pulled up on her forearms as she struggled to stand, and the fluffy blond wig on her head caught on the shoulder belt and slithered off her tiny head like a shy hedgehog. It flipped backward into the driver's seat behind her, leaving her own scanty hair waving about in the ocean breeze.

"Dear, can you get that for me?" Chloe murmured unperturbed and let go of my arms long enough to allow me to retrieve the wig from her beaded seat cover. "It's Jasper's favorite."

I handed the pelt of nylon to Chloe, and she slapped it back on her head like a beret, not bothering to tuck her own wispy strands back under it. I made sure Chloe had her book bag before I shut the car door behind her.

"My dears, the most amazing miracle has occurred!" Bunny gushed as we came up the short walk to her front door stoop. "Just look!" she said proudly and gestured behind her at the tray of charred cakes on Ginger's baking sheet. Chloe sniffed the air as we drew near and then peered shortsightedly at the lumps.

"Seed cake?" she warbled and poked a finger at one. "That's not a miracle. I can make those."

"No, dears, no." Bunny and Ginger stepped back to allow us into the front door of the house. "Look at the big one. Can't you see it?"

"Yes," Chloe answered, unperturbed by the question. "Of course, I can see it. It's the size of my head."

Poor wee Chloe. Even dinner rolls were the size of her head.

"It came out of the oven just like this!" Ginger said. His normally booming voice was lowered in hushed reverence. "It looks just like the crown of thorns!"

"You put thorns in your seed cake?" Chloe warbled and made her way to the kitchen where we usually had our lesson. "I don't think I'd care for one, then. Thank you anyway. I believe I'll just have my usual cup of tea."

"Ginger's tea cake is yet another miracle!" Bunny gushed. "Just like the lint ball of Saint Thomas!"

"I'm going to send it to my daughter!" Ginger said happily, putting the tray of burnt baking on the stove before wrapping the chosen black lump in a white handkerchief. He inserted the bundle into the front pocket of his baggy pants. "We've just been looking up the account of it in Saint Matthew."

"I'd like a cup of Earl Grey, please," Chloe said placidly and settled herself in her usual seat by the Aga cooker and put her book bag on the table to wrest her literature free. "But today, if I may, I'd like quite a bit of sugar in it. I have to put a bit more weight on. Jasper said—"

"Jasper, my dear?" Bunny clapped her arthritic hands and then clutched them to her bosom. "Don't tell me. That lovely Jasper Penhallow? Did he ask you, then? You're getting married?"

"Another miracle!" Ginger intoned in a hushed voice and then leaned forward to touch the back of Chloe's veiny hand. "Congratulations, my dear."

"Thank you." Chloe beamed happily. I fished my Bible and publications from my book bag and put them on the table in front of me. "Isabella's little brother is going to be ring bearer. He'll be a darling."

"He's certainly a beautiful little boy," Bunny gushed and then noticed my books on the table. "Oh, dear Bella, that reminds me. Violet came by early this morning and asked me if I had any history on your family. I found a book that my dear Papa had acquired. I'm not sure where he got it, but it's in wonderful shape for being so old. Ms. Dilly had found out that I had it and had made me an offer for it. Ms. Dilly at the library, you know. But I would never sell it. It's a family heirloom. Let me just go and get it."

She rose from the table as Ginger busied himself with the kettle on the kitchen counter beside us, getting the tea things together for our customary pot of tea. I hoped that the burnt seed cakes weren't going to be offered as part of the hospitable refreshments. Chloe has been known to spit her teeth out on the table just to fish a raspberry seed from under her tongue. Bunny came back just as the kettle began to boil.

"Here, my dear. Keep this as long as you'd like. I know you'll be careful." She sat down and handed me a huge tome. "I hope this will be of use. I know Violet had talked about local village history. She had seemed to be interested in the time period before Prince George."

"Thank you very much," I said and placed the book in my book bag. I was dying to forage through Bunny's borrowed treasures, but I knew that my explorations would have to wait until later.

After we finished our study, we left Bunny and Ginger to themselves, getting into Chloe's Volvo so she could drop me off at home. My grandparents were driving in from the ferry that morning, and they were expected to arrive close to lunchtime. As a precaution, Clive Chaucer was to be one of the lunch guests in case the excitement proved to be a little much for my great-aunts. I came into the kitchen just as my mother was putting the finishing touches on a fruit salad.

"Have a good day, *bocciolo*?" she greeted me warmly, stilling the machete-sized knife in her hand as she accepted my kiss on her cheek. The kitchen smelt of freshly baked lavender bread.

"Very," I answered her and watched as she sliced off another round of pineapple. "Do you need any help?"

"Not really." She smiled and began to trim the thorny peeling from the slice. "You can go ahead and change if you'd like, then round up your baby brother, and make sure he's presentable. Your grandparents just called, and they should be here any moment."

I stole a kiwi chunk from the bowl, popped it in my mouth, and then went upstairs to change into white cotton pants and a dark blue pullover. I was just finger-combing my hair when Michael knocked on my doorjamb and leaned in.

"Have you seen Aunt Astrid?"

"No. Why?"

"Aunt Aurora said that her bed is undisturbed, and she can't find her."

"Her bed is undisturbed?" I turned from the vanity mirror and looked at Michael warily. "Were they supposed to be taking a nap?"

He nodded and then slapped the side of the doorjamb before pushing himself away from the wall.

"Help me find her, there's a good little girl." He grinned and disappeared down the hall.

"I have to get Gabriel ready first!" I called out to his retreating back and got a grunt in reply. I gathered my hair into a ribbon and then went in search of my little brother. I found him at my mother's vanity painting his lips with a tube of Ruby Flirt as he peered into the triple mirror.

"Not good," I said, yanked him from the elegant little bench seat, took him to the bathroom for a quick swipe with a washcloth, and then gently shoved him in the direction of the stairs.

"Go down, *cucciolo*, and ask Mom if she needs help," I said, did a last-minute check of my own face in the mirror, and then followed him down the stairs to look for Aunt Astrid. I met up with Great-aunt Aurora in the hallway beside the kitchen.

"Isabella, dear, I can't seem to find Sister." She peered at me in the dim light. "Have you seen her? Is she with you?"

"No, Aunt Aurora," I said. "When did you see her last?"

"Before my nap," she said and pressed a tremulous hand to her bosom. I heard the odd sound of crackling paper. "We didn't sleep very well last night, I'm afraid. We're both so excited about seeing Bryn. We haven't seen her since she married your dreadful grandfather. Oh my. I do wonder where Sister is."

"Have you asked Mom?"

"No, dear, she's so busy right now."

Just then the phone rang in its little cubbyhole under the staircase. There is an extension in the kitchen and another extension upstairs in my parent's bedroom. Aunt Aurora and I jumped at the unexpected sound of loud buzzing, and I heard my mother's voice calling out from the kitchen as Aunt Aurora pressed her hand to her bosom. Once again I heard the very distinct sound of paper crackling from Aunt Aurora's ample cleavage.

"Can you get that, *bocciolo*?" my mother's voice floated plaintively into the hallway. "My hands are a bit messy right now."

"Okay!" I answered her and started toward the phone nestled on the hallstand. Aunt Aurora trotted alongside me as the phone continued its unrelenting summons.

"Oh my," Aunt Aurora breathed, obviously distressed by the insistently jarring sound, and then without warning, she suddenly veered slightly and toddled off toward my father's study. I jerked to a puzzled stop and watched as she opened the door to the vacant room. "Hello?" she answered the empty doorway. "Who is it?"

The phone rang again, and I paused, watching Aunt Aurora as she wandered cautiously into the unoccupied room, obviously on a mission to seek out the mischievous sprite that kept ringing the buzzer in her head and running away.

"Uh-oh," I said blankly. My mother's voice floated down the hallway again, urging me to answer the phone before the caller tired and disconnected without leaving a message.

"It might be your grandparents!" she called out. "Wait a moment, I hear a knock!"

"I'll go ahead and get the phone!" I called back to her and ran the few remaining steps toward the insistently ringing phone, leaving Aunt Aurora to wander about the study. There wasn't much she could do to hurt herself unless she opted to stab herself in the eye with a pencil or dart about brandishing Dad's letter opener.

Before I could reach the phone, however, the answering machine picked up the call. I froze with surprise when I heard Great-aunt Astrid's voice answering back.

"Hello? Luc? If it's not too much trouble, can you come get me?" she said and then hung up.

"No!" I howled, lunged for the phone as I heard her disconnect, and stubbed my toe on one of the age-warped floorboards. I went flying and nearly demolished the answering machine with my chin.

"Are you all right?" Michael's voice and hands suddenly descended on me, and his feet came into my horizontal line of vision. I nodded, momentarily stunned, and then rolled over in time to see Great-aunt Aurora hove into view over me like a benign zeppelin. She held Dad's stapler to her ear.

"I answered it, dear." She smiled at me over her bosom as Michael gently eased me into a sitting position under the phone table. "Don't get up. I think it's a wrong number anyway. I only hear breathing."

Then several things happened at once. The phone began ringing again, my parents shunted into view with my grandparents, whom I hadn't seen in a year, and Aunt Astrid abruptly wandered out of the linen cupboard. She looked lost and had someone's mobile phone pressed to her ear. I reached up over my head and lifted the ringing phone from its cradle.

"Hello?" I said cautiously into the receiver. "Aunt Astrid?"

"Yes. Who's this?"

Jude came into the hallway just then, whistling a creatively mangled snatch of Vivaldi, and greeted our grandparents.

"Hello, Grandfather. Grandmother, you're looking beautiful." He grinned, lifted her off her feet in a hug, and then looked over her head at Aunt Astrid. "Thanks for finding my phone. I thought I'd left it here."

We all looked at each other for a beat of three seconds; then my parents sprang into action, herding my grandmother and Aunts Astrid and Aurora together for a tearful and somewhat befuddled reunion, returning the mobile phone to a highly amused Jude, returning me to my feet, and returning the stapler to the desk, all the while managing to intercept Gabriel in full careen down the hallway before he could inadvertently explode the group hug of my grandmother and great-aunts like a bowling ball knocking down pins.

Dante and Brandt suddenly emerged into the joyful melee from wherever they'd been and greeted Grandfather as he stood surveying his wife's long-overdue embrace of her sisters. My grandfather hugged his two oldest grandsons, and then turned and scowled at his weeping sisters-in-law.

"*Fuist,* now! *Fuist! Bryn anseo,*" my grandfather said in Gaelic, his voice deepening and cat's tongue rough. "I've brought her. Don't carry on so. Hush!" He frowned and turned toward my brothers. "Women!"

"Hi, Grandfather," I said. He looked down at me, giving me a double take.

"You've grown, lass," he said gruffly. He gave me his customary hooded stare from unreadable black eyes, then grunted, and ruffled my head as if I were a good spaniel. He looked around the hallway for Gabriel. "Where's the runt of the litter?"

My mother had tactfully taken my little brother with her when she had withdrawn into the kitchen, leaving my father to cope with my great-aunts while she coped with quickly finishing lunch.

"Oh, Bryn!" Aunt Aurora sniffled and broke from her sisters to accept the handkerchief proffered by my amused father. She dabbed at her nose, ignoring my grandfather's impatient frown. "I can't believe it! It's been so long! We've all gotten so old!"

"It was that dreadful Finghin's fault," Aunt Astrid wailed indistinctly into the clot of their embrace.

My grandfather grunted, spun on his heel, and left the overcrowded hallway.

"I'll see to him." Dante grinned and followed my grandfather to the front room. I stayed a few minutes more, watching my grandmother's reunion with her younger sisters, and then made my way to the kitchen to see if my mother needed any help. I ended up putting together a tray of tea things and taking it into the front room. I took Gabriel with me. Once I cleared the threshold with the laden tray, my little brother bounded past me and swarmed my grandfather where he sat on one of the huge armchairs.

"Hi, Grandfather!"

"Hello, yourself, *cna'dai*," he answered back, his brogue pronounced, and reached out a calloused hand to fondle Gabriel's head.

Dante took the tray from me and put it on an end table as the others finally entered the room. My mother was beaming as my grandmother and great-aunts sat down together in a tangle on the couch. They wouldn't let go of each other's hands, putting my grandmother in the middle. My grandfather snorted again and accepted a cup of tea from Dante.

My brother grinned at me, then went back to pour tea for Aunts Astrid and Aurora.

As everyone found a seat, I was left stranded. The only comfortable seat left open was beside my grandfather. I started toward it, then veered away as my courage faltered, going to the smaller sofa to make Brandt and Michael scoot apart. I inserted myself into the narrow space and crossed my arms.

"Chicken," Michael murmured.

There was a cheerful tattoo on the front door, and a second later Clive Chaucer peered around the foyer's threshold.

"Am I late?"

"Come in." My father grinned. "Just in time for a cup of tea before lunch."

Of course, when lunch rolled around, my exuberant little brother begged to sit between my grandparents during the meal. He seemed unduly impressed with the work-roughened scars on Grandfather's huge hands and with Grandfather's shaggy silver hair.

Dressed in black jeans, a black tee shirt, and his black boots, my grandfather had obviously refused to dress up for the reunion. His short ponytail was tied back with the thin end of a worn horsewhip, and I grinned in my soup, remembering Zinnia Bunt-Joliet's fond memory of my grandfather when he tore the whip in two and tossed it out of reach on the stable roof.

I watched Gabriel finger a distinctive scar on my grandfather's left hand, and my grin died, remembering how the ridged mark had gotten there. I was eight years old at the time, and we were in Ireland, visiting my grandparents for the week, when I had unobtrusively followed my grandfather out to one of the paddocks next to his stables.

Having no idea of what was about to happen, I watched as he led a half-grown stallion out into the omnipresent Irish drizzle and into a smaller holding pen. He secured the restless stallion in his makeshift stall, then, standing ankle deep in mud, he raised a knife and proceeded to geld the horse.

Those are polite euphemisms. "Gelding" isn't a verb, and that wasn't exactly mud that he was ankle deep in.

The horse and I pretty much started screaming at the same time. I can still see the flash of silver as the wicked-looking knife slipped in my startled grandfather's hand and cut, not only the horse exactly where he had planned, but one of my grandfather's ungloved fingers. Blood sprayed everywhere, Gaelic curses floated over the misty drizzle, I passed out facedown in the "mud," and the horse certainly was never the same again.

The resultant ten stitches made my grandfather's forefinger look as if a mad scientist had sewed it on one stormy night.

I looked over at my grandmother sitting between Gabriel and Aunt Aurora. She caught my eye and flashed me a smile, her careworn face looking suddenly young.

Dressed in a red floral print of poppies, my grandmother had wrapped a black velvet ribbon at the end of her long braid and had fastened a brilliant choker of colorful glass beads about her throat. I was reminded of Zinnia Bunt-Joliet again and her impressive tangle of Murano glass tinkling like wind chimes every time she moved.

The mealtime discussion seemed to center around Great-uncle Desmond and his bizarre games. My grandmother and great-aunts had kept up with one another all their years apart, so there was very little news of their lives that could be classified as new. Great-uncle Desmond's treasure seemed to be the only undiscussed nugget.

"The man was an idiot when I knew him," my grandfather grunted at the end of the meal in a one-sentence summation and pushed his chair back, throwing his napkin on the table next to his silverware. "I'm going out for some air."

After lunch, I went to my room to finish studying for the meeting. That night was one of our longer meetings, nearly two hours of Bible instruction compared to the one hour of the Bible study the night before last.

My grandmother and great-aunts had opted for a long predinner nap since they wanted to go to the meeting later, my mother was finishing up the dishes herself, my father was with his father on the beach, Dante and Brandt were back at their cottage polishing up their parts for the meeting, and Michael and Jude were outside playing soccer with Gabriel. I could hear my older brothers' laughter and Gabriel's delighted shrieks floating up to my bedroom window from the strip of lawn outside.

It didn't take me long to finish studying what I had started earlier that morning, and once finished, I dug out the history book that Bunny Dawlish had lent me, sitting on the comfortable expanse of my bed with the tome. I tucked my legs under me Indian style and hefted the heavy book onto my lap.

Bound in battered black calf and full of miniscule print, it was almost two inches thick. Curious, I checked its title page and was surprised to see that it had been published only six decades ago. I thumbed through its crabbed-looking contents and was further surprised to see photographs and reproductions of actual correspondence and documents. Feeling like I was holding a goldmine, I hurriedly flipped back to the table of contents and ran my eyes down the sections and chapters.

The book dealt with everything that anyone had ever wanted to know about Halfmoon Village. I found chapters that dealt with agriculture, livestock, properties, local politics, family lines, and even the Moonstone pub. The Moonstone's original owners seemed to have been a family with the unsurprising name of Tregaren. Swing a cat anywhere in Cornwall, and you'll hit a Tregaren.

Having a brainstorm, I decided to check the extensive glossary in the back for the unusual name of Wildeve. Wildeve may have been English, but it was definitely not a name native to Cornwall. How did the Wildeves get so much property, and where did they come from? And why on earth weren't more of them tucked away in the village?

I found five references to "Wildeve" in the back.

I looked up the first reference to the family name and found myself looking at a sepia photograph of Tanglewood. It covered the whole page, and I had to skew the book sideways to see the picture the right way around. I would have never recognized the manor without the accompanying caption labeling it.

The photograph had been taken from the front lawn, and judging by the scope of the picture, the photographer had to have been standing very close to the cliff's edge to be able to sight the whole property in the camera's lens. All the greenery, from the lawn to the ivy climbing up the building, was lush, clipped, and obviously manicured. The fountain of mermaids was lichen free, wet, and functioning; and the drive was smooth, graveled, and in perfect repair. The manor's windows were sparkling and salt free. Flowers abounded, trees thrived, and the enormous planters around the sweeping front steps were filled with topiary and cascading plants.

On the front steps like a tiered school picture was a large battalion of people. I realized by all the leather and cloth aprons that I was looking at the servants and workers who were responsible for keeping the property up. I peered closely at the faces in the picture, made too tiny for details, and realized with a start that in the center of the workforce, standing on the top step, was a couple dressed in elegant formal attire. The man, dressed in the stiff collar and black serge of a formal suit, towered over the slight wispy woman holding a ruffled parasol.

My great-grandparents?

I looked at the caption: Sir James Wildeve and his bride, Sarah Prudence Entwhistle.

So this was a photograph of the unfortunate Sarah, taken sometime before Great-uncle Desmond had been born. I got up, found the enameled magnifying glass that I kept in my desk, and brought it back to the bed to peer through it at Sarah's face. She was still too tiny and blurred to make out the details of her features. I could just barely discern her expression. She looked serene and radiant. I wondered when her mental train had begun to derail.

I applied my magnifying lens to my great-grandfather. I could only see a nose, a chin, a brow, and thick dark hair. His eyes were pools of black shadowed by his own thick eyebrows. He looked vigorous, robust, and protective of his tiny and nearly translucent bride.

I got up, found a notebook and pen, and then tore a strip of paper to insert between the pages, writing the words "Tanglewood photo" on the sliver that stuck out over the binding.

I went back to the glossary and looked up the second reference listed for the name "Wildeve." It turned out to be a mention of two ancestors inserted into a single paragraph:

> William Augustus Horatio Algernon Wildeve received a land grant and five hundred pieces of gold from the king at the turn of the sixteenth century and proceeded to build the fortress of what was then called "Wildeve Manor" on his property

> bordering the shoreline. It wasn't until two hundred years later in the late eighteenth century that the estate was renamed Tanglewood and the borders redefined when the current owner lost over half of the land to the then-ruling government.

I read the rest of the paragraph out loud:

> Until Cromwell, Wildeves were staunch royalists, fighting for king, for government, for England, and it wasn't until George Harry Wildeve lost the land that they completed their transformation into rebels. The family line began to lose strength, and many Wildeves either died in battle or by decree of law.

I scanned the rest of the page, but the writer had moved on to local politics without any more mention of my ancestors.

It wasn't, however, until the third reference to Wildeve that I hit the goldmine I was after. I had found James George Wildeve, the smuggler. He stared out at me with bold dark eyes, his portrait reproduced in the archives from a painting hanging in an obscure museum near London.

Fascinated, I studied it through my magnifying lens. Dressed in the fancy dress of his day, he stood against a dark background next to a teetering pile of books. He was an impressive conglomeration of lace, gold buttons, braid, embroidered velvet, satin, earrings, black curls, silky goatee, arrogant confidence, humor, intelligence, and my father's slashed eyebrows. He seemed to be a complete caricature of a villain until you looked at his eyes. Then you realized that he regarded everything as a joke, even himself. Life was one big humorous con.

And then I noticed the ring on his little finger. Holding the heavy tome up to a shaft of soft light, I peered at the blob that the artist had painted on the canvas. It wasn't clearly etched, merely an impression of a signet ring. It looked like a soft cabochon of metal surrounded by a tiny braid, part of it lost in the shadows of his cuff. I could barely make out the scrolled *W* swirled into its mounded center.

His hand was cupped over the edge of the stack of books beside him, and I realized that the artist had painted titles on the books' spines. The spines were skewed away from the viewer, and I had to squint for some time before I could decipher the letters. Disappointed, I realized that once again I was looking at Latin.

Taking the pen and paper I had brought to the bed, I scribbled down each title as best I could and left my room in search of a phone to call Basil Brett for a translation. I used the phone in my parents' bedroom, getting Basil once again on the second ring. I read the letters off to him, and he promised to call back in a few minutes.

I ran back to my room, snagged the history book, and went back to my parents' bed to await the results. As I waited, I looked up the fourth reference in the tome to the name "Wildeve."

It referred to James George's death at sea and to the subsequent change of estate owners when Tanglewood and the surrounding land went to my great-great-grandfather, Henry Bertrand Wildeve, evicting the then-present tenant, who left to marry Algernon Wycliffe. I stopped, feeling like I was supposed to see something important in that simple sentence, but for the life of me, I couldn't figure out what it was. I reread it out loud. I still couldn't see what made me pause with my finger snagged on the paragraph. By "present tenant" did they mean "guest" or perhaps "housekeeper" who was often the last to go, sometimes staying with the house when it changed hands? And who was Algernon Wycliffe? Why did that name sound familiar?

A memory nagged, and I turned back in the book to the second reference to "Wildeve." A William Augustus Horatio Algernon Wildeve had been given the land grant and five hundred pieces of gold from the king at the turn of the sixteenth century. Algernon wasn't a common-enough name to forget. Not like James George. Or all the Harrys in the family line, not to mention Huberts.

The phone rang, and I hurriedly picked it up, anticipating Basil's call.

"Hello, my angel," Basil's plumy voice vibrated the phone wires. "I have translated the Latin for you. May I ask where you found the words?"

"I have a history book that was lent to me, and in it I found a portrait of one of the Wildeve ancestors. He was one of the original owners of Tanglewood and a cousin of my great-great-grandfather. His name was James George, and he was a smuggler who died at sea in 1793. In his portrait he is standing next to a stack of books, and the Latin I read off to you are the books' titles. Why?"

"Well, my dear, I don't believe they are the titles of real works of literature. After what you've just told me, I believe that the artist had inserted into the portrait what sounds like the subject's epitaph. Let me read it off to you, my angel, and you decide."

"I'm ready," I said and reached for the pen and paper I had laid on a pillow.

"I'm assuming that you started with the topmost book and read off the titles going downward, like you would a document. What you read to me doesn't rhyme in Latin, but it certainly does in English if you chose your words carefully. It's a poem, my dear. Are you ready?"

"Very." I grinned at the phone receiver under my chin and readied the pen and paper in my hands as Basil began to read.

"Starting with the first title and going down, it reads, 'Soon when I die, and I will die soon, gold and silver lie beyond star and moon.' It rather sounds like man's idea of heaven, doesn't it?"

I frowned and thought about the irreverent humor I had seen in the portrait's eyes.

"Would the artist have done something like that?" I asked. Basil made a noise of assent.

"If the subject was religious, many times they requested that a biblical reference be painted into the portrait, somehow."

"A biblical reference?"

"There was a lot of symbolism in art, then. This seems a bit more direct, but it would follow the trends of the times."

"Maybe," I said, thinking of treasure and not of epitaphs beaming the subject to heavenly glory. The mention of gold and silver combined with the eyes in the portrait didn't seem very pious to me. I had treasure on the brain, and I wasn't going to get it out of my thoughts until we found whatever it was that Great-uncle Desmond had left for his sisters.

"Thank you," I said and folded up the square of paper, inserting it into the book next to James George's portrait. "I guess I'll see you this evening."

"Indeed you will, angel. Have fun."

I hung up and took my book, paper, and pen back to my bedroom and climbed back onto my bed. Glancing up at the windows, I suddenly noticed that moving clouds had long since obscured the sun. The wet sky was blue with dark smudges hidden under the damp fluff, and I knew that it would be raining before midnight. I got back up and peered out at the world beyond my windows.

The family's wing overlooked a private strip of green lawn and gardens, leaving the more spectacular view of ocean and sheltered rosebushes for the paying guests billeted in the other side of the inn. I rested my forearm on the glass panes above my forehead and stared up at the cooling sky, smelling ozone wafting in from outside. I looked down and noticed that Gabriel, Michael, and Jude had long since finished their game of soccer and had left the strip of private lawn, probably going inside.

I sighed and went back to my bed, looking up the last reference to "Wildeve" in the history book and found another treasure in the book's goldmine of information. I had found an unexpected photograph of Destiny, my great-grandmother.

She was listed in a group portrait of a garden party somewhere other than Tanglewood. I didn't recognize any of the other names of the guests as they lounged in the white wicker and flowers, but I recognized my great-grandmother almost immediately, double-checking the list of names to make sure I had picked her out correctly.

Sitting on the arm of another woman's chair, Destiny had one stocking-clad leg tucked up under the other, her dress nothing but a beaded rainbow with straps. She looked like an exotic orchid of the Roaring Twenties. Her shiny black hair had been bobbed into ebony wings touching her cheekbones, and her full lips were painted deep scarlet. In the black-and-white photograph, her lipstick looked as dark as her hair.

I snatched up my magnifying lens and studied her right cheek. One deep dimple bracketed her smile. I grinned and got up from the bed, the book and lens in my hand as I went in search of Brandt. Brandt who sported the lone dimple in his right cheek, the dimple that mystified my parents, the dimple with no known genetic origin. The dimple that had Brandt jokingly claim that he was evolving out of the family gene pool.

I pocketed the magnifying lens, tucked the book under my arm, went down the stairs, and left through the back door.

The cooling air outside was heavily laced with ozone and ocean salt. I breathed it in, looked up at the slowly darkening sky, and set off for the flagstone pathway that would lead me past the wild apple trees to my brothers' cottage on the back of the property.

The cottage rose up invitingly out of the tall hedge that encircled its narrow lawn and back drive, its sculpted thatch looking like you were about to encounter a fairy tale dwelling beyond the arched gate. The reality was much more prosaic once you passed the hedge. Solid-looking lawn furniture was scattered around a hammock strung between two trees, and an enormous barbeque pit was built on to the ground with fire-resistant bricks the size of safety deposit boxes. A spanner was planted in a flowerpot along with a healthy wood fern and a clump of earth.

I pulled the spanner out as I passed, knowing that it had been forgotten, not abandoned, and tucked it into the back pocket of my slacks before knocking on the front door. I went in, not waiting for an answer, and looked around the masculine front room of massive leather furniture and massive fireplace. Spotting an abandoned laptop computer on a low table, I set the spanner down beside it and went in search of Brandt. I found him in the kitchen pouring a cup of something hot. Dante was sitting at the narrow table nursing his own cup of coffee.

"What's up, *poca?*" Brandt asked amiably from his spot beside the kitchen counter and turned when I set the book down in front of Dante, opening it up to the photograph of Destiny at the garden party. I didn't say anything as I watched Dante's expression.

He frowned in curiosity, leaned forward, not touching the book, and studied the picture in front of him. Putting the French press pot of coffee back on the counter beside his cup, Brandt wiped his hands on a dishtowel and came over to stand behind us.

"It's you, Brandt," Dante's deep laugh rumbled beside, me and he finally touched Destiny's figure with a careful finger. "You even have her eyebrows."

"Who?" Brandt asked curiously and leaned over me to see where Dante was pointing. I moved out of his way so he could see his great-grandmother clearly.

"You're the masculine version of Destiny," I said. "I found this picture in a history book that Bunny Dawlish had lent me."

"It's you all right," Dante continued to chuckle. "Destiny's genes seemed to have skipped a couple of generations before resurfacing."

"Here," I said and slipped the magnifying lens from my pocket, handing it to Brandt, who sat down at the table and held the book up to the light. He held the lens to the photograph, and after a few seconds, I could see a slight smile curve his mouth.

"So that's why I'm Grandmother's favorite," he joked and slid the book back to me.

"Did you find anything more?" Dante asked, taking a sip of coffee, and leaned back in his chair. I sat down with them.

"I found this as well," I said and turned to the portrait of James George, unfolding the Basil-translated poem and spreading it out beside the book. "I called Basil Brett, and he translated the books' Latin titles for me." I watched as my brothers studied my find. "What does it sound like to you?"

"Soon when I die, and I will die soon, gold and silver lie beyond star and moon," Brandt read out loud and leaned backward in his chair to snag his cup of coffee waiting on the counter behind him. "What did Basil say that it meant?"

"He said that it was probably an epitaph dictated to the artist by the subject. He said that it sounds like a reference to heaven after death."

"Not to me," Dante rumbled beside me. I watched as they scooted the book between them. "It sounds like a private joke."

"To me too," Brandt agreed and studied the portrait. "He doesn't look like a man who intends to go to heaven."

"Do you think that he had really died in 1793?" Dante regarded Brandt over the rim of his coffee cup as he took another sip. "Soon when I die, and I will die soon." He looked at me, setting his cup down with a decisive thump. "How close to the time he was lost at sea was this portrait painted?"

"Are you thinking that he had faked his own death?" I asked, startled. Dante shrugged philosophically.

"Perhaps. It would get him and his crew away from hanging if Customs and Excise were getting suspicious."

"It sounds to me as if he knew it would eventually come to that and had already planned out the details." Brandt grinned, still studying the figure in the portrait. He leaned back, his hand resting on the book's open pages. "It sounds like a private joke. A taunt. It sounds like he had already stored up enough portable wealth somewhere to start a new life when the need arose."

"Would he have left Tanglewood for his cousin to take over?"

"He couldn't take it with him, and life without Tanglewood would be preferable to capital punishment," Brand said, glancing at Dante. "Perhaps 'beyond star and moon' refers to life beyond the village."

"Halfmoon," I said, suddenly seeing what they were reading into the Latin translation. "Oh, my goodness," I said feebly.

"What else did you find, *poca*?" Dante asked and slipped the heavy book toward me. "What do the words 'Tanglewood photo' refer to?"

I opened the book to the estate photograph and pushed it back toward the center of the table.

"That's a picture of Great-grandfather and his first wife."

"The crazy Sarah Entwhistle," Brandt murmured under his breath and took the first look. "Obviously taken before all her marbles rolled away." He slid the book over to Dante, who studied the large photograph.

"She looks frail and unhealthy," was his only comment.

I took the book back and found the reference to James George's death at sea and to the subsequent change of estate owners when Tanglewood and the surrounding land went to our great-great-grandfather, Henry

Bertrand Wildeve. I read the sentence aloud, stressing the statement about the eviction of the then-present tenant, who had left to marry Algernon Wycliffe.

"I imagine it was his housekeeper, someone too unimportant back then to mention by name, or they definitely would have, but I'm curious to find out who Algernon Wycliffe is. They don't mention the housekeeper's name, but they mention her groom's name like he's somebody we should know."

"Have you looked it up in the back, *poca*?" Dante asked. I shook my head.

"I actually hadn't thought of that," I admitted and watched curiously as Dante reached for the book and opened it up to the glossary. He perused the alphabetized references, shrugged, and opened the book back to the reference I had just shown him.

"This is the only listing of the name," he said. Brandt shifted to reach the wall phone behind him. He handed the cordless receiver to me.

"Call Tamsin and ask her to look him up."

"Good idea," I said, knowing that my friend was overseeing the library for Ms. Dilly on one of its slow days. I dialed the library's number, and Tamsin picked it up on the fifth ring.

"Halfmoon's lending library," she said, sounding out of breath. "Ms. Dilly isn't in right now. This is Tamsin Hugo."

"Tamsin, it's me. How is it going?" I asked, suddenly aware of the burst of voices filtering past Tamsin. It sounded like I had inadvertently dialed the number to the psychiatric ward during a full moon. "What's all that noise?"

"Heaven help me," Tamsin pleaded. "Pansy Bliss just dropped off her whole brood, and I'm up to my eyeballs in darting children."

"Do you need for me to come over?"

"No, but thank you," Tamsin laughed. "I had just enlisted the help of Marjorie Stoat, and she's rounding them up even as we speak."

Marjorie Stoat is a regular patron of the library, spending long hours sitting on one of the padded armchairs reading and rereading Agatha Christie mysteries. She is built like a tank, wears chiffon scarves and fingerless gloves, carries a stout-walking stick of blackthorn, and smells like the apple brandy she keeps hidden in her purse. I heard a strangled shriek cut off in midgurgle, and I pictured Marjorie gagging a Bliss child with one of her ubiquitous floating dusters.

"What's up?" Tamsin asked, shattering my musings. I frowned in sympathy for my friend.

"It sounds like you're too busy," I said, but she forestalled me before I could back out of my request.

"Not after the Bliss children leave. Pansy is due back in a few minutes. What do you need?"

"I have a new name for you to look up."

"That's no problem. I haven't gotten to do any of the other research yet, but things should die down soon enough once Pansy returns to get her children. I just hope she doesn't decide to stay and browse. What name do you want me to research?"

"Algernon Wycliffe," I said and heard a loud crash echo over the phone lines. "What happened? Are you all right?"

"Marjorie had just decided that Lark Midnight was not going to race Zorro Delighte on the book cart," she giggled. "Never challenge an angry lady who carries a walking stick." She paused. "Is that Wycliffe with a *y* or an *i*?"

# 13

Lamond Makumba met me at the door right before the meeting as I came up the steps behind my grandparents. He detained me with a hand so blue-black it glowed like varnished ebony. His pleasant face broke into a gold-colored smile that moved both ears.

"Ms. Isabella," he said in his heavily accented English. "I must apologize about my words."

"Apologize?" I said and moved out of the way of the narrow threshold, making room for my parents and Gabriel to enter the upper room of the Drown'd Man.

Right now all sixty-seven of us in the Halfmoon congregation are meeting in a huge room over the Drown'd Man, a pub off the High Street. We're hoping to qualify soon for a new ground floor building all to itself since we are also an old congregation for the most part. Three percent of the congregation is over ninety years of age, 50 percent can't get up the pub's back stairs on stormy nights, and 90 percent have broken-hip phobias.

Okay, I know that 3 percent of 67 is 2.01. You can't have 2.01 almost-centenarians in a group of sixty-seven humans, but I'm counting Beatrix Plimpton as 1.01 instead of one. Beatrix Plimpton has six fingers on her left hand and an extra toe somewhere in her geriatric shoes. No matter how you look at it, even without the Pomeranian named Buttons that she habitually carries around in her purse, she should count for a little extra.

"Apologize?" I said again. "What words?"

"I called you 'unruly' last Thursday when I had meant that your hair itself was 'curly.' Your hair I can now say properly. Clive Chaucer corrected me after you had gone into the lavatory. Your hair is blond, not *white*, and beautiful and curly." His smile widened. "It is not politically correct to say that you yourself are white, is it not?"

"Well, I don't . . . ," I faltered, spying Jude's amused smile as he overheard our conversation. "I don't really mind. I am white."

"No. You do not have the milky skin. You have the colored skin." He searched his mental word bank and then suddenly grinned, finding a descriptive term that obviously delighted him. "You are beige with the beigeness of the hairy coconut!"

I blinked at him, having nothing to say to his declaration.

"And your eyes, they are like the marbles I had lost as a boy." He smiled at me triumphantly and nodded his head. "Yes, they are the violet of laxative bottles. The shiny blue of beetles. Yes, very blue." He paused and stared at me, still delighted. "Yes. I like them as much as I like your hair. I like them as much as I like peppermints," he joked. "We do not have chewy peppermints in Nairobi."

"Describe her nose," Jude said interestedly, leaning into our conversation with a wicked grin on his face.

"Shut up," I murmured, eyeing the bathroom door over Lamond's shoulder.

"It's occupied," Jude said amiably. "Aunt Astrid is in there."

"Her nose?" Lamond wrinkled his own nose and scrutinized my face with a thoughtful expression on his. "It is unremarkable. It is not large and not too small. It is straight and does not go off to the side. I like her nose. It does not shout for attention. It is polite. It is well-mannered."

"I don't know," Jude said thoughtfully and grasped my chin between his forefinger and thumb, tilting my face up into his gaze. "I think her nostrils tend to flare like a horse's when she's perturbed." He turned my face back to Lamond. "What do you think?"

"What is 'perturbed'?" Lamond asked innocently and waited for Jude's answer.

"Disconcerted. Disturbed," Clive's amused voice came from somewhere behind me. "Who's perturbed?"

"No. I do not see a flare. Her nostrils are as delicate as dragonflies."

"If you're sure," Jude said doubtfully and let go of my face. "I would have described her nose differently. I certainly wouldn't have said 'well-mannered.'"

The bathroom door across the entry opened, and Aunt Astrid strode out, her hair freshly dried and patted back into its customary helmet. I darted free and made it to the lavatory just as Chloe O'Rourke tottered up the stairs and into the room.

"It's wet out there." She quavered and pressed her wig to her head. "How's my hair?" she asked of no one in particular. I heard literal-minded Lamond's polite observation just before I shut the door behind me.

"Dangerous in a fire. I should not wear that on a plane, Sister Chloe."

Locking the door, I peered at my reflection in the mirror over the sink. The dampness outside had lifted my loose curls into Medusa-like snakes waving about my head. Groaning in frustration, I grabbed a wad of paper towels and pressed hunks of hair between them in an effort to dry the drizzle from the strands. And to tame them a bit. My mother's hair never waved about, I thought miserably. Why did mine have to?

There was a knock on the door, and Elsie Schnitzler's phlegmatic shout vibrated the thin walls.

"Hello in there! I haff taken medication, and I cannot wait!"

I tossed the damp paper into the trash and hurriedly unlocked the bathroom door in an unsuccessful effort to forestall a second nugget of unnecessary information.

"Isabella, you haff a bit of loo roll on your shoe!" she bellowed as I came out. I quickly extracted it and darted out of her way.

Up ahead of me at the stairwell door, I saw my father welcoming a couple I had never seen before. The man had a solid body, graying blond hair, a moustache, and was quite a bit shorter than my father. His narrow face was lean and almost Danish with its fine angles. The woman standing with him was slender, with glowing dark skin and black hair pinned up into a French twist. I guessed them to be husband and wife since the woman had her hand tucked into the crook of the man's elbow.

Curious, I went over to stand behind my father. The woman saw me and smiled. Her pleasant smile was like white sunlight.

My father noticed me standing behind him and turned, bringing me forward with a hand on my shoulder.

"This is my daughter, Isabella," he said. I shook hands with them. "They're friends of Alec Lytton. They met him at Brooklyn."

"Daniel Barnes and this is my wife, Marian," the man said, his accent unmistakably American.

Alec Lytton was a Cornish transplant to Brooklyn Bethel in New York and a periodic visitor of his grandfather, Riley Lytton, a vigorous eighty-something-year-old. Riley was even shorter than I was and used his silver-headed cane like a third arm, doing everything with it, from picking wild apples to dragging eight-year-old Aura Callahan off the stage when she wasn't supposed to be there.

Alec, his grandson, wasn't much taller. Stocky, with short brown hair and cheerful blue eyes, Alec was a favorite with all the elderly sisters in the congregation. I looked past the newcomers' shoulders and saw Riley, Alec's grandfather, climbing the stairwell toward us.

Elsie Schnitzler suddenly jerked open the bathroom door and held up a tampon like it was a scepter, and she was crowning me queen.

"Isabella! You haff forgotten something!"

"But it's not mine," I said, startled, feeling a blush engulf my face.

"Well," she trumpeted with a show of humor, "it cannot be mine! I am over eighty!" She tossed it into the trash behind her and turned off the bathroom light, coming out to stare curiously at the new couple.

"My mother is German," the man contributed, his expression unreadable. Elsie drew herself up to her full height of five feet.

"I am not German! I am from Vienna!" She waddled over to us and peered up at the brother's face. He started smiling. "I am Elsie Schnitzler!"

"Hello, Elsie! I could hear you out in the car park!" Alec suddenly swanned up the stairs and allowed himself to be welcomed into Elsie's substantial bosom. "Have you met my friends from Patterson?"

I heard my Gabriel's awestruck voice come unexpectedly from somewhere behind my hips.

"You're from Bethel? In America?" he breathed out, his squeaky voice reverential. "Can I sit by you?"

During the meeting, I had nervous knots in my stomach that had nothing to do with the fact that Tamsin hadn't showed yet or that Great-aunt Aurora was lapsing back into Spanish with every other sentence. I had developed full-blown intestinal macramé when I found out that I was sitting next to my grandfather. I knew that I was overreacting, but this was my grandfather's very first meeting, and we were all walking on eggshells.

On the Aran Islands, where my grandparents live, there is no place for my grandmother to meet in. The Aran Islands get worked every so often by Gaelic-speaking special pioneers that come over on a boat, and that, combined with the biannual visits from the circuit overseer, have been the only association that my grandmother had been able to enjoy over the years.

Still dressed in his black clothes, the only concession my grandfather had made to attend his first meeting was the neat rubber band that my grandmother had made him substitute for the torn scrap of horsewhip he had been wearing earlier.

During the opening song, my great-aunts shared their one English songbook with my grandmother, who only had one in Gaelic, leaving me to hold my own open songbook under my grandfather's fierce eyes. He looked down at the small brown book like an eagle staring at a mouse and frowned mightily through the whole first verse.

By the time we got to the chorus, the nervous sweat trickling from my hairline was beginning to look like shiny little slug trails. Acting nonchalant, I continued to hold my songbook under his frown, too petrified with awkwardness to move, let alone lower it from his chin, which unexpectedly turned out to be a good thing. When the second verse began, his voice suddenly rolled down over me in a lilting baritone, and I saw my grandmother glance up at him and raise an eyebrow in surprise.

Afterward, as Brandt, our school instructor, introduced the Theocratic Ministry School, Tamsin scooted into the first row and sat down in front of me. Relieved, I settled back to concentrate on the meeting, doing my best to ignore the disconcerting presence of my grandfather beside me. As it turned out, my fragile peace was doomed before it had time to gel, shattering during Lamond Makumba's delivery of the instruction talk.

Lamond had just directed us to read a scripture, so no one was looking up when Great-aunt Aurora suddenly spiraled out of orbit. The first intimation that something was wrong came from Tamsin's gasp. It was barely audible, and I was the only one close enough to hear it. I looked up at the hiss and saw Great-aunt Aurora mounting the stage with her purse slung over her arm. Horrified, I looked around me to see who had noticed, hoping that at least my father would, or one of my brothers, but everyone was deep into Lamond's accented reading of the scripture.

Paralyzed, I watched as Aunt Aurora walked up to the podium and rapped on it loudly, startling an exclamation out of Lamond. He dropped his Bible, and notes scattered everywhere like thrown leaves.

"Hello, little boy." Aunt Aurora smiled tremulously at Lamond's rump as he scrabbled on the floor for his fallen notes. "Are your parents home?"

Her only answer was Elsie's unfortunate response from somewhere in the back of the hall.

*"Oh mein gott!"* she boomed in horrified sympathy. Jude and Clive, who were attendants for the evening, finally reached the platform. They gently took Aunt Aurora's elbows and turned her around, easing her off the stage's high step and down the wide center aisle.

We all reacted differently. My parents got up from their seats and met Clive, Jude, and Aunt Aurora halfway, walking to the back with them. My grandmother hurriedly got up and followed them, her face a mask of anxiety. Great-aunt Astrid looked around at the audience in a discombobulated fashion. Tamsin whirled around in her seat to stare at me in powerless horror. My grandfather belched.

A gentle cloud of secondhand ravioli settled around us, snapping me out of my helplessness, and I suddenly stood, handing him my Bible and songbook and grabbing my purse.

"I'm coming with you," Tamsin hissed and followed me to the back of the room. Lamond resumed talking.

We converged in the tiny entryway by the bathroom doors.

"Where's Astrid?" Aunt Aurora said loudly in a plaintive voice. My father stepped past the tight clot of bodies, peered into the men's loo, and then opened the door wider to the unoccupied haven and jerked us all inside, shutting the door behind us. He turned the lock, his eyes never leaving Great-aunt Aurora's face.

"She's at the meeting," he said gently and put a hand to his aunt's face, turning her toward the light coming from the dim bulb over the sink. Jude and Clive never let go of her elbows, turning with her as she shifted, and I felt the porcelain of the toilet against the back of my knees. Everyone swayed at the shift of bodies, and I fell back, sitting down hard on the cold seat. Tamsin tucked herself against the wall, standing beside me, her brown eyes as round as golf balls.

It was just as well that Aunt Astrid was mystified and befuddled with fatigue and still in her seat on the second row. The only way another person could join us would be to start stacking.

"Are you all right, Aunt Aurora?" my father continued. I noticed that while he held her attention, Clive was busily taking her pulse.

"As fit as a fiddle." Aunt Aurora beamed tremulously and pressed a hand to her bosom for emphasis. The crackle of paper was unmistakable in our small confined space. I saw my mother's eyes swivel down toward Aunt Aurora's chest in a bewildered frown.

"So far, everything seems fine," Clive said, and letting go of Aunt Aurora's arm, he peered into her eyes and raised a forefinger. Instead of focusing on it, Aunt Aurora looked up at the ceiling.

"I don't see it, dear," she said gently, her forehead puckering.

"Just look at my finger, luv," Clive said cheerfully and waited until she complied. "Now follow it with your eyes. Keep watching it."

He moved his hand to the left, to the right, up, down, and then finally in an ever-widening circle.

"So far, still fine," Clive murmured, more in reassurance to the rest of us than to Aunt Aurora. Aunt Aurora seemed to regard his examination as a mildly interesting game she was playing with a stranger. The doorknob suddenly rattled peremptorily somewhere behind Aunt Aurora's ample buttocks, and we all jumped as if we'd been shot. I knocked the spare loo roll off the back of the toilet, and it rolled under the sink.

"Just a minute!" three male voices called out in unison as Clive, Jude, and my father responded to the urgent-sounding attempt to get in.

"Coming!" Aunt Aurora warbled on heels of their peremptory male chorus. "I'm almost done!" Then she leaned over and flushed the toilet under me.

It sounded like a condensed snippet of operatic relay. My father and Jude glanced at each other and grinned. I didn't dare look up at Tamsin. I was glad that my father had chosen the men's bathroom to dart into. If it had been the women's bathroom, no doubt Elsie's medication would have kicked in again, and the whole congregation would have been privy to Elsie's shouted plea for admittance.

"I have my medical bag in my car." Clive patted Aunt Aurora's shoulder and then turned to my parents. "She's fine, just exhausted. My guess is that she has been too excited to sleep deeply, and exhaustion has its own vicious cycle. Why don't I take her back home, do a more thorough examination just to be sure, then get her to bed, and give her a sedative to help her sleep. A good-night's sleep will help, and then we'll look into stepping up their homeopathic remedies."

"Luc," my mother's careful voice floated past the male bodies blocking her. They shifted. She came into view, looking worried. "I'll go with them, but I'll need you to find a quick substitute for my talk. It's coming up in a few minutes."

I stood up, being the obvious person to substitute for her, and took a deep breath to propose a simpler solution; but before I could say a word, the doorknob rattled again, this time sounding even more urgent, and my father leaned past everyone and unlocked the door, opening it to my grandfather.

"Fancy meeting you here," Grandfather said in a rare burst of dark humor. "Is everything all right?"

My father leaned out and pulled him into the bathroom, shutting the door and locking it again. I fell back onto the toilet with a jarring thud.

"How's Astrid? Did you leave her up there by herself?" my grandmother barked out at him before anyone else could speak, obviously agitated at the turn of events. He rolled his eyes exaggeratedly until they came to rest on her.

"She's looking up scriptures, so she seems dandy, woman," he said dryly. "But as to whether they are the right ones, only heaven and Violet Pengarth knows. Yon little woman moved up to sit with her."

"Listen, Mom, go ahead and do your talk," I said quickly, interrupting before my grandmother could serve the answering retort I could see hovering on her lips.

"Who said that?" My grandfather looked around and finally spotted me hunkered down on the toilet seat.

"I'll go with Clive and put Aunt Aurora to bed. I'll sit with her," I said, ignoring my grandfather. "I'm the only one in the family who doesn't have an assignment tonight. It will be easiest."

"I don't know, *cara mia*—," she began. I hesitantly cut her off.

"It would be easier for me to sit with her than to give your talk without seeing your notes until I'm on the stage," I said and looked at my father. "I'll be fine."

"I'll go with her," Tamsin said quietly.

"It should be fine," Clive supplemented in a professionally reassuring voice. "The sedative is strong enough to put her to sleep where she stands. I could administer it outside, but it would be easiest to wait until she's tucked in bed. I'll stay until it takes effect."

"If you're certain," my mother said uncertainly. My grandfather surprised us all by putting a gentling hand on her shoulder.

"They'll be fine, Raphaela," he said gruffly and lowered his pirate eyebrows in a fierce expression that would have sent toddlers fleeing. "I'll go back with them."

"No," I cried out, dismayed that he was going to miss his first meeting and then belatedly realized what my outburst had sounded like. I would be lying if I said that it wouldn't have been my second concern, but it certainly wasn't what had prompted my horrified exclamation. My grandfather ignored me.

"I should go," my grandmother said, sounding distressed. My grandfather transferred his hand from my mother to his wife.

"You'll stay here, woman. I'll not want you and Aurora chattering at me."

"Finghin, I don't—"

"You'll stay."

"No, I—"

"Woman, I'll not listen to you and Aurora, and I'll not sit with Astrid up in the front seats!" he bellowed, flustered, obviously intimidated by the thought of being left behind at the meeting without his wife. Everyone but my father and Aunt Aurora stared at him in surprise.

"It's settled, then," my father said, forestalling the words that rose to my grandmother's lips.

"Let's get on with it," Clive said cheerfully. My father unlocked the door, and we began the difficult task of unobtrusively hustling Great-aunt Aurora quietly out of the Hall and down the stairs to the back door of the pub below.

"I think, my dears, that I would like a wee tot of brandy," she trumpeted loudly as we shuffled her unwilling figure toward the head of the staircase.

"Not tonight, luv," Clive said good-naturedly as my grandmother and mother stayed behind, closing the upper storey door behind us.

We went down the stairs and left the pub, stepping out under the streetlamp. The drizzle that had dampened everyone earlier had spent itself, leaving a cool mist that smelled of ozone. I looked up and saw the huge blurred orb of a full moon behind the moving gauze overhead. Patches of cold-looking stars peeked through the rips. I could tell that the rain wasn't over. In fact, it was just taking a breather before gearing up. My father and Jude handed Aunt Aurora into the backseat of Clive's Toyota while I got in beside her and secured the safety belt. My grandfather climbed in the front with Clive. We started out, driving as carefully as the lead car in a parade, with Tamsin bringing up the rear in her red Mini Cooper.

By the time we got home, Great-aunt Aurora had escalated from confused docility to adamant paranoia. I think it was the sight of my grandfather in the front seat that triggered some sort of emotional memory in her distressed brain. The vague tirade had been getting worse with every street, and now the focus became obvious as we neared the inn.

"You aren't marrying her," she said plaintively as we swept through the inn's front gates. "I won't let you."

We passed the fountain on the front lawn and crunched over the gravel to the family's private entrance.

"You reek of whisky, and your hair is too long." She sniffled, and I helplessly patted her hand. "You're a handsome rogue, Finghin, with an eye for the ladies, but you'll not turn my sister's head. She's much too good for you."

Clive pulled to a stop in front of the doors to our wing and put the car into park, cutting off the engine and the headlights. Outside the car, the wind suddenly intensified, swirling around trees and rustling leaves.

"I've seen the women falling at your feet, staring at you, and I'll not have her marry some sort of dangerous hound. You are a rogue and a . . . oh . . . ," she broke off and stared out of the window at the inn with curiosity. "Oh, dear. What an interesting place. Deja vu. I feel I've been here before. Where are we?"

"You're doolally, woman," Grandfather snorted in disgust and got out of the car. Tamsin pulled up behind us and turned off her engine, getting out with her purse slung over her shoulder.

It took all four of us to get Aunt Aurora out of the car and into the house. She resisted our efforts to herd her toward the doors, and every time my grandfather would take her arm with any sort of force, she would pull herself free from his grasp and hit him.

"For goodness' sakes, woman!" he finally bellowed, giving up on being gentle as he strong-armed her over the inn's threshold when I unlocked the front door. Clive chuckled and grasped her upper arms.

"Now now, Aurora," he chided gently in an amused voice as he steered her toward her suite on the bottom floor. "Easy does it." Her response was to break free and aim another wallop at my grandfather, who let go of her to duck.

Clive continued to murmur soothingly, unable to keep the amusement from his voice.

"Relax, there's a good girl," he crooned.

"That's for stopping Bryn from going to the meetings!" she said and smacked a fist against my grandfather's stomach, catching him before he could dodge a second time.

He grunted loudly.

"You hound!" She smacked him again.

"You're doing fine, luv," Clive chuckled and managed to maneuver Aunt Aurora toward her ruffled bed with its mound of fat pillows. "Come on, now. You're expending yourself. Come on. Relax."

Together we managed to plant Aunt Aurora's bottom on her mattress and hold her arms while Clive hurriedly broke open his black bag and readied the sedative and syringe. He rolled up the sleeve of her dress, the syringe in his hand poised over her plump arm, and swiped an alcohol-soaked cotton ball over a spot of skin.

"Hurry up, man," my grandfather growled. Clive quickly stuck the needle in her flesh and efficiently plunged the sedative into her system.

"How long before it takes effect?" I asked as Clive popped the used needle off the syringe and disposed of it in a lidded box. He dropped the syringe and box back into his black bag.

"Only a moment or two," he said cheerfully and snapped his bag closed. At the sound of his voice, Aunt Aurora's eyes rolled up at Clive, looking at him, and then continued rolling until they disappeared into the back of her head. We stared in fascination as her muscles seemed to settle in on each other, and her head slumped forward. My grandfather caught her ample weight with a startled grunt and then looked up at the doctor.

"That was a bit of an understatement, man," he said dryly.

Tamsin and I undressed her, heaving her sleeping body about the bed with the help of Clive while my grandfather waited in the kitchen, nursing a finger of scotch. It didn't take us long.

We stripped her to her petticoat and slid a heavy flannel nightgown over her while she snored delicately in the big fat bed. Trying not to disturb her more than was necessary, we left her flat on the mattress while we worked. It was a bit like stuffing a soft rubber log into support hose. Bits of hooks and straps kept catching on the gewgaws of flannel, and it was with a loud sigh of relief when we finally rolled her under the covers and tucked her in. She smiled angelically at the ceiling when I smoothed a stray poodle curl from her forehead.

"Are you sure she's out?" I asked, disconcerted when it seemed that she smiled at my touch.

"Probably dreaming," Clive said, standing behind Tamsin and me as we huffed and puffed over her peaceful figure like steam engines, trying to get our breath back. He put his hands on our elbows and chuckled. "She sure gave your grandfather a workout, didn't she?"

"Bella," Tamsin's voice sounded funny. I looked at her. She pointed at the bosom of my great-aunt. "What's that?"

I looked in the direction of her gaze and was a bit startled to see a sliver of parchment poking out of the neck of her gown. I leaned over and tugged on it, working it free from her tightly ensconced cleavage. It came out with a breathy slurp, and I unfolded the scrap of yellowed paper.

"Don't tell me your great-uncle managed to plant a clue there," Clive chuckled, recognizing the waxy sheen of the old parchment.

"It's just a line of letters and numbers," I said and held it up for Tamsin and Clive to see.

"I thought I kept hearing the crackle of paper every time she moved," Clive said and took the paper from me. "So what is it?"

"I have no idea," I said and leaned over to peer at the parchment's back. "That's all it is. Just letters and numbers."

"From your uncle Desmond?" Clive asked and handed it back to me. I nodded.

"It looks like it."

Aunt Aurora suddenly snorted and rolled over, tucking the pillow deeper under her neck.

"Let's go ahead and leave her to it, then. Let me just listen to her heart and breathing for a minute and get her blood pressure, and then I'll meet you in the kitchen when I'm done." Clive smiled and patted our shoulders, gently steering us toward the hallway. "Go ahead and get yourself changed into more comfortable clothes, and then we can try to figure out the numbers on the parchment over a cup of tea."

Tamsin and I left him and went up the uneven staircase to my bedroom. I hurriedly and distractedly changed into a pair of jeans and a tee shirt while Tamsin changed into the pair of jeans she keeps stashed in my closet. We went downstairs with the slip of paper.

"Sit down and drink this." Clive had made it to the kitchen ahead of us and was there when we entered. He handed us huge mugs of fragrant hot tea. "You both need the sugar."

My grandfather was at the table with his scotch, one booted foot resting on his knee as he leaned back in his chair. He regarded me out of brooding eyes, and I had no idea what he was thinking. I didn't know at that point what I was even thinking.

"Thank you," I told Clive and sat down at the table across from my grandfather. My grandfather and I studied each other for a minute over Clive's black medical bag, and I was the first to look away, reaching into my pocket for the parchment. I unfolded it and slid it around the bag and across the tabletop toward him.

"We found this in Aunt Aurora's . . . uh . . . dress," I finished lamely, refusing to utter the word "cleavage" to my dark-browed grandfather. I noticed that a shock of silver hair had worked loose from its mooring of rubber band and had fallen over his forehead. I saw Tamsin staring at him in open fascination, the exact thoughts behind her brown eyes unreadable.

My grandfather put his glass down and pulled the scrap of parchment toward him.

"Smells like talcum," he growled and frowned at the numbers straggling across the paper. "Did my wife's loony half brother write this?"

"It looks like his writing," I said cautiously. Clive sat down at the heavy wooden table with his own mug of tea.

"How's Aunt Aurora?" I asked, looking at Clive. He smiled, his gray eyes crinkling tiredly behind his glasses.

"Sleeping like a baby." He paused and took a large swallow of tea. "She's fine. Nothing but exhaustion."

Just then his expression changed, and he shifted to pull his vibrating pager from his pocket, turning its tiny screen up to the light to peer at it. He sighed.

"I certainly hope this isn't what I think it is," he said and stood, putting his mug down on the table. "Excuse me while I make a phone call." As he left us in the kitchen, he pulled his mobile phone from his pocket and flipped it open to turn it on and punch in a number.

My grandfather put the parchment back down on the table and picked up his glass of scotch. A jagged streak of lightning suddenly shot over the horizon in the distant sky, and Tamsin's eyes jerked up. We looked through the uncovered panes at the spectacular flickers.

"Yon figures look like the combination to a safe," my grandfather grunted, ignoring the flicker of lightning shooting out behind his head.

"A safe?" I said, surprised. "What safe?"

"I wouldn't know, lass," my grandfather grumbled disagreeably and downed the rest of his scotch, slapping the empty glass on the table beside the parchment. I leaned forward and retrieved the paper. Looking at it again, I noticed for the first time that the letters *R* and *L* preceded every number.

"You're right," I said, surprised, and held the paper out to Tamsin. "Was there a safe in Tanglewood?"

A faint crash of thunder echoed ominously in the distance, and I frowned.

"Relax," my grandfather said gruffly. "It won't break for an hour. It's still too far out."

"I have to go." Clive strode into the room just then, sounding grim and preoccupied. He snatched his bag from the table, touching my shoulder briefly as he leaned over me. "Tell your parents to call me when they get in, and I'll try to make it back to check on your aunt Astrid."

"Okay," I said, feeling suddenly marooned as I watched him walk out of the room on his way to the front door, his mind obviously racing elsewhere. "Thank you." A second later, I heard the front door slam.

Silence suddenly stretched around us, and the hush in the kitchen swelled and became nearly as intense as the gathering storm outside. Tamsin and I fiddled silently for a moment with our mugs, stealing glances at each other, aware of the electric brooding presence of my grandfather. Even though he didn't speak, he seemed to fill the kitchen.

I sighed and looked back at Tamsin.

"Did you find out anything at the library?"

I was unprepared for the effect my innocent question had on Tamsin. Her eyes darted up, suddenly wide, and I could swear her pupils dilated as she pressed her fingers to her mouth.

"How could I forget?" She moved her fingers long enough to utter her question, then slapped her hand back to her mouth.

"What?"

"Bella." Tamsin took her hand off her mouth and suddenly stuck out both hands to grab the edge of the table as if she needed mooring. She leaned toward me. "I found Algernon Wycliffe in the French connection. You'll never believe it. Oh . . . ," she started, looking around herself, and then spotted her purse on the floor by her feet. "I'll have to show you."

Taking a deep breath, she pulled her shoulder bag to her lap, and reaching inside, she pulled a sheaf of papers free. She unfurled the first one and handed it to me. A distant spark of lightning flickered again as I took it from her.

It was a copy of something written in copperplate so ornate I could barely make out the letters, realizing suddenly that it had been written in French.

"I can't read this," I said helplessly. But Tamsin waved my complaint away.

"You don't have to. I know what it is. It's Algernon Wycliffe's marriage lines. Look at the names on the bottom."

I did and saw the name of the bride. The name of the tenant of Tanglewood that had been evicted at the death of James George Wildeve.

"Destiny Ophelia Wycliffe?" I said a second later, not trusting my eyes. I looked up at Tamsin and could feel my own pupils dilate. "Destiny. Clarisse's Destiny? She was alive?"

Tamsin nodded solemnly, her brown eyes shining and intense, and then she unfurled the second paper in her hand and held it out to me.

"I found a portrait. It's in a museum outside of Chartres, France. They faxed it to me at the library. That's why I was very nearly late to the meeting. I had to wait for it."

I took the paper, expecting to see the ruffled figure of Destiny Ophelia simpering out at me in her eighteenth-century costume. But I was wrong. It wasn't of Destiny. I gaped at the reproduction.

"Who is this?" I managed to breathe out. And Tamsin looked at me like I was crazy.

"It's Algernon Wycliffe. Why?"

"No, it's not," I said and felt my pupils shrink back to normal. I felt as if the air was suddenly sucked from the room, and I looked up to grin at my friend, my heart beating hard in my excitement. "It's a picture of James George Wildeve, the smuggler."

# 14

I let myself in the back door of my brothers' cottage and found the history book that I had left on their kitchen table. I hadn't wanted to risk getting it wet when I had to go back home in the drizzle earlier that evening.

Tamsin and Grandfather were waiting in the inn's kitchen for me to retrieve the heavy tome and bring it back. Well, at least Tamsin was openly eager to compare the two portraits. It was hard to know what my grandfather was thinking. He had merely pinned me with unreadable eyes and grunted in a way that could have meant anything from his blessing to indigestion.

Lightning was now forking the distance with ominous regularity, and the wind had grown, whipping the tops of the trees into a chaotic dance. Patchy clouds were racing past the full moon, rolling shadows past me, and I could smell the damp sharp scent of the approaching storm. My hair kept whipping around my face and into my eyes as I made my way back to the inn in the frenetic darkness.

I let myself back into the kitchen, embracing the book to my chest, and was surprised to see my grandfather up at the counter staring at the bag of coffee beans in his huge bony hand like he had just found a sack of rabbit pellets in the freezer. Tamsin was still in her seat at the table, her eyes glued unblinkingly to my grandfather's broad back.

"Would you like a coffee, Grandfather?"

"Haven't the Italians heard of instant?" he grunted, his soaring eyebrows plunging down over his eyes in a spectacular *V*. He shot a sideways glare at the brushed chrome espresso machine tucked away beside the toaster and grunted. "How does your mother work that thing?"

"I'll make it," I said and handed the book to Tamsin, opening it up to James George's portrait before taking the sack of coffee beans from my grandfather. While I ground the beans and made the espresso, my grandfather and Tamsin peered in turns at the portraits. I watched their expressions as the fragrance of coffee filled the kitchen.

Tamsin seemed fascinated and kept flicking her eyes back and forth between what was obviously the same man while my grandfather had taken only one look at the portraits and had shoved the book back to the center of the table with a grunt.

I poured my grandfather a cup of espresso and topped it with steamed milk, making a cappuccino even though he hadn't asked for one. He looked at it suspiciously and then accepted the mug from my hand, taking a sip.

"Tastes like mule urine." He slammed the cup down on the table with a grimace. Steamed milk rose up in a miniature volcano and spattered the back of his hand.

"Of course, and we all know instant coffee doesn't," I said dryly, then sat down, cupping my chin in my hand as I leaned an elbow on the table. "And by the way, when did you last drink mule urine?"

*"Fuist, cna'dai'!"* he grunted, his mouth twitching at one corner. And I saw Tamsin's gaze bounce between us. "You have a mouth like your father. Just remember, you aren't too big to put over my knee."

Tamsin's eyes widened uneasily. I grinned at her, doing my best not to be intimidated by my grandfather, and slipped the book from her hand to open it to the section that referred to Tanglewood's tenant marrying Algernon Wildeve, which we now knew to be Destiny Ophelia and James George. I listened as Tamsin read the passage out loud.

"So what was she doing at Tanglewood?" I asked.

"Fleeing the French Revolution, lass," my grandfather grunted.

Tamsin and I looked up in unison, our mouths parted, and I felt my own eyebrows twitch.

"But how did she get here?"

"By boat?" my grandfather answered sardonically and took another sip of his "mule urine," his mouth grimacing in distaste as he swallowed.

"James George's smuggling boat," I said slowly. "Brandy and lace wasn't the only thing he took out of France."

"Bella," Tamsin said slowly. I turned to look at her.

"What?"

"The painting, Bella," she said quietly. "The painting of the shipwreck over your great-grandmother's mantel. It was signed 'Destiny.'"

"So it really was a signature. She must have been the one who painted that." It took a second for words to come out. I was thinking furiously even though at the moment I felt as if a cricket bat had just smacked my brain into another room. Guesses and deductions were falling into place too fast for me to assimilate them. "She had to have painted it, then, while she was here. It wasn't a Wildeve who had painted that. It was Destiny Wycliffe. But what shipwreck did she paint?"

"Who said she had painted a real shipwreck?" Tamsin asked curiously. I raised my eyebrows at her.

"If you'd seen the painting in a good light and not by torchlight, you wouldn't ask. It's real, all right, and it's of the beach below Tanglewood."

"Well, James George's boat was caught in a storm in 1792, and a piece of the hull was damaged," she said, blinking at me. I stared at her. "No, really. I found an account of it by one of the local families. It came up cross-referenced to the name of James George Wildeve."

"An account by one of the local families," I repeated and slowly grinned at her. "Tamsin, that means that James George's shipwreck did happen here. If that is the shipwreck that Destiny painted, then my guess is that she was on that boat when it was driven into the cliff rocks below the manor."

"Why do you say that?"

"The date on the back of the painting," I said. "It was framed in 1792. Put that with the fact that the date on Clarisse's urn is the same year, and I would be willing to bet that Destiny's crossing from France was on the same run that ended up smashing a hole in the smuggling boat. Tamsin, it all happened in the same year, and there wouldn't have been enough time for it all to have happened on another smuggling run. Besides, there was real fear in that painting."

I remembered an entry in one of my great-grandmother's diaries, and it suddenly fell into its place in the jigsaw of bits that Great-uncle Desmond had planted everywhere.

"Tamsin, do you remember the journal from my great-grandmother that Dante had found shoved into the riding boot?"

"In the tower room that used to be your great-grandmother's bedroom? What about it?"

"I finally understand why Great-uncle Desmond separated it from the other journals. The main batch of journals disclosed the fact that Desmond wasn't from Great-grandmother Destiny, but the single journal he had separated had a more specific clue that makes sense now." I paused, trying to remember the exact wording of the two odd sentences that had struck me at the time. "In it my great-grandmother had written a strange entry. She wrote that she had found another Destiny, and if it had gone properly, she wouldn't be here today."

"I don't understand," Tamsin said and scooted her cooling mug of tea aside, ignoring my grandfather's enlightened grunt.

"If she had somehow found the old oil painting here after she had married my great-grandfather, then she would have noticed that the artist had signed the painting with the same name of Destiny. It makes me think that she was curious enough to do some research. She must have somehow found out what we had. If James George hadn't fled the country with Destiny Ophelia, then Tanglewood would have never ended up with my great-grandfather."

Tamsin suddenly grinned.

"There's another clue that makes more sense now."

"Which one?"

"One of your great-uncle's rhymes: 'Roses are red. Violets are blue. Men aren't the dead. This is a clue.'" She waited for me to make the connection. "Bella, your great-uncle must have been referring to the fact that James George's crew obviously didn't die at sea in a shipwreck. The men aren't dead."

A crash of thunder rolled overhead, startling me, and I looked past my grandfather to the sky framed in the windows. The bushes on the lawn intensified their wild dance.

"None of this makes a difference," my grandfather's gruff voice suddenly popped our bubble. "A person can speculate all they want about what happened two hundred years ago, but they would still have no idea where the silly fool hid the treasure."

Before I could say anything, there was a peremptory knock on our front door. The sound traveled faintly to the kitchen, and I paused, not sure that I had heard what I had thought I had heard. The knock sounded again.

"That must be Clive," I said, wondering why he didn't just come in. I got up and went through the lamp-lit house to the foyer and opened the front door. I was surprised to see Patrick McCauley, Halfmoon's only taxi driver. I peered around his wiry little body and saw his shiny black sedan parked in the drive behind Tamsin's Mini. He looked over his shoulder at the direction of my gaze, then turned back to me, and fixed me with his customary grin.

"Why, hello, my lovely. The old lady said you would pay me."

"Who is it?" I asked curiously and waited for whomever it was still ensconced in the taxi to alight. I wondered if my grandmother had decided to ignore my grandfather and leave the meeting early.

"I don't know, do I?" He ran a hand through his red hair, shoving it off his forehead. "Beastly night, isn't it? There's a real one brewing out over the ocean. That will be two pounds."

"Why aren't they getting out?" I asked, ignoring his outstretched hand. Who could possibly be arriving this late?

"Why aren't they getting out, my lovely?" He grinned and pushed his hand through his hair again. "Why, they already got out, didn't they?"

"Who, Patrick?" I persisted. His grin widened.

"You don't know? She came from your own house, and you don't know who had sent for me?"

"What?" I felt my breath seize up.

"All I know, my lovely, is that I got a call to come here, and I picked up some old lady in a pink raincoat. She told me she wanted to go home. So I took her. Two pounds, my lovely." He held his hand out again.

I slammed the door in his face, turned, and ran all the way to Aunt Aurora's room, skidding to a stop beside her empty bed.

"Oh no." I sucked in air. "Grandfather! Tamsin! Grandfather! Tamsin!" I ran back to the front door and yanked it back open. Patrick was still there, looking startled and somewhat leery of me. He took a step backward when I lunged out and wrapped my fingers around his wrist.

"Where did you take her? To the Tanglewood Estate?" I could feel poor Patrick's sinews tightening under my grip. A strong hand descended on my shoulder, I was yanked free of the cheerful little taxi driver, and was spun around to face my grandfather.

"What is it, child?" his agitated baritone vibrated through me.

"Aunt Aurora's gone! She must have woken up and called Patrick to take her to the manor in his taxi."

"Old woman must have the constitution of an ox." My grandfather marveled, sounding incredulous, and turned to Patrick. "Where did you take her, man?"

"Like the girl said." Patrick looked worried. "To Wildeve Manor. Tanglewood. Why? What's up?"

"Oh no," I wailed. My grandfather gave me an impatient shake.

*"Fuist!"* he said, his voice gruff. I felt Tamsin's fingers grip mine from somewhere behind me. I thought of the cliffs bordering the drive and felt sick.

"Get your keys," I said to Tamsin. She nodded, breaking away to get her purse in the kitchen. I looked back at Patrick who was looking like he was now wishing he hadn't returned for his two pounds. "Where exactly did you drop her off? Did she go inside the manor?"

"Well, no." Patrick's eyebrows collided in a worried frown. "She wandered around the back. I thought it was barmy at the time, what with the storm nearly here, but I figured she would be fine. She was old enough to know her own business."

At least she didn't wander in the direction of the cliffs, I thought. With Aunt Aurora's habit of dithering, if we hurried, we might still find her in the garden. She might even fall asleep out there and never even leave the walled greenery.

"How did she seem?" I asked, hoping against hope that her short nap had worked wonders and that she was no more vague than usual.

"Hard to tell, my lovely. She never talked to me on the drive. The only thing she said when she got out was to come back for the money."

I knew then that Great-aunt Aurora must not have taken her purse, so she was apparently without the manor's house keys as well. Tamsin came up just then, my purse over her arm along with her own, and shoved the leather bag at me. I took it and started out of the door.

"Child, wait!" my grandfather's voice was like a whip as I took off running for the Mini, and my body jerked involuntarily to a stop. "Calm down!"

Patrick took a step back and nervously fingered his collar as my grandfather stepped out onto the doorstep.

"We don't know for certain, child. Have ye checked the whole house?"

"No, but—"

*"Fuist!"* He roared, his brogue getting more pronounced with every word. I could tell that Tamsin was having a hard time deciphering the musical vowels rolling across the drive at us in the darkness. "Listen to me! I'll not have ye running around in the storm alone looking for her! She'll be fine."

"I have to, Grandfather," I said, twisting my purse strap into knots. "I will be safer than she will. I have to go find her."

"Aye, and can ye control her once you do?" One of his fierce eyebrows arched. "I'm not saying you cannot help. We'll go after I leave a message at yon pub for your father."

"I guess you don't need me, then." Patrick backed down the front step and turned, hurriedly making his way back to his taxi as he yelled over his shoulder at us, "Forget the two pounds, my lovely. It's on the house!"

My grandfather left as Patrick drove away in his taxi, coming back only a minute later with two torches in his hand. He handed one to me and kept the other one for himself.

"I cannot find a third . . . You two will not separate once we're there," he instructed gruffly as we strode to his car. "And ye'll go only where I say."

A vortex of cold ozone and flying leaves whipped around us. Clouds continued to flee overhead, and my hair lashed my eyes when I looked up at the distant flickers of lightning.

Who knew that gentle, sweet fluffy Aunt Astrid could defy not only my grandfather but also Clive Chaucer's best shot?

Sick with worry, I jumped into the backseat of my grandfather's car, and Tamsin and I huddled together for dubious comfort. By the time we got to the manor and got out of the car, the clouds out over the water were flickering with spasms of internal lightning. I felt like we were standing under a celestial bug zapper in a swarm of midges. The display was spectacular enough to halt me in midstride.

"Stop dawdling, ye daft child." My grandfather's hand grasped my arm and sucked me back into his wake. I felt like his ball and chain as I stumbled and was jerked with every stride over the uneven ground. "Turn on your torch!"

I did as he asked, trotting to keep up, and he let go of my arm. I felt Tamsin's long fingers scrabble at my back and intertwine in a handful of my tee shirt.

"Are we going to the garden?" I asked my grandfather as we rounded the side of the house. "I'll never find the way in through the wall in the dark. I'm not sure I can even find it in the daylight."

"I remember the way in," my grandfather growled. He didn't elaborate, and I wondered how much time he had spent at Tanglewood wooing my grandmother. I wondered if he remembered all the secret passages as well.

"Aunt Aurora!" I yelled. "Where are you?" My voice was whipped away by the wind and carried up.

"She'll not hear ye," my grandfather said gruffly. "Not over the winds, child, and certainly not past those infernal pixies in her head."

We made our way around the house, and instead of following the winding flagstone path that led to the garden wall, my grandfather set off at an angle over the terraced back lawn. He walked unerringly to the yew-covered gate and fished through the brambles. The gate swung open without the telltale click of the latch at the same time that Tamsin spied Aunt Aurora's white scarf caught in the yew.

"Bella, is that hers?" She yanked on my arm and pointed at it. I shined my light at the white smudge flapping erratically in the chaotic wind and nodded.

"It looks like it."

My grandfather glowered at the scrap of fabric and pushed wide the unlatched gate. Aunt Aurora must not have closed it behind her.

"Get inside," he commanded and held the yew back until we were all in, shutting the gate firmly behind him until the latch clicked. "Do you have a watch?"

Tamsin and I both nodded.

"We'll meet back here in an hour," he said and strode off into the darkness. I suddenly felt like crying with frustration.

"This place is so big we'll never find her," I wailed as Tamsin checked her watch to mark the time.

"Aunt Aurora!" we yelled into the banshee winds and started off in the direction of the Adam and Eve fountain. Maybe she had decided to return to the glade where she had spent many hours playing with her sisters as a child. I knew I could find the glade where the Destiny grave was if I followed the wisteria path that began at the fountain. After a few moments, I spied the fountain up ahead.

"Come on. Let's check the clearing where the secret tunnel to the boiler is."

We followed the wisteria-hung path. Torn white petals swirled around us, and more than once we tripped, not looking where we were stepping, but instead looking around in the dense greenery for a glimpse of Aunt Aurora's new pink raincoat. We made it to the glade, and no one was there.

"Aunt Aurora!" I screamed again. My only answer was the wail of the wind and the whip and creak of branches. Gnarled vines scraped together with every gusty breath and the long grass bent and whipped the ground around us. I looked up at the sky. Clouds had engulfed the fragmented moonlight, and I could see that the storm was directly above us.

"Aunt Aurora!" I looked around at the wind-shredded wisteria, trying to figure out where we should try next.

"Bella!" Tamsin had to yell over the swirl of wind. "Where would she go to sit down? She still has to be feeling the effects of the sedative."

"I don't even know what's in the garden." I spun around to look at her. Her short dark hair was leaping about her face. "I only know about the ruins, the burial plot, and a maze." I thought for a moment, then pointed the beam of my torch behind her. "Jude said that the maze is somewhere over there. Aunt Astrid said that there is a folly inside the center. Let's try that."

"She could be anywhere," Tamsin said, depressingly honest. I snatched her hand as I started walking, towing her behind me so we wouldn't get separated. I could feel the tension in her grasp as she continued thinking out loud. "I just hope she's in the garden and not wandering about in someone's pasture. I'm afraid of the storm."

I knew that being "afraid of the storm" was her less distressful euphemism for "afraid Aunt Aurora will be struck by lightning," a possibility I refused to imagine. I was more afraid of the nearby cliffs, the cold rain, and her age. Great-aunt Aurora wasn't acclimatized to the weather of Cornwall with its unexpected bursts of rain and ocean-cooled nights.

We found the maze quickly, unmistakable as an untamed tall solid wall of yew. I stopped and stared at the endless mass of growth. It looked like it had been dropped down in one solid celestial clump from space, absorbing all sound and light, even the maniacal winds. The black hole of Tanglewood. I wondered what monster lived inside of it.

"Where's the opening?" Tamsin's anxious voice brought me back to earth. And I swung my torch beam helplessly down its sides.

"I can't see one. What if it's like the hidden gate to the garden? All leafed over and closed up?"

"Come on." This time it was Tamsin who tugged on me, dragging me with her as she started walking alongside the yew line.

Above us the clouds had curled up and thickened. Lightning danced frenetically behind the black mass, flickering and skipping across the sky, and I felt the hair on the back of my neck stand up.

"Does yew attract lightning?" I shouted over the growing wind. Tamsin abruptly dropped my hand.

"I was just wondering the same thing," she said with grim humor. "Maybe we should make a smaller target. Besides, you're the one holding the metal torch."

"Very funny!" I yelled. A streak of lightning suddenly shot earthward and hit the cliffs on the other side of the manor, cracking the air open in a green flash. We screamed and took off running.

"Wait!" Tamsin shrieked as I passed her, my knees almost meeting my chin. I snagged her arm as we ran, spotted the black yawning mouth of yew, and plunged into it, not caring if we were going to be caught in its brambles.

The beam of my torch bobbed all over the interior of greenery, violently erratic, and we rounded the curve still holding on to each other.

I didn't know what we were running from. It wasn't as if the lightning was unable to hit the moving targets of our bodies. Running probably drew lightning just like it drew snarling dogs to chase you down the street. We kept running because I think we just couldn't stop. At least not until one of us exploded. And by the way my lungs were rasping, I knew that it was going to be me.

A dark shadow suddenly rose up in front of us, blocking our way, and I cannoned straight into it before I could check myself. It wasn't Aunt Aurora. It was like hitting a brick wall of sharp protrusions. Tamsin had breath enough to scream. What breath I had left shot out of my lungs as I bounced backward and landed flat on my back. Tamsin turned, still screaming, and tried to save me, dragging my prone figure behind her roiling legs in a valiant effort to take me with her.

It was slow going. I couldn't get my feet under my body as she dragged me, and besides that, I was struggling and twisting to avoid having my head dented by her churning heels. Tamsin has very long legs, and she can use them like a giraffe.

A string of raspy Gaelic shot through the air, piercing our panic like an icicle shot from a bazooka. Tamsin gave one last scream and collapsed. For one horrified moment, I didn't know if she had abruptly lost her adrenaline burst in relief, or she had died.

"Of all the daft things!" my grandfather roared. "I'll not leave either of ye out here looking! Up! Up! Get up and go to the car!" His brogue was so thick by that point that I knew that all Tamsin heard was the agitated bellow. I rolled over on my hands and knees and crawled over to my prone friend, falling on her in relief as she rolled over, the whites of her eyes glinting like peeled eggs in the dark. I shined my torch on her. It was still in my hand. In fact, it was going to take pliers to pry my convulsed fingers off the cylinder.

"He wants us to get up and go back to the car," I said, my voice almost as raspy and my grandfather's. I could feel Tamsin shaking under me, and I wasn't much steadier.

"What about your aunt Aurora?" Tamsin wailed. I could barely hear over my irate grandfather.

"Get up, now!" A hand descended on my upper arm and hauled me to my feet. "Don't carry on. You're all right!" A hand hauled Tamsin up. "Now do as I say!"

"What about Aunt Aurora?" I asked and was shushed.

"I'll find the daft woman," he said irritably. But I still protested.

"She'll only run from you—," I began and was silenced by a hard, sharp slap to the seat of my jeans. It echoed like a gunshot in the tunnel of overgrown yew, and I gasped.

"I said get in the car!"

I grabbed my stinging flesh with my free hand and stared blankly at him. He towered over me, glowering, and then suddenly, in a move so uncharacteristic of him, I was shocked into stupefied compliance. His fierce expression suddenly moderated into something less like an Irish gargoyle, and he gently cupped the side of my head in one of his large hands. His laserlike eyes pinned me to Tamsin who was standing behind me as if my body was an adequate shield to my grandfather's ire.

"I said go to the car, child," he said gruffly. "I'll not let your aunt come to harm. I'll not let you and your friend, either. Do as I say."

I took a deep breath in an attempt to press down my anxiety.

"Yes, sir," I said and then groped behind me for Tamsin's hand. Somewhere over our yew cocoon, a rumble of thunder exploded and vibrated the air.

"I said get in the car and do it quickly! The storm is about to break."

"Yes, sir," I said, the spent adrenaline suddenly making me nauseous. Tamsin and I clutched at each other, turned, and ran back to the maze's exit.

By the time we emerged from the sheltering greenery, the storm was starting to break. Still grasping hands, Tamsin and I set off toward the garden gate, trotting faster and faster until the sky suddenly rent open. Then we broke into a dead run as if rabid badgers were chasing us.

We eventually broke from the garden and neared my grandfather's car parked in the shelter of the manor's bulk. I slowed, letting go of Tamsin to press my knuckles to the stitch in my side. Rain pelted us like icy marbles.

I couldn't stop worrying that we weren't going to find Aunt Aurora in time. I paused, sucking in air, and stood only ten feet from the car, irresolute and afraid. Tamsin stopped and turned to look at me, her hand on the back door of the car.

"Come on, Bella," she yelled over the wet wind slanting the raindrops sideways. "Let's at least get in the car and think. Maybe we can figure out where she might have gone."

I swung my torch around us ineffectively and panted, feeling frustration and helplessness swell into unmanageable proportions. I knew that I was too tired and worried to think rationally, but I couldn't help but feel that we weren't trying hard enough to find her.

"Let me just check the cliffs," I said, thinking about the scrap of chiffon scarf we had seen on the garden yew. I couldn't easily dismiss the fact that it was snagged quite a distance away from the gate and not on the inside of the garden where we had imagined her to be. If I could just make sure she wasn't beyond or near the cliffs, I could wait a lot more easily for my grandfather to find her. I set off for the far edge of the front lawn.

"No, Bella! Wait!" Tamsin called out and let go of the car door. "You'll get blown over!"

"I won't!" I yelled back. A fierce gust shot the hair straight off my head to wave at the sky, my drenched curls nothing but a flying mop. "It's blowing in right now from the water and up the cliff's side! If anything, it will blow me back to the car!"

"I'm coming with you!"

"Well, hurry up before Grandfather gets here! I don't want his belt macerating my buttocks!"

"Neither do I!" She grinned wetly and then gurgled as another sudden gust blew rainwater into our facial orifices. I tucked my face down, thinking of how turkeys drowned in storms because they looked up at the sky to see where all the water was coming from. I twined my arm in hers and forged ahead over the flattened muddy grass toward the cliff side.

The cliffs rose from the beachside in a series of jagged switchbacks that somebody, probably James George "the Smuggler," had carved into rough steps. In dry weather and in bright daylight, the steps were fairly accessible if you wore suction cups all over your body and were attached to mountain goats, but in wet weather, the steps were extremely treacherous. You might as well throw yourself over the edge and be done with it than to attempt to descend.

The vortex of rain and wind intensified the closer we got, and by the time we crept up to the edge, holding on to each other, we were bent double with our faces so close to the ground we could have grazed like cows as we went.

"This is insane!" Tamsin gasped. I was about to agree with her when I saw a white glove snagged on a boulder ahead of us. A fierce squeeze of fear shot through me like a pain, and I froze. Tamsin looked at me and then followed the direction of my stare.

"Bella!" she yelled as I let go of her hand and went toward it, the beam of my torch barely penetrating the rain. "It doesn't mean anything! It could have blown over here like the scarf!"

"I know!" I yelled back. But before I could reach the cloth glove to pick it up, another vortex of wind pried it free from the rock and slung it past us like an airborne sponge. It sailed by, and Tamsin whirled to watch its progress over the lawn.

Hunkering down, I quickly crawled the last twenty feet to the edge of the cliff and peered over at the beach below, scared to death that I was going to see Aunt Aurora's broken body impaled on the rocks like a forked sausage.

"Bella!" I heard Tamsin's horrified protest behind me. I waved her back.

"I'm just looking!" The waves below were pounding the thin strip of beach. It wasn't quite high tide yet, and I could see the phosphorescent glow of the ocean's relentless spew. My torch didn't quite reach the water, so I swept it from ledge to ledge, assuming that unless Aunt Aurora had shed her pink raincoat along with her scarf and gloves, she wasn't down there, or I would have seen her. Then I spotted the second glove on a step about fifty feet below me. I cried out and rose to my knees. It was a foolish time to forget the storm raging about us.

Lightning shot over us, a crack of thunder boomed deafeningly, and a squall of wind rushed up over the cliff face, unbalancing me. I grabbed at air and promptly went over the edge. I heard Tamsin's scream as I slithered down what seemed like a mile of gut-ripping stones and onto a ledge somewhere below me. I landed facedown and stuck like a limpet, my arms outstretched and my fingers crooked in a grip that even a crowbar couldn't have shifted.

Somewhere I had lost the torch. I had probably flung it out over the ocean when the thunder had detonated the sky above us.

I sucked in air, too scared to move, and tried to assess what was under me. By the slant of my body and the gouging of ledges, I realized that I had landed on a stretch of steps. Feeling around me inch by inch, I found a ridge of cliff side and curled my fingers around it like a handle, pulling myself up far enough to see.

I was on the ledge very close to Aunt Aurora's glove. I raised myself up, the wind pinning me to the cliff face, and looked above me at a dim white blob hovering over the edge. It was frantically screaming something.

"I'm fine!" I yelled. "I'm on a ledge! I won't fall, but I don't think I can climb back up! Get Grandfather!"

Without argument, Tamsin's frantic face withdrew, and I felt a new and inappropriate fission of fear, not exactly sure that a furious grandfather would be the lesser of two evils.

I carefully pushed myself up into a sitting position and looked around me, assessing my options. I wasn't in particular danger of falling unless I did something stupid again, but I could see that I was definitely in danger of being skewered by a bolt of lightning. I was a quivering wet target of fry-able flesh clinging to sea-blasted rock that had been weathering lightning strikes since Noah saw the first raindrop. It was time to get out of the way.

I had two options: slither up or slither down.

My mind was made up for me when a bolt of lightning hit the top ledge of the cliff. Sparks of electricity, the size of cricket bats, bounced and shot into the air like spears. I screamed and tried to tuck my body into the steps.

Unfortunately, now only one of the two options was possible. Gravity, plus the fact that I was now only thirty feet from the beach as opposed to nearly fifty feet from random bolts of lightning and my grandfather's belt, made going down the only thing I could do to reach dubious safety. But going down to what?

I untucked my body from the nonexistent protection of the open rocks and peered at the beach below, looking frantically for a spot that would provide some sort of safety and shelter from the frenetic lightning flying about.

The encroaching tide was slapping against the beach, surging closer and closer after each ebb, and I knew that it would only be a matter of minutes before the sand was covered in a dangerously roiling riptide.

I spotted the rock that Great-uncle Desmond's body had been found on, knowing that its wind-scoured surface would stay above the highest of high tide. But it was surrounded by water. If I ever made it to the rock, I would be nothing but a bull's-eye for the next bolt of celestial electricity.

Brilliant lightning erupted overhead, stabbed the back of my eyeballs, and lit up the cliff face in a brilliant flickering strobe, revealing every nook and cranny. And then I suddenly saw something that I wagered only Great-uncle Desmond knew about. Great-uncle Desmond who "swam like a fish" according to Pansy Bliss's granny. And now I knew why Napoleon was planted in the bathtub with a snorkel and flippers.

Below me was the jagged relief of a slit in the rocks. The hole was wide enough and tall enough to take a dinghy once high tide flowed into it, but right now it was standing out of the water. Just barely. It wouldn't be long before the floor of the cave and the narrow outcropping leading to it would be submerged in lashing waves.

In daylight the opening would be shadowed and would melt into the irregularity of the cliffs, too high in low tide for anyone on the beach to see it and all but submerged in high tide. In the flicker of wild lightning, it looked like the mouth of a monster, complete with jagged rocks lining the sides like fangs. I was willing to wager that the cave was part of James George's smuggling setup. And if I were right, then it would no doubt lead somewhere safe and dry. It was my best option and, for the moment, my only chance.

Now for the hard part.

I flattened myself on the slippery steps and proceeded to lower myself inch by painful rock-gouging inch, going feet first and on my stomach so I could adhere to the steps like a limpet. Gusts kept slamming up the vertical face of the cliffs around me. Lightning flickered, thunder crashed, rain was flung, waves pounded, and I prayed and slithered spastically from step to uneven step. Then, stupidly, I fell, miscalculating the distance from the last landing to the outcropping beside the cave's mouth. Slipping, I lurched sideways on the slick rocks and tried to cushion my landing with an outstretched hand. I hit a loose stone the size of my head, shot sideways when it rolled under my grip, and fell shoulder first into a shallow cleft of rock right in front of the cave. Stunned, I sprawled sideways in the icy rain-lashed puddle and stared up at the sky like a bewildered flounder.

Talk about jumping from the frying pan and into the fire. I suddenly found to my panic that I couldn't move. My right hand was plunged wrist deep between two boulders above my head and caught fast like a rat in a sprung trap. Lightning forked overhead, snapping me out of my daze, and I started flailing, trying frantically to jerk my imprisoned hand free.

If I died, my parents would kill me.

Lightning continued to burst and shoot above me, and while I thrashed and jerked on my arm, I thought of Aunt Aurora, wondering in a surreal one track thought if she was all right. I called myself names and tried to position myself with my feet bunched up on the boulders, trying to use my much stronger leg muscles to shift the stones clamped on my hand. I screamed in frustration and clawed at the gritty edges. I rocked back and forth, rubbing a raw bracelet on my wrist as I tried to find a way to slide it out.

Nothing worked. I dropped back onto the rock and rested my forehead on a coarse edge of stone. I was exhausted and numb except for the almost-unbearable throbbing of my wrist. Maybe Aunt Aurora was dead. And my grandfather. And even Tamsin. All three of them picked off by lightning in a meteorological skeet shoot.

I knew I was going to die too.

# 15

"Bella!" a faint shout penetrated the pounding noise of the waves and rain. I looked up. A figure carrying a torch was descending the steps, hugging the slanting rocks like they were scaling the cliff's face. "Hold still! I'll be there in a second!"

Of all my possible rescuers, I couldn't believe my ears. What was he doing here?

"Dad!" I screamed so loud my ears popped and fizzed like blown lightbulbs.

"It's all right, *leanba'n*, stay still!" he called and descended the rest of the steps, jumping the last few to land beside my prone figure. He put the torch down and knelt, running his fingers over my trapped arm. "Is it broken?" he asked. I shook my head, close to tears.

"I don't think so. I think I can move my fingers."

"That doesn't necessarily mean that a bone isn't cracked," he said grimly and felt around the edges of the boulders clamping on my wrist. "When I move the rock, I want you to pull free, but be careful with your hand."

I nodded and watched as he braced his hands on the jagged lip of the largest boulder, the one that was trapping the stone crushing my wrist. The muscles in his shoulders tightened, and the stone suddenly shifted and moved. I jerked my hand free once the rock left my flesh, sat up, and cradled my arm to my chest.

"Let me see." My father let the heavy stone fall back into its weather-grooved slot and leaned over me, gently freeing my throbbing hand from my clutch to explore it with quick fingers. "You're fine, *leanba'n*. You're going to be all right," he said, hushing me, his voice reassuring, and tucked my arm back to my chest. "Come on, let's get out of this lightning."

He lifted me from my rain-pelted puddle, and I was blissfully wrapped in anorak and arms.

"There's a cave we can go into," I said, shutting my eyes tightly in case we were going to proceed up the cliff stairs wrapped around each other like a human burrito. I wasn't in any shape to weather thrills.

"I know, *leanba'n*, I see it," he rumbled. I felt him walk the short distance into the unexpected haven. The rain stopped pelting my skin, and the musty smell of grit and wet rock overwhelmed my nose. I opened my eyes as he set me carefully on a ledge. He took his dark slicker off and wrapped it around me.

"Aunt Aurora," I said. My teeth suddenly started chattering like castanets, and he hushed me, wrapping his arms around me.

"She's fine, child. She's fine. Your grandfather found her wandering through the ruins. She's wet, but otherwise fine. Your grandfather and Tamsin are with her now, and Clive is already on his way."

I shifted to stare up at his jaw in stupefied relief. He looked down, and a smile touched his mouth.

"Don't cry, *leanba'n*," he said gently and smoothed a steadying hand on my face. "Everyone is safe."

"I know. I know." I hiccupped, angry for some reason, and pressed the heel of my good hand to my eyes. "Grandfather is going to kill me."

"No, he won't," my father's dismissive laugh rumbled comfortingly around me, and he rocked me, letting the beam of his torch rove the rough walls of the cathedral-sized room. The lash of the storm sounded even more frenetic outside, and lightning strafed the cave's entrance.

"How did you find me?" I asked. My arm throbbed from my fingertips to my shoulder, and my face was numb with cold, sticky, and leaking from every orifice. I tried to tune out the loud roar of the water on the other side of the cave's narrow mouth.

"When I pulled up, Tamsin was darting about in the dark without a torch, changing direction every time lightning lit up the grounds." The hand cradling my head shifted to push the sodden hair from my face. "Poor child looked like a wet pinball. I almost ran over her when she saw my headlights and darted toward the car. But before she could point to what part of the cliff you had fallen over, your grandfather came around the side of the house with your aunt Aurora. They were struggling. He was trying to hold on to her, and she was trying to get away."

He suddenly laughed in genuine amusement, and the rumble went through me. I pressed myself closer, shivering like a wet dog, and watched the pyrotechnics outside.

"They would have looked like they were waltzing except I could hear the grunts and the string of Gaelic floating over the storm. I gave Tamsin the keys to the manor and ran to find you."

I leaned away to wring the water from the stomach of my shirt and swipe the stickiness from my face.

"I imagine they're still waltzing, except I hope it's in the manor and out of the storm," he said and gently pulled me off the ledge to set me on my feet. "Move around, child. Let's get some blood moving and get out of here before the tide slides in."

My wet feet landed in icy water, and I looked down, kicking in the darkness and feeling the unmistakable slosh of high tide surging around my ankles.

"The tide is already sliding in," I said, dismayed, and looked at him as he played the torch's beam over the stone walls.

"I know. It's all right. I see stairs."

"Where?" I waded closer and peered around a giant wedge of wall. A narrow flight of roughly carved steps spiraled upward and out of sight in a tight curve of hewn tunnel. "I was right. Another tunnel from James George." I slid the frozen fingers of my unhurt hand into my father's, trying to warm them. "We just found the answer to another clue."

"You'll not rest until you find it, will you?" He towed me toward the steep slant of crooked stairs. "I'm more concerned with getting you safe and warm, child, than with finding the treasure."

"Do you think the treasure is somewhere here?" I asked as he guided me to the foot of the stairs and let go of my hand.

"I don't know. Watch your step. I'll be right behind you with the torch," he said and urged me forward. "By the way, child, how did you come to be wedged at the bottom of the cliff between two boulders? Tamsin had merely said that you had slid down part way and were stuck on the steps."

As I carefully began mounting the rough treads, I told him what had happened, part of my mind tiredly wondering if I was seeing the passage in much the same way that it had appeared to the smugglers two hundred years ago with their swinging lanterns. Blazing torches wouldn't have worked with the wind swirling upward from the cave's entrance, much as it was doing now. More than one greasy head of hair would have caught fire.

"What?" my father's amused voice boomed behind me in the narrow spiral of stone.

"I'm just imagining James George and what it must have been like to haul contraband up these steps at night."

The flight through stone kept ascending and at one point I had to pause just to pump air back into my lungs. A stitch pierced my side, and I leaned a shoulder against the gritty wall. My arm was still throbbing, and my fingers felt poised to explode like weenies in a microwave. I supported my injured wrist with my other hand while I looked around.

The stone had changed from cliff rock to roughly hewn blocks, and I knew that we must be close to our destination, wherever that was. Perhaps it would be an exit into the house, or an entrance, depending on your point of departure.

"Are you all right, child?" my father asked. I gasped, my stomach pumping my lungs like bellows and just nodded. My father clamped the torch under one arm, reached into the somewhat damp breast pocket of the slicker he had draped over me, and pulled his mobile phone from the pocket. He opened it up and checked its screen.

"Surely you can't have reception down here," I said. He shook his head.

"I'm checking to see if it's still working. It looks as if at some point we'll be above ground, and I'll be needing to call your brothers then." He closed the phone and inserted it back into the pocket. "I'm just thinking that your grandfather won't know what happened to us if we're down here much longer without contact. Are you ready?"

I nodded and set off again, continuing my climb of tread after tread in a never-ending curve to the right. We had ascended only seven steps higher when I noticed something on the outer wall that stopped me in my tracks. Surely I couldn't be seeing what I thought I was seeing.

"Dad," I said and groped behind me to touch his arm, not taking my eyes from the hewn block I was looking at in case I couldn't find it again. "Shine the torch up there."

He directed the beam to where I was pointing, and I went up the next few steps to get a closer look. On the left side of the tunnel, away from the spiral's core, was a familiar carving. My father came up to stand behind me.

"It's the same thing we saw in the tunnel that went from Destiny's grave in the garden to behind the boiler in the cellars," I said excitedly and watched as my father felt the etched circle and its encircling band of cross marks. As in the other tunnel, this one was too high for me to reach.

"A moon and stars," my father said quietly, his fingers following the etched grooves. I swiveled my head to stare up at him.

"So that's what that is," I said, recognition dawning, and looked back at the stone's etching. "Soon when I die, and I will die soon, gold and silver lie beyond star and moon," I said softly, quoting the words painted on the book spines in James George's portrait. And then I remembered something else in the painting. The ring on James George's hand wasn't merely a seal ring with his monogram of a scrolled *W* etched on the gold. It was the artist's impression of a scrolled *W* on a moon surrounded by stars.

"In the last clue we found behind the boiler, Great-uncle Desmond had written, 'You went where this led, and you found the main clue.' And then on the back he wrote, 'Put it all together and look.' We had thought that the gold buckle we had found was the main clue." I huddled in the warming depths of the enormous bell of slicker and tried to stop my convulsive shivering. "It wasn't the main clue. This etching is. Dad"—I felt my eyes swivel to stare up at my father, barely getting out the next words—"we've found the treasure."

My father looked down at me, his eyes narrowing in amusement as he grinned.

"And how do you figure that, child?" he asked.

I looked up at him, uncomprehending, then belatedly realized that he didn't know about the things that Tamsin and I had put together in the kitchen while Aunt Aurora was making her great escape.

Then suddenly I felt my own balloon of excitement deflate when I remembered our deductions. It couldn't be the treasure. James George had to have taken the gold and silver with him when he left Tanglewood to escape capital punishment. What Uncle Desmond had found must be something else, and so far, no one knew what it could be or where it really was. All we had solved was the enigma of James George and Destiny.

I told my father about the portrait of James George that Tamsin had located in France, painted when James George was Algernon Wildeve and hiding with Destiny, who had, at one point, been a smuggled-from-France guest of Tanglewood Estate.

My father listened patiently to my garbled recital. I had to admit that it didn't sound quite as impressive with bouts of shivering and clacking teeth as it had when we had talked about it over hot tea in the kitchen.

"But it can't be the treasure," I finished up, sighing and clacking my teeth, sounding like I was shaking dice in a cup. "James George took it with him when he eloped to wherever and changed his identity."

My father laughed and reached over me to wring rain and ocean spew from my hair.

"Not necessarily, child. What has your great-uncle's wild goose chase been about if there isn't any treasure left behind?" He smiled. "So far, what you and Tamsin have worked out have all been inspired guesses. We don't know what had really happened two hundred years ago other than James George escaped with his life. Let's see what's here first before we decide we're wrong."

Our conversation in the boiler's tunnel came back to me at his words, and I remembered our speculations as to why Great-uncle Desmond had never cashed in on the wealth, leaving it for his sisters instead. If it were contraband that James George had no right to, something that he had to leave behind because he couldn't shift it, then it would also be something that Aunts Astrid and Aurora also had no right to, and Great-uncle Desmond's last joke.

"Hold the beam steady on the wall," he said, sliding my sleeve up and handing me the torch, then laughed when the beam shivered with the rest of me, bobbling all over the stone with convulsive abandon. "Or as steady as you can, *leanbh*."

When I had first spotted the carved moon and stars on the hewn block and had thought that we had found the treasure, my mind had immediately gone to all the secret rooms and tunnels we had already discovered. The hewn block was obviously a marker for something. I could tell that my father had assumed the same thing and that if we didn't try to trigger the mechanism now, we'd probably never find the faint etching again.

I moved back, going up the staircase a few more steps until I was out of his way.

He put the flat of his hand on the carved block and pushed. At first nothing happened. I sucked in a great lungful of cold air and held my breath, trying to keep the beam steady on the wall.

And then it moved. The whole wall. The hewn block under my father's hand had suddenly shifted inward, triggering some kind of counterbalance; the wall in front of him shifted, groaned, grated, and screeched, and a narrow doorway to two hundred years ago slowly opened. A blackness that smelt surprisingly stale wafted out like slow smoke, and in my excitement I was hard-pressed not to clear the steps in one jump to land beside it. I coughed at the grit of disused air and dry stone and quickly descended the uneven steps. My father took the torch from me and shined it inside the small room.

Highlighted in the torch's beam was a stone ledge, and on the ledge was a trunk. The trunk was roughly three feet by four feet, made of cracked leather and solid wood, and bound in a greenish metal that looked like hammered bronze. A piece of parchment had been placed on the trunk's lid and anchored in place by a chunk of metal. It took me a second to realize that the chunk of metal was actually the padlock that would have been on the hasp of the trunk's lid.

My father stepped in and picked up the paper to read Great-uncle Desmond's last words.

*"Audentes fortuna juvat,"* my father read aloud, sounding amused. And I stared down at the torn piece of parchment.

"What?"

"It's Latin," my father laughed and translated for me. "Fortune favors the bold." He turned the parchment over, and as usual there was an age-faded inking of words on the reverse side. "*A' bientot.*"

"That's French for 'good-bye, I'll see you later,'" I said, my voice echoing weirdly in the narrow room.

My father was silent a moment, then looked at the trunk with an odd expression.

"Child, I'm not so sure that your great-uncle Desmond wrote this."

My father and I looked at each other for a moment, silent, and then I took the parchment from my father's hand to look closer at the faded ink. Great-uncle Desmond's handwriting looked exactly like the tracks of an inebriated spider. This handwriting, in spite of the flaking ink, was larger, bolder, heavier, and sharper. I thought of the portrait of James George, a man who seemed to regard everything from humorous eyes, and realized that he must have regarded his escape as one huge joke. He couldn't resist a parting shot for whoever found the hidden trunk.

I was holding a two-hundred-year-old note from a smuggler. I took a deep breath and handed the parchment back, my hand involuntarily covering my mouth.

This had to be the treasure.

"Want to open it and take a quick look, *leanbh*?" My father raised a wicked eyebrow and grinned. I nodded and felt my eyeballs nearly extrude from their sockets.

"Can you hold this again?" he laughed and held out the torch, waiting until I took it before moving the heavy brass lock from the top of the trunk's lid. He put the lock on the stone ledge, lifted the thick hasp, and opened the trunk.

My imagination expected to see heaps of jewels and gold. The more realistic side of me expected to see silver with valuable hallmarks hammered in their bottoms. Or perhaps stray pieces of jewelry among other more portable things like dishes, documents, or other household pickings. Maybe old and rare books, though I didn't see how they would have survived. There would be some sort of damage even though the airless room had been securely sealed away from the elements.

What things of value would James George have smuggled to Cornwall but couldn't take with him to France? The note proved that he had willingly left the trunk behind. He wasn't caught short. He left under his own steam and with his gold and silver.

I was totally unprepared for what the opened lid revealed. I stared at the stale fabric in blank bewilderment.

Reaching in, my father lifted out a dark velvet cloak with a ruff of molting fur. He shook it out, and tiny hairs from the ruff floated away in the torch beam, looking like airborne silver filaments.

"What is that? Someone's evening cloak?" I asked, shivering and tucked my throbbing arm close to my midriff. My hand felt like a swollen udder. I wasn't sure I wanted to look down at it. "Could it be valuable?"

"I'm not sure." My father frowned and draped it over the lifted lip of the trunk's lid. "The trunk seems to be full of clothes."

He reached back into the trunk and pulled out a gown. It unfolded itself in a vigorous billow of spring-loaded whalebone and heavy cream-colored satin. I had never seen a dress unfurl like an explosion before. Short underskirts of whalebone insets must have been sewn in as part of the dress.

Perhaps it had once been white. Shell pink rosebuds were embroidered in the heavy satin, and billows of pink gauze were caught at the shoulders of the long sleeves with tiny green silk leaves.

My father squinted critically when he held it up.

"It's beautiful," I whispered, shivering and clacking like a castanet, forgetting for a moment that we were supposed to be looking for a treasure.

"It would fit you, child. And it's dry and warm and almost as good as a blanket," he said and laid it back in the trunk. He took the torch from my hand and set it on the ledge beside the trunk, its beam shining upward toward the low ceiling. "Let's get those wet clothes off."

"I can't wear that!" I gasped. "I'll ruin it!"

"I'll not have you going into shock." Though my father's voice was grim, brooking no argument, his hands were gentle as he moved my throbbing arm from my stomach and took his slicker from my shoulders before I could protest any further. He put the slicker on the ledge, freeing his hands, and began stripping free my sodden shirt and jeans, carefully helping me past the pain and clumsiness of my swollen arm. Lifting the antique cloak from the lid of the trunk, he draped it around my frigid skin.

I gave an inarticulate screech when I realized what he was suggesting, looking down with dismay at the ancient velvet blotting up the dirt, rain, and saltwater from my body. Fur from the cloak's edging stuck to my clammy body, making me look like a molting sheepdog, and I saw my father's concerned expression lighten into a grin.

"This is terrible," I said grimly and tried not to choke on the two-hundred-year-old smell of who-knows-what clogging the back of my throat as I used the antique velvet to dry off.

"You'll both launder good enough, later," my father laughed and reached for the dress once I was done. He slipped the heavy gown over my head, carefully avoiding my sodden hair, dropped it into place, and turned me around so that my back faced the glow of the torch, doing up a few of the tiny pearls that made up the buttons. Then turning me around to face the light again, he stepped back and surveyed me in the golden glow.

"Well, *leanbh*, that seems to be much better. Are you ready to find our way back out to civilization?"

I jerked my head up in dismay.

"No," I nearly wailed and looked over at the trunk. Silvery blue brocade shimmered in the torch glow. "We haven't looked through the trunk yet."

"We can look later, child," my father said and closed it, draping the damp cloak out over its lid. He put the slicker on me and closed its snaps, covering up the top half of the exquisite ball gown. The lower half poofed out in an exuberant froth of heavy warming fabric, lace, and embroidery; and I looked like an upside-down mushroom. "You need your hand looked to, Bella. It's getting worse by the minute. If I had known how bad it was, I wouldn't have stopped to find the trunk. I'm not altogether sure that a bone or two isn't broken, and the others need to know that we're fine."

"But we've only been gone for a few minutes. Please?" I pleaded. "I'm dry and much warmer now, and it will take only seconds to just look. My hand isn't going to get any worse in the few seconds it will take. I can't stand not knowing what's in there. Please? I've worked so hard to find this."

My father stared down at me, the torch in his hand, and I watched his face as he considered my protests. Tolerance for my pleading won, but I could tell that it wasn't an easy battle. He sighed, looking troubled, and then capitulated.

"Okay, Bella, but we're just glancing through the contents. Your brothers and I will come back later to take the trunk out of the cave." He handed me the torch with a rueful smile. "Just be glad your mother isn't here, *leanba'n*. She's better at resisting her children."

I trained the torch's beam on my father and held my breath again, watching as he quickly lifted out a ball gown of silvery blue silk brocade. When he held it up, it billowed out like the first one. The dress seemed to fill the room. Tiny crystal beads sewn into the skirt and bodice glittered like ice chips in the glow of the torchlight. I could only imagine how it looked when Destiny danced in the candlelight.

Even though I wondered why it hadn't been taken back to France, I had no doubt that we were looking at a trunk full of Destiny Ophelia's clothes.

The third dress my father yanked from the chest was of delicately embroidered cherry-colored silk. The birds and flowers embroidered across the hem of the skirt were nothing more than black swirls, but an occasional spark showed that the thread was actually real silver strands beaten so fine it was a wonder they hadn't already fallen into tarnished dust. Even ruined with age and neglect, the dress was still breathtaking. He laid the dress to the side with the one made of silvery blue brocade.

Then my father pulled out a smooth sheet of parchment. On the sheet of parchment in the center of the lower edge was a red ribbon, and attached to the red ribbon was a small box.

"Is that from Great-uncle Desmond?"

"I don't think so, child," my father said quietly. "This is genuinely old."

"What does it say?" I whispered, suddenly wondering if this was the treasure.

"I don't know." My father shook his head as he scanned the inked words. "My Latin isn't up to this."

"It's in Latin?" I moved closer and peered at the unfamiliar script.

"This is something better left for Basil," my father said, an odd note to his voice, and then reached back into the trunk to pull out a rigid choker made of something that gleamed dully in the torch's light.

"Is that gold?" I gasped and reached out to touch one of the tiny carved leaves.

"I think so, child," my father said, put the necklace of hammered gold back into the now-empty trunk, and took the torch from me to shine it on the faded document in his hand.

"Is that the provenance to the necklace?" I asked and peered into the trunk at the decorated circlet of impure gold.

"You could say that." He smiled and set the parchment with its accompanying box back in the bottom of the trunk with the jewelry, piling the clothes back on top of it. I noticed that he didn't bother to fold the dresses or the damp cloak.

"So what is it?" I asked. His eyes moved thoughtfully from the trunk to me as he shut the lid on the billow of cloth.

"I only caught a few words, child."

"What did it say?" I persisted. "Is it the treasure that Great-uncle Desmond talked about?" He smiled and absently smoothed the flat of his hand over my forehead, shoving the clinging strands of wet hair from my eyes.

"It's the treasure, *leanbh*."

"Really?" I could barely get the word out. "We found the treasure!" The only thing stopping me from dancing manically in front of the trunk was the pain that continued to shoot from my fingers like tiny bolts of lightning.

"Calm down, child," my father laughed. "We won't know exactly what's entailed until we get Basil to look at it."

"But we found the treasure," I said. He guided me back out of the secret room and on to the stairs still spiraling up into blackness.

"Yes. We found the treasure."

I gathered up as much of my full skirt as I could in my good arm and started climbing the staircase.

"Dad? What is the treasure?" I asked, gritting my teeth against the pulsing ache. "Is it the gold necklace?"

"It's part of it. I'd rather wait before I say any more. I could be greatly wrong in my guess. I could only decipher enough to realize that it was what your great-uncle had been hinting at. But I still don't know what all of it is or why it could be so valuable."

"Will you tell me even a little bit?" I pleaded, climbing tread after tread after tread of the never-ending staircase.

"The parchment came from King Edward."

"King Edward?" I asked, trying to keep my mind off my revolting arm. I was finding it hard to concentrate. "Which one? Weren't there hundreds of them?"

"Eight," my father laughed. "My guess is the sixth one, or perhaps one later. I had seen something on the trunk that makes me think it was sometime after 1525."

"Really?" I looked at him over my gauze-clad shoulder, something easy to do since we weren't ascending in a straight line.

"Watch out," my father commanded, grasping the collar of the anorak. "You're about to run into a door, child."

I turned in time and saw the enormous oak door set in on a landing I had just stepped up to. I had thought that it was just another tread. I was going to dream about stairs tonight.

"Is there a latch?" my father asked and leaned past me to shine the light on the petrified planks with its iron hinges.

"Just a ring."

"Let's hope it isn't barred on the other side," my father said and pulled. It swung open unwillingly, grating on the uneven floor, and I realized that it was balanced in such a way that it would swing shut unless it was secured.

A long, even, straight tunnel unfurled in front of us, looking endless in the beam of my father's torch.

The tunnel seemed to go on forever, and I wondered at the strength and stamina of James George's crew. I couldn't imagine carrying case after case of illicit brandy and wine or rolling barrel after barrel of the stuff, let alone dragging bale after bale of cloth and numerous bolts of lace. Maybe they had wagons and carts like coal miners.

They must have been paid well.

"Are you doing all right, child?" my father asked behind me. I nodded, stifling a shiver of pure fatigue.

"I was just thinking, even if the other side is inaccessible or blocked, then we still have a way out. We can just wait for low tide and go back up the cliff steps."

"I hope not," my father said dryly. "I'm afraid that your brothers will try to come down that way to find us. I need to get aboveground to call Dante."

"I hope Aunt Aurora is all right," I fretted. My father's hand brushed the coils of my soggy hair.

"I'm sure she is. As bad tempered as your grandfather is, he's capable. Don't forget that Clive should be there now."

"Are Dante, Brandt, Jude, or Michael coming?" I asked and frowned. "They can't leave the meeting. They have parts."

"Only the announcements and the first part. Jude was going to get Lamond to substitute as an attendant for him, and they're coming as soon as they can." He checked his watch in the torchlight. "They should already be here. Dante said he was going to take Brandt's truck and that Michael and Brandt would follow as soon as they could in Michael's Saab."

"But Aunt Aurora is already found," I said. "I know Dante and Jude are probably already here, but wouldn't Clive have called the rest of them at the pub and told them not to worry?"

"But we're missing, *leanbh*," my father said gently.

I thought of the high waves battering the cliff side and the lightning shooting everywhere.

"How are Mom, Grandmother, and Aunt Astrid getting home?" I asked a moment later, realizing that they would still be at the meeting.

"You're worrying too much," my father laughed. "Violet said she would take them home. I imagine she and your grandmother are having their hands full of Astrid right now."

Up ahead we could see the faint glimmer of something solid touch the edge of the torch's glow.

"Is that a door?" I squinted in the dim light but could only make out that we had reached the end of our long straight stretch. For all I knew it was merely a turn in the tunnel, and we would have to continue our endless trek.

"It looks like stairs," my father said. As we approached the far-off mirage, I realized he was right. But they were steps that went straight up into the ceiling. The closer we drew to the oddity, the more disoriented I felt.

"So what are we supposed to do?" I asked helplessly, coming to a dead stop at the first tread and looking up.

"It's obviously a way out," my father laughed, put his hands on my shoulders, and gently moved me out of the way. "You're tired, lass."

It was an understatement. I was past tired, I realized with a sigh, and slumped against the wall in my exquisite two-hundred-year-old satin ball gown of rosebuds and silk gauze. The only thing keeping me awake and off the floor was the unrelenting pain my arm and the enormous oddly spring-loaded skirt that propped me up. At least I was dry and much warmer than ten minutes ago.

I watched as my father shined his torch on an iron ring bolted into the slab of metal above us. He reached up and merely slid the ceiling aside. A blast of ozone, salt, and fresh air swirled in. I sucked in a great lungful, reviving a bit at the coldness that swirled in with it. My father mounted the steps, hauling me up and out with him.

We had emerged onto a mosaic of gold and blue tiles. I looked down at the swirls of the sun underneath my feet and then turned around to look at the skipping cherub behind me. The tiny marble statue was on a pedestal of lacy fretwork atop a displaced chunk of metal, and I realized that it was standing beside the slab that my father had just moved to let us out.

"Where are we?" I asked, looking up at the domed ceiling overhead. The roar of the storm was still raging around us, though it was muted, and a crash of thunder vibrated the air. Encircling us were skinny marble columns and backless benches. My father shined his torch over the quivering mass of damp greenery ten feet from the pavilion we seemed to be standing in, then pulled his mobile from his pocket, opening it and punching in a number.

"I think we're in the center of the maze."

I went to a marble bench and tried to sit down. My skirt billowed and bunched in spite of the slicker, and I soon gave up, barely listening to my father's words. He had apparently reached Dante, and I listened to the one-sided conversation with half an ear, waiting until he hung up to find out what was going on. He eventually pocketed the phone and wiped a tired hand over his scalp, pushing his wet black hair back from his forehead, then smiled at me, and held out a hand.

"Come here, child." I went over to him, and he wrapped comforting arms around my shoulders. "Your aunt Aurora has been taken to the hospital for monitoring. Clive is going to admit Aunt Astrid too, just as soon as your mother gets home from the meeting, collects some things, and gets Aunt Astrid to the hospital. They're both going to be perfectly fine."

"Where's Tamsin?"

"She went with Clive and Aunt Aurora to the hospital. Clive needed her to keep your great-aunt calm. I imagine Clive is also trying to keep Tamsin safe and out of the storm. It was only afterward that your grandfather realized that we weren't anywhere to be found and obviously hadn't made it back up the cliff steps." My father laughed, and his breath puffed warmly across my forehead. "Apparently he knew about the cave and where it led. He'd found it decades ago when he was wooing your grandmother."

"Why didn't he say anything?" I reared back and looked at him.

"He didn't know that he was the only one who knew about it. He had told Desmond about it all those years ago, and your great-uncle said that he already knew about it. No one knows how long Desmond had known, but I know that your grandmother and great-aunts always visited the beach along the village, never this one. This one was too dangerous."

"So how did Grandfather know that we had found the cave?"

"He didn't. After he got your Aunt Aurora bundled off, he came looking for us and even went as far down the steps as he could, but had to give up at the waves. He came back up when a streak of lightning hit the rocks above him, and he realized that he couldn't see us anywhere. He guessed that we must have seen the cave and gone down to it." My father paused as thunder reverberated over us, waiting for the echoes to roll away before continuing. "Dante and Jude arrived just then and insisted on trying the cliff steps themselves to look for us. Your grandfather told them about the cave before they went down, but, of course, the opening was almost completely underwater by the time they got down to it. They were forced to come back up to try to get to the tunnel through the maze entrance we just came through."

"So are they on their way?" I asked, tiredly trying to figure it out. So far it all sounded chaotic.

"They're on their way, child. It has been fifty years since your grandfather had been in the maze, and it's all grown up. He's having a hard time remembering the key."

I sighed and rubbed my good hand over my eyes. It felt like I was rubbing in slivers of glass.

"Where are Brandt and Michael? Are they already on their way here to the manor?"

"They're already here and with the others. They'll all be here in a minute," he laughed. "Apparently, when they were courting, your grandfather used to get your grandmother lost in here so he could have her to himself for a few minutes. Apparently, he proposed to her in this folly."

"Did you tell them we found the treasure?"

"I did, child."

I suddenly heard my grandfather's irate voice floating over the noise of the storm still raging somewhere beyond the thick barrier of yew maze. My brothers and grandfather suddenly burst through a gap in the overgrown hedge, each one carrying a torch, and just then lightning suddenly streaked overhead, lighting up the whole tableau with perfect timing. We gaped at each other in the brilliant light. The scene flickered painfully, imprinting itself in my retinas and searing itself into the back of my tired brain before I could even blink, making me suddenly disoriented and dizzy.

My brothers stared, grim, obviously anxious, and not very amused with their hands full of my irate grandfather. My grandfather's long hair had long since lost its customarily neat ponytail, and silver strands were pasted on the sides of his head. Thick black eyebrows scowled in his weathered face, and dark eyes shot sparks that reached me where I stood frozen beside my father.

"Lass, are you all right?" he roared in Gaelic, his face looking abruptly like a gargoyle's with its lean angles and blazing eyes. "Child, you're not hurt badly, are you?"

They swarmed the tiny folly, and Dante was the first to reach us, cupping a protective hand on the back of my head. Hands skimmed my hair, my shoulders, my frigid face, and exclamations flew over my head. With his eyes still shooting sparks, my grandfather's wild rain-wet gargoyle's head suddenly swooped over me and blotted out everything else.

"Lass, answer me. Are you all right?"

"She's fine," my father intervened. "Other than injuring her wrist."

"What happened?" Brandt gently lifted my purpling hand to examine it in the beam of his torch. "Dante said it's dislocated."

"She slid belly first down the loose scree near the top of the cliff and landed on the steps more than halfway down. She managed to fall again on her way down to the cave and lodged her hand between two boulders."

Put like that, I sounded a bit of an idiot. Apparently, my grandfather thought so as well. He snorted at my father's words, clamped a hand on my good shoulder, imperatively and carefully commandeered me from my cocoon of slickers and voices, and lowered his exasperated face to mine.

"Why did you disobey me, child?" he roared over the storm at me and was magnificently underscored with a crash of thunder. Lightning flickered the air around us like a berserk strobe light. Sparks flew from his wet silver head. "Why did you do that to me, lass?"

When I involuntarily took a step back, he imprisoned my shoulders with a hard arm and then suddenly and disconcertingly pulled me to his rather rocky bosom. For one horrified moment, I was totally and completely disoriented, not sure whether he was going to embrace me or pop my head off with a deft pinch.

"You do that again, lass," he growled feelingly into my ear, and I felt the thumping of his heart against my face, "and I'll hammer your backside to my knee with my belt so hard you'll not sit down until your wedding. Do you hear me?"

I nodded dumbly.

"Daft child," he growled. A calloused hand then passed fleetingly over the side of my face, and I was released to my father.

"Have you called your mother and told her that Aunt Aurora is all right?" my father asked my brothers as I cupped myself back into the shelter of his arm. I shut my eyes and listened to the voices bouncing over my head.

"We'd already left a message on the machine. Apparently they weren't home from the meeting yet," Dante answered. "We told her to go ahead and pack some things and take Aunt Astrid up to the hospital as well, and Clive will check her in with Aunt Aurora."

"How was your mother when you left her?"

"As you'd expect," Brandt answered him. "I talked to her before Michael and I left. She said that she and Grandmother will go home as soon as Violet can leave the meeting. They'll stay put with Aunt Astrid and keep her calm until they hear."

"Bryn should know by now her sister is safe," my grandfather rumbled overhead gruffly. "They're on their way to the hospital, no doubt, having heard the message."

"Come on, let's get Bella to the hospital so Clive can set her wrist. She doesn't have much left in her," my father said, firmly drawing his slicker tighter around my shoulders.

"I'm fine," I said tiredly, opening my eyes, but my words were drowned out in a crash of thunder.

We traipsed to a shaggy slit in the wall of yew, my father and I behind my grandfather while my brothers brought up the rear. By the time we got to the end of the maze and exited out into the storm, I was starting to feel every plodding step in my bloated hand. It was with great relief that I allowed myself to be bundled into the front of the Range Rover and buckled in. The seat was tilted back, my door shut, along with several other car doors opening and slamming, and my father started the Rover's engine. A blast of hot air shot up from the floorboard vents, and goose bumps the size of pennies flooded me as the warmth traveled up the cramped bell of my skirt and over my skin.

"Hang in there, *leanbh*," my father said. And I felt the brush of his thumb on my chin. "Clive will give you a pain killer, and then you can sleep in your bed tonight."

"I want a bath too," I murmured. "I stink like a compost bin, thanks to Destiny's cloak."

My father laughed, pulled forward down the rutted lane, and then, one by one, I heard the convoy of cars that had been parked around the front sweep of Tanglewood pull into formation behind us.

"What a night," I murmured feelingly and concentrated on immobilizing my arm against the dips and bumps of the stony drive.

When we got to the tiny hospital lodged on the road between Halfmoon and the neighboring village, I was shivering again. The adrenaline caused by Aunt Aurora's disappearance, my slide down the cliff, and the discovery of the treasure had oozed away during the drive and left me wobbly and as slow as a drugged sloth. By the time we pulled up under the portico of the emergency entrance, my legs were shaking, and my brain felt embedded in sludge.

My father smiled reassuringly at me, making no move to get out, and I was momentarily discombobulated when my door opened unexpectedly beside me. Brandt leaned in, unbuckled my seatbelt, and eased me out of the seat and onto the rain-blown pavement.

"I'll be in after I park," my father said before Brandt shut the door behind me. I allowed myself to be led like Helen Keller into the hospital and up to the front desk where Brandt gave the grimly efficient nurse my name.

"It's about time," she stated crabbily, rose from her desk, and trotted over to a line of wheelchairs placed against the wall by the doors. "Dr. Chaucer said to put you in cubicle 4 when you get in and then give him a buzz."

She came up behind me with the sagging wheelchair. There was a rusty stain on the armrest that could have been anything from dried blood to engine oil. There isn't a lot of engine oil in a hospital. I looked up at my brother.

"Please don't make me ride in that. I can walk."

"That's against hospital regulations," Nurse Ratched replied thinly and competently aborted any further argument by ramming the seat of the wheelchair against the back of my legs. I fell backward, surprised, and the bell of my skirt creaked ominously, nearly popping the slicker's snaps open. For a moment I was afraid the slicker would give, and the skirt would rise up to smack me in the face.

"I'll take over, Nurse," Clive's sedate voice floated overhead from somewhere. I tried to tuck the musty skirt around my thighs. "Go finish torturing the old gent in cubicle 2 when you're done up here. You left the IV in his arm. Please remove it so he can check out."

The wheelchair pivoted, and I found myself propelled to the hallway, through a set of double doors and down a row of curtained cubicles.

"I'll check you in and be there is a second, *bambina*," Brandt's deep voice floated reassuringly. Floated. Everything was floating. Voices. The wheelchair. My head. Everything but my hand. It was the throbbing weight that anchored the universe.

"How are you holding up, luv?" Clive asked cheerfully. I tried to peer through the swinging doors behind me at the lobby where I had left Brandt verbally wrestling with Nurse Ratched over my admittance forms.

"Fine. Where's Aunt Aurora?"

"She's in the back wing in a private room. She's in excellent shape considering what she'd just been through. Tamsin had volunteered to stay with her until she settled to sleep." The room spun abruptly as he pivoted me again in my wheelchair and backed me into a cubicle, empty except for a wheeled bed. Hands under my arms helped me to stand, and I was backed up to the edge of the high gurney and helped onto its spotless cover. Clive eased me back against the elevated head of the bed and onto the pillows. There was a loud cracking sound from below my bosom, my father's slicker popped open with the strain of unfurled whalebones, and the skirt billowed out with the vigor of a parachute in the middle of a skydive. A rush of cold air blasted my clammy skin, and Clive jumped backward from the bed as if I had just exploded.

I started, nearly levitating from the bed myself, and for one humiliating moment, I thought my eyes were going to roll up in my head. This was not a position I wanted to pass out in. Especially when I heard the agitated bellow of my grandfather telling the nurse at the front desk to get her hands off him. I could only assume that to her unaccustomed eyes, my wet and glaring grandfather looked like an unfortunate casualty blown in by the storm.

"Let him back, Nurse!" Clive called out. Frantically and ineptly, I tried to force my skirt back to a shape less like a bell with my legs as clappers. Seemingly unaware of my agitation, Clive lifted a folded blanket from the bed railing, opened it, and draped it over me.

"There you go, luv. That will keep you warm while we see to your injuries."

The weight of the blanket was negligible and merely draped over the bell of skirt in an enormous pregnant bubble. I looked like Humpty Dumpty in surgery. The sound of footsteps swelled in the hallway, and after a noisy moment, the familiar faces of the male members of my family popped one by one into the curtained cubicle. My father was suddenly at my side, and his steadying hand cupped the top of my wet head.

Unperturbed at the sudden crowd, Clive freed my arm from the blanket and the slicker, and held it up to his eyes, turning it this way and that, prodding it while he made professional noises under his breath.

"The wrist is certainly dislocated. I'll order an x-ray as well," Clive murmured and drew the blanket down past my waist, letting its gathered edge rest precariously on the exuberant bell of fabric. "Do you hurt anywhere else, luv?"

Before I could answer, I was aware of a swirl of disturbance beyond the curtains. The nurse's loud protestations swelled up, abruptly died, and a second later my grandfather lurched forward as if he had been rammed from behind by an angry small rhino. His habitual expression of impatience changed abruptly into one of blank surprise as he was unceremoniously bumped aside.

*"Per favore!"* my mother exploded into the room, swirling the bodies of my brothers like so much flotsam in the wake of a speedboat. "*Voglio vederia!* I want to see her! *Voglio mia figlia!* I want my daughter!"

She struck out from side to side as she surged to the bed, agitatedly slapping and pounding male chests out of her way as she went.

"Why didn't you tell me?" she raged, thumping Dante soundly in the shoulder. If he had been twenty years younger, he would have gotten a furiously firm swat on his bare behind. "Why didn't you tell me my *bambina* had fallen over a cliff?"

"Raphaela!" my father interjected before she could blindly thump Clive as well and hurriedly caught her to his chest. "She's all right! Calm down, love! Bella's fine!"

"Mom!" I interjected and tried to sit up without rolling off the bed. "Mom! I'm all right!"

*"Leanbh!"* My grandmother's distressed voice was suddenly added to the melee. I jerked around to see her on the other side of the bed with an anxious Tamsin and an utterly befuddled Aunt Astrid tied to each other in a clot of clasped arms and hands. I wasn't sure who was holding on to whom, and for a moment, I wondered if Aunt Astrid had been trying to escape them.

"Oh, Bella!" my mother cried, pushed away from my father, and gathered up as much of me as she could. For a fleeting moment, I was afraid I was going to come completely undone in the familiar embrace and howl in her bosom like a baby.

"Well, isn't this nice!" Aunt Astrid said inexplicably. "Anyone care for a second anchovy?"

"Come away, dear," Violet Pengarth's voice chirped from somewhere in the cubicle. I pulled away from my mother's shoulder to see Violet's hand gently grasp Aunt Astrid and disentangle her from Tamsin's clutch.

"Come with me, and we'll go on out and sit in those lovely orange chairs in the lobby."

"I left instructions with the nurse out there," Clive's voice rose over Aunt Astrid's confused reply. He managed to sound highly amused, concerned, and slightly baffled at the same time. "Just give her Astrid's name, and I'll see to her once Nurse settles her in the room with Aurora."

"Oh, Aurora is scouting the shores of Lake Titicaca, dearest, looking for wild bananas," Aunt Astrid said, her voice fading away as she walked with Violet down the hallway.

"What happened, *tesoro?* Where are you hurt?" My mother leaned away and began smoothing the damp hair from my face.

"Oh, Bella," Tamsin's voice wobbled over me breathlessly. It took me a second to identify the waver as awe. "You should have been there. Violet did a U-turn in the lane going about forty. I thought we were going to roll the Uno."

"How did you find out about Bella?" Dante asked my mother, grinning slightly as he rubbed his shoulder. Tamsin answered him timidly before my mother could say anything.

"I told them. They were bringing your Aunt Astrid in, and when I saw them, I asked if Bella was all right. I'm sorry. I didn't know that you hadn't told them."

"Poor Astrid," my grandmother sighed. "We didn't even check her in. We just turned around and ran back to Violet's little Fiat."

"We passed you on our way to the manor, and I knew you were going to the hospital. That's when Violet turned the car and tried to follow." My mother continued to smooth the dank hair from my face. Then she caught sight of my injured hand resting on the bed like an obscene purple udder. She gave a maternal screech, and Clive intercepted the burgeoning panic before it could manifest itself into another spate of passionate Italian.

"Her right wrist is merely dislocated," Clive answered her soothingly and carefully disentangled us, waiting until my father gently pulled her away from me and back into the shelter of his arm. "We need some x-rays before I set it back in place. But before that, I'm going to sedate her."

"We'd better step out to give him room to work," Brandt said and held an arm out for my mother.

"I'm not leaving, *figlio*," my mother said firmly. My father cupped her face and kissed her forehead.

"She'll be all right, my *ro'so'g fi'ain*." My father gently handed her off to my brother. "Go with Brandt."

"You'll need to, luv," Clive told her cheerfully. "I'll need her father and perhaps one of her brothers in here to steady her while I set it. There really won't be room."

"I'll stay," Dante volunteered. My grandfather reached out a hand to pat my mother, dwarfing her shoulder.

"Come on, Raphaela," my grandfather said gruffly. "Yon skinny man is right. He'll need no distractions while he sets the joint."

"Come, Raphaela, let's go and check on Astrid and Violet." My grandmother bent down, kissed my sticky forehead, gave me a worried smile, then turned, and took my mother's arm.

"I'll be just outside the curtains, *bambina,*" my mother said, twisting slightly between Brandt and my grandmother to throw me a protectively maternal look over her shoulder. I saw my brothers exchange looks over her head with each other and with my father.

"We'll take her to the lobby," Jude said quietly, catching my father's eye, then groped under the bell of blanket and skirt until he found my foot, squeezing it gently before filing out of the cubicle with Tamsin and Michael.

"Don't worry, *bambina,*" Dante said and came over to grasp my good hand. "It will be over in a second."

I rolled my eyes, feeling beads of anticipatory sweat break out on my forehead, and focused mindlessly on the fluorescent tubing over my bed while my father continued to stroke my hair. Clive noisily washed his hands in the nearby sink.

*"I love sixpence, pretty little sixpence . . . ,"* Brother Chaucer crooned in a falsetto over the splash of water. *"I love sixpence better than my life . . . I spent nothing, I lent nothing, I love nothing better than my wife . . ."* Unperturbed, Clive finished his ditty, turned casually from the sink, shook the water from his hands before pulling a paper towel from the dispenser, and grinned at me. "Ready, luv?"

The blanket was ceremoniously undraped, and I was rolled onto my left side. I tumbled about into position on the gurney with all the grace of an elephant doing tricks, and a syringe the size of a turkey baster was plunged into my flesh. Clive dispensed the painkilling sedative into my bloodstream and looked up at my father as he removed the straw-sized needle from my hip.

"This is the strongest I have without knocking her all the way out. She'll be seeing colors in a few moments." He grinned and pressed a cotton ball to the puncture. "Lovely colors, from what I hear."

I skewed my eyes to my father, not quite understanding Clive's prediction. My father just smiled in comprehension and continued to rub a comforting hand over the top of my damp hair.

Moments later, I did see colors. Rays emanating from the fluorescent tubing overhead like blue sunbeams. Sparks glinting from my father's white teeth. A halo surrounding Dante's head. I stared dreamily at the framed medical chart of the ear canal, and Clive's face drifted into my line of vision.

"She's ready," he said, his voice sounding like molasses sliding down a drain. The slicker was carefully removed and my body tucked back under a heavier blanket. "Let me call the technician for a couple of quick x-rays."

The gurney ride through the halls was what I had always imagined a Disney ride to be. Wonderfully fantastic colors slid by, bringing a lump to my throat, and I was aware of a delicious sensation of warmth creeping through my limbs like warmed honey. I didn't even mind the cold, hard metal of the x-rays.

In what seemed like no time lapse at all, I was wheeled back to my slot in the cubicle and parked between my father and Dante.

"Are you all right, *leanbh?*" My father calmly wiped the tears from my temples where my eyes had leaked onto the pillow. I nodded, deeply moved.

"She looks like she'd just had a vision," Dante remarked and leaned over my face. The nimbus surrounding his head glittered and flowed like melting moonlight. "That's some shot."

After some minutes Clive came back in, checked my pupils under my draped eyelids. His thumbs felt like damp kisses on my eyes, and I smiled dreamily as he let my lids flop back into place.

"The x-rays showed no broken bones, but there were two dislocated bones in her wrist that also displaced her ulna. It's going to be somewhat tricky." He paused. "You might want to scoot that basin by the sink a bit closer to us."

Hands drifted over me, arms encircled limbs, someone's breath touched my cheek, and I was gently, firmly, and carefully anchored into place. I was utterly immobilized, supported, and mindless. I was dimly aware of Clive lifting my hand, grasping it in hard fingers, positioning it, and counting softly to three.

"One, two, three . . ."

"Four," I started to murmur languorously and then gave a short sharp scream like an aborted air-raid siren at the sharp twist and jerk that nearly yanked me off the gurney. Gristle cracked, tendons stretched, and bones snapped back into place like exploding firecrackers that jarred me to the core.

"Quick, get the basin!" Clive commanded. I was hurriedly rolled over like a termite-infested log coming apart and hung over the edge of the gurney. I had a split second to notice the stainless steel under my nose before I lost my stomach into it.

It was over.

The ride back home was infinitely more entertaining than the ride to the hospital had been. The sedative was still coursing through my bloodstream, making me feel wonderfully liquid, muffling the ceaseless throb in my newly splinted arm, and making every oncoming headlight a symphony of prisms. I sat in the front passenger seat beside my father, my body as boneless as hot taffy, buckled in and tilted back with Destiny's odiferous dress still wafting pervasively about my person. My father hit a slight dip in the road as he passed a meandering van, and my dress shot up to wave exuberantly at the befuddled occupants. My father pressed the skirt back down with a distracted hand as he talked and drove, deftly tucking its exuberance under my knees. My legs rose up from the seat, and I felt as if I was riding on a pillow of brittle snakes.

My mother sat behind me, carefully trying to untangle my Rastafarian nest of wet, storm-ratted hair. Her fingers felt like moths caught in my curls. Tamsin sat in the seat beside her, listening raptly to my father's calm recital of our discovery of the cliff-side cave and its concealed treasure. In my sedative befuddled state, his voice had taken on the musical quality of a lilting rumble, a bit like distant thunder rolling down Irish hills.

I had found out later that my grandfather had taken my grandmother with him in their car while Dante and Brandt followed in Brandt's truck, and Michael and Jude brought up the rear in Michael's Saab. Gabriel had been kept blissfully ignorant of Aunt Aurora's escapade and the subsequent panic, having been taken by Alec Lytton and his New York guests to Alec's grandfather's house for the night. My mother had enough foresight to ask Alec to keep my little brother once she heard of Aunt Aurora's wild escape.

We pulled up in front of the house, and my parents invited Tamsin to stay overnight. She declined in a voice like lilting Welsh bells. By then the back-and-forth conversation in the car was beginning to sound like only so much slow noise in my exhausted sedative-raddled brain. I tried to add my persuasion to my parents' invitation, but I think I ended up saying something about sausages. I must have been hungry. I gave up and let my eyes roll up in my head, which was where they had been steadily trying to go since we'd entered the outskirts of the village.

At some point, Tamsin took her leave. I wasn't aware of her departure. Her presence just seemed to dissolve. The car door beside me opened, letting in the stinging rain, which revived me enough to pry my eyes open. I could see the light over the inn's door through the slashing downpour. Its welcoming beams flowed into the rain-soaked night like the aurora borealis, and I felt my mouth flop open in wonderment at the lantern's intense beauty. Someone laughed above my head. It sounded like a foghorn.

And then I was deftly and magically borne upward with my face to the sky, buoyant, blissful, and weightless, with the bell skirt of my magnificent frock unfurling heavenward like an enormous, smelly blossom. I tried unsuccessfully to lift my leaden arms to fly, feeling a lava flow of pure joy bubble out of my heart and to my fingertips. I was a floating butterfly. A dragonfly of joy.

"More like Tinkerbell under the influence." Dante's laughter cascaded down the deep tunnels of my ears. I must have voiced my heavenly bliss out loud. "Someone help me with this ridiculously fiendish dress. I can't see."

Hundreds of hands batted my legs and forcefully tucked the gently malodorous blossom around my knees. Which were starting to feel numb. I floated and floated, slowly and dreamily from the soaking-wet darkness and suddenly into warmth. Yellow warmth.

"Where do you want her?"

I unglued my lids. Dante's chin was only a few inches away from my eyeballs.

"The bathroom," my mother's voice penetrated my superb mental fog. "Your grandmother and I are going to get her into a bath."

"Can I have a drink?" I whooshed out loosely, my lips like two slinkies, and tried to figure out why I was still floating. "My tongue is as dry as Gandhi's flip-flop."

# 16

When I woke up the next morning, brilliant sunlight was streaming in my windows and falling across the foot of my bed. I turned to look blearily at my clock, and my mother appeared out of nowhere to press a cool hand to my face. She smiled and then bent down to kiss me.

"Well, good morning, *cara mia. Come stai?*"

"Vile," I croaked and shifted to dig my hot arm out from under the covers. It was bandaged, and the protruding fingers were slightly lavender. The rest of my scraped arms were rusty with iodine and greasy with salve.

"Do you feel up to getting out of bed?"

"What time is it?" I tried to look at my clock again, but the numbers seemed to dance and flicker.

"It's early yet." My mother shifted the blankets from me as I tried to untangle myself.

"Where's—oh, my head," I groaned when I sat up and pressed my free hand to my face.

"It's that painkiller that Clive gave you in a shot last night. He said that it has the effect of a hangover once it starts to wear off." My mother tucked a tangle of hair behind my ears, and the light behind her head shimmered. I shifted my gaze to watch its painful, surreal darting about. "He left some painkillers here for you to take when you wake up. *Bocciolo*, are you sure you feel good enough to come down?"

"Where's Dad?" I yawned, trying heroically not to drool, and pieced together my memories of the night before. Snatches kept floating by and falling into place.

"He went with your grandfather and brothers to bring the trunk home. They should be back soon." She paused. "How about a little breakfast after you get dressed?"

"Sounds wonderful." I yawned again. "But I need to go to the bathroom first."

"Come on, *cara mia*, I'll help you," she said and raised me to stand on wobbly legs. As we began to make our way awkwardly toward the door and down the hallway to the loo, the blood began to flow painfully to the ends of my limbs and wake up my nerves. Even my toes began to throb.

"Good morning, child." My grandmother seemed to materialize out of the shadows and floated toward us from the end of the hallway. Her long hair was in its customary braid, and she carried a large black leather purse on her arm. She embraced me in a cloud of flower scent. "How are you, *leanbh*?"

"She's a bit . . . I suppose the English word is 'wonky,'" my mother answered for me, laughing. My grandmother pulled back and put a dry hand on my forehead and then my cheek, frowning at my mother.

"Her eyes are a bit dilated. I don't like that."

"I noticed that," my mother said. I looked longingly at the bathroom. "Clive said that it couldn't be helped. She'll be fine once the shot wears all the way off, though I'm not totally sure about the painkillers he left. He said they're pretty potent."

"Well, do you need any help, dear?"

My mother shook her head.

"We'll be fine. Go ahead and enjoy your visit. Give my love to Astrid and Aurora. Tell them we'll come and see them later this afternoon after they have time to get a little more rest."

"If you're sure you'll be all right." My grandmother touched my mother's cheek much the same way she had mine. "I won't be back for lunch, dear. I imagine I'll stay with them until dinner."

"You know we're having Basil and Clive over this morning? They want to see the trunk once Luc, Finghin, and the boys bring it back. Tamsin was coming as well, but the librarian called her, and the poor child is going to have to fill in at the front desk until the afternoon. It seems that Ms. Dilly has just been commissioned this morning to finish a research project."

"How are Aunt Astrid and Aunt Aurora?" I asked, two beats behind them. "And Tamsin? Is she okay?"

"They're all fine, sweetheart." My grandmother smiled at me. "You'll see Tamsin this afternoon, apparently, and Astrid and Aurora will be back soon. Don't worry, *leanbh*, just get your rest."

I started to answer, but the soft pink light coming from my grandmother's face distracted me. It looked so beautiful darting about her peach-colored dress.

"Oh, dear," my grandmother sighed and patted me, looking quickly at my mother. I reached out and touched the sparks shooting from my grandmother's necklace. "Don't let her around the stairs, Raphaela."

"I won't," my mother laughed. "I promise."

My father, grandfather, and brothers came home with the trunk when I was in the kitchen eating an omelet. Even though I was ravenous, the fluffy eggs weighed heavily in the pit of my stomach like feathery little bites of lead. I was washing down the last bite with a swallow of orange juice and painkillers when we heard their voices entering the front door.

"Is that Gabriel I hear with them? They must have retrieved him from Alec's." My mother frowned uncertainly and left the kitchen, a dishtowel in her hand. I put my empty glass down by my empty plate, considered taking them to the sink, and then decided against it when I stood up. Still feeling a bit unsteady, I made my way carefully through the dining room and to the front room where the voices were mixing.

"Bella!" Gabriel exploded at me as I cleared the threshold. I was hurled back against the doorjamb. Skinny arms wrapped around me, and we nearly slid down the wall and onto my backside in a tightly wrapped clot.

"Careful!" Michael's hand shot out and caught me before we could complete our inelegant descent to the floorboards. "Gabriel, be gentle. She's hurt."

"I know," the voice said in my stomach, and the arms tightened into a vise that nearly shoved my navel past my spine.

"I'm all right, *cucciolo*," I laughed weakly as Michael unpinned Gabriel's fierce little figure from my middle.

"How are you, my *fi'ain coca'n ro'is*?" My father loomed up beside us and carefully enveloped me in a hug. Gabriel broke free from my brother's restraining hand and slid back into place, inserting himself between us.

"Better," I said, trading a quick kiss before Gabriel's knotty little forehead could pop my spleen.

"So that's the treasure?" I heard my mother's amused voice as my father gently released us. She stood over the trunk and wrinkled her nose at the musty smell pervading the room.

"How are you, *bambina*?" Brandt came up beside me and brushed my hair away to peer into my eyes. He grinned. "Welcome back to reality."

"If I ever swan off a cliff like Bella and wedge myself somewhere, I want the shot she got," Jude stated calmly and planted a kiss on my head as he passed me. "Is there coffee?"

"In the kitchen," my mother said, glancing up from the trunk as Jude left the room in search of caffeine. "Gabriel, *cucciolo*, let go of your sister."

"Get Grandfather some coffee," Dante called out to Jude's retreating figure and came up to me to lift my face in his hand. I submitted meekly to his frowning scrutiny, not sure what he was scanning my face for. After a second, he rubbed a thumb across my cheek to dislodge a renegade crumb of something. Probably a bit of omelet. I had blearily missed my mouth a couple of times while I was eating breakfast and had to clean egg chunks from my lap more than once. "How are you this morning?"

"Fine."

"*Bambina,* don't ever do—"

"I've already told that to the lass," my grandfather interrupted with a growl and reached past Dante to clamp his large bony grasp around my shoulder. He pulled me from the doorway and steered me into the room. "I meant it, child. I'll not stand for disobedience. Now go sit on yon sofa. You look plowed over, lass."

As my grandfather towed me to the sofa, Michael grinned and quickly rearranged the pillows into a fat nest of petit point, looking over his shoulder at my mother as my grandfather levered me onto the cushions. "Is there something to eat?"

"I'll get something, *figlio*," my mother said, giving the musty trunk another amused once-over before leaving the room.

"Here's a bite of omelet," I said, frowning into the neckline of my shirt. I reached in and fished out a fluffy blob of yellow. "You can have that if you want."

"Don't blather, lass," my grandfather growled. I dropped the bite of egg onto the coffee table, having no idea what else to do with it, and sank backward into the fat pillows. Michael picked up the chunk with quick fingers, grinned at me, and tossed it into the fireplace when my grandfather turned away.

There was a cheerful short rap on the front door.

"That should be either Clive or Basil," Dante said as my father answered the summons. Brandt peered out of the window and touched my hovering baby brother on the crown of his head.

"It's Clive," he said and urged Gabriel toward the kitchen where my mother was foraging. "Go tell Mom we have company." Gabriel careened away just as my father admitted Clive Chaucer into the front room.

"Would you like some coffee or tea?" my father asked. Clive declined absentmindedly, greeting everyone with a brisk nod.

"Not just now, thank you. I've just been to see Astrid and Aurora," he said cheerfully, sat on the low table in front of me, and gently freed my bandaged arm from the barricade of pillows. He began to undo the immobilizing splint. "They're fine. Actually, they're having the time of their lives in their private room with Bryn and all the shimmering bricks of gelatin that they can possibly eat. I haven't restricted their diet just yet, and I've left instructions with the nurses to cater to their every whim."

He grinned at my mother as she came into the room. Jude was following her, carrying two mugs of fragrant coffee in his hands while Gabriel hung from his back like a skinny little wombat. Jude handed a mug to my grandfather who gave a grunt of acceptance as he took it. My mother greeted Clive, who grinned at her.

"Raphaela, I've a message from Astrid and Aurora. They said that steamed vegetables at the hospital are all very nice, but nothing compares to your tiramisu." He set the splint on the table in front of the sofa and began prodding the heel of my hand. "Tell me if it gets to be too much, luv."

"That looks grisly," Dante commented, sitting on the other side of me on the sofa. "How long will it be like that?"

"From the feel of it, only a week or two at the most," Clive said cheerfully and then looked pointedly at the rather obvious trunk clogging up the middle of the room like a corpse. "So that's the treasure."

"The man was an idiot," my grandfather growled, aiming his epithet at Great-uncle Desmond. "He didn't have to keep it hidden."

Clive grinned at my grandfather's words and continued to examine my wrist, making me wriggle my fingers under his grip. Once he was done, he resplinted my arm, grasped my chin, and turned my face toward the light.

"How are you feeling otherwise?" he asked and stretched my lids wide open with his thumb to peer at my eyeballs. "Still seeing colors? It looks like the sedative is wearing off."

"Basil Brett is here!" Gabriel announced abruptly and dropped off Jude with a thump, careening to the front door and opening it before Basil could knock. "Look! We have the treasure!" he said, towing Basil into the room by one of his fingers. Basil was carrying a heavy-looking leather case in his free hand. He set it down as he passed an unoccupied chair.

"So I see, my exuberant little friend."

"Would you like a coffee? Espresso? Cappuccino?" My mother smiled, and Basil nodded at her as he allowed Gabriel to tow him toward the trunk.

"Thank you. I would very much like an espresso, my dear lady." He turned when he spied me on the sofa. "And how's beautiful Bella today?"

I smiled at him.

"Pretty numb, thanks to the painkillers," I said as my mother motioned for Gabriel to let go of Basil.

"Come on, *cucciolo*," she said and reeled my baby brother to her side. "I'll need someone strong to help me carry the food in."

"I can do that," Gabriel said happily. "I'll carry the heavy stuff, if you'd like." He began hopping on one foot all the way to the doorway. "And I'll do it for a kiss, beautiful lady."

My mother paused at the threshold and threw my father an amused look mingled with exasperation before following her youngest son out of the room.

"It looks like you brought a few reference books." My father turned and shook hands with Basil, gesturing toward the huge satchel. "Debretts?"

"Among other things. How did you know?" Basil stood beside the trunk and looked down at it squatting promisingly at his feet. "After you described what you had found, I made an appointment with the lord chancellor's office and decided that I had better bring my computer so I could connect up with the British Museum and the British Archives as well."

He looked over at me. I was totally at sea as I listened to their exchange.

"It seems that you, dear child, had found the French connection a step ahead of me. When we had gone to lunch at the Moonstone, I had already been considering the possibility of looking through French records for our answers, but it wasn't until I found the wine that I started to figure a small part of it out."

"What made you think of France?" I asked. A faint trace of red wiggled just outside of my line of vision, and I rubbed a hand over my eyes as Basil answered.

"The mannequins in the secret passageway were wearing undergarments trimmed with antique French lace. I also considered the figure of Napoleon in the bathtub, my dear. But I wasn't certain until I did a little research on the name of Clarisse De Mornay."

"I thought you looked like you were on to something." Jude grinned. "I assumed you would tell us once you were sure."

"So when are you going to look at the document?" my grandfather asked gruffly and stood up to help my mother carry in the tray of coffee, cups, and plates, setting it down on the low table in front of the sofa. Gabriel followed, painstakingly carrying the homemade biscotti like he was transporting a baby on a slick slaver. My mother began to pour the coffee out into the fragile cups.

"Now that Raphaela is here, we can begin if no one has any objections," Basil answered my grandfather and watched as my father and Brandt raised the lid on the trunk. A burst of smell erupted from it, and Clive waved his hand over his face with a grin.

"It seems like you've discovered Pandora's box, luv," he said, patting my shoulder, then stood up to look into the trunk with Basil. "Apparently it's been alive and well and hiding out in a Cornish cave."

"Does that make Uncle Desmond the troll under the bridge?" Jude grinned. "Or am I mixing my stories?"

Basil stared at the open lid, dropped very slowly to his aged knees, and ran a hand over the lid's rim. For the first time I could see gilded words carved into the wooden lip.

"Oh my," Basil breathed reverentially. I struggled to sit up higher so I could see. My mother snagged Gabriel before he could hop over on one foot to join them. "The gilt is still fresh enough to read. Could someone get a pencil and paper out of my case?"

My father bent to comply, and Basil began to dictate the words as he found them.

"*Hoc op fiebat Ao Dni MCCCCCXXV,* blah, blah, blah, blah . . ."

At least that's what it sounded like to me as Basil read on. Clive wasn't kidding when he had told my mother that the painkillers were potent. Either that or last night was more of an ordeal than I had thought. I struggled to focus. Not that it would have mattered anyway since the only Latin I knew was the proper name for the climbing rose under my window.

"Latin," Dante commented under his breath once Basil had finished. "I understood only part of it."

"That's because many words seem to be abbreviated," Basil said and then gingerly pushed himself to his feet, reaching for the paper that my father held out to him. "This shouldn't take long."

He tottered over to the chair where he had put his case and sat down, digging in the leather satchel to pull out an enormous book.

"Is that what you saw that made you think of Edward VI?" I asked my father. He nodded, bending down to get a couple of fingers of pistachio biscotti, giving one to his father, who sat enthroned in the brown leather wingback like the family patriarch that he was. Grandfather looked at me looking at him and grunted irritably. I grinned and shifted my eyes to watch Basil pore over his book.

"Is that a translation book?" my mother asked and let go of Gabriel long enough for him to snatch a finger of biscotti from the plate. He came over to where I was sitting and climbed up onto the sofa's armrest beside me. He leaned gently on my head and started gnawing on the hard Italian cookie.

"It certainly is, my dear lady," Basil said, flipping busily through the book. True to his word, it took him only a few minutes of peering and writing before he was finished. He stood up and began to read his finished product aloud.

"Here is what has been carved on the trunk." He smiled suddenly, and I wondered if his unvoiced suspicions were proving correct. "This was made in the year of our Lord 1525 for Henry Wycliffe, son of Henry Thomas, son of Flavia, son of Henry, husband of Ophelia, daughter and heiress of Edward Wycliffe, on whose house may God have mercy."

"Wycliffe?" I frowned. "I thought James George "the Smuggler" had renamed himself Algernon Wycliffe. So this is his trunk and not Destiny's?"

"Who are those other people?" My mother sat down in the wingback beside Basil's.

"Luc told me about what Bella and Tamsin had worked out from the portraits they had found." Basil turned to me. "Very good research, my dear Bella. Very good. Now, if I may see what's in the trunk, I might be able to answer all the questions."

My father put his coffee down on the table beside my grandfather and pulled out the red velvet cloak, spreading it out in front of Basil. He and my father shared a grin, and Basil ran a fastidious finger over the shedding fur ruff.

"You are absolutely right. It is stoat." He took a handkerchief from his pocket and carefully wiped the tiny hairs from his fingertip.

"Stoat?" Brandt's eyes narrowed as he looked from the cloak to Basil and my father. "You mean ermine?"

"Ermine," Dante repeated and went over to touch the cloak with gentle hands. "Red velvet and ermine." He grinned. "Well, I'll be."

I looked at my mother, who shrugged helplessly at me with a small smile.

"I like the word 'stoat' better," Gabriel intoned thoughtfully and put the half-gnawed biscotti back into his mouth.

"Let's see the chapeau." Basil smiled and stepped back as my father draped the velvet and stoat cloak on the open lid. Together Brandt and Dante pulled out the two ball gowns, but before they could drape them over a chair, my mother gave a discreet screech. They grinned and took them to the foyer to drape them over the coat hooks. My father reached into the trunk and pulled out the gold circlet that I had thought was a necklace, handing it to Basil. Basil had called it a chapeau. A hat? I watched curiously as Basil took it from my father's hands with reverential fingertips.

"I have never held one," he said quietly and turned it over and over in his hands, examining every detail of the formed gold. "Strawberry leaves."

"Is that the design?" my mother asked and got up to pour Clive another cup of coffee.

"It is," Basil said happily and handed the dull gold back to my father. My father put it on the low table next to the coffee tray.

"And here," my father said, delving into the bottom of the nearly empty trunk, "I have the letters patent."

My grandfather grunted. Whether it was a belch or a comment, no one knew, and he didn't make it clear. He fixed his eyes on the parchment and waited for Basil's pronouncement.

"I certainly hope so, Luc. I certainly hope so." Basil took the large document and studied it for a moment before reading it aloud. Since he read it in its original form of Latin, I couldn't understand a word he said.

"*Edwardus Dei gracia rex Anglie dominus Hibernie et Dux Aquitannie omnibus ad quos presentes littere pervenerint salutem*. Ahhh. That seems clear enough. I've seen this kind of thing before in books and archives. It says, 'Edward, by the grace of God, King of England, Lord of Ireland—"

My grandfather grunted derisively.

"And Duke of Aquitaine, to all those into whose presence these letters might come, greeting."

"King of England! Did you just say King of England?" My mother raised her eyebrows, and Basil looked into the tiny box that had been affixed to the document by the red ribbon.

"Certainly, dear lady. In the box is the royal seal of Edward II enthroned recto, on horseback verso."

"Fool," my grandfather grunted again. No one knew if he was remarking on Great-uncle Desmond again or on Edward II. Basil looked at my father and smiled widely, showing nearly all his perfectly polished teeth.

"You're right, my dear fellow. It is a letters patent."

"What does the rest of the Latin say?" Jude asked curiously as Gabriel reached for another biscotti.

"Last one before lunch, *cucciolo,*" my mother murmured. Gabriel nodded happily as he settled beside me, offering me first bite of his cookie, which I declined with a smile.

"He graciously makes this promise on behalf of himself and his heirs . . . ," Basil cleared his throat and continued reading. "*Sibi et successoribus suis aut masculi aur mulieres pariter imperpetuum* . . . . To the subject of this letter and his heirs in perpetuity. His heirs . . . on equal terms. Coronet and the same robes to be worn by both male and female . . . Ahhh, here it is. Eldest son, and failing sons the eldest daughter, equal rights and honors of inheritance . . . Oh my."

"What?" Michael and I said in unison.

"The Duchy of Fayrfax."

No one knew what he was talking about, except, perhaps, for my father, but we were all silent, mainly out of respect for Basil's obvious awe. No one wanted to interrupt his moment. After a few moments, Basil stirred himself, then fixed his glowing eyes on my father's amused face.

"My dear fellow, I need to make sure of something first." Basil seemed beside himself. "Does Bella still have the certificate naming Clarisse De Mornay as Destiny Ophelia's mother?"

"Not Great-grandmother Destiny," Gabriel clarified under his breath and looked at me for confirmation.

"No," I answered him. "Great-grandmother was Destiny Olivia Wildeve. Basil wants the certificate that Tamsin found of the Destiny that came over here from France two hundred years ago. She was Destiny Ophelia, not Destiny Olivia." I looked at my father. "It's in my knapsack in my room."

"I'll get it," Michael said and left. We could hear his swift ascent up the staircase. A moment later, he came back with a sheaf of papers in his hand, giving them in one chunk to Basil, who sorted them out on the table by the gold chapeau. After a second, Basil held up one of the papers and peered at it.

"I was right. One more thing to check and if I prove right on this little detail, then I can tell you why your uncle Desmond hid this. Even why James George had it walled up in the cliff tunnel."

He grinned and held up the sheet he had singled out from the rest of the papers.

"I can tell you this much, Luc. Destiny Ophelia, Clarisse's daughter, also daughter of Henry Thomas Wycliffe, became the rightful Duchess of Fayrfax at her parents' death in the French Revolution."

I realized that my mouth was open, and I closed it quickly. Too many chaotic questions were sliding around in my brain, and I tried to separate them. Where is the Duchy of Fayrfax? Does it even still exist? And why did James George rename himself with the surname of Wycliffe if Destiny Ophelia's name was Wycliffe as well? And what was a letters patent, anyway?

"So Destiny Ophelia wasn't fully French, either," my mother murmured. "Like Luc's grandmother."

"No, dear lady, apparently she was half English as well," Basil answered, putting the document down on the table next to the gold chapeau of strawberry leaves. I saw Gabriel eyeing it speculatively, and I nudged him.

"Don't even think about it," I whispered. He grinned, pretending that he hadn't even heard me. I looked back at Basil. "What is a letters patent? Is it what I think it is?"

"Probably." Basil smiled and began to dig out his laptop computer. "Anymore they're issued through the office of the lord chancellor and sealed with the Great Seal of England, but back then"—he gestured to the document—"it could be issued directly from the king."

"They're official documents conferring an exclusive right or privilege," my father clarified. "As in this case, it's conferring the right to a title of nobility."

"So this one was issued by King Edward conferring the title of duke or duchess to follow the family line of Henry Thomas?" my mother mused out loud and got up to pick up the chapeau. "I suppose this was worn by those who inherited the title."

"And the crimson velvet robe trimmed in ermine." Basil's blue eyes looked dreamily at my mother. "The ceremonial robe and coronet they were required to wear at state occasions."

"You made me dry off with the ceremonial robe of a duchess?" I gasped and stared at my father, thinking about all the salt and dirt the velvet had blotted up. "Did you know that's what it was when I used it?"

"Child, it's only a piece of cloth," my father laughed. "And, yes, I knew what it probably was. You forget how much Renaissance art I've studied over the years. The paintings in the museums and history books are full of these."

"But it's valuable," I protested. My father's grin softened a bit.

"So are you child," he said dryly. "The robe would have to be seen to by a professional restorer, anyway. No lasting harm was done to it."

"Excuse me, Luc, but I assume you have Internet in the inn?" Basil tucked his tiny silver laptop under his arm and looked questioningly at my father, who nodded.

"Come in my study. My desk is convenient." He paused. "Do you need privacy?"

"No, not really." Basil looked around at us. "I don't mind if you want to watch, but I don't imagine it will make sense to anyone until I can explain."

"We'll wait," my mother said firmly and put the coronet back down on the low sofa table. "I'm sure you don't need the distraction."

"Very well." Basil smiled cheerfully and then followed my father out of the room to his study.

I settled back against the sofa and felt Gabriel's fingers entwine absently in a chunk of my hair.

"So how valuable do you think this is?" Dante broke the short silence, pulling us all back from our thoughts. Clive shrugged at his question.

"I've seen these coronet things under glass in museums, but whether they are there because they're rare and valuable or because they merely have historic value, I don't know."

"Where's the Duchy of Fayrfax?" Brandt asked and bent down to break off a piece of biscotti, putting the whole chunk in his mouth.

"I suppose that's one of the things Basil is looking up," Dante said.

"I've never heard of it." I nudged my little brother and pointed at the biscotti plate. "Can you get me one of those, please?"

"For a kiss, beautiful lady." My little brother regarded me out of grave eyes.

I laughed, and my mother looked accusingly at my older brothers.

"Did you teach him that?"

Jude held his hands up in defense, laughing and shaking his head.

"No," he protested. "The other day he caught a lady's eye while she was eating in the dining room, approached her, and told her that he was named after an angel."

"But I was," Gabriel said innocently and scampered off the cushions to fetch a finger of biscotti for me, clambering back up to his spot at my shoulder to trade the cookie for a kiss. "And she was really pretty too. I think I was in love."

My mother gave an exasperated sigh, and Clive chuckled.

"Girls are expensive, Gabriel." Clive grinned at my little brother. "Be careful. If you really do fall in love, you'll be giving them all your pennies."

"Maybe," Gabriel said pensively, "but I don't mind. Girls smell nice."

"So he's Italian." Dante grinned at my mother, but my grandfather grunted.

"He takes after his father."

"Who does?" My father walked into the room just then and went to put an arm around my mother. "So what do you think of all this, *a'lainn*?"

"I don't know what to think." She smiled up at him. "I'm glad it's over, though. I wonder what Aunt Astrid and Aunt Aurora are going to think of all this."

"I wish Tamsin could be here," I sighed, holding the biscotti up to my mouth, but not taking a bite. "She did most of the work, and now she can't even be here to see it."

Basil entered the room just then and snagged his waiting espresso from the table. He heard my complaint.

"Ah, not so, beautiful Bella. She will soon be in the thick of it. She certainly hasn't been left out." He smiled at me and left the room to go back to his computer. "You'll soon see."

I watched his retreating back until he disappeared into the hallway and then looked at my parents.

"What I can't figure out is why the Wycliffe name is woven through the whole thing," I sighed and finally took a nibble of biscotti. "Why did James George call himself that when it was Destiny's name?"

"Perhaps that's why," Dante said reasonably. "Why not take on your wife's name, using her papers and identity to establish a false one of your own? She could have claimed that he was a cousin, and who would dispute that? Especially back then."

"Is Grandmother already telling Aunt Astrid and Aunt Aurora about the treasure trunk, or is she going to wait until they can take the excitement?" Jude asked and settled on the far end of the sofa beside Michael.

"I advised her to keep the conversation light for the next few days," Clive answered, looking thoughtfully at the robe draped over the trunk lid. "You know, there's a lot of history in that thing."

"I wonder what Basil is doing," I said and chewed another chunk of biscotti. It sounded like I was eating rocks, and I had to pause to hear my father's answer.

"He's online at the Royal College of Heralds."

"Why?" I gaped at him, the biscotti slowly dissolving in my cheek.

"He didn't say, but I know that he also wants to get in touch with the British Museum's baronial archive. My guess is that he's checking the letters patent and making sure that his deductions are correct."

"You mean whether or not Destiny Ophelia Wycliffe was the Duchess of Fayrfax," Brandt said. "I'm willing to wager that James George and his new wife didn't go to France when they left here. At least not until the revolution was over, and it was safe for Clarrise's daughter to return. I wonder where they did go."

"We'll never know that, son," my grandfather said gruffly, eyeing my older brother from hooded eyes. He looked bored. Or perhaps thoughtful. It was hard to tell with my grandfather's hawklike face. "Perhaps yon Welsh child can find that out."

"Tamsin?" I looked thoughtfully at my grandfather and struggled to get to my feet. "She's at the library right now. Maybe she can look it up. It might not take her that long—"

"Sit down, child," my grandfather said. "Yon little man is on the phone line. You'll not call."

I sank back in my cushions, and Gabriel fell sideways onto my shoulder.

"What about one of your mobile—," I began. But my father shook his head.

"Don't worry, *leanbh*. Tamsin will be here soon enough, and you can talk to her then."

I felt we were in limbo waiting for Basil's return with nothing but questions and speculations to make the minutes stretch into longer units than they already were. I sighed and wished I could go to sleep until Basil finished and came back with answers.

I settled back under Gabriel's armpit, let him drape himself over my head, and closed my eyes, sinking deep into the cushions. I think I was starting to dream when a brisk knock on the door woke me up as if I had been slapped.

"It's just Tamsin," Michael said soothingly as I started. He was peering out of the window. "I see her Mini."

"I'll get it," my mother said and left to open the foyer door. I could hear the soft exclamations and greetings, and after a second, my mother escorted her into the front room. Tamsin was carrying an enormous folder and looked bewildered, slightly gobsmacked, and anxious all at once.

"Tamsin," I greeted her. She whirled around to stare somewhat blankly at the sofa. I seemed to be camouflaged by Gabriel and cushions and was a bit hard to spot.

"Oh, Bella," she said breathlessly, finally seeing me, and bent over to hug my head as I sat up. "I'm so glad you're better." She straightened up and whirled back around to look questioningly at my mother. "Ms. Dilly sent me here with this. I'm supposed to give this to Basil Brett."

"So Basil was the one who commissioned her this morning," my mother said, enlightenment dawning in her eyes. "It was about all this." She looked down at the folder in Tamsin's hand. "Come this way, *bambina*, and you can give it to him yourself."

As they left the room together, my mother put an arm around her and squeezed.

"We want to thank you for . . . ," her voice faded from my hearing as they left the room together.

"Research?" I gaped at the threshold where they had disappeared.

"It seems Basil is one step ahead of us," my father chuckled. "We'll see what this is about."

"Did you know about this too?" Michael asked. My father nodded.

"He told me a bit of what he was doing, but not why. I think he didn't want to disappoint us if he turned out to be wrong."

"Wrong about what?" I asked.

"No one knows yet, *poca*," Dante laughed.

A few minutes later, Basil came excitedly into the room, followed by a breathless Tamsin and my amused, but bewildered, mother carrying the older man's espresso. Basil nearly pranced to his chair, his normally prim tread buoyant and energized.

"Oh, my dears." He carried the folder that Tamsin had delivered from Ms. Dilly. It had been opened, and a sheaf of papers had been extracted. He held them carefully in his hand as if he was afraid to crumple the words. "It's as I had suspected once I was told of the letters patent. Just as I had hoped."

"Sit down, man, and tell us," my grandfather demanded and shifted uncomfortably in his wingback.

"I had commissioned Ms. Dilly, the head librarian at the Halfmoon lending library, to research the names Algernon Wycliffe, Destiny Ophelia Wycliffe, and also Destiny Olivia Wildeve, and to give it to Tamsin to bring it so that she may be included in this little bit of fun."

"So that's it," my father said slowly and then raised his eyes to stare at Basil with dawning comprehension. Something Basil had just said had put two pieces together in my father's mind. He sounded almost unsettled by his realization.

"What, Luc?" My mother looked up at him. "Do you know?"

"I'm beginning to," my father said quietly. Basil beamed.

"Makes sense now, doesn't it, my dear fellow?"

"His first clue," my father said, frowning in thought as he continued to stare at Basil's glowing grin. "And why Desmond couldn't cash in on this."

"Tell us," I pleaded. Gabriel sprang up from his seat at my shoulder to tug at Tamsin's hand, dragging her back to the sofa with him.

"Here, pretty lady, have my seat."

Tamsin stumbled and nearly fell onto the sofa's arm beside me. Gabriel lunged at the tray of biscotti, selected one for Tamsin, handed it to her, and then ran to my grandfather to clamber up on his lap.

"Sit, child, and listen," my grandfather said gruffly and cupped the crown of Gabriel's dark head. "Hush, now."

"Tell us, Basil, old fellow," Clive laughed and shifted to perch on the edge of his chair. "The suspense is killing all of us."

"While I was in Luc's study, I used my mobile to call Liza Weebs, one of Halfmoon's oldest residents, and asked her to cast her mind back to the day Destiny Olivia, Luc's grandmother, came into town as a World War I refugee fleeing France. After I promised her a bribe of éclairs and a bottle of single malt whiskey, she confirmed my suspicions."

Basil paused and looked down at the sheaf he held in his fist as if making sure they were still there.

"She remembers a huge canvas in Destiny's cart. Liza described what I now know to be the painting of the shipwreck that Destiny had eventually put up over the fireplace mantel in the tower bedroom."

He waited for his statements to sink in, letting us picture the fleeing Destiny in her traveling dress with all her belongings strapped to the cart bringing her in from the train station miles away.

"That painting was hers before she came here?" I asked and cradled my bandaged arm over my stomach. "She didn't find it in Tanglewood where Destiny Ophelia had left it?"

"No, my dear girl." Basil smiled and continued, choosing his next words carefully. "I know why you must have surmised that. But, no, the painting was already hers before she met your great-grandfather."

"So that's it," Dante quietly echoed my father's words earlier.

"Everyone gets it but me," I said. My mother glanced at my frustrated expression.

"Not everyone, *bocciolo*." She smiled, looking back at Basil. "Why is that significant?"

"My dear, dear Raphaela." Basil turned on the full wattage of his beam. "It's significant in that the shipwreck painting is a family heirloom. Family, dear. Destiny Olivia Wildeve, your husband's grandmother, is a direct descendant of James George "the Smuggler" and Destiny Ophelia Wycliffe."

"Wycliffe!" I suddenly exclaimed and nearly slapped my forehead with my hand, stopping myself before I connected. "Why, oh, why, did I forget that?"

"Forget what, child?" my father asked curiously. I looked at Tamsin.

"I forgot to tell anyone." I looked back at my father. "Liza Weebs told me that Destiny Olivia's mother was a Wycliffe before she married. I never made a connection. I had completely forgotten."

"What does all this mean, man?" my grandfather interrupted impatiently. Basil turned delighted eyes on him, sitting in his chair with Gabriel on his lap.

"It means, my dear sir, that you"—he paused to point—"are married to a duchess. Bryn is the legal heir to the title of Duchess of Fayrfax."

*"Che?"* my mother burst out, sounding like the air had been sucked from her lungs by her one-word comment. "What?"

"The title descended to Grandmother?" Jude raised both eyebrows and grinned. "You mean the title is still active?"

"Anyone who wants to claim a title and can prove their descent, which Ms. Dilly has kindly documented right here"—Basil waved the papers in his fist about—"goes to the chancellor. If he's satisfied, which he eventually will be, the documents go to the House of Lords for a writ of summons, which, once issued, creates the title again, and it is active."

"So what does that make Luc as the firstborn?" my mother stated anxiously and looked up at my father.

"A duke once he inherits. Then Dante will be heir to the title as his firstborn." Basil smiled.

"Duke Luc." Jude grinned, then got up from his seat on the sofa to snatch another biscotti. "That's almost as bad as Finghin Quinn, eh, Grandfather?"

My grandfather grunted, looking crabby about the whole Duchess of Fayrfax thing.

"That's better than Duke Dante." Dante frowned. "That sounds a bit like a digestive condition."

"Don't tell Rayvyn," Michael murmured feelingly.

"So what do we do?" my mother asked. My father laughed gently at her obvious anxiety, putting both arms around her to pull her up against his chest. He kissed the top of her head, grinning, and started to rock her as if they were dancing together.

"Don't worry, me *fi'ain ro'so'g*. Titles are easily revoked by an act of parliament," he said, his brogue almost as marked as my grandfather's had been. "I have a feeling, however, that the title isn't what Desmond had bequeathed when he made Aunt Astrid and Aunt Aurora his heirs. What a joke from James George and Desmond. What a tremendous joke."

"You are correct," Basil said and shifted through the papers in his hand, finding one that he consulted before continuing. "Your uncle had mentioned that what he had left was worth much money. A title isn't valuable by itself, but the property entailed to a title can be."

"Property?" My mother looked out of the shelter of my father's arms. She looked confused. I was still reeling from my grandmother having to go to parliament to have them take away her title of duchess. My grandmother, the duchess. What on earth would that make Grandfather?

"In this case," Basil cleared his throat suddenly and looked a bit wobbly before he continued, looking down at the paper topmost in his fist. "In this case, Bryn will own certain properties to the tune of well over three and a half million pounds, including real estate."

*"Che?"* my mother burst out again.

"What?" my grandfather roared. Gabriel jumped in his lap. My grandfather put a restraining arm around him and moderated his voice to a decibel that didn't cause brain damage. "My wife inherits three and a half million pounds? Ye're crazy, man!"

"And real estate, Grandfather," Brandt laughed. "Don't forget that."

"I assure you I am not crazy," Basil said smugly and patted the papers in his hand. "I was in contact with my solicitor early this morning. He was able to pull some of his more influential strings and find out the particulars quickly enough. It seems that the said property is already in probate court right now as there seems to be a question as to where and who the proper heir is. It seems that the wealth traveled through one of Destiny Ophelia's distant cousins once she was given up for dead after the French Revolution, and that the last kin was somewhat eccentric and had died intestate with no near relatives still alive."

"So once Bryn establishes her descent from Destiny Ophelia, then it will belong to her?" my mother asked. Basil nodded.

"Absolutely."

"How long will all the red tape take?" Clive asked. I looked past Tamsin to the doctor on his chair by the fireplace. He had been so quiet and still that I had nearly forgotten about him. He looked pleased at Basil's assertions and vastly entertained as if he had just been watching dinner theatre with his coffee and biscotti.

"Who knows?" Basil shrugged. "Perhaps a year. Perhaps less, maybe more. It depends on the solicitors we hire to get this thing moving."

"I don't believe it," my grandfather grumbled behind his hand and then wiped his fingers and palm wearily over his eyes, returning his hand to his chin. "Yon Desmond was a daft idiot to hide this."

"So Bryn won't actually be taking anyone's expectations away," my mother murmured. My father shook his head, his arms still around her.

"No, *a'lainn*. It's lost money until she claims it."

"Does she have to claim the title as well?" I asked. My father shook his head again.

"No, child. Not necessarily. She can go to parliament once she proves her descent from Destiny Ophelia and have it revoked before it's made active." He looked at Basil. "I assume that the title went dormant when they couldn't find Destiny Ophelia after the revolution."

"It did."

"That's why Great-uncle Desmond couldn't cash in on it," I sighed, feeling a throb start up in my wrist as I repositioned it. I wondered when I was allowed my next set of painkillers. "Great-uncle Desmond couldn't. He didn't come from Great-grandmother Destiny. No wonder he said that it belongs, not belonged, to Destiny. The title is still hers."

"And the taunt that Great-aunts Astrid and Aurora had no sense of heritage. That was a clue in itself," Michael remarked.

"It's also clear why the trunk with the robe, coronet, and letters patent was left behind when Destiny and James George escaped England," my father said. My bemused mother left his arms to stack the used refreshment dishes on the tray. "She dared not claim it if she wanted to marry her smuggler. Being married to a duchess is no way to escape discovery. So she made her choice."

"No wonder he left a last note," I said, thinking again about the portrait's eyes with their secret joke.

"I suppose that the parchment that Great-uncle Desmond used to write the clues on was another clue in itself," Jude said thoughtfully and settled deeper into the sofa. "It drew attention to the floor plans in the library. James George had probably done that specific set of plans, omitting the real tunnels that he had constructed so that no one would know of their existence."

"A double bluff." Dante grinned. "A smuggler's insurance in case his house was searched."

"Oh, wait a minute." I sat up, Jude's word of "parchment" triggering something. I looked at Tamsin. "What did we do with that piece we found in Aunt Aurora's . . . dress?"

"You had found something in Aunt Aurora's dress?" my mother asked quietly. Clive grinned, not saying anything.

"Yes. Uh . . . she had stored it for safekeeping, apparently. She must have found it in Great-uncle Desmond's study and put it in her purse that day we all went to Tanglewood. We found it last night when we put her to bed. Clive said that it looked like the combination to a safe. Did Great-uncle Desmond have one of those? Did he have a safe?" I looked at my father.

"I hadn't seen one."

"You'll have to ask your Aunt Aurora once she's up to remembering," my mother suggested. "Luc, *caro*, can you put the trunk somewhere else until we know what to do with it? That smell is overpowering."

"I'll put it in storage," my father laughed.

"Where is that note?" I fretted, ignoring them.

"Lass, I know where the note is." My grandfather met my eyes over Gabriel's head. "I put it under yon coffee contraption in the kitchen."

"That was a clue?" My mother's eyes widened, and she put the dish-laden tray in her hands back down on the sofa table and hurried off. "Oh, my goodness. I thought that was trash, and I put it in the bin under the coffee grounds."

"Good thing it had been written on indestructible parchment," Dante laughed and, picking up the tray, followed her scurrying figure to the kitchen.

# 17

It turned out that the parchment did, indeed, hold the combination to a safe, and we found the safe that afternoon. It all started with our family's visit to Aunts Astrid and Aurora at the hospital.

Basil and Clive had long since left the inn, Basil with his computer and documents, taking the sheaf of papers to his solicitor to sort out for my grandmother before presenting them to her, and Clive to go back to the surgery. The rest of us piled into two vehicles for the excursion. My father drove the Range Rover with my mother, grandfather, Tamsin, and myself as passengers while Michael drove his Saab with Dante, Brandt, Jude, and Gabriel stuffed inside its cramped interior. Dante's antediluvian Peugeot was still parked at their cottage with a major chunk of its machinery dismantled in the tiny shed where Jude had been working on it.

When we arrived, a young nurse the size of a sturdy pony escorted us to the nurses' station outside of their room. We were only allowed to enter in trios, and my mother, father, and Gabriel went in first. After five minutes of visiting, they were escorted out by the nurse, and Jude, Grandfather, and I were allowed in next.

The room was small, but bright and airy with its double windows overlooking the rolling green lawns outside. Aunts Astrid and Aurora were sitting up in their beds, looking serene and slightly confused in their flowered bed jackets. The roses from my parents perfumed the room, its vase propping up Gabriel's offering of a flying red hippo drawn on the inn's stationery. I squinted at the picture, seeing Gabriel's blocky signature under the stars hanging from the hippo's feet, and the words "I love you" crayoned on the hippo's voluptuous belly.

Jude and I kissed my great-aunts and my grandmother, and I handed the grapes we had brought to Great-aunt Aurora. My grandmother, having risen from her chair, sidled close and patted me on the cheek.

"Thank you, *leanbh*. How are you feeling? Are they taking good care of you?"

"I'm fine," I told her, having swallowed another set of painkillers before we left for the hospital. I was so numb and relaxed, I could have taken a bullet and not noticed.

"Hello, Finghin, dear." She smiled at my grandfather, and he leaned down to accept her kiss on his cheek, grunting, his hooded eyes roving over the faces of my great-aunts as they peered at us. At least one was.

"Woman, why is Aurora shutting her eyes?"

I looked at the bed. Aunt Aurora's face was screwed up as tightly as a wilted peony.

"I'm so ashamed of the way I acted," Aunt Aurora answered him in a tremulous voice before my grandmother could. Her blue eyes popped back open. "Can you ever forgive me?"

"For what?" my grandfather asked laconically. Aunt Aurora looked nonplused.

"For . . . ," she faltered, then looked at my grandmother. "What had I done?"

"You told him that you wouldn't let Sister marry him, and then you punched him," Aunt Astrid answered her calmly, forestalling the words rising to my grandmother's lips. "You were trying to make him go away, you said."

"Oh, my goodness," Aunt Aurora sounded startled and looked even more bewildered than a moment ago. "I said that?"

"You did." My grandfather gave a dark smile. "But you'll have to try harder than that if you want to get rid of me, you silly woman. Perhaps if you wait long enough, I'll die of old age."

"Have some fruit, Aunt Aurora," I intervened hastily and pointed at the bag of fat grapes resting on her blanketed knees. "You like grapes, don't you?"

"Yes, I love them." Aunt Aurora's confused eyes swiveled from my grandfather to the bag of fruit, and she reached out a plump hand to snag a glistening cluster, offering them to her sister. "Look, Astrid, we have fruit. It's been years since I'd had grapes."

"Are there no grapes in Peru?" My grandfather's eyebrows rose lazily. "What's Peruvian wine made from? Llama—"

"Finghin!" my grandmother said sharply. Jude and I locked eyes, trying not to smile. "I know what you're doing! You're deliberately aggravating her when you know she's not responsible for her reactions!"

My grandfather's dour face broke into a wicked grin, but he refrained from saying anything. I hastily stepped over to the bed and lifted Gabriel's drawing, turning it toward the light.

"Bella!" Aunt Astrid gasped and reached from her bed to clutch at my tee shirt, noticing for the first time the splint swallowing up my purple fingers. "Is that what you had done to yourself when you slid off the edge of the cliff? Bryn said that you had hurt your arm, but she said that Clive had taken care of it."

"Oh, my goodness, dearest, did you break it?" Aunt Aurora asked, her eyes as round as blue golf balls behind her thick glasses.

"No. It will be fine in a week or so. It's fixed, just a bit sore," I said hastily, reassuring them. But Aunt Aurora leaned over to cluck and pat my splint-covered wrist. I smiled at her and studied Gabriel's drawing of the astral hippopotamus. I pointed to the pendants hanging from the hippo's neck. "Obviously a girl hippo. But what's this?"

"The moon, dear." My grandmother came up behind me, smiling, and ran a finger over the slashes of color. "The moon and stars."

"The moon and stars," I repeated and turned to look at her, frowning. "Wait a minute. You've just reminded me of something."

"What?" Jude asked, his question quiet. But I barely heard him, thinking. My grandmother's phrase nudged a thought in the back of my brain. Something I had forgotten, but shouldn't have. I sighed, blaming the befuddling effects of the painkillers and studied the childish drawing for inspiration.

"What about the moon and stars, lass?" my grandfather grunted and leaned over to pluck a grape from one of the clusters in the bag, putting it in his mouth. "You aren't thinking of yon smuggler?"

"That's it!" I turned and looked at Jude. "The first moon and stars we found. In the tunnel where we found the buckle and one of Desmond's clues."

"The tunnel from the garden to the boiler?" Jude asked, reading my mind. "We never checked, did we?"

"We didn't know that it marked a door," I said, putting the drawing back in its place of honor beside the vase of roses. "We'd thought that Desmond had scratched it in the stone to make us think of James George. Remember, though, what his clue said?"

"To put it all together and look." Jude grinned, his arms crossed over his chest as he leaned against the wall behind him. "It takes on a different meaning when you know that James George and not Uncle Desmond had chiseled the figures into the stones."

"Who's James George?" Aunt Aurora asked fuzzily, busily plucking the rest of the grapes from their stems to line them up across her lap in formation.

"Are you thinking of going back and seeing what's behind yon wall?" my grandfather asked, then shrugged darkly. "Come on then, lass. Let's get it over with. We'll take one of the cars back." He leaned down to kiss my grandmother.

"*Sla'n leat*, dear," she said, accepting his kiss on the corner of her mouth. "Tell Raphaela and Luc that I'll be back for dinner."

"Speaking of our son, the future duke," he said dryly and paused at the door as Jude and I kissed Aunts Astrid and Aurora good-bye, "you might want to ask him what I should call you now. I was waiting to tell you all about it myself, but it looks like it isn't over."

"What do you mean?" She frowned at him, and he abruptly gave her one of his rare grins. His eyes darkened, and his ends of his eyebrows soared. He looked thoroughly amused.

"You, *a'lainn*, are the Duchess of Fayrfax and will probably inherit over three and a half million pounds. Ask Luc to explain. It will take too long for me to tell you now." He opened the door and left. We could hear his voice echoing faintly as the door started to swoosh shut. "I'll not trust Bella out of my sight until yon lass is satisfied. Come on, lass, hurry up, and let's put to rest yon mess made by that idiot Desmond."

"What did you just say? Finghin!" my grandmother called out ineffectually, then turned to Jude. "Can you tell me what on earth he's talking about?"

"The trunk that Dad and Bella found held the legal documents conferring the Duchy of Fayrfax to the firstborn descendents of Destiny Ophelia. The title comes with property and wealth, apparently."

"Destiny Ophelia?"

"Dad told you last night." Jude grinned. "The original Destiny that ran off with James George 'the Smuggler.'"

"How does that make me—"

"You are the firstborn descendent of Destiny Ophelia. It all goes to you."

My grandmother put a hand to her chest and staggered back until she was sitting on Aunt Aurora's feet. Grapes rolled everywhere.

"Dad." I stepped out of the door and got my father's attention. "Grandfather and Jude just dropped the bomb on Grandmother, and I think she needs you to explain. Is it all right if I go with Grandfather back to the house to check on the first set of moon and stars that we found in the garden tunnel?"

"So your grandfather just said." My father grinned. I looked at my grandfather's retreating back as he continued to stride down the long hospital corridor then looked back at my parents. My mother looked worried, and I knew that she was about to refuse to let me go with Grandfather.

"I'll be fine," I pleaded.

My grandfather's roar rolled down the hallway, earning an indignant stare from the sturdy nurse behind her station, "Come on, lass! I'll not wait! I want this over with!"

"Go ahead," my father said and stepped forward to catch the door as Jude stepped out into the hallway behind me. "Jude, son, go with her and look after her. Make sure she doesn't overdo it."

"Can I go?" Tamsin stood up uncertainly from her plastic orange chair.

"Of course." I grinned, and I motioned for her to follow. "Come on."

In the end, my grandfather drove the Saab back to the inn. We were filled to capacity with Tamsin, Jude, my mother, Gabriel, and myself. We dropped my mother and Gabriel back home and picked up a handful of torches before continuing on to Tanglewood.

I felt a queer lurch in the pit of my stomach when we pulled to a stop in front of the manor. I peered sideways at the distant horizon falling away from the cliff's edge, thinking of my plunge the night before. Far from being threatening, however, the water and the sky were as innocent as aquamarines in the storm-washed light. Unable to help myself anyway, I averted my eyes skittishly from the cliff as we got out of the Rover.

We made our way to the garden, my grandfather leading the way to open the hidden door. Once in the garden, it took only a few minutes to reach the tunnel marked as Destiny's grave. My grandfather strode impatiently over the flowers and blazed a straight swath through the exuberant blooms to the tunnel's entrance, but it wasn't until we reached the grave that we realized the unwelcome result of having left the slab open the night before. At that time, none of us could find the trigger to close the entrance, so it had been left open until one of my brothers could come back in the daylight to look.

We shone our torches at the rainwater from last night's storm that had flooded into the tunnel. It obscured the stone floor in slicks of motionless black sludge. Tamsin drew back in dismay and looked at me.

"You don't have to if you don't want to," I told her. She stared at me indecisively and bit her lip.

Without ceremony, my grandfather and Jude began to descend into grave's depths.

"It's not deep," Jude called out reassuringly over the echoing splashes of their footsteps. "It's only a few inches."

"I'll be back in a few minutes," I told her and began to clamber over the high edge of the grave, lowering myself step by step, deciding to jump the last few steps into the water. I just wanted to get it over with before fastidious common sense kicked in and froze me on the drier treads. I landed in the sloshing blackness, and icy water splashed my ankles.

"Bella!" Tamsin called down, blotting out the light coming through the opening above my head. "I'm not afraid of the water! It's the drowned rats floating down there that I was thinking of."

Just then something swam over my foot. My toes abruptly curled in my sneakers, and I almost levitated back up to her silhouette. I shrieked, earning an exasperated scowl from my grandfather, and tried to climb Jude. I slipped and would have gone facedown into the bubonic-ridden water if my brother hadn't snagged me with a surprised arm and kept me aloft.

"Bella!" he steadied me. "Calm down or you're going to hurt yourself."

My grandfather snorted impatiently.

"If there are drowned rats down here, then they're only what's blocking yon small opening in the wall under the boiler. It's either that or washed up leaves clogging up the cellar hole. Besides, lass, rats swim."

Tamsin screeched and withdrew. There was an answering squeak from the water beside my brother's boot. I stared downward, horrified into immobility. Somehow, swimming rats were worse than dry ones.

"Here," Jude laughed, unperturbed at the black splash of water moving past his foot, and hoisted me unceremoniously higher on his back, taking a couple of shrugs to swing me around and place me. "Just try not to choke me with your splint."

My grandfather grunted, watching us, then turned on his heel and began to stride down the tunnel, not bothering to wait. He raked his light over the walls above our heads, obviously searching for the etched moon and stars we had found earlier.

"I wonder where the tomcat is," I murmured in Jude's ear. He grinned.

"He's fine. He's obviously survived worse."

"You know we'll never catch him. He's going to roam the garden, attacking everyone until he dies of old age."

"As long as he cleans out the rats, I don't much care how antisocial he is."

"Do you think there's another room behind the moon and stars?"

"I don't know," Jude answered. I sighed, resting my chin on his shoulder. We continued to plod on, our lights searching the hewn blocks for the etching. It was my grandfather who had finally spotted the circle and cross marks above his head.

"Is this it?" he asked, stopping directly under it to shine the full beam of his torch on the marks. "How did your father move the stones in the other tunnel, lass?"

"He used the flat of his hand to push on the block it was etched on," I answered, adding my light to my grandfather's. "The wall beside it moved like it was on some kind of balancing pivot. It just moved to the side."

My grandfather grunted, put a large bony hand against the block, braced himself, and gave the wall a carefully controlled push. A screeching grate of stone on wet stone filled the tunnel and rolled down both ends. I hunched my shoulders against the uncomfortable sound and watched as the wall opened up, shifting and sliding at a slight angle over the other stones to expose a narrow slit to another room.

All three of us eagerly shined our torch beams into the aperture. A ledge against the back wall, identical to the ledge in the other secret room, held a squat black box the size of a supersized flour cannister.

"What is it?" I asked blankly. My grandfather stuffed his large frame through the narrow opening, blocking it from sight.

"I think, *poca*," Jude said slowly, following him, "we've just found the safe."

I heard my grandfather grunt, the sound echoing eerily in the cramped room.

"Call your mother and ask her the combination," he said dryly, his light playing over the shiny chrome dial. "I'll not be carrying this contraption up to the house."

Jude lowered me onto the high ledge next to the safe.

"Stay here with grandfather, and I'll go up into the garden where I can get reception." He left us, sloshing back out into the tunnel. "And behave yourself. I don't want any fighting while I'm gone."

I looked at my grandfather to see how he took Jude's parting joke and was rewarded with a sardonic rise of his brows and a level gaze from black eyes. They glinted diabolically in the reflected torchlight, mesmerizing me, and I stared back at him. I felt like a guinea pig caught in the considering gaze of a python. After a short moment, my grandfather stirred restlessly.

"And just what are you staring at, lass?" he asked quietly, his tone ironic. I crossed my arms across my chest.

"What are *you* staring at?" I countered apprehensively. I heard Jude's amused voice floating down the long tunnel in an eerie echo.

"Don't make me separate you two."

I tightened my arms over my chest, and my grandfather made an impatient gesture, turning his gaze to the safe plopped between us like a sword. His profile was lean and brooding.

"I'll not eat you, lass," he said after a moment, his gruff voice surprisingly mild, and his mouth curved up in grim humor. "Besides, I take bigger tidbits than you."

I dropped my gaze from his profile and shined my torch beam over the hewn blocks that made up the tiny room. There were no other marks on the stones, and the safe seemed to be the only object that had been hidden inside the cramped space.

We had figured out all the clues, but one.

"Grandfather . . . ," I began hesitantly. His black gaze swung up to mine. "Tamsin and I had found a slab outside of the garden, and it had some words chiseled on it in Latin."

He grunted, and I took it as encouragement to continue.

"It said, 'I wait beyond the flames. Where I dance above light, silver are my feet and black is my crown.' Had you ever seen anything like that in the garden or in the manor? Do you know what it might mean?"

He studied me for a long moment and then shifted restlessly, moving his booted feet in the water as if something had crawled over them. I backed up from the ledge's edge until my body was flat against the wall behind me.

"The maze."

I frowned at his answer and cast my mind back to what I knew of the maze, which was nothing. I hadn't even gotten a good look at it while I was in it.

"What's in the maze?" I asked curiously. My grandfather raised an eyebrow.

"The folly, lass. Did ye not even open your eyes last night?"

"What does that have to do with the engraving?"

"What did you and yon father climb out of?" He frowned impatiently, and his eyebrows came down over his nose in lopsided slashes.

"We came out from under a statue of something." I frowned back at him, wondering what it was I was supposed to have seen, but obviously hadn't. And then I remembered. "Oh, I know. The statue is on a floor mosaic of the sun. 'Where I dance above light—"

"Silver are my feet, and black is my crown," my grandfather finished the rest of the engraving. "Yon statue is standing on a slab of silver marble."

"What is 'black is my crown'?" I asked. He shifted, hearing Jude's approach down the waterlogged tunnel.

"The dome of the folly, lass," he grunted, his attention already off my question and on Jude who carried back the safe's combination. "It's made of black slate."

"Hold the lights steady," Jude's voice echoed down the tunnel, "and I'll open it. I've got the combination."

As I complied, I wondered what the first part of the etched words meant then, if the rest of the engraving referred to the folly. It made sense since the folly was the cave's egress, the escape hatch for James George's men and their contraband.

"I wait beyond the flames," I murmured as Jude entered the tiny room. And then I knew. For once our surmises had been correct. We were correct in our guess that it was the original slab that had covered the tunnel to the boiler in the cellars. It seemed that James George's dark humor extended to planting clues all over the place for the Excise men to discover if they were only bright enough.

Jude bent down until he was eye level with the chrome dial of the squat safe and began to spin it deftly to the memorized numbers in his head. After only a few spins in either direction, he tugged down on the latch, and the door clicked open. I let my breath out in a loud whoosh. I hadn't even been aware that I had been holding it. My grandfather merely grunted as Jude swung the door of the small safe wide.

Inside were two small velvet boxes and a folded square of parchment. Jude reached for the parchment first and opened it. Great-uncle Desmond's shaky handwriting crawled over the paper in the bright glow of our torches.

Jude read the penned words out loud, his normally deep voice eerily quiet in the cramped space and the darkness, "I found these in your mother's things, so I set about finding out who Destiny and her beloved James were. So now, my dear sisters, I will say good-bye. Or, perhaps, I won't. Perhaps I will see you again. It was a pleasant diversion, figuring out this little charade. Either way, I hope you have been happy in your chosen lives. Until we meet again, Desmond."

Jude's words echoed quietly in the tiny room, and I felt a faint hand from the past brush down my spine. I shivered, not knowing if I felt the memories of James George and Destiny stirring inside of me, or pity for Great-uncle Desmond.

"Idiot," my grandfather said wearily, bringing us back to the present with a solid thump. "Open yon boxes, son, and let's see what the fool hid."

Jude took the largest one from the safe and opened its lid. Inside was a tiny porcelain miniature edged in dull gold filigree. The face and shoulders painted on its oval surface was of a young girl in lace. Her black hair was unbound and wild, flying over her beautiful face in a smoky cloud, and her emerald eyes were bright enough to see by the torchlight.

"Bryn!" my grandfather sounded as if my grandmother's name was jerked out of him. He touched the face in the miniature. "She looks like Bryn."

"That's Grandmother?" I asked. He shook his head, taking the velvet box from Jude.

"No, lass. It's Destiny."

Forgetting myself and the swimming rats, I clambered over the safe to stand behind my grandfather, leaning eagerly over his shoulder as he stared at the portrait. He lifted it from its velvet box and turned it over gently, his fingers dwarfing the delicate miniature. The back was encased in gold with words engraved on its dull surface: "To my beloved James." I slowly deciphered the intricate writing in a hushed voice. "From your Destiny."

"She must have painted it herself," Jude said quietly and then reached for the second velvet box sitting forlornly in the center of the nearly empty safe. He flipped open the tiny lid and shined his light into the cushioned depths. A dull wink of gold flickered in the torchlight. Jude shifted the box to the palm of his hand and lifted the object out with a fingertip. On his finger were the moon and stars.

"James George's ring." I reached out and touched it. I couldn't get my voice above a whisper as I traced a fingertip over the worn gold. "Great-grandmother had his ring."

Jude carefully slid the circle of gold onto the forefinger of his right hand where it fit perfectly.

When we got back, my father, Grandmother, Dante, Brandt, and Michael were in the kitchen at the enormous block table with their cups of coffee while my mother pottered about cooking dinner. Gabriel seemed to be taking his predinner bath. I could hear the faint splashes coming from the hallway as he played with his usual noisy exuberance.

"How did it go?" My father raised an eyebrow at us. I stripped my wet shoes and socks from my feet, grateful for Tamsin's supporting hand.

"We opened the safe." I grinned, towing Tamsin behind me as we made our way to a couple of chairs beside him and sat down.

"There was a last message from Great-uncle Desmond inside." Jude went to the coffeepot to pour a mug of black coffee. He held the mug up to my grandfather.

"Put a finger of whiskey in that, and it would be welcome," my grandfather grunted and reached into his hip pocket to pull the parchment free, unfolding it and handing it to my grandmother. He lowered himself onto the chair beside her and stretched his long solid legs in front of him like fallen tree trunks. "I assume Luc explained everything."

"Yes," my grandmother said quietly, taking the parchment. I peered at her expression but could only see a slight veneer of puzzlement over fatigue.

"Your brother was an idiot," my grandfather stated calmly and accepted the hot mug of Irish coffee that Jude handed him. "Well, Bryn, *na' bi' buartha*, we'll sort it all out."

My grandmother gave his profile an unreadable look and then turned her attention to the parchment, reading the words out loud. She sighed when she was done.

"Poor Desmond," my mother said quietly into the aftermath of silence, slicing a mound of mushrooms with a lethal carving knife.

"Well," my grandmother said philosophically, "he was right about one thing. We probably will see him again, though not where he obviously thinks."

"What does he mean, 'I found these in your mother's things'?" Dante asked and reached for the parchment that was still in my grandmother's fingers. "Was there something else in the safe?"

Jude finished pouring out his mug of coffee, took a quick sip, held his hand up to frown at the ring still on his finger, then worked it loose with his thumb, dropping it on the gouged surface of the block table. It hit the wood with a dull clink and rolled. Dante caught it and held it up.

"Well, well . . . ," he said softly, rolling it between his thumb and forefinger. Late-afternoon sunlight gave the impure gold a mellow glow.

"Is that James George's ring?" Michael asked. Dante handed it to him. He held it up, scrutinizing it with a frown before passing it on to Brandt's open hand. "What else was there?"

"There was only the parchment, the ring, and this," I said, grinning, and dug the velvet box holding the miniature from my pocket. I handed the box to my father. He opened the lid and stared for a moment at the exquisite miniature nestled on the black velvet. I watched his face. His expression was unreadable, and I wondered what he was thinking.

"So this is who painted the shipwreck," he said in a low voice after a moment, one black eyebrow twitching. He handed the velvet box to my grandmother. "She looks like you."

My grandmother held the boxed miniature up so my mother could look at it over her shoulder.

"She does," my mother gasped.

"Maybe when I was sixteen, but hardly now," my grandmother snorted, then handed it back to my father, who took it from her with a grin. "This must be the woman you had gotten your talent from, dear."

"That's several generations." My mother looked up at my father, who kept staring bemusedly at the tiny portrait. "Would it travel like that?"

"Up to six generations." My father grinned, shrugging. "And I'm her great-great-great-grandson, making me only the fifth. Who knows?"

Tamsin stirred timidly.

"Even though I noticed it, I didn't really put it together at the time, Bella," she interjected hesitantly, "but your father is also the spitting image of James George."

"The smuggler?" My mother looked up, vastly amused, and then cast her grin at my father, who sat regarding her with one eyebrow raised. "I would love to see the portraits of James George that you and Bella had found."

"I still have the book that has a reproduction of the first portrait," I said, started to get up from my seat at the table, and then abruptly sat back down again at a sudden thought. "The second portrait, Tamsin. The one that was faxed to you from a museum in France."

"What about it?" she asked genuinely puzzled. "You have that. It's on one of those papers in your room. Would you like for me to go up and get the book and the faxed portrait?"

"I was just thinking," I said, feeling a slow grin spread across my face as I switched my gaze to my father, "we should find out who the painting is attributed to. I wonder if the artist signed it."

"Destiny?" my father gave a brief laugh, his eyes still fixed on my mother. "Probably, child."

I thought of the face in the portrait with the wicked eyebrows so exactly like my father's. I continued to gaze at my father and felt a bolt of surprised recognition when he turned his own amused gaze to me and winked. Tamsin was right. Put my father in late-eighteenth-century dress, and you have James George "the Smuggler." No wonder my father wore long wild hair, a goatee, and a pirate's gold earring when he was young. My ancestor's heart still beat in my father. Genetics are tricky things.

I stared at him openmouthed, and he grinned.

"What is it, *leanbh*?"

"Tamsin's right," I said. "You do look like him. Exactly."

"There's something engraved on the inside of this ring," Brandt interrupted us, his voice curious. He stood up from the table and went to a slant of bright sunlight streaming in from one of the windows. He held the ring up and squinted at the words engraved on the inside of the band. "It's in Latin."

"Let me see, son." My father stood up and went over to him. "Perhaps I can decipher it."

Brandt handed my father the ring, and we all waited quietly as my father studied the thick circlet of gold. After a moment, his face broke into a wide grin, and he laughed.

*"Dux femina facti."* He laughed again, genuinely amused, and closed his fingers around the tiny object. "*Dux femina facti.* 'A woman was leader of the exploit.'"

"Poor fool," my grandfather grunted, his heavy brows meeting over his black eyes in a mighty frown as he ignored my grandmother's ironic stare. "That explains everything. The poor man didn't stand a chance."

"I wonder if he knew Destiny Ophelia in France," Michael murmured thoughtfully. I shifted my gaze from my father to stare at my older brother. "He'd been to France enough."

"Do you mean that he might have been in love with her before he smuggled her out of the country?" I asked and was interrupted by my mother's soft voice.

"Luc? What is it?" At my mother's question, we all stopped gaping it each other and turned to look again at my father. He was staring at the inside of the ring again and grinning quietly.

"You're right, *Daid.* He didn't stand a chance," he laughed softly. "There's more engraved behind the moon. *Amor vincit omnia.*"

"What does that mean, Luc?" my mother asked and carefully put her knife down by the mound of mushrooms.

*"Amor vincit omnia,"* he said, raising his eyes to my mother's. "Love conquers all."

My grandfather skewed his black eyes to my grandmother's thoughtful profile, grunted, then stared at his mug of Irish coffee, letting his eyes give nothing else away.

# 18

Great-aunts Astrid and Aurora were coming home. They had been in the hospital for over three weeks and seemed to be recovering nicely. They were still prone to moments of abstraction, and if they missed enough sleep, they still tended to think they are back in Peru. Or think that they are children back again in Tanglewood. Or, once, in the case of Aunt Aurora when she had a restless night due to a burgeoning bedsore, she insisted she was Juanito, which I found out later was a favorite doll of hers that had gone missing when she was little more than a toddler. The mind is a funny thing. At least, Aunt Aurora's is.

My parents talked my grandmother into keeping back a third of her inheritance as Duchess of Fayrfax, though she is in a ponderous trek through red tape to lose the duchess part before it can stick to her.

Grandmother had decided to use the money coming to her as a bargaining chip to persuade my grandfather to retire. Or at least, partially retire, since she knows that he will never leave horses or be idle. I think the money is also going to be used to further the first part of my grandmother's campaign to move from the Aran Islands and on to the mainland. She's aiming for Halfmoon so she can be closer to her family, go to the meetings, and perhaps even regular pioneer with the rest of us. She had always wanted to, but it's hard to get your monthly time in answering others' questions when the island you live on is so small that you can throw rocks from any window of your home and kill a fish.

She had tried to bestow some of the money she had kept back on us as well, including Tamsin, but no one is taking any of it. Except Aunts Astrid and Aurora. In this, my grandmother is the stronger of the three and refuses to take a refusal. So Aunt Astrid is already planning to buy a small car and get her driver's permit, which is causing my parents sleepless nights already. Aunt Aurora, however, just wants a new hat. Jude had suggested a crash helmet in case her sister does, indeed, succeed in getting a new car.

The rest of the money is going to fund the missionary work my great-aunts had been part of for so long. No one has worked out how much exactly since the estate will take some time to settle. Grandmother had already talked to the couple we had met at the last meeting, the husband and wife from New York who had been visiting Alec Lytton. They promised to get in touch with the legal department once they fly back to Patterson.

And as to Tanglewood Estate, my great-aunts had decided to let the house go to the National Trust. It was too dilapidated to deal with, having been neglected for so long. Instead, they had gotten permission to take a few family heirlooms with them, but no one knows yet what they're going to choose. Tamsin and I want to go with them when they do. We haven't gotten to slide down the stairs in a tea tray yet.

Ambrose Hobhouse, Uncle Desmond's solicitor, told us that the National Trust had planned to turn Tanglewood Manor into a sort of historical tour complete with roaming docents dressed as Destiny and James George.

I can't imagine anything sillier.

Except, perhaps, for the new hobby Rayvyn has taken up. Her fascination with everybody's colon has waned a wee bit, and she has taken up tofu carving. She has already presented Michael with a five-pound block of carved curd shaped like a dead horse.

She says it a nonrepresentational sculpture of childbirth, but no matter how hard I squint, I just can't see it.